NORTHWEST
Readers

Other Titles in the Northwest Readers Series

Series Editor: Robert J. Frank

Hive of Dreams

Contemporary Science Fiction
from the Pacific Northwest

edited by Grace L. Dillon

Oregon State University Press
Corvallis

The paper in this book meets the guidelines for permanence and
durability of the Committee on Production Guidelines for Book Longevity
of the Council on Library Resources and the minimum requirements of
the American National Standard for Permanence of Paper for Printed
Library Materials Z39.48-1984.

Library of Congress Cataloging-in-Publication Data
Hive of dreams : contemporary science fiction from the Pacific Northwest
/ edited by Grace L. Dillon.
    p. cm. – (Northwest readers)
  ISBN 0-87071-555-0 (alk. paper)
  1. Science fiction, American–Northwest, Pacific. 2. American
fiction–Northwest, Pacific. 3. Northwest, Pacific–Fiction.
I. Dillon, Grace L. II. Series.
  PS570.H58 2003
  813'.08762089795–dc21

                                                  2003012104

Oregon State University Press
101 Waldo Hall
Corvallis OR 97331-6407
OREGON STATE 541-737-3166 • fax 541-737-3170
UNIVERSITY
http://oregonstate.edu/dept/press

Series Preface

In 1990 the Oregon State University Press issued its first two books in the Northwest Reprint Series, *Oregon Detour by* Nard Jones, and *Nehalem Tillamook Tales, edited by Melville Jacobs.* Since then, the series has reissued a range of books by Northwest writers, both fiction and nonfiction, making available again works of well-known and lesser-known writers.

As the series developed, we realized that we did not always want to reissue a complete work; instead we wanted to present selections from the works of a single author or selections from a number of writers organized around a unifying theme. Oregon State University Press, then, has decided to start a new series, the Northwest Readers Series.

The reasons for the Northwest Readers Series are the same as for the Northwest Reprint Series: "In works by Northwest writers, we get to know about the place where we live, about each other, about our history and culture, and about our flora and fauna."

RJF

Dedication

With much love to Tracy, Beth, and Sean,
my three "honeys"

The hive of dreams, windows heaped against the sky. I can see the pictures, but there is no path. I know you've come from there, but it's there ... isn't there!

William Gibson, *Idoru*

Contents

The following symbol is used to show where text has been omitted from the original:

Introduction

Individualism and innovation. The Northwest character exudes both. Cataracts and coastlines, rushing rivers and boiling skies, daily remind us that a natural order infuses our lives. At the same time, silicon forests of high-tech business proliferate, monuments to a human drive that wills imagination into being. It is not hard to see the tension between a growing affinity with technology and concerns about protecting the environment as characteristic of the Northwest spirit. From the first forest logged by pioneers to the Bonneville dam and beyond, the effects of harvesting nature in an effort to enhance our lives have raised hard questions. How do we exploit technology while simultaneously preserving a natural order? To what degree is technology an extension of a natural order? To what degree are humans merely a species of technology?

A number of writers in this collection confront such questions in a regional literature marked by both a distinctively Northwest character and an increasingly global awareness. The juxtaposition of old-growth forest and silicon factory provides inspiration for these authors, who work on the frontiers of science fiction, pioneering ecoliterature (more popularly dubbed "ecolit") and cyberpunk/post-cyberpunk, or cybernetic, literature (which we'll call "cyberlit"). Since the 1960s, science fiction has concerned itself with ecological issues, exploring the consequences of technology and industry on a fragile planet. In fact, it is widely noted that science fiction is one of the contemporary genres that most clearly confronts environmental issues and human and nonhuman nature. The work of Brian Aldiss, John Brunner, Ursula K. Le Guin, and Joanna Russ in the 1960s and 1970s established the trend, which was expanded by Carl Emery, David Brin, Kim Stanley Robinson, Scott Russell Sanders, Neal Stephenson, and others in the 1980s and 1990s.

Unlike the "golden age" of science fiction associated with luminaries like Stanislaw Lem, Robert Heinlein, Arthur C. Clark, and Isaac Asimov, which could posit fantastic worlds in distant futures as backdrops for speculations about our fate, ecolit and cyberlit science fiction grounds us in worlds that are close to our immediate experience. This quality lends a sense of urgency to the work. When reading of alien worlds millennia away that may echo ours, we are hardly challenged to address the social ills portrayed. Ecolit and cyberlit represent mandates to act on the concerns expressed, and to act now. They capture a prevalent Northwest sensibility regarding our place in nature and our responsibility for developing an ecologically sustainable future. While ecolit reflects a growing ethic regarding our interaction with nature, cyberlit emphasizes our increasingly computer-dependent existence. Since both often are set only five to twenty years in the future, they share similarities; environmental stories often examine our reactions to computer technology, and cybernetic tales often take up environmental issues in exploring the consequences of the cycle of high-tech buildup and decay.

For these reasons, the present volume offers something new: a juxtaposition of two pioneering sub-genres of science fiction that have more in common than has been previously recognized. That commonality arises partially from the human response to the grandeur—the incredible beauty—of nature in places like our Northwest paradise. The stories arranged in section one of this collection typify evolving thought experiments in ecoliterature, while those in the second section focus on contributions to cybernetic literature. This is for simplicity's sake. As I've suggested, and as the volume illustrates, there is much crossover.

The seeds of what I call ecoliterature originated in the New Wave movement, a term coined by writer Judith Merril in a 1966 essay in *The Magazine of Fantasy and Science Fiction*. The New Wave shifted emphasis from the physical to the social sciences, radicalized notions of community, and acknowledged that science and technology can be used for negative ends. New Wavers experimented with gender, relationships, and ideas of the self as a series of constructed identities influenced more by social, political, and economic forces than by biological states. Ecolit finds its more immediate antecedent in ecofeminist science fiction, which boomed in the late 1960s and in the 1970s with groundbreaking works such as Ursula K. Le Guin's *The Left Hand of Darkness* (1969) and Joanna Russ's *The Female Man* (1975). The effect was a shift in science fiction from "hard science" and a desire to portray a world of unimagined technological advances, to "soft science" that emphasizes the interpersonal and psychological. Along with an explosive interest in gender construction, this intersected with the 1970s ecological movement labeled "ecofeminism," which linked the oppression of women with the domination of nature.

Such science fiction began primarily as a reaction against a mechanistic worldview. It questions the notion that natural and social systems are like smoothly running machines, and is disturbed by the resulting ethic of domination and the reduction of nature to a commodity. In a mechanistic world, hierarchies prevail: people dominate nature, men dominate women, the rich dominate the weak. Ecolit authors turn this view upside down, creating worlds where nature and culture subtly and intricately interconnect, where things aren't all black or white, where traditionally dominant institutions devolve into close-knit and caring communities. This prevalent feature has been strongly maintained in more contemporary ecoliterature.

On the surface, this literature seems predominantly concerned with the split between culture and nature—or, more precisely, with eradicating the notion that culture and nature are split. It portrays a world where culture and nature are interdependent, a web where reciprocating forces exist holistically. Earlier forms of ecofeminist science fiction tended to reflect pastoral settings that in turn suggested a return to primitive and pure times before we became the victims of our own technology. More recent experiments in ecolit redefine the environment to include both rural and urban landscapes. This shift allows for the Robledo community in Octavia Butler's *Parable of the Sower*, where residents create a walled town filled with acorn trees and gardens to preserve a safer way of life than exists in the city surrounding them.

An additional characteristic is a reexamination of humanity's historical attitudes toward nature, such as Le Guin explores in "The Rock That Changed Things." Often ecolit provokes environmental-ethical reflection, as Molly Gloss's *The Dazzle of Day*. It can also transgressively reinscribe the logic of domination, as in "The Rock That Changed Things" and Ted Chiang's "Story of Your Life." Sometimes a distinct crossover between ecolit and early cyberpunk occurs when authors delineate the ecologies of cities, such as the overpopulated, overcluttered, excessive vertical density of William Gibson's aptly named "Sprawl," the futuristic eastern American coast in *Neuromancer*. These stories sometimes become studies of how to place a local region and its recent human history into an increasingly overpowering global context, as in Neal Stephenson's *The Diamond Age*. Gloss's *The Dazzle of Day* expresses the human spirit's strong resistance to environmentally debilitating consumption, and delineates the advance of human degradation and its effect on the spirit. Others concentrate on the emergence of environmental destruction and to a degree trace its cultural origins. Butler, Stephenson, and Ted Chiang in his "Story of Your Life," for example, investigate the ways in which these cultural origins were created to enforce ethnic, economic, and class divisions.

Exploding on the scene in the 1980s, cyberwriters addressed environmental concerns and often depicted dystopian consequences of the problems that ecoliterature addresses. The term "cybernetic literature" therefore is intended to suggest a tradition encompassing several postmodern movements and extending the discussion of ecological sustainability.

Cybernetics (from the Greek *kubernetes* or pilot) is a term coined in the 1940s, and is often used to characterize emerging communication technologies; its meaning has come to suggest someone who could control and direct flows of information. The first crest of this new wave is cyberpunk, whose luminaries include William Gibson, Pat Cadigan, Bruce Sterling, and Nicola Griffith. Cyberpunk stories are "cyber" because they depict characters who control information technology and who are, ironically, controlled by it. These characters are "punk" because their central value is social resistance, particularly resistance against media and multinational corporations that recycle people's desires into commodities for sale. In section two, you'll meet punks like Case, a disillusioned former cyberspace cowboy, in Gibson's *Neuromancer*.

The dominant themes of cyberlit include the breakdown of the classic opposition between nature and culture, and a questioning of the privileged status of humans over machines. In earlier science fiction, notably the work of influential writers such as Philip K. Dick, the idea that machines can be "more human than human" finds disturbing application; in an increasingly technological world, humans risk becoming automatons, devoid of empathy, existing as mechanistic devices rather than as souls in organic bodies. In cyberlit, by contrast, the distinctions blur. Humans can be part machine, machines can be part human; in fact, the synthesis of human and machine is viewed as an inevitable step on the evolutionary ladder.

Cybervisions imagine a potentially nonnatural future populated by cybernetically enhanced humans whose organic nature becomes superceded by hybrid cyborg forms. Even the original cyberpunk thus acknowledges that the Alien or Other resides within us. The possible variations on human existence are manifold. One can exist in a physical, organic body, or one can exist as a series of electronically captured memories on CDs played in cyberspace, such as Gibson's Dixie Flatliner in *Neuromancer*. Organic bodies may be augmented with prosthetic limbs, implanted circuitry, cosmetic surgery, and genetic alteration while the mind makes use of brain-computer interfaces, artificial intelligence, and neurochemistry. In John Varley's *Steel Beach*, humans possess digital circuitry that enables a central computer to resurrect them whenever they die. What is human, and what is self, in the bold new world that cyberpunks imagined ten to twenty years ago? More recent cyberlit follows Donna Haraway, whose influential "The Cyborg Manifesto" acknowledges that this bold new world has already arrived.

Since the 1980s, cyberlit has moved through postmodern phases to encompass chaos/complexity theory; Nicola Griffith, Neal Stephenson, Ted Chiang, and William Gibson in his more recent work are among the authors venturing into this newer territory. Chaos/complexity theory suggests that we may rely too heavily on the deterministic, linear equations we use to predict the behavior of simple mechanisms. In a world where small causes may trigger large effects, chaos abounds. The ecological models originating in chaos/complexity theory have been applied in biological, neurological, genetic, and molecular biological studies. More recently, this theory has been applied to sustainable or steady state economics, which defines economic practices as subsystems of the ecosystem. Why has this theory become an integral part of much cyberlit writing? Because these writers grapple with the implications of multinationals and the increasing globalization of capitalism, chaos/complexity theory is appealing for its ecological explanation of the world economy. As heirs to the cyberpunk world in which existence is dominated by a society that represents the ultimate triumph of advanced capitalism, cybervisionaries embrace chaos/complexity theory because it offers hope for the individual trapped in an overwhelming system. If a butterfly's wings can blow a tornado into being, as a popular précis of chaos/complexity has it, then the actions of a single individual can bring about social change and a rebirth of political consciousness.

Another significant emerging technology of interest to cyberwriters is nanotechnology, an experimental science used to manipulate matter at the molecular level in order to build molecular computers and make essentially anything. The alchemical machine predicted by nanotechnologists would be able to turn hay seed into filet mignon. The extraordinary outcomes predicted include the eradication of poverty, hunger, and aging, as nanotechnology promises to give humans utter control over physical matter, a cornucopia of previously scarce commodities. The original conception of this revolutionary science came from Nobel laureate Richard Feynman, but it was Eric Drexler who popularized the theory. Within our region, nanotechnology is among the University of Washington's cutting-edge research interests, while Portland State University has established a Center for Nanoscience Research.

As explored by science fiction writers, the application of nanotechnology raises troubling questions and generates cautionary tales. In *The Diamond Age* Neal Stephenson, for example, challenges the assumption that this new biological manipulation will facilitate global egalitarianism. In his view, the wealthy will have greater access to the fruits of this technology, creating a more pronounced divide between those who have and those who need. Greg Bear's prognostications in */Slant* suggest that the development of nanotechnology will parallel that of atomic fusion, originally conceived as a means of providing benign and abundant energy but ultimately appropriated by the military. In *Idoru*, William Gibson adds to these threats and suggests the possibility that the creatures produced by nanotechnology will self-perpetuate, in turn creating alien architectures that will blur the distinction between what is organic yet ersatz and what is natural.

Ultimately, innovations in cyberlit reflect the mainstreaming of science fiction itself. No longer isolated on worlds far away in space and time, cyberlit concerns itself with not only predicting what's to come but also with reflecting what already exists. As noted cyberpunk author Bruce Sterling argues in *Mirror Shades*, a prevailing feature of cyberlit is its immersion in the images and activities of popular culture, including television, advertisements, movies, and music. Perhaps *Neuromancer* began the trend by strongly evoking "Blade Runner," Ridley Scott's cinematic adaptation of Philip K. Dick's *Do Androids Dream of Electric Sheep?*. Neal Stephenson has said that he often writes while listening to the music of Seattle rock bands like Sound Garden, Nirvana, and Pearl Jam—loud.

The inclusion in this collection of excerpts from Douglas Coupland's *Microserfs* and from Richard Powers' *Plowing the Dark* forces us to ask, what is contemporary science fiction? While most readers would not consider *Microserfs* science fiction, it is cyberlit in its emphasis on computer-producing multinationals and the changing lifestyles that accompany high-tech research. The assorted friends depicted in the novel feel that their work campus is the "sci-fi world" where new inventions and technological advances resemble the stuff of science fiction novels. Powers' *Plowing the Dark* was chosen in preference to his critically lauded science fiction offering, *Galatea 2.2. Plowing the Dark*, a novel about virtual reality, takes up virtually all of the dominant themes of cyberlit—especially its disenchantment with the commodification practices of postcapitalism and its resurrection of the more mysterious elements of cyberspace—but generally is regarded as a mainstream novel and is most often placed in "fiction" rather than "science fiction" sections of bookstores. Both selections share the postmodern characteristic of dissolving the boundaries of genre.

In bringing Pacific Northwest practitioners of the new science fictions into one volume, this collection suggests that our regional landscape has naturally induced ecolit and cyberlit writers alike to live and work here. The collection begins in the forests and mountains of the Northwest with Le Guin's "The Good Trip" and ends in the cities and multinational conglomerates of the Pacific Rim with Gibson's *Idoru*, yet one might choose to emphasize instead that it begins in the city buses of Portland and ends on the quiet beaches of the Oregon coast. The communities that are both extolled and denigrated in these stories are neither completely rural nor completely urban. They reflect lifestyles unique to our region and themes popularized by a growing tradition of science fiction.

Will our growing dependence on technology displace us from nature? The authors collected here offer diverse visions of possible worlds where the distinctions between technology and biology, utopian wishfulness and cynical realism, urban and rural, virtual and real, blur. That these worlds resemble the Northwest ahead offers both caution and hope.

Part I

Ursula K. Le Guin

Among the more widely read Pacific Northwest authors, Ursula K. Le Guin (b. 1929) has enjoyed critical success and continues producing memorable stories for aficionados of science fiction, fantasy, and children's literature. Her work is not so easily categorized, however. It has been characterized as anthropological science fiction, magical realism, and speculative fiction, suggesting both the range of Le Guin's interests and the qualities that make a good book worth reading no matter what genre you use to label it. Some common themes do emerge from her writing, including the fine lines between utopia and dystopia, democracy and dictatorship, language and understanding, and male and female. Above all, Le Guin's fiction addresses her concern that we are trained not to exploit our powers of imagination. Her worlds challenge us to do so by questioning our perceptions of reality.

Le Guin was born and grew up in Berkeley, California, the daughter of anthropologist Alfred Kroeber and writer Theodora Kroeber, whose combined interests provided important early influences on the direction of her career. Her father owned a library of science fiction and fantasy novels, and Le Guin began making her contributions to the field as early as the age of eleven, when she submitted a short story about time travel to *Amazing Stories*. At Radcliffe she began her study of French and Italian Renaissance literature, earning a B.A. degree in 1951 and then an M.A. from Columbia in 1952. On a Fulbright fellowship to France in 1953 she met her future husband Charles Le Guin, who also was studying on a Fulbright scholarship. He became a professor of French history at Portland State University in Portland, Oregon, where they have lived for over forty years.

In 1962 Le Guin published her first fantasy story, "April in Paris," in *Amazing Stories*. She followed this in 1966 with her science fiction novel, *Rocannon's World*. *The Wizard of Earthsea*, part one of the *Earthsea* trilogy, appeared in 1968 and received the Boston Globe-Horn Book Award in 1969. Le Guin's critically acclaimed *The Left Hand of Darkness* firmly established her as a major presence in science fiction as well as a rising voice in feminist studies.

Le Guin has won five Hugo Awards: in 1970 for best novel for *The Left Hand of Darkness*, "The Word for World is Forest" (1973 short fiction), "The Ones Who Walk Away from Omelas" (1974 short stories), *The Dispossessed: An Ambiguous Utopia* (1975 novel), "Buffalo Gals, Won't You Come Out Tonight?" (1988 novelette). She has won five Nebula Awards from the Science Fiction and Fantasy Writers of America: *The Left Hand of Darkness* (1969 novel), *The Dispossessed: An Ambiguous Utopia* (1974 novel), *Tehanu: The Last Book of Earthsea* (1990 novel), "The Day Before the Revolution" (1974 short story), "Solitude" (1990 novelette). She received a Newberry Honor for *The Finest Shore* (1972), the Pilgrim Award for her entire body of work in 1989, and a 1995 World Fantasy Award for Live Achievement, among others. She is the only science fiction author to have won a National Book Award (1973, *The Farthest Shore*). Her recent works include the third installment in her Hainish cycle, *The Telling* (2000), *Tales From Earthsea* (2001), and *The Birthday of the World and Other Stories* (2002).

Set in a landscape that juxtaposes the urban and the sublime in the forms of Portland and Mount Hood, Oregon, "The Good Trip" (from *The Wind's Twelve Quarters,* 1976) can be read in the tradition of utopian tales that project an imaginative vision of the end at which social life aims. Notable early utopian works include Margaret Cavendish's *The Blazing World* (1666), which recent observers have called the original science fiction story instead of the more popularly known *Frankenstein* by Mary Shelley; Francis Bacon's *The New Atlantis*, a title Le Guin uses for her own novella of Portland as tyrannical utopia; and Samuel Butler's *Erewhon* (1872), a satirical utopia referenced in the following, which Le Guin has called a "psychomyth," a surrealistic fantasy that takes place outside of time. Le Guin was studying Italian and translating Dante's *Comedia* at the time she wrote this story, so fans of Dante and Beatrice will recognize the allusions.

The Good Trip

As HE SWALLOWED THE STUFF HE KNEW HE SHOULDN'T SWALLOW the stuff, knew it for sure, knew it as a driver knows the truck coming straight at him at 70 mph: suddenly, intimately, finally. His throat shut, his solar plexus knotted up like a sea anemone, but too late. Down the hatch it went, the bit of bitter candy, the acid-drop, the sourball, the peppy packet of power, etching a little corroded trail of terror behind it all the way down his esophagus like a poisoned snail swallowed whole. It was the terror that was wrong. He was afraid and hadn't known it, and now it was too late. You can't afford to be afraid. Fear fouls it all up, and sends those few, those unhappy few, a very small percentage, to the loony bin to cower in corners not saying anything …

You have nothing to fear but fear itself.

Yes sir. Yes sir Mr. Roosevelt sir.

The thing to do is relax. Think good thoughts. If rape inevitable—He watched Rich Harringer open up his little packet (accurately compounded and hygienically wrapped by a couple of fellows putting themselves through grad school in chemistry by the approved American method of free enterprise, illegitimate to be sure but this is not unusual in America where so little is legal that even a baby can be illegitimate) and swallow the small sour snail with formal and deliberate enjoyment. If rape inevitable, relax and enjoy. Once a week.

But is anything inevitable besides death? Why relax, why enjoy? He would fight. He would not go on a bad trip. He would fight the drug consciously and purposefully, not in panic but with intent, and we'll see who wins. In this corner LSD/alpha, 100 micrograms, plain wrapper, the Tibetan Whirlwind; and in this corner, ladies and junglemen, L.S.D./B.A., MA, 166 lbs, the Sonoma Sniveller, wearing white trunks, and red suitcases, and blue cheekpouches. Let me out of here, let me out of here! *Clang.*

Nothing happened.

Lewis Sidney David, the man with no last name, the Jewish Kelt, cornered in this corner, stared warily around him. His three companions all looked normal, in focus if out of touch. They did not have auras. Jim was lying on the verminous sofa-bed reading *Ramparts,* a trip to Vietnam he wanted maybe, or to Sacramento. Rich looked torpid, he always looked torpid even when serving free lunch in the park, and Alex was nitpicking around on his guitar. The infinite satisfaction of the chord. The silver cord. Sursum corda. If he carries a guitar around why can't he play a tune on it? No. Irritability is a symptom of loss of self-control: suppress it. Suppress everything. Censor, censor. Fight, team, fight!

13

Lewis got up, observing with pleasure the ready ease of his responses and the perfection of his sense of balance, and filled a glass of water at the vile sink. Beard hairs, spat-out Colgate, rust and radish droppings, a sink of iniquity. A small sink, but mine own. Why did he live in this dump? Why had he asked Jim and Rich and Alex to come share their sugarlumps with him here? It was lousy enough without being an opium den too. Soon it would be littered with inert bodies, eyes dropping out like marbles and rolling under the bed to join the dust and ruin lurking there. Lewis carried the glass of water over to the window, drank half of it, and began to pour the rest gently around the roots of a seedling olive tree in a mended ten-cent pot. "Have a drink on me," he said, looking closely at the tree.

It was five inches high but looked very like an olive tree, gnarled and durable. A bonsai. Banzai! But where's satori? Where's the significance, the enhancement, all the shapes and colors and meanings, the intensification of the perception of reality? How long does it take the damned stuff to work? There sat his olive tree. No less, no more. Unenhanced, insignificant. Men cry Peace, peace, but there is no peace. Not enough olive trees to go around, due to population explosion of human species. Was that a Perception? No, any undrugged meat-head could have perceived it. O come on, poison, poison me. Come, hallucination, come, so that I may fight you, reject you, refuse you, lose the fight and go mad, silently.

Like Isobel.

That was why he lived in this dump, and that was why he had asked Jim and Rich and Alex here, and that was why he was off on a trip with them, a pleasure-cruise, a holiday in picturesque Old Erewhon. He was trying to catch up with his wife. What is most difficult about watching your wife go insane is that you can't go with her. Farther and farther away she walks, not looking back, a long trip down into silence. The lyre falls dumb, and the psychiatrists are liars too. You stand behind the glass wall of your sanity like one at an airport watching a crash. You shout, "Isobel!" She never heard. The plane crashed in silence. She could not hear him call her name. Nor could she speak to him. Now the walls that divided him from her were brick, very solid, and he could do what he liked with his own glass house of sanity. Throw stones. Throw alphas. Tinkle, crash.

LSD/alpha did not drive you insane, of course. It did not even unravel your chromosomes. It simply opened the door to the higher reality. So did schizophrenia, he gathered, but the trouble there was that you couldn't speak, you couldn't communicate, you couldn't say what.

Jim had lowered his *Ramparts.* He was sitting in a noticeable fashion, inhaling. He was going to get with reality the right way, like a lama, man. He was a true believer and his life now centered upon the LSD/a experience as a religious mystic's upon his mystical discipline. Could you keep it up once a week for years, though? At thirty? At forty-two? At sixty-three? There is a terrible monotony and adversity to life; you'd need a monastery. Matins, nones, vespers, silence, walls around, big solid brick walls. To keep the lower reality out.

Come on, hallucinogen, get with it. Hallucinogenate, hallucinogenize. Smash the glass wall. Take me on a trip where my wife went. Missing person, age 22, ht 5'3", wt 105 lbs, hair brown, race human, sex female. She never was a fast walker. I could catch up with her with one foot tied behind me. Take me where she walked to.

No.

I'll walk there by myself, said Lewis Sidney David. He finished pouring the water in little dribbles around the roots of the olive tree, and looked up, out the window. There through smeary glass was Mount Hood, forty miles away, two miles high, a volcanic cone possessing the serene symmetry peculiar to volcanic cones, dormant but not officially extinct, full of sleepy fires and surrounded by its own atmosphere and climate different from that of lower altitudes: snow and a clear light. That was why he lived in this dump. Because when you looked out the window of it, you saw the higher reality. Eleven thousand feet higher.

"I'll be damned," Lewis said aloud, feeling that he was on the edge and verge of perceiving something really important. But he had that feeling fairly often, without chemical assistance. Meanwhile there was the mountain.

A lot of muck, freeways and disposable office buildings and high-rises and urban renewal bombsites and neon elephants washing neon cars with dotted showers of neon, lay in between him and the mountain, and the base of it was hidden along with its foothills in a pale smog, so that the peak floated.

Lewis felt a strong impulse to cry and to say his wife's name aloud. He repressed this impulse, as he had been doing for three months, ever since May when he had taken her to the sanitarium, after the silent months. In January, before the silence began, she had cried a great deal, all day long some days, and he had become frightened of tears. First tears, then silence. No good. O God get me out of this! Lewis let go, quit fighting the impalpable enemy, and begged for release. He implored the drug in his bloodstream to work, to do something, to let him cry, or see colors, or go off his rocker, anything.

Nothing happened.

He finished pouring the water in little dribbles around the roots of the olive tree, and looked up, at the room. It was a dump, but big, and it had a good view of Mount Hood, and the wisdom-tooth crest of Mount Adams on clear days too. But nothing would happen here. This was the waiting room. He picked up his coat off a broken chair and went out.

It was a good coat, lambswool lining and a hood and all that, his sister and mother had clubbed to get it for him for Christmas, making him feel like R. R. Raskolnikov. But he was not going to murder any old pawnbrokers today. Not even a pseudocide. On the stairs he passed the painters and plasterers with their ladders and buckets, three of them, going up to do his room over, peaceful-looking, fresh-faced men in their forties and fifties. Poor bastards, what would they do with the sink? with the three alphies, Rich and Jim and Alex, who on honeydew had fed and drunk the milk of Paradise? with his notes on LeNotre, Olmsted and McLaren, with his fourteen pounds of photographs of Japanese domestic architecture, with his drawing board and fishing tackle, his *Collected Works of Theodore Sturgeon* bound in sensational cardboard, the 8' x 10' unfinished oil of an ataxic nude by a painter friend whose auto loan co. had attached his paintings, Alex's guitar, the olive tree, the dust and eyeballs under the bed? That was their problem. He went on down the rooming-house stairs that smelled of old tomcat, and heard his hiking boots clomping heartily. He felt that all this had happened once before.

It took him a long time to get out of the city. Since public transportation was forbidden to people in his condition, of course, he couldn't get on the Gresham bus which would have saved a lot of time, taking him through the suburbs and halfway there. But there was plenty of time. The summer evening would stay light; he could count on it. Lenient and sweet in their length are the twilights of a latitude halfway between equator and pole: no tropic monotonies, no arctic absolutes, but a winter of long shadows and a summer of long dusks: gradations and accommodations of brightness, attenuations of clarity, subtleties and leisures of the light. Children scuttered in the green parks of Portland and down long side streets, all at one great game over all the city, the game of Young. Only here and there a kid went alone, playing Solitude, for higher stakes. Some kids are gamblers born. Bits of trash scraped along the gutters moved by a warm wind now and then. There was a great, sad sound far off over the city as if lions were roaring in cages, walking and lashing their gold sides with gold-tasselled tails and roaring, roaring. Sun set, somewhere west over roofs, but not for the mountain that still burned with a white fire away up high. As Lewis left the last of the city and went through a pleasant land, hilly and well farmed, the wind began to smell of wet earth, cool, complex, as it will as night comes on; and past Sandy there was darkness under great increasing forests on the rising slopes. But there was plenty of time. Above and ahead the peak stood white, faintly tinged with apricot, in sunlight. As he climbed the long, steep road he came out again and then again from the dark forests into gulfs of yellow clarity. He went on until he was up above the forests and up above the darkness, on heights where there was only snow and stone and air and the vast, clear, enduring light.

But he was alone.

That wasn't right. He hadn't been alone when this had happened. He had to meet with— He had been with— Where?

No skis no sled no snowshoes not even an inner tube. If I had got the commission for this landscape, God, I would have put a path along here. Sacrificing grandeur for convenience? But only a little path. No harm. Only a little crack in the Liberty Bell. Only a little leak in the dike, fuse on the bomb, maggot in the brain. O my mad girl, my silent love, my wife whom I sold into bedlam because you would not hear me speak, Isobel, come save me from yourself! I've climbed after you up above all the paths and now I stand here alone: there isn't any way to go.

Daylight died away and the white of the snow went somber. In the east, above endless darkening ranges and forests and pale, hill-enfolded lakes, Saturn shone, bright and saturnine.

Lewis did not know where the lodge was; somewhere on the timberline, but he was above timberline. He would not go down. To the heights, to the heights. Excelsior! A youth who bore mid snow and ice a banner with this strange device HELP HELP I AM A PRISONER OF THE HIGHER REALITY. He climbed. He climbed unclomben slopes, unkempt, and as he climbed he wept. His tears crawled down over his face and he crawled up over the mountain's face.

The very high places are terrible, alone at dusk.

The light no longer stayed for him. There was no longer plenty of time. He had run out of time. Stars came out and looked at him eye to eye out of the gulfs of darkness whenever he glanced aside from the huge white uptilted plain, the higher plane he climbed. On either side of him there was a gap, with a few stars in it. But the snow kept its own cold light, and he kept climbing. He remembered the path when he came across it. God or the state or he himself had put a path there on the mountain after all. He turned right, and it was wrong. He turned left, and stood still.

He did not know which way to go, and shaking with cold and fear he cried out aloud to the death-white summit above him and to the black places in between the stars his wife's name, "Isobel!"

She came along the path out of the darkness. "I began to get worried about you, Lewis."

"I went farther than I meant to," Lewis said.

"It stays light so long up here you sort of think it'll go on forever …"

"Right. I'm sorry I worried you."

"Oh, I wasn't worried. You know. Lonesome. I thought maybe your leg had slowed you down. Is it a good hike?"

"Spectacular."

'Take me along tomorrow,"

"Didn't you enjoy skiing?"

She shook her head. "Not without you," she muttered, shamefaced. They went leftward down the path, not very fast. Lewis was still slightly hobbled by the pulled muscle that had kept him off skis the last two days, and it was dark, and there wasn't any hurry. They held hands. Snow, starlight, stillness. Fire underfoot, darkness around; ahead of them, firelight, beer, bed. All things in their due time. Some, born gamblers, will always choose to live on the side of a volcano.

"When I was in the sanitarium," Isobel said, pausing so that he too stopped and there was no longer even the noise of their boots on the dry snow, no sound at all but the soft sound of her voice, "I had a dream like this. Awfully like this. It was the … most important dream I had. Yet I can't recall it clearly—I never could, even in therapy. But it was like this. This silence. Being up high. The silence above all … above all. It was so silent that if I said something, you would be able to hear it. I knew that. I was sure of it. And in the dream I think I said your name, and you *could* hear me—you answered me—"

"Say my name," he whispered.

She turned and looked at him. There was no sound on the mountain or among the stars. She said his name.

He answered saying hers, and then took hold of her; both of them were shaking.

"It's cold, it's cold, we've got to go down."

They went on, on their tightrope between the outer and the inner fires.

"Look at that enormous star."

"Planet. Saturn—Father Time."

"Ate his children, didn't he," she murmured, holding hard to his arm.

"All but one of them," Lewis answered. Down a long clear slope before them now they saw in grey starlight the bulk of the upper hut, the towers of the ski-lift vague and gaunt, and the vast down-sweep of the lines.

His hands were cold and he slipped off his gloves a minute to beat them together, but this was hard to do because of the glass of water he was holding. He finished pouring the water in little dribbles around the roots of the olive tree and set down the glass beside the mended flowerpot. But something still remained in his hand, folded into the palm like a crib for a high-school French final, *que je fusse, que tu fusse, qu'il fût*, small and sweat-stuck. He opened his hand and studied the item for some while. A message. From whom, to whom? From grave, to womb. A little packet, sealed, containing 100 mg of LSD/a in sugar.

Sealed?

He remembered, with precision and in order, opening it, swallowing the stuff, the taste of it. He also remembered with equal order and precision where he had been since then and knew that he had not been there yet.

He went over to Jim who was just exhaling the breath he had been inhaling as Lewis began to water the olive tree. Deftly and gently Lewis tucked the packet into Jim's coat pocket.

"Aren't you coming along?" Jim asked, smiling a mild smile.

Lewis shook his head. "Chicken," he murmured. It was hard to explain that he had already come back from the trip he had not made. Besides, Jim wouldn't hear him. He was off where people don't hear and can't answer, walled in.

"Have a good trip," Lewis said.

He got his raincoat (dirty poplin, no fleece lining, hold on, wait) and went down the stairs and out into the streets. The summer was ending, the season changing. It was raining but not dark yet, and the city wind blew in great cool gusts that smelled of wet earth and forests and the night.

Joanna Russ

n this excerpt from her pioneering novel of gender and culture, Joanna Russ (b. 1937) wittily portrays utopia in the guise of Whileaway, a future society composed exclusively of women. An experiment in nonhierarchical forms of social organization, *The Female Man* emphasizes simpler lifestyles that stress less-polluting "soft" technologies.

Russ is particularly known for her use of ironic language to expose the foibles of mainstream America. Her works include *How to Supress Women's Writing* (1983), *Zanzibar Cat* (1984), *Extra(Ordinary) People* (1984), *The Adventures of Alyx* (1986), *To Write Like a Woman: Essays in Feminism and Science Fiction* (1995), and *What Are We Fighting For?: Sex, Race, Class, and the Future of Feminism* (1998). She is a 1983 Hugo Award winner for her novella *Souls* and a 1972 Nebula Award winner for her short story "When It Changed."

The Female Man is among the essential works of ecolit, exploring the ways in which individuals construct their own identities. Russ portrays four versions of self: Jeannine, a librarian; Janet, inhabitant of a utopian earth; Joanna, a feminist from the 1970s; and Jael, a woman from the near future. Russ wrote the novel while working as a professor at the University of Washington in Seattle.

from *The Female Man*

Part One V

THE FIRST MAN TO SET FOOT ON WHILEAWAY APPEARED IN A FIELD of turnips on North Continent. He was wearing a blue suit like a biker's and a blue cap. The farm people had been notified. One, seeing the blip on the tractor's infrared scan, came to get him; the man in blue saw a flying machine with no wings but a skirt of dust and air. The county's repair shed for farm machinery was nearby that week, so the tractor-driver led him there; he was not saying anything intelligible. He saw a translucent dome, the surface undulating slightly. There was an exhaust fan set in one side. Within the dome was a wilderness of machines: dead, on their sides, some turned inside out, their guts spilling on to the grass. From an extended framework under the roof swung hands as big as three men. One of these picked up a car and dropped it. The sides of the car fell off. Littler hands sprang up from the grass.

"Hey, hey!" said the tractor-driver, knocking on a solid piece set into the wall. "It fell, it passed out!"

"Send it back," said an operator, climbing out from under the induction helmet at the far end of the shed. Four others came and stood around the man in the blue suit.

"Is he of steady mind?" said one.

"We don't know."

"Is he ill?"

"Hypnotize him and send him back."

The man in blue—if he had seen them—would have found them very odd: smooth-faced, smooth-skinned, too small and too plump, their coveralls heavy in the seat. They wore coveralls because you couldn't always fix things with the mechanical hands; sometimes you had to use your own. One was old and had white hair; one was very young; one wore the long hair sometimes affected by the youth of Whileaway, "to while away the time." Six pairs of steady curious eyes studied the man in the blue suit.

"That, *mes enfants,*" said the tractor-driver at last, "is a man."

"That is a real Earth man."

VI

Sometimes you bend down to tie your shoe, and then you either tie your shoe or you don't; you either straighten up instantly or maybe you don't. Every choice begets at least two worlds of possibility, that is, one in which you do and one in which you don't; or very likely many more, one in which you do quickly, one in which you do slowly, one in which you don't, but hesitate, one in which you hesitate and frown, one in which you hesitate and sneeze, and so on. To carry this line of argument further, there must be an infinite number of possible universes (such is the fecundity of God) for there is no reason to imagine Nature as prejudiced in favor of human action. Every displacement of every molecule, every change in orbit of every electron, every quantum of light that strikes here and not there—each of these must somewhere have its alternative. It's possible, too, that there is no such thing as one clear line or strand of probability, and that we live on a sort of twisted braid, blurring from one to the other without even knowing it, as long as we keep within the limits of a set of variations that really make no difference to us. Thus the paradox of time travel ceases to exist, for the Past one visits is never one's own Past but always somebody else's; or rather, one's visit to the Past instantly creates another Present (one in which the visit has already happened) and what you visit is the Past belonging to that Present—an entirely different matter from your own Past. And with each decision you make (back there in the Past) that new probable universe itself branches, creating simultaneously a new Past and a new Present, or to put it plainly, a new universe. And when you come back to your own Present, you alone know what the other Past was like and what you did there.

Thus it is probable what Whileaway—a name for the Earth ten centuries from now, but not *our* Earth, if you follow me—will find itself not at all affected by this sortie into somebody else's past. And vice versa, of course. The two might as well be independent worlds.

Whileaway, you may gather, is in the future.

But not *our* future.

VII

I saw Jeannine shortly afterward, in a cocktail lounge where I had gone to watch Janet Evason on television (I don't have a set). Jeannine looked very much out of place; I sat next to her and she confided in me:

"I don't belong here." I can't imagine how she got there, except by accident. She looked as if she were dressed up for a costume film, sitting in the shadow with her snood and her wedgies, a long-limbed, coltish girl in clothes a little too small for her. Fashion (it seems) is recovering very leisurely from the Great Depression. Not here and now, of course. "I don't belong here!" whispered Jeannine Dadier again, rather anxiously. She was fidgeting. She said, "I don't *like* places like this." She poked the red, tufted leather on the seat.

"What?" I said.

"I went hiking last vacation," she said big-eyed. "That's what I like. It's healthy."

I know it's supposed to be virtuous to run healthily through fields of flowers, but I like bars, hotels, air-conditioning, good restaurants, and jet transport, and I told her so.

"Jet?" she said.

Janet Evason came on the television. It was only a still picture. Then we had the news from Cambodia, Laos, Michigan State, Lake Canandaigua (pollution), and the spinning globe of the world in full color with its seventeen man-made satellites going around it. The color was awful. I've been inside a television studio before: the gallery running around the sides of the barn, every inch of the roof covered with lights, so that the little woman-child with the wee voice can pout over an oven or a sink. Then Janet Evason came on with that blobby look people have on the tube. She moved carefully and looked at everything with interest. She was well dressed (in a suit). The host or M.C. or whatever-you-call-him shook hands with her and then everybody shook hands with everybody else, like a French wedding or an early silent movie. *He* was dressed in a suit. Someone guided her to a seat and she smiled and nodded in the exaggerated way you do when you're not sure of doing the right thing. She looked around and shaded her eyes against the lights. Then she spoke.

(The first thing said by the second man ever to visit Whileaway was, "Where are all the men?" Janet Evason, appearing in the Pentagon, hands in her pockets, feet planted far apart, said, "Where the dickens are all the women?")

The sound in the television set conked out for a moment and then Jeannine Dadier was gone; she didn't disappear, she just wasn't there any more. Janet Evason got up, shook hands again, looked around her, questioned with her eyes, pantomimed comprehension, nodded, and walked out of camera range. They never did show you the government guards.

I heard it another time and this is how it went:

MC: How do you like it here, Miss Evason?

JIB (looks around the studio, confused): It's too hot.

MC: I mean how do you like it on—well, on Earth?

JIB: But I live on the earth. (Her attention is a little strained here.)

MC: Perhaps you had better explain what you mean by that—I mean the existence of different probabilities and so on—you were talking about that before.

JIB: It's in the newspapers.

MC: But Miss Evason, if you could, please explain it for the people who are watching the program.

JIB: Let them read. Can't they read?

(*There was a moment's silence. Then the MC spoke.*)

MC: Our social scientists as well as our physicists tell us they've had to revise a great deal of theory in light of the information brought by our fair visitor from another world. There have been no men on Whileaway for at least eight centuries—I don't mean no human beings, of course, but no men—and this society, run entirely by women, has naturally attracted a great deal of attention since the appearance last week of its representative and its first ambassador, the lady on my left here. Janet Evason, can you tell us how you think your society on Whileaway will react to the reappearance of men from Earth—I mean our present-day Earth, of course—after an isolation of eight hundred years?

JIB (*She jumped at this one; probably because it was the first question she could understand*): Nine hundred years. What men?

MC: What men? Surely you expect men from our society to visit Whileaway.

JIB: Why?

MC: For information, trade, ah—cultural contact, surely. (*laughter*) I'm afraid you're making it rather difficult for me, Miss Evason. When the—ah—-the plague you spoke of killed the men on Whileaway, weren't they missed? Weren't families broken up? Didn't the whole pattern of life change?

JIB (*slowly*): I suppose people always miss what they are used to. Yes, they were missed. Even a whole set of words, like "he," "man" and so on—these are banned. Then the second generation, they use them to be daring, among themselves, and the third generation doesn't, to be polite, and by the fourth, who cares? Who remembers?

MC: But surely—that is—

JIB: Excuse me, perhaps I'm mistaking what you intend to say as this language we're speaking is only a hobby of mine, I am not as fluent as I would wish. What we speak is a pan-Russian even the Russians would not understand; it would be like Middle English to you, only vice-versa.

MC: I see. But to get back to the question—

JIB: Yes.

MC (*A hard position to be in, between the authorities and this strange personage who is wrapped in ignorance like a savage chief: expressionless, attentive, possibly civilized, completely unknowing. He finally said*): Don't you want men to return to Whileaway, Miss Evason?

JIB: Why?

MC: One sex is half a species, Miss Evason. I am quoting (and he cited a famous anthropologist). Do you want to banish sex from Whileaway?

JIB (*with massive dignity and complete naturalness*): Huh?

MC: I said: Do you want to banish sex from Whileaway? Sex, family, love, erotic attraction—call it what you like—we all know that your people are competent and intelligent individuals, but do you think that's enough? Surely you have the intellectual knowledge of biology in other species to know what I'm talking about.

JE: I'm married. I have two children. What the devil do you mean?

MC: I—Miss Evason—we—well, we know you form what you call marriages, Miss Evason, that you reckon the descent of your children through both partners and that you even have "tribes"—I'm calling them what Sir calls them; I know the translation isn't perfect—and we know that these marriages or tribes form very good institutions for the economic support of the children and for some sort of genetic mixing, though I confess you're way beyond us in the biological sciences. But, Miss Evason, I am not talking about economic institutions or even affectionate ones. Of course the mothers of Whileaway love their children; nobody doubts that. And of course they have affection for each other; nobody doubts that, either. But there is more, much, much more—I am talking about sexual love.

JIB (*enlightened*): Oh! You mean copulation.

MC: Yes.

JIB: And you say we don't have that?

MC: Yes.

JE: How foolish of you. Of course we do.

MC: Ah? (*He wants to say, "Don't tell me."*)

JIB: With each other. Allow me to explain.

She was cut off instantly by a commercial poetically describing the joys of unsliced bread. They shrugged (out of camera range). It wouldn't even have gotten that far if Janet had not insisted on attaching a touch-me-not to the replay system. It was a live broadcast, four seconds' lag. I begin to like her more and more. She said, "If you expect me to observe your taboos, I think you will have to be more precise as to exactly what they are." In Jeannine Dadier's world, she was (would be) asked by a lady commentator:

How do the women of Whileaway do their hair?

JIB: They hack it off with clam shells.

❀

Part Three IV

Whileawayans are not nearly as peaceful as they sound.

V

Burned any bras lately har har twinkle twinkle A pretty girl like you doesn't need to be liberated twinkle har Don't listen to those hysterical bitches twinkle twinkle twinkle I never take a woman's advice about two things: love and automobiles twinkle twinkle har May I kiss your little hand twinkle tinkle twinkle. Har. Twinkle.

VI

On Whileaway they have a saying: When the mother and child are separated they both howl, the child because it is separated from the mother, the mother because she has to go back to work. Whileawayans bear their children at about thirty—singletons or twins as the demographic pressures require. These children have as one genotypic parent the biological mother (the "body-mother") while the non-bearing parent contributes the other ovum ("other mother"). Little Whileawayans are to their mothers both sulk and swank, fun and profit, pleasure and contemplation, a show of expensiveness, a slowing-down of life, an opportunity to pursue whatever interests the women have been forced to neglect previously, and the only leisure they have ever had—or will have again until old age. A family of thirty persons may have as many as four mother-and-child pairs in the common nursery at one time. Food, cleanliness, and shelter are not the mother's business; Whileawayans say with a straight face that she must be free to attend to the child's "finer spiritual needs." Then they go off by themselves and roar. The truth is they don't want to give up the leisure. Eventually we come to a painful scene. At the age of four or five these independent, blooming, pampered, extremely intelligent little girls are torn weeping and arguing from their thirty relatives and sent to the regional school, where they scheme and fight for weeks before giving in; some of them have been known to construct dead falls or small bombs (having picked this knowledge up from their parents) in order to obliterate their instructors. Children are cared for in groups of five and taught in groups of differing sizes according to the subject under discussion. Their education at this point is heavily practical: how to run machines, how to get along without machines, law, transportation, physical theory, and so on. They learn gymnastics and mechanics. They learn practical medicine.

They learn how to swim and shoot. They continue (by themselves) to dance, to sing, to paint, to play, to do everything their Mommies did. At puberty they are invested with Middle-Dignity and turned loose; children have the right of food and lodging wherever they go, up to the power of the community to support them. They do not go back home.

Some do, of course, but then neither Mother may be there; people are busy; people are traveling; there's always work, and the big people who were so kind to a four-year-old have little time for an almost-adult. "And everything's so *small*," said one girl.

Some, wild with the desire for exploration, travel all around the world—usually in the company of other children—bands of children going to visit this or that, or bands of children about to reform the power installations, are a common sight on Whileaway.

The more profound abandon all possessions and live off the land just above or below the forty-eighth parallel; they return with animal heads, scars, visions.

Some make a beeline for their callings and spend most of puberty pestering part-time actors, bothering part-time musicians, cajoling part-time scholars.

Fools! (say the older children, who have been through it all) Don't be in such a hurry. You'll work soon enough.

At seventeen they achieve Three-Quarters Dignity and are assimilated into the labor force. This is probably the worst time in a Whileawayan's life. Groups of friends are kept together if the members request it and if it is possible, but otherwise these adolescents go where they're needed, not where they wish; nor can they join the Geographical Parliament nor the Professional Parliament until they have entered a family and developed that network of informal associations of the like-minded which is Whileaway's substitute for everything else but family.

They provide human companionship to Whileawayan cows, who pine and die unless spoken to affectionately.

They run routine machinery, dig people out of landslides, oversee food factories (with induction helmets on their heads, their toes controlling the green-peas, their fingers the vats and controls, their back muscles the carrots, and their abdomens the water supply).

They lay pipe (again, by induction).

They fix machinery.

They are not allowed to have anything to do with malfunctions or breakdowns "on foot," as the Whileawayans say, meaning in one's own person and with tools in one's own hands, without the induction helmets that make it possible to operate dozens of waldoes at just about any distance you please. That's for veterans.

They do not meddle with computers "on foot" nor join with them via induction. That's for *old* veterans.

They learn to like a place only to be ordered somewhere else the next day, commandeered to excavate coastline or fertilize fields, kindly treated by the locals (if any) and hideously bored.

It gives them something to look forward to.

At twenty-two they achieve Full Dignity and may either begin to learn the heretofore forbidden jobs or have their learning formally certificated. They are allowed to begin apprenticeships. They may marry into pre-existing families or form their own. Some braid their hair. By now the typical Whileawayan girl is able to do any job on the planet, except for specialties and extremely dangerous work. By twenty-five she has entered a family, thus choosing her geographical home base (Whileawayans travel all the time). Her family probably consists of twenty to thirty other persons, ranging in age from her own to the early fifties. (Families tend to age the way people do; thus new groupings are formed again in old age. Approximately every fourth girl must begin a new or join a nearly-new family.)

Sexual relations—which have begun at puberty—continue both inside the family and outside it, but mostly outside it. Whileawayans have two explanations for this. "Jealousy," they say for the first explanation, and for the second, "Why not?"

Whileawayan psychology locates the basis of Whileawayan character in the early indulgence, pleasure, and flowering which is drastically curtailed by the separation from the mothers. This (it says) gives Whileawayan life its characteristic independence, its dissatisfaction, its suspicion, and its tendency toward a rather irritable solipsism.

"Without which" (said the same Dunyasha Bernadetteson, q.v.) "we would all become contented slobs, *nicht wahr?*"

Eternal optimism hides behind this dissatisfaction, however; Whileawayans cannot forget that early paradise and every new face, every new day, every smoke, every dance, brings back life's possibilities. Also sleep and eating, sunrise, weather, the seasons, machinery, gossip, and the eternal temptations of art.

They work too much. They are incredibly tidy.

Yet on the old stone bridge that links New City, South Continent, with Varya's little Alley Ho-ho is chiseled:

You never know what is enough until you know what is more than enough.

If one is lucky, one's hair turns white early; if—as in old Chinese poetry—one is indulging oneself, one dreams of old age. For in old age the Whileawayan woman—no longer as strong and elastic as the young—

has learned to join with calculating machines in the state they say can't be described but is most like a sneeze that never comes off. It is the old who are given the sedentary jobs, the old who can spend their days mapping, drawing, thinking, writing, collating, composing. In the libraries old hands come out from under the induction helmets and give you the reproductions of the books you want; old feet twinkle below the computer shelves, hanging down like Humpty Dumpty's; old ladies chuckle eerily while composing The Blasphemous Cantata (a great favorite of Ysaye's) or mad-moon cityscapes which turn out to be do-able after all; old brains use one part in fifty to run a city (with checkups made by two sulky youngsters) while the other forty-nine parts riot in a freedom they haven't had since adolescence.

The young are rather priggish about the old on Whileaway. They don't really approve of them.

Taboos on Whileaway: sexual relations with anybody considerably older or younger than oneself, waste, ignorance, offending others without intending to.

And of course the usual legal checks on murder and theft—both those crimes being actually quite difficult to commit. ("See," says Chilia, "it's murder if it's sneaky or if she doesn't want to fight. So you yell 'Olaf!' and when she turns around, then—")

No Whileawayan works more than three hours at a time on any one job, except in emergencies.

No Whileawayan marries monogamously. (Some restrict their sexual relations to one other person—at least while that other person is nearby—but there is no legal arrangement.) Whileawayan psychology again refers to the distrust of the mother and the reluctance to form a tie that will engage every level of emotion, all the person, all the time. And the necessity for artificial dissatisfactions.

"Without which" (says Dunyasha Bernadetteson, op. cit.) "we would become so happy we would sit down on our fat, pretty behinds and soon we would start starving, *nyet?*"

But there is too, under it all, the incredible explosive energy, the gaiety of high intelligence, the obliquities of wit, the cast of mind that makes industrial areas into gardens and ha-has, that supports wells of wilderness where nobody ever lives for long, that strews across a planet sceneries, mountains, glider preserves, culs-de-sac, comic nude statuary, artistic lists of tautologies and circular mathematical proofs (over which aficionados are moved to tears), and the best graffiti in this or any other world.

Whileawayans work all the time. They work. And they work. *And they work.*

Michael G. Coney

B orn in Birmingham, England (1932), Michael Coney is the author of numerous science fiction short stories, novellas, and novels, as well as several nonfiction works relating to the forests of Vancouver Island, British Columbia, where he has made his home since the early 1970s. His novels include *Cat Karina* (1982), two volumes in the *Song of the Earth* series—*The Celestial Steam Locomotive* (1983) and *Gods of the Greenaway* (1984)—and two novels that reflect his interest in Arthurian legend: *Fang, the Gnome* (1988) and its sequel *King of the Sceptre'd Isle* (1989). He is a Nebula and Hugo Award nominee for the novelette *Tea and Hamsters*.

This playful story questions appearances. Is Gran crazy or enlightened? The fine line separating human nature from the natural order thins to a blur as Coney examines our inherent tendency to perpetuate dualisms and hierarchies.

The Byrds

GRAN STARTED IT ALL.

Late one afternoon in the hottest summer in living memory, she took off all her clothes, carefully painted red around her eyes and down her cheeks, chin and throat, painted the rest of her body a contrasting black with the exception of her armpits and the inside of her wrists which she painted white, strapped on her new antigravity belt, flapped her arms and rose into the nearest tree, a garry oak, where she perched.

She informed us that, as of now, she was Rufous-necked Hornbill, of India.

"She always wanted to visit India," Gramps told us.

Gran said no more, for the logical reason that Hornbills are not talking birds.

"Come down, Gran!" called Mother. "You'll catch your death of cold."

Gran remained silent. She stretched her neck and gazed at the horizon.

"She's crazy," said Father. "She's crazy. I always said she was. I'll call the asylum."

"You'll do no such thing!" Mother was always very sensitive about Gran's occasional peculiarities. "She'll be down soon. The evenings are drawing in. She'll get cold."

"What's an old fool her age doing with an antigravity unit anyway, that's what I want to know," said Father.

The Water Department was restricting supply and the weatherman was predicting floods. The Energy Department was warning of depleted stocks, the Department of Rest had announced that the population must fall by one-point-eight per cent by November or else, the Mailgift was spewing out a deluge of application forms, tax forms and final reminders, the Tidy Mice were malfunctioning so that the house stank …

And now this.

It was humiliating and embarrassing. Gran up a tree, naked and painted. She stayed there all evening, and I knew that my girlfriend Pandora would be dropping by soon and would be sure to ask questions.

Humanity was at that point in the morality cycle when nudity was considered indecent. Gran was probably thirty years before her time. There was something lonely and anachronistic about her, perched there, balancing unsteadily in a squatting position, occasionally grabbing at the trunk for support then flapping her arms to re-establish the birdlike impression. She looked like some horrible mutation. Her resemblance to a Rufous-necked Hornbill was slight.

"Talk her down, Gramps," said Father.

"She'll come down when she's hungry."

He was wrong. Late in the evening Gran winged her way to a vacant lot where an ancient tree stood. She began to eat unsterilized apples, juice flowing down her chin. It was a grotesque sight.

"She'll be poisoned!" cried Mother.

"So, she's made her choice at last," said Father.

He was referring to Your Choice for Peace, the brochure which Gran and Gramps received monthly from the Department of Rest. Accompanying the brochure is a six-page form on which senior citizens describe all that is good about their life, and a few of the things which bug them. At the end of the form is a box in which the oldster indicates his preference for Life or Peace. If he does not check the box, or if he fails to complete the form, it is assumed that he has chosen Peace, and they send the Wagon for him.

Now Gran was cutting a picturesque silhouette against the pale blue of the evening sky as she circled the rooftops uttering harsh cries. She flew with arms outstretched, legs trailing, and we all had to admit to the beauty of the sight; that is, until a flock of starlings began to mob her. Losing directional control she spiralled downward, recovered, levelled out and skimmed towards us, outpacing the starlings and regaining her perch in the garry oak. She made preening motions and settled down for the night. The family Pesterminator, zapping bugs with its tiny laser, considered her electronically for a second but held its fire.

We were indoors by the time Pandora arrived. She was nervous, complaining that there was a huge mutation in the tree outside, and it had cawed at her.

Mother said quickly, "It's only a Rufous-necked Hornbill."

"A rare visitor to these shores," added Father.

"Why couldn't she have been a sparrow?" asked Mother. "Or something else inconspicuous." Things were not going well for her. The little robot Tidy Mice still sulked behind the wainscoting and she'd had to clean the house by hand.

The garish Gran shone like a beacon in the morning sunlight. There was no concealing the family's degradation. A small crowd had gathered and people were trying to tempt Gran down with breadcrumbs. She looked none the worse for her night out, and was greeting the morning with shrill yells.

Gramps was strapping on an antigravity belt. "I'm going up to fetch her down. This has gone far enough."

I said, "Be careful. She may attack you."

"Don't be a damned fool." Nevertheless Gramps went into the toolshed, later emerging nude and freshly painted. Mother uttered a small scream of distress, suspecting that Gramps, too, had become involved in the conspiracy to diminish the family's social standing.

I reassured her. "She's more likely to listen to one of her own kind."

"Has everyone gone totally insane?" asked Mother.

Gramps rose gracefully into the garry oak, hovered, then settled beside Gran. He spoke to her quietly for a moment and she listened, head cocked attentively.

Then she made low gobbling noises and leaned against him.

He called down, "This may take longer than I thought."

"Oh, my God," said Mother.

"That does it," said Father. "I'm calling the shrink."

Dr. Pratt was tall and dignified, and he took in the situation at a glance. "Has your mother exhibited birdish tendencies before?"

Father answered for Mother. "No more than anyone else. Although, in many other ways, she was— "Gran has always been the soul of conformity," said Mother quickly, beginning to weep. "If our neighbours have been saying otherwise I'll remind them of the slander laws. No—she did it to shame us. She always said she hated the colours we painted the house—she said it looked like a strutting peacock."

"Rutting peacock," said Father. "She said rutting peacock. Those were her exact words."

"Peacock, eh?" Dr. Pratt looked thoughtful. There was a definite avian thread running through this. "So you feel she may be acting in retaliation. She thinks you have made a public spectacle of the house in which she lives, so now she is going to make a public spectacle of you."

"Makes sense," said Father.

"Gran!" called Dr. Pratt. She looked down at us, beady little eyes ringed with red. "I have the personal undertaking of your daughter and son-in-law that the house will be repainted in colours of your own choosing." He spoke on for a few minutes in soothing tones. "That should do it," he said to us finally, picking up his bag. "Put her to bed and keep her off berries, seeds, anything like that. And don't leave any antigravity belts lying around. They can arouse all kinds of prurient interests in older people."

"She still isn't coming down," said Father. "I don't think she understood."

"Then I advise you to fell the tree," said Dr. Pratt coldly, his patience evaporated. "She's a disgusting old exhibitionist who needs to be taught a lesson. Just because she chooses to act out her fantasies in an unusual way doesn't make her any different from anyone else. And what's *he* doing up there, anyway? Does he resent the house paint as well?"

"He *chose* the paint. He's there to bring her down."

We watched them in perplexity. The pair huddled together on the branch, engaged in mutual grooming. The crowd outside the gate had swollen to over a hundred.

On the following morning Gran and Gramps greeted the dawn with a cacophony of gobbling and screeching.

I heard Father throw open his bedroom window and threaten to blast them right out of that goddamned tree and into the hereafter if they didn't keep it down. I heard the metallic click as he cocked his twelve-bore. I heard Mother squeal with apprehension, and the muffled thumping of a physical struggle in the next room.

I was saddened by the strain it puts on marriages when inlaws live in the house—or, in our case, outside the window.

The crowds gathered early and it was quickly apparent that Gramps was through with trying to talk Gran down; in fact, he was through with talking altogether. He perched beside his mate in spry fashion, jerking his head this way and that as he scanned the sky for hawks, cocking an eye at the crowd, shuddering suddenly as though shaking feathers into position.

Dr. Pratt arrived at noon, shortly before the media.

"A classic case of regression to the childlike state," he told us. "The signs are all there: the unashamed nakedness, the bright colours, the speechlessness, the favourite toy, in this case the antigravity belt. I have brought a surrogate toy which I think will solve our problem. Try luring them down with this."

He handed Mother a bright red plastic baby's rattle.

Gran fastened a beady eye on it, shuffled her arms, then launched herself from the tree in a swooping glide. As Mother ducked in alarm, Gran caught the rattle neatly in her bony old toes, wheeled and flapped back to her perch. Heads close, she and Gramps examined the toy.

We waited breathlessly.

Then Gran stomped it against the branch and the shattered remnants fell to the ground.

The crowd applauded. For the first time we noticed the Newspocket van, and the crew with cameras. The effect on Dr. Pratt was instantaneous. He strode towards them and introduced himself to a red-haired woman with a microphone.

"Tell me, Dr. Pratt, to what do you attribute this phenomenon?"

"The manifestation of birdishness in the elderly is a subject which has received very little study up to the present date. Indeed, I would say that it has been virtually ignored. Apart from my own paper—still in draft form—you could search the psychiatric archives in vain for mention of Pratt's Syndrome."

"And why is that, Dr. Pratt?"

"Basically, fear. The fear in each and every one of us of admitting that something primitive and atavistic can lurk within our very genes. For what is more primitive than a bird, the only survivor of the age of dinosaurs?"

"What indeed, Dr. Pratt?"

"You see in that tree two pathetic human creatures who have reverted to a state which existed long before Man took his first step on Earth, a state which can only have been passed on as a tiny coded message in their very flesh and the flesh of their ancestors, through a million years of Time."

"And how long do you expect their condition to last, Dr. Pratt?"

"Until the fall. The winters in these parts are hard, and they'll be out of that tree come the first frost, if they've got any sense left at all."

"Well, thank you, Dr.—"

A raucous screaming cut her short. A group of shapes appeared in the eastern sky, low over the rooftops. They were too big for birds, yet too small for aircraft, and there was a moment's shocked incomprehension before we recognized them for what they were. Then they wheeled over the Newspocket van with a bedlam of yells and revealed themselves as teenagers of both sexes, unclothed, but painted a simple black semi-matt exterior latex. There were nine of them.

In the weeks following, we came to know them as the Crows. They flew overhead, circled, then settled all over the garry oak and the roof of our house.

They made no attempt to harass Gran or Gramps. Indeed, they seemed almost reverential in their attitude towards the old people.

It seemed that Gran had unlocked some kind of floodgate in the human unconscious, and people took to the air in increasing numbers. The manufacturers of antigravity belts became millionaires overnight, and the skies became a bright tapestry of wheeling, screeching figures in rainbow colours and startling nakedness.

The media named them the Byrds.

"I view it as a protest against today's moral code," said Dr. Pratt, who spent most of his time on panels or giving interviews. "For more years than I care to remember, people have been repressed, their honest desires cloaked in conformity just as tightly as their bodies have been swathed in concealing garb. Now, suddenly, people are saying they've had enough. They're pleasing themselves. It shouldn't surprise us. It's healthy. It's good."

It was curious, the way the doctor had become pro-Byrd. These days he seemed to be acting in the capacity of press-agent for Gran—who herself had become a cult-figure. In addition, he was working on his learned paper, The Origins and Spread of Avian Tendencies in Humans.

Pandora and I reckoned he was in the pay of the belt people.

"But it's fun to be in the centre of things," she said one evening, as the Crows came in to roost, and the garry oak creaked under the weight of a flock of Glaucous Culls, come to pay homage to Gran. "It's put the town on the map—and your family too." She took my hand, smiling at me proudly.

There were the Pelicans, who specialized in high dives into the sea, deactivating their belts in mid-air, then reactivating them underwater to rocket Polaris-like from the depths. They rarely caught fish, though; and frequently had to be treated for an ailment known as Pelicans' Balloon, caused by travelling through water at speed with open mouth.

There were the Darwin's Tree Finches, a retiring sect whose existence went unsuspected for some weeks, because they spent so much time in the depths of forests with cactus spines held between their teeth, trying to extract bugs from holes in dead trees. They were a brooding and introspective group.

Virtually every species of bird was represented. And because every cult must have its lunatic fringe, there were the Pigeons. They flocked to the downtown city streets and mingled with the crowds hurrying to and fro. From the shoulders up they looked much like anyone else, only greyer, and with a curious habit of jerking their heads while walking. Bodily, though, they were like any other Byrd: proudly unclothed.

Their roosting habits triggered the first open clash between Byrds and Man. There were complaints that they kept people awake at night, and fouled the rooftops. People began to string electrified wires around their ridges and guttering, and to put poison out.

The Pigeons' retaliation took place early one evening, when the commuting crowds jammed the streets. It was simple and graphic, and well-coordinated. Afterwards, people referred to it obliquely as the Great Deluge, because it was not the kind of event which is discussed openly, in proper society.

There were other sects, many of them; and perhaps the strangest was a group who eschewed the use of antigravity belts altogether. From time to time we would catch sight of them sitting on the concrete abutments of abandoned motorways, searching one another for parasites. Their bodies were painted a uniform brown except for their private parts, which were a luminous red. They called themselves Hamadryas Baboons.

People thought they had missed the point of the whole thing, somehow.

Inevitably when there are large numbers of people involved, there are tragedies. Sometimes an elderly Byrd would succumb to cardiac arrest in mid-air, and drift away on the winds. Others would suffer belt malfunctions and plummet to the ground. As the first chill nights began to grip the country, some of the older Byrds died of exposure and fell from their perches. Courageously they maintained their role until the end, and when daylight came they would be found in the ritualistic "Dead Byrd" posture, on their backs with legs in the air.

"All good things come to an end," said Dr. Pratt one evening as the russet leaves drifted from the trees. It had been a busy day, dozens of groups having come to pay homage to Gran. There was a sense of wrapping up, of things coming to a climax. "We will stage a mass rally," said Dr. Pratt to the Newspocket reporter. "There will be such a gathering of Byrds as the country has never known. Gran will address the multitude at the Great Coming Down."

Mother said, "So long as it's soon. I don't think Gran can take any more frosts."

I went to invite Pandora to the Great Coming Down, but she was not at home. I was about to return when I caught sight of a monstrous thing sitting on the backyard fence. It was bright green except around the eyes, which were grey, and the hair, which was a vivid yellow. It looked at me. It blinked in oddly reptilian fashion. It was Pandora.

She said, "Who's a pretty boy, then?"

The very next day Gran swooped down from the garry oak and seized Mother's scarf with her toes, and a grim tug-of-war ensued.

"Let go, you crazy old fool!" shouted Mother.

Gran cranked her belt up to maximum lift and took a quick twist of the scarf around her ankles. The other end was wrapped snugly around Mother's neck and tucked into her heavy winter coat. Mother left the ground, feet kicking. Her shouts degenerated into strangled grunts.

Father got a grip of Mother's knees as she passed overhead and Gran, with a harsh screech of frustration, found herself descending again; whereupon Gramps, having observed the scene with bright interest, came winging in and took hold of her, adding the power of his belt to hers.

Father's feet left the ground.

Mother by now had assumed the basic hanging attitude: arms dangling limply, head lolling, tongue protruding, face empurpled. I jumped and got hold of Father's ankles. There was a short, sharp rending sound and we fell back to earth in a heap, Mother on top. Gran and Gramps flew back to the garry oak with their half of the scarf, and began to pull it apart with their teeth. Father pried the other half away from Mother's neck. She was still breathing.

"Most fascinating," said Dr. Pratt.

"My wife nearly strangled by those goddamned brutes and he calls it fascinating?"

"No—look at the Hornbills."

"So they're eating the scarf. So they're crazy. What's new?"

"They're not eating it. If you will observe closely, you will see them shredding it. And see—the female is working the strands around that clump of twigs. It's crystal clear what they're doing, of course. This is a classic example of nest-building."

The effect on Father was instantaneous. He jumped up, seized Dr. Pratt by the throat and, shaking him back and forth, shouted, "Any fool knows birds only nest in the spring!" He was overwrought, of course. He apologized the next day.

By that time the Byrds were nesting all over town. They used a variety of materials and in many instances their craftsmanship was pretty to see. The local Newspocket station ran a competition for The Nest I Would Be Happiest To Join My Mate In, treating the matter as a great joke; although some of the inhabitants who had been forcibly undressed in the street thought otherwise. The Byrds wasted nothing. Their nests were intricately-woven collections of whatever could be stolen from below: overcoats, shirts, pants, clothesline, undergarments, hearing-aids, wigs.

"The nesting phenomenon has a two-fold significance," Dr. Pratt informed the media. "On the one hand, we have the desire of the Byrds to emulate the instinctive behavioural patterns of their avian counterparts. On the other hand, there is undoubtedly a suggestion of— how can I say it?—aggression towards the earthbound folk. The Byrds are saying, in their own way: join us. Be natural. Take your clothes off. Otherwise we'll do it for you."

"You don't think they're, uh, sexually *warped?*" asked the reporter.

"Sexually liberated," insisted Dr. Pratt.

The Byrds proved his point the next day, when they began to copulate all over the sky.

It was the biggest sensation since the Great Deluge. Writhing figures filled the heavens and parents locked their children indoors and drew the drapes. It was a fine day for love; the sun glinted on sweat-bedewed flesh, and in the unseasonable warmth the still air rang with cries of delight. The Byrds looped and zoomed and chased one another, and when they met they coupled. Artificial barriers of species were cast aside and Eagle mated with Chaffinch, Robin with Albatross.

"Clearly a visual parable," said Dr. Pratt. "The—"

"Shut up," said Mother. "Shut up, shut up, shut up!"

In the garry oak, Rufous-necked Hornbill mated with Rufous-necked Hornbill, then with Crow; then, rising joyously into the sky, with Skua, with Lark, and finally with Hamadryas Baboon, who had at last realized what it was all about and strapped on a belt.

"She's eighty-six years old! What is she thinking of?"

"She's an Earth Mother to them," said Dr. Pratt.

"Earth Mother my ass," said Father. "She's stark, staring mad, and it's about time we faced up to it."

"It's true, it's true!" wailed Mother, a broken woman. "She's crazy! She's been crazy for years! She's old and useless, and yet she keeps filling in all that stuff on her Peace form, instead of forgetting, like any normal old woman!"

"Winter is coming," said Dr. Pratt, "and we are witnessing the symbolic Preservation of the Species. Look at that nice young Tern up there. Tomorrow they must come back to earth, but in the wombs of the females the memory of this glorious September will live on!"

"She's senile and filthy! I've seen her eating roots from out of the ground, and do you know what she did to the Everattentive Waiter? She cross-wired it with the Mailgift chute and filled the kitchen with self-adhesive cookies!"

"She did?"

And the first shadow of doubt crossed Dr. Pratt's face. The leader of the Byrds crazy?

"And one day a Gameshow called on the visiphone and asked her a skill-testing question which would have set us all up for life—and she did the most disgusting thing, and it went out live and the whole town saw it!"

"I'm sure she has sound psychological reasons for her behaviour," said Dr. Pratt desperately.

"She doesn't! She's insane! She walks to town rather than fill out a Busquest form! She brews wine in a horrible jar under the bed! She was once sentenced to one week's community service for indecent exposure! She trespasses in the Department of Agriculture's fields! You want to know why the house stinks? She programmed the Pesterminator to zap the Tidy Mice!"

"But I thought ... Why didn't you tell me before? My God, when I think of the things I've said on Newspocket! If this comes out, my reputation, all I've worked for, all ..." He was becoming incoherent. "Why didn't you tell me?" he asked again.

"Well, Jesus Christ, it's obvious, isn't it?" snapped Father. "Look at her. She's up in the sky mating with a Hamadryas Baboon, or something very much like one. Now, that's what I call crazy.

"But it's a *Movement*.... It's free and vibrant and so basic, so—"

"A nut cult," said Father. "Started by a loonie and encouraged by a quack. Nothing more, nothing less. And the forecast for tonight is twenty below. It'll wipe out the whole lot of them. You'd better get them all down, Pratt, or you'll have a few thousand deaths on your conscience."

But the Byrds came down of their own accord, later that day. As though sensing the end of the Indian summer and the bitter nights to come, they drifted out of the sky in groups, heading for earth, heading for us. Gran alighted in the garry oak with whirling arms, followed by Gramps. They sat close together on their accustomed branch, gobbling quietly to each other. More Byrds came; the Crows, the Pelicans. They filled the tree, spread along the ridge of the roof and squatted on the guttering. They began to perch on fences and posts, even on the ground, all species intermingled. They were all around us, converging, covering the neighbouring roofs and trees, a great final gathering of humans who, just for a few weeks, had gone a little silly. They looked happy although tired, and a few were shivering as the afternoon shortened into evening. They made a great noise at first, a rustling and screeching and fluid piping, but after a while they quieted down. I saw Pandora amidst them, painted and pretty, but her gaze passed right through me. They were still Byrds, playing their role until the end.

And they all faced Gran.

They were awaiting the word to Come Down, but Gran remained silent, living every last moment.

It was like standing in the centre of a vast amphitheatre, with all those heads turned towards us, all those beady eyes watching us. The Newspocket crew were nowhere to be seen; they probably couldn't get through the crowd.

Finally Dr. Pratt strode forward. He was in the grip of a great despondency. He was going to come clean.

"Fools!" he shouted. A murmur of birdlike sounds arose, but soon died. "All through history there have been fools like you, and they've caused wars and disasters and misery. Fools without minds of their own, who follow their leader without thought, without stopping to ask if their

leader knows what he is doing. Leaders like Genghis Khan, like Star-
busch, like Hitler, leaders who manipulate their followers like puppets in
pursuit of their own crazy ends. Crazy leaders drunk with power. Leaders
like Gran here.

"Yes, Gran is crazy! I mean certifiably crazy, ready for Peace. Irrational
and insane and a burden to the State and to herself. She had me fooled
at first." He uttered a short, bitter laugh, not unlike the mating cry of
Forster's Tern. "I thought I found logic in what she did. Such was the
cunning nature of her madness. It was only recently, when I investigated
Gran's past record, that I unmasked her for what she is: a mentally
unbalanced old woman with marked antisocial tendencies. I could give
you chapter and verse of Gran's past misdemeanors—and I can tell you
right now, this isn't the first time she's taken her clothes off in public—
but I will refrain, out of consideration for her family, who have suffered
enough.

"It will suffice to say that I have recommended her committal and the
Peace Wagon is on its way. The whole affair is best forgotten. Now, come
down out of those trees and scrub off, and go home to your families, all
of you.

He turned away, shoulders drooping. It was nothing like the Great
Coming Down he'd pictured. It was a slinking thing, a creeping home, an
abashed admission of stupidity.

Except that the Byrds weren't coming down.

They sat silently on their perches, awaiting the word from Gran.

All through Dr. Pratt's oration she'd been quiet, staring fixedly at the
sky. Now, at last, she looked around. Her eyes were bright, but it was an
almost-human brightness, a different thing from the beady stare of the
past weeks. And she half-smiled through the paint, but she didn't utter a
word.

She activated her belt and, flapping her arms, rose into the darkening
sky.

And the Byrds rose after her.

They filled the sky, a vast multitude of rising figures, and Pandora was
with them. Gran led, Gramps close behind, and then came Coot and
Skua and Hawk, and the whole thousand-strong mob. They wheeled
once over the town and filled the evening with a great and lonely cry.
Then they headed off in V-formations, loose flocks, tight echelons, a
pattern of dwindling black forms against the pale duck-egg blue of
nightfall.

"Where in hell are they going?" shouted Dr. Pratt as I emerged from
the shed, naked and painted. It was cold, but I would soon get used to it.

"South," I said.

"Why the hell south? What's wrong with here, for God's sake?"

"It's warmer, south. We're migrating."

So I activated my belt and lifted into the air, and watched the house fall away below me, and the tiny bolts of light as the Pesterminator hunted things. The sky seemed empty now but there was still a pink glow to the west. Hurrying south, I saw something winking like a red star and, before long, I was homing in on the gleaming hindquarters of a Hamadryas Baboon.

Octavia E. Butler

O ctavia Estelle Butler (b. 1947), a leading African-American science fiction author, began writing professionally in 1970 after receiving encouraging words from science fiction powerhouse Harlan Ellison. Her works typically explore the themes of African-American history, environmental racism, and speculations on the future of culture. Her first novel, *Patternmaster* (1976), started a five-volume series including *Mind of My Mind* (1977), *Survivor* (1978), *Wild Seed* (1980), which received the James Tiptree, Jr. Award, and *Clay's Ark* (1984). Her other works include the trilogy, *Dawn: Xenogenesis* (1987), *Adulthood Rites* (1988), and *Imago* (1989); *Kindred* (1979); and *Bloodchild and Other Stories* (1995), the title story of which won the Hugo Award and Nebula Award. *The Parable of the Sower*, from which the following excerpt is taken, was a finalist for the Nebula Award and a New York Times Notable Book of the Year. Its sequel, *Parable of the Talents*, was published in 1998. In 1995, Butler received a $295,000 MacArthur Foundation fellowship in recognition of her blending of science fiction and African-American themes.

Formerly a resident of Los Angeles, she moved to Seattle after teaching several Clarion West workshops there and discovering that the Emerald City is one of the most livable she has ever resided in. In *The Parable of the Sower*, she portrays the Northwest as a potential Edenic land of plenty. Lauren Olamina's family community in Los Angeles, Robledo, is burned to the ground; she and a few others from this walled community manage to survive and go on a journey with the intention of reaching the paradise of Oregon, Washington, British Columbia, and Alaska. Interwoven is Lauren's development of a new religion, Earthseed, and the fact that she is a "sharer" crippled with a hyperempathy syndrome that causes her to share the pain of others, including animals. It is worth noting that, along with the themes of literacy and the transformative powers of an utterly embodied woman, *The Parable of the Sower* extends Butler's earlier novel, *Wild Seed*. There Doru collects people he calls "wild seed," the name he creates to signify their genetic potential or those who are "too valuable to be casually killed." He represents a slave-master ideology that treats humans as seeds to be sown and harvested or as farm animals to be bred and used by their owners. In the excerpt below, on the other hand, Lauren disperses Earthseed thoughts—thoughts of change taking root in companions like Harry and Zahra. Butler has called the novel a thought experiment in how to remain human in the face of violent circumstances.

from *The Parable of the Sower*

Chapter 15

WE WALKED DOWN TO THE FREEWAY—THE 118—AND TURNED WEST. We would take the 118 to the 23 and the 23 to U.S. 101. The 101 would take us up the coast toward Oregon. We became part of a broad river of people walking west on the freeway. Only a few straggled east against the current—east toward the mountains and the desert. Where were the westward walkers going? To something, or just away from here?

We saw a few trucks—most of them run at night—swarms of bikes or electric cycles, and two cars. All these had plenty of room to speed along the outer lanes past us. We're safer if we keep to the left lanes away from the on and off ramps. It's against the law in California to walk on the freeways, but the law is archaic. Everyone who walks walks on the freeways sooner or later. Freeways provide the most direct routes between cities and parts of cities. Dad walked or bicycled on them often. Some prostitutes and peddlers of food, water, and other necessities live along the freeways in sheds or shacks or in the open air. Beggars, thieves, and murderers live here, too.

But I've never walked a freeway before today. I found the experience both fascinating and frightening. In some ways, the scene reminded me of an old film I saw once of a street in mid-twentieth-century China—walkers, bicyclers, people carrying, pulling, pushing loads of all kinds. But the freeway crowd is a heterogeneous mass—black and white, Asian and Latin, whole families are on the move with babies on backs or perched atop loads in carts, wagons or bicycle baskets, sometimes along with an old or handicapped person. Other old, ill, or handicapped people hobbled along as best they could with the help of sticks or fitter companions. Many were armed with sheathed knives, rifles, and, of course, visible, holstered handguns. The occasional passing cop paid no attention.

Children cried, played, squatted—did everything except eat. Almost no one ate while walking. I saw a couple of people drink from canteens. They took quick, furtive gulps, as though they were doing something shameful—or something dangerous.

A woman alongside us collapsed. I got no impression of pain from her, except at the sudden impact of her body weight on her knees. That made me stumble, but not fall. The woman sat where she had fallen for a few seconds, then lurched to her feet and began walking again, leaning forward under her huge pack.

Almost everyone was filthy. Their bags and bundles and packs were filthy. They stank. And we, who have slept on concrete in ashes and dirt, and who have not bathed for three days—we fitted in pretty well. Only our new sleepsack packs gave us away as either new to the road or at least in possession of new stealables. We should have dirtied the packs a little before we got started. We will dirty them tonight. I'll see to it.

There were a few young guys around, lean and quick, some filthy, some not dirty at all. Keiths. Today's Keiths. The ones who bothered me most weren't carrying much. Some weren't carrying anything except weapons.

Predators. They looked around a lot, stared at people, and the people looked away. I looked away. I was glad to see that Harry and Zahra did the same. We didn't need trouble. If trouble came, I hoped we could kill it and keep walking.

The gun was fully loaded now, and I wore it holstered, but half covered by my shirt. Harry bought himself a knife. The money he had snatched up as he ran from his burning house had not been enough to buy a gun. I could have bought a second gun, but it would have taken too much of my money, and we have a long way to go.

Zahra used the shoe money to buy herself a knife and a few personal things. I had refused my share of that money. She needed a few dollars in her pocket.

The day she and Harry use their knives, I hope they kill. If they don't, I might have to, to escape the pain. And what will they think of that?

They deserve to know that I'm a sharer. For their own safety, they should know. But I've never told anyone. Sharing is a weakness, a shameful secret. A person who knows what I am can hurt me, betray me, disable me with little effort.

I can't tell. Not yet. I'll have to tell soon, I know, but not yet. We're together, the three of us, but we're not a unit yet. Harry and I don't know Zahra very well, nor she us. And none of us know what will happen when we're challenged. A racist challenge might force us apart. I want to trust these people. I like them, and. . .they're all I have left. But I need more time to decide. It's no small thing to commit yourself to other people.

"You okay?" Zahra asked.

I nodded.

"You look like hell. And you're so damned poker-faced most of the time....

"Just thinking," I said. "There's so much to think about now."

She sighed her breath out in a near whistle. "Yeah. I know. But keep your eyes open. You get too wrapped up in your thinking, and you'll miss things. People get killed on freeways all the time."

Chapter 16

Earthseed
Cast on new ground
Must first perceive
That it knows nothing.

Earthseed: The Books of the Living

Monday, August 2, 2027
(cont. from notes expanded August 8)

Here are some of the things I've learned today:

Walking hurts. I've never done enough walking to learn that before, but I know it now. It isn't only the blisters and sore feet, although we've got those. After a while, everything hurts. I think my back and shoulders would like to desert to another body. Nothing eases the pain except rest. Even though we got a late start, we stopped twice today to rest. We went off the freeway, into hills or bushes to sit down, drink water, eat dried fruit and nuts. Then we went on. The days are long this time of year.

Sucking on a plum or apricot pit all day makes you feel less thirsty. Zahra told us that.

"When I was a kid," she said, "there were times when I would put a little rock in my mouth. Anything to feel better. It's a cheat, though. If you don't drink enough water, you'll die no matter how you feel."

All three of us walked along with seeds in our mouths after our first stop, and we felt better. We drank only during our stops in the hills. It's safer that way.

Also, cold camps are safer than cheery campfires. Yet tonight we cleared some ground, dug into a hillside, and made a small fire in the hollow. There we cooked some of my acorn meal with nuts and fruit. It was wonderful. Soon we'll run out of it and we'll have to survive on beans, cornmeal, oats—expensive stuff from stores. Acorns are home-food, and home is gone.

Fires are illegal. You can see them flickering all over the hills, but they are illegal. Everything is so dry that there's always a danger of campfires getting away from people and taking out a community or two. It does happen. But people who have no homes will build fires. Even people like us who know what fire can do will build them. They give comfort, hot food, and a false sense of security.

While we were eating, and even after we'd finished, people drifted over and tried to join us. Most were harmless and easily gotten rid of.

Three claimed they just wanted to get warm. The sun was still up, red on the horizon, and it was far from cold.

Three women wanted to know whether two studs like Harry and me didn't need more than one woman. The women who asked this may have been cold, considering how few clothes they had on. It's going to be strange for me, pretending to be a man.

"Couldn't I just roast this potato in your coals?" an old man asked, showing us a withered potato.

We gave him some fire and sent him away—and watched to see where he went, since a burning brand could be either a weapon or a major distraction if he had friends hiding. It's crazy to live this way, suspecting helpless old people. Insane. But we need our paranoia to keep us alive. Hell, Harry wanted to let the old guy sit with us. It took Zahra and me together to let him know that wasn't going to happen. Harry and I have been well-fed and protected all our lives. We're strong and healthy and better educated than most people our age. But we're stupid out here. We want to trust people. I fight against the impulse. Harry hasn't learned to do that yet. We argued about it afterward, low voiced, almost whispering.

"Nobody's safe," Zahra told him. "No matter how pitiful they look, they can steal you naked. Little kids, skinny and big-eyed will make off with all your money, water, and food! I know. I used to do it to people. Maybe they died, I don't know. But I didn't die."

Harry and I both stared at her. We knew so little about her life. But to me, at that moment, Harry was our most dangerous question mark.

"You're strong and confident," I said to him. "You think you can take care of yourself out here, and maybe you can. But think what a stab wound or a broken bone would mean out here: Disablement, slow death from infection or starvation, no medical care, nothing."

He looked at me as though he wasn't sure he wanted to know me anymore. "What, then?" he asked. "Everyone's guilty until proven innocent? Guilty of what? And how do they prove themselves to you?"

"I don't give a piss whether they're innocent or not," Zahra said. "Let them tend to their own business."

"Harry, your mind is still back in the neighborhood," I said. "You still think a mistake is when your father yells at you or you break a finger or chip a tooth or something. Out here a mistake—one mistake— and you may be dead. Remember that guy today? What if that happened to us?"

We had seen a man robbed—a chubby guy of 35 or 40 who was walking along eating nuts out of a paper bag. Not smart. A little kid of 12 or 13 snatched the nuts and ran off with them. While the victim was distracted by the little kid, two bigger kids tripped him, cut his pack straps, dragged the pack off his back, and ran off with it. The whole thing happened so fast that no one could have interfered if they'd wanted to. No one tried. The victim was unhurt except for bruises and abrasions— the sort of thing I had to put up with every day back in the neighborhood. But the victim's supplies were gone. If he had a home nearby and other supplies, he would be all right. Otherwise, his only way of surviving might be to rob someone else—if he could.

"Remember?" I asked Harry. "We don't have to hurt anyone unless they push us into it, but we don't dare let our guard down. We can't trust people."

Harry shook his head. "What if I thought that way when I pulled that guy off Zahra?"

I held on to my temper. "Harry, you know I don't mean we shouldn't trust or help each other. We know each other. We've made a commitment to travel together."

"I'm not sure we do know each other."

"I am. And we can't afford your denial. You can't afford it."

He just stared at me.

"Out here, you adapt to your surroundings or you get killed," I said. "That's obvious!"

Now he did look at me as though I were a stranger. I looked back, hoping I knew him as well as I thought I did. He had a brain and he had courage. He just didn't want to change.

"Do you want to break off with us," Zahra asked, "go your own way without us?"

His gaze softened as he looked at her. "No," he said. "Of course not. But we don't have to turn into animals, for godsake."

"In a way, we do," I said. "We're a pack, the three of us, and all those other people out there aren't in it. If we're a good pack, and we work together, we have a chance. You can be sure we aren't the only pack out here."

He leaned back against a rock, and said with amazement, "You damn sure talk macho enough to be a guy."

I almost hit him. Maybe Zahra and I would be better off without him. But no, that wasn't true. Numbers mattered. Friendship mattered. One real male presence mattered.

"Don't repeat that," I whispered, leaning close to him. "Never say that again. There are other people all over these hills; you don't know who's listening. You give me away and you weaken yourself."

That reached him. "Sorry," he said.

"It's bad out here," Zahra said. "But most people make it if they're careful. People weaker than us make it—if they're careful."

Harry gave a wan smile. "I hate this world already," he said.

"It's not so bad if people stick together."

He looked from her to me and back to her again. He smiled at her and nodded. It occurred to me then that he liked her, was attracted to her. That could be a problem for her later. She was a beautiful woman, and I would never be beautiful—which didn't bother me. Boys had always seemed to like me. But Zahra's looks grabbed male attention. If she and Harry get together, she could wind up carrying two heavy loads northward.

I was lost in thought about the two of them when Zahra nudged me with her foot.

Two big, dirty-looking guys were standing nearby, watching us, watching Zahra in particular.

I stood up, feeling the others stand with me, flanking me. These guys were too close to us. They meant to be too close. As I stood up, I put my hand on the gun.

"Yeah?" I said, "What do you want?"

"Not a thing," one of them said, smiling at Zahra. Both wore big holstered knives which they fingered.

I drew the gun. "Good deal," I said.

Their smiles vanished. "What, you going to shoot us for standing here?" the talkative one said.

I thumbed the safety. I would shoot the talker, the leader. The other one would run away. He already wanted to run away. He was staring, open-mouthed, at the gun. By the time I collapsed, he would be gone.

"Hey, no trouble!" the talker raised his hands, backing away. "Take it easy, man.

I let them go. I think it would have been better to shoot them. I'm afraid of guys like that—guys looking for trouble, looking for victims. But it seems I can't quite shoot someone just because I'm afraid of him. I killed a man on the night of the fire, and I haven't thought much about it.

But this was different. It was like what Harry said about stealing. I've heard, "Thou shalt not kill," all my life, but when you have to, you kill. I wonder what Dad would say about that. But then, he was the one who taught me to shoot.

"We'd better keep a damn good watch tonight," I said. I looked at Harry, and was glad to see that he looked the way I probably had a moment before: mad and worried. "Let's pass your watch and my gun around," I told him. "Three hours per watcher."

"You would have done it, wouldn't you?" he asked. It sounded like a real question.

I nodded. "Wouldn't you?"

"Yes. I wouldn't have wanted to, but those guys were out for fun. Their idea of fun, anyway." He glanced at Zahra. He had pulled one man off her, and taken a beating for it. Maybe the obvious threat to her would keep him alert. Anything that would keep him alert couldn't be all bad.

I looked at Zahra, kept my voice very low. "You never went shooting with us, so I have to ask. Do you know how to use this?"

"Yeah," she said. "Richard let his older kids go out, but he wouldn't let me. Before he bought me, though, I was a good shot."

Her alien past again. It distracted me for a moment. I had been waiting to ask her how much a person costs these days. And she had been sold by her mother to a man who couldn't have been much more than a stranger. He could have been a maniac, a monster. And my father used to worry about future slavery or debt slavery. Had he known? He couldn't have.

"Have you used a gun like this before?" I asked. I re-engaged the safety and handed it to her.

"Hell, yeah," she said, examining it. "I like this. It's heavy, but if you shoot somebody with it, they go down." She released the clip, checked it, reinserted it, rammed it home, and handed it back. "I wish I could have practiced with you all," she said. "I always wanted to."

Without warning, I felt a pang of loneliness for the burned neighborhood. It was almost a physical pain. I had been desperate to leave it, but I had expected it still to be there—changed, but surviving. Now that it was gone, there were moments when I couldn't imagine how I was going to survive without it.

"You guys get some sleep," I said. "I'm too wound up to sleep now. I'll take the first watch."

"We should gather more wood for the fire first," Harry said. "It's burning low."

"Let it go out," I said. "It's a spotlight on us, and it messes up our night vision. Other people can see us long before we see them."

"And sit here in the dark," he said. It wasn't a protest. At worst, it was grudging agreement. "I'll take the watch after you," he said, lying back and pulling up his sleepsack and positioning the rest of his gear to serve as a pillow. As an afterthought, he took off his wrist watch and gave it to me. "It was a gift from my mother," he said.

"You know I'll take care of it," I told him, He nodded. "You be careful," he said, and closed his eyes.

I put the watch on, pulled the elastic of my sleeve down over it so that the glow of the dial wouldn't be visible by accident, and sat back against the hill to make a few quick notes. While there was still some natural light, I could write and watch.

Zahra watched me for a while, then laid her hand on my arm. "Teach me to do that," she whispered.

I looked at her, not understanding,

"Teach me to read and write."

I was surprised, but I shouldn't have been. Where, in a life like hers, had there been time or money for school. And once Richard Moss bought her, her jealous co-wives wouldn't have taught her.

"You should have come to us back in the neighborhood," I said. "We would have set up lessons for you."

"Richard wouldn't let me. He said I already knew enough to suit him."

I groaned. "I'll teach you. We can start tomorrow morning if you want.

"Okay." She gave me an odd smile and began ordering her bag and her few possessions, bundled in my scavenged pillowcase. She lay down in her bag and turned on her side to look at me. "I didn't think I'd like you," she said. "Preacher's kid, all over the place, teaching, telling everybody what to do, sticking your damn nose in everything. But you ain't bad."

I went from surprise into amusement of my own. "Neither are you," I said.

"You didn't like me either?" Her turn to be surprised.

"You were the best looking woman in the neighborhood. No, I wasn't crazy about you. And remember a couple of years ago when you tried your hardest to make me throw up while I was learning to clean and skin rabbits."

"Why'd you want to learn that, anyway?" she asked. "Blood, guts, worms.... I just figured, 'There she goes again, sticking her nose where it don't belong. Well, let her have it!'"

"I wanted to know that I could do that—handle a dead animal, skin it, butcher it, treat its hide to make leather. I wanted to know how to do it, and that I could do it without getting sick."

"Why?"

"Because I thought someday I might have to. And we might out here. Same reason I put together an emergency pack and kept it where I could grab it."

"I wondered about that—about you having all that stuff from home, I mean. At first I thought maybe you got it all when you went back. But no, you were ready for all the trouble. You saw it coming."

"No." I shook my head, remembering. "No one could have been ready for that. But. . . . I thought something would happen someday. I didn't know how bad it would be or when it would come. But everything was getting worse: the climate, the economy, crime, drugs, you know. I didn't believe we would be allowed to sit behind our walls, looking clean and fat and rich to the hungry, thirsty, homeless, jobless, filthy people outside."

She turned again and lay on her back, staring upward at the stars. "I should have seen some of that stuff," she said. "But I didn't. Those big walls. And everybody had a gun. There were guards every night. I thought. … I thought we were so strong."

I put my notebook and pen down, sat on my sleepsack, and put my own pillowcased bundle behind me. Mine was lumpy and uncomfortable to lean on. I wanted it uncomfortable. I was tired. Everything ached. Given a little comfort, I would fall asleep.

The sun was down now, and our fire had gone out except for a few glowing coals. I drew the gun and held it in my lap. If I needed it at all, I would need it fast. We weren't strong enough to survive slowness or stupid mistakes.

I sat where I was for three weary, terrifying hours. Nothing happened to me, but I could see and hear things happening. There were people moving around the hills, sometimes silhouetting themselves against the sky as they ran or walked over the tops of hills. I saw groups and individuals. Twice I saw dogs, distant, but alarming. I heard a lot of gunfire— individual shots and short bursts of automatic weapons fire. That last and the dogs worried me, scared me. A pistol would be no protection against a machine gun or automatic rifle. And dogs might not know enough to be afraid of guns. Would a pack keep coming if I shot two or three of its members? I sat in a cold sweat, longing for walls—or at least for another magazine or two for the gun.

It was nearly midnight when I woke Harry, gave him the gun and the watch, and made him as uncomfortable as I could by warning him about the dogs, the gunfire, and the many people who wandered around at night. He did look awake and alert enough when I lay down.

I fell asleep at once. Aching and exhausted, I found the hard ground as welcoming as my bed at home.

A shout awoke me. Then I heard gunfire—several single shots, thunderous and nearby. Harry?

Something fell across me before I could get out of my sleepsack— something big and heavy. It knocked the breath out of me. I struggled to get it off me, knowing that it was a human body, dead or unconscious. As I pushed at it and felt its heavy beard stubble and long hair, I realized it was a man, and not Harry. Some stranger.

I heard scrambling and thrashing near me. There were grunts and sounds of blows. A fight. I could see them in the darkness—two figures struggling on the ground. The one on the bottom was Harry.

He was fighting someone over the gun, and he was losing. The muzzle was being forced toward him.

That couldn't happen. We couldn't lose the gun or Harry. I took a small granite boulder from our fire pit, set my teeth,and brought it down with all my strength on the back of the intruder's head. And I brought myself down.

It wasn't the worst pain I had ever shared, but it came close. I was worthless after delivering that one blow. I think I was unconscious for a while.

Then Zahra appeared from somewhere, feeling me, trying to see me. She wouldn't find a wound, of course.

I sat up, fending her off, and saw that Harry was there too.

"Are they dead?" I asked.

"Never mind them," he said. "Are you all right?"

I got up, swaying from the residual shock of the blow. I felt sick and dizzy, and my head hurt. A few days before, Harry had made me feel that way and we'd both recovered. Did that mean the man I'd hit would recover?

I checked him. He was still alive, unconscious, not feeling any pain now. What I was feeling was my own reaction to the blow I'd struck.

"The other one's dead," Harry said. "This one. ... Well, you caved in the back of his head. I don't know why he's still alive."

"Oh, no," I whispered. "Oh hell." And then to Harry. "Give me the gun."

"Why?" he asked.

My fingers had found the blood and broken skull, soft and pulpy at the back of the stranger's head. Harry was right. He should have been dead.

"Give me the gun." I repeated, and held out a bloody hand for it. "Unless you want to do this yourself."

"You can't shoot him. You can't just ..."

"I hope you'd find the courage to shoot me if I were like that, and out here with no medical care to be had. We shoot him, or leave him here alive. How long do you think it will take him to die?"

"Maybe he won't die."

I went to my pack, struggling to navigate without throwing up. I pulled it away from the dead man, groped within it, and found my knife. It was a good knife, sharp and strong. I flicked it open and cut the unconscious man's throat with it.

Not until the flow of blood stopped did I feel safe. The man's heart had pumped his life away into the ground. He could not regain consciousness and involve me in his agony.

But, of course, I was far from safe. Perhaps the last two people from my old life were about to leave me. I had shocked and horrified them. I wouldn't blame them for leaving.

"Strip the bodies," I said. "Take what they have, then we'll put them into the scrub oaks down the hill where we gathered wood."

I searched the man I had killed, found a small amount of money in his pants pocket and a larger amount in his right sock. Matches, a packet of almonds, a packet of dried meat, and a packet of small, round, purple pills. I found no knife, no weapon of any kind. So this was not one of the pair that sized us up earlier in the night. I hadn't thought so. Neither of them had been long-haired. Both of these were.

I put the pills back in the pocket I had taken them from. Everything else, I kept. The money would help sustain us. The food might or might not be edible. I would decide that when I could see it clearly.

I looked to see what the others were doing, and was relieved to find them stripping the other body. Harry turned it over, then kept watch as Zahra went through the clothing, shoes, socks, and hair. She was even more thorough than I had been. With no hint of squeamishness, she hauled off the man's clothing and examined its greasy pockets, seams, and hems. I got the feeling she had done this before.

"Money, food, and a knife," she whispered at last.

"The other one didn't have a knife," I said, crouching beside them. "Harry, what—?"

"He had one," Harry whispered. "He pulled it when I yelled for them to stop. It's probably on the ground somewhere. Let's put these two down in the oaks."

"You and I can do it," I said. "Give Zahra the gun. She can guard us."

I was glad to see him hand her the gun without protest. He had not made a move to hand it to me when I asked, but that had been different.

We took the bodies down to the scrub oaks and rolled them into cover. Then we kicked dirt over all the blood that we could see and the urine that one of the men had released.

That wasn't enough. By mutual consent, we moved camp. This meant nothing more than gathering our bundles and sleepsacks and carrying them over the next low ridge and out of sight of where we had been.

If you camped on a hill between any two of the many low, riblike ridges, you could have, almost, the privacy of a big, open-topped, three-walled room. You were vulnerable from hill or ridge tops, but if you camped on the ridges, you would be noticed by far more people. We chose a spot between two ridges, settled, and sat silent for some time. I felt set-apart. I knew I had to speak, and I was afraid that nothing I could say would help. They might leave me. In disgust, in distrust, in fear, they might decide that they couldn't travel with me any longer. Best to try to get ahead of them.

"I'm going to tell you about myself," I said. "I don't know whether it will help you to understand me, but I have to tell you. You have a right to know."

And in low whispers, I told them about my mother—my biological mother—and about my sharing.

When I finished, there was another long silence. Then Zahra spoke, and I was so startled by the sound of her soft voice that I jumped.

"So when you hit that guy," she said, "it was like you hitting yourself."

"No," I said. "I don't get the damage. Just the pain."

"But, I mean it felt like you hit yourself?"

I nodded. "Close enough. When I was little, I used to bleed along with people if I hurt them or even if I saw them hurt. I haven't done that for a few years."

"But if they're unconscious or dead, you don't feel anything."

"That's right."

"So that's why you killed that guy?"

"I killed him because he was a threat to us. To me in a special way, but to you too. What could we have done about him? Abandon him to the flies, the ants, and the dogs? You might have been willing to do that, but would Harry? Could we stay with him? For how long? To what purpose? Or would we dare to hunt up a cop and try to report seeing a guy hurt without involving ourselves. Cops are not trusting people. I think they would want to check us out, hang on to us for a while, maybe charge us with attacking the guy and killing his friend. I turned to look at Harry who had not said a word. "What would you have done?" I asked.

"I don't know," he said, his voice hard with disapproval. "I only know I wouldn't have done what you did."

"I wouldn't have asked you to do it," I said. "I didn't ask you. But, Harry, I would do it again. I might have to do it again. That's why I'm telling you this." I glanced at Zahra. "I'm sorry I didn't tell you before. I knew I should, but talking about it is ... hard. Very hard. I've never told anyone before. Now. ..." I took a deep breath. "Now everything's up to you."

"What do you mean?" Harry demanded.

I looked at him, wishing I could see his expression well enough to know whether this was a real question. I didn't think it was. I decided to ignore him.

"So what do you think?" I asked, looking at Zahra.

Neither of them said anything for a minute. Then Zahra began to speak, began to say such terrible things in that soft voice of hers. After a moment, I wasn't sure she was talking to us.

"My mama took drugs, too," she said. "Shit, where I was born, everybody's mama took drugs—and whored to pay for them. And had babies all the time, and threw them away like trash when they died. Most of the babies did die from the drugs or accidents or not having enough to eat or being left alone so much ... or from being sick. They were always getting sick. Some of them were born sick. They had sores all over or big things on their eyes—tumors, you know—or no legs or fits or can't breathe right. ... All kinds of things. And some of the ones who lived were dumb as dirt. Can't think, can't learn, just sit around nine, ten years old, peeing in their pants, rocking back and forth, and dripping spit down their chins. There's a lot of them."

She took my hand and held it. "You ain't got nothing wrong with you, Lauren—nothing worth worrying about. That Paracetco shit was baby milk."

How was it that I had not gotten to know this woman back in the neighborhood? I hugged her. She seemed surprised, then hugged back.

We both looked at Harry.

He sat still, near us, but far from us—from me. "What would you do," he asked, "if that guy only had a broken arm or leg?"

I groaned, thinking about pain. I already knew more than I wanted to about how broken bones feel. "I think I'd let him go," I said, "and I'm sure I would be sorry for it. It would be a long time before I stopped looking over my shoulder."

"You wouldn't kill him to escape the pain?"

"I never killed anyone back in the neighborhood to escape pain."

"But a stranger ..."

"I've said what I would do."

"What if I broke my arm?"

"Then I might not be much good to you. I would be having trouble with my arm, too, after all. But we'd have two good arms between us." I sighed. "We grew up together, Harry. You know me. You know what kind of person I am. I might fail you, but if I could help myself, I wouldn't betray you."

"I thought I knew you."

I took his hands, looked at their big, pale, blunt fingers. They had a lot of strength in them, I knew, but I had never seen him use it to bully anyone. He was worth some trouble, Harry was.

"No one is who we think they are," I said. "That's what we get for not being telepathic. But you've trusted me so far—and I've trusted you. I've just put my life in your hands. What are you going to do?"

Was he going to abandon me now to my "infirmity"—instead of me maybe abandoning him at some future time due to a theoretical broken arm. And I thought: One oldest kid to another, Harry; would that be responsible behavior?

He took his hands back. "Well, I did know you were a manipulative bitch," he said.

Zahra smothered a laugh. I was surprised. I'd never heard him use the word before. I heard it now as a sound of frustration. He wasn't going to leave. He was a last bit of home that I didn't have to give up yet. How did he feel about that? Was he angry with me for almost breaking up the group? He had reason to be, I suppose.

"I don't understand how you could have been like this all the time," he said. "How could you hide your sharing from everyone?"

"My father taught me to hide it," I told him. "He was right. In this world, there isn't any room for housebound, frightened, squeamish people, and that's what I might have become if everyone had known about me—all the other kids, for instance. Little kids are vicious. Haven't you noticed?"

"But your brothers must have known."

"My father put the fear of God into them about it. He could do that. As far as I know, they never told anyone. Keith used to play 'funny' tricks on me, though."

"So … you faked everyone out. You must be a hell of an actor."

"I *had* to learn to pretend to be normal. My father kept trying to convince me that I was normal. He was wrong about that, but I'm glad he taught me the way he did."

"Maybe you are normal. I mean if the pain isn't real, then maybe—"

"Maybe this sharing thing is all in my head? Of course it is! And I can't get it out. Believe me, I'd love to."

There was a long silence. Then he asked, "What do you write in your book every night?" Interesting shift.

"My thoughts," I said. "The day's events. My feelings."

"Things you can't say?" he asked. "Things that are important to you?"

"Yes."

"Then let me read something. Let me know something about the you that hides. I feel as though … as though you're a lie. I don't know you. Show me something of you that's real."

What a request! Or was it a demand? I would have given him money to read and digest some of the Earthseed portions of my journal. But he had to be eased into them. If he read the wrong thing, it would just increase the distance between us.

"The risks you ask me to take, Harry. … But, yes, I'll show you some of what I've written. I want to. It'll be another first for me. All I ask is that you read what I show you aloud so Zahra can hear it. As soon as it's light, I'll show you."

When it was light, I showed him this:

> *"All that you touch*
> *You Change.*
>
> *All that you Change*
> *Changes you.*
>
> *The only lasting truth*
> *Is Change.*
>
> *God*
> *Is Change."*

Last year, I chose these lines to be the first page of the first book of *Earthseed. The Books of the Living.* These lines say everything. Everything!

Imagine him asking me for it.

I must be careful.

Molly Gloss

I n this novel, winner of the Pen Center USA West fiction prize (1997) and Nebula Award nominee (1998), a group of Quakers builds a biosphere called Dusty Miller to travel through space in search of a more sustainable world than the deteriorating Earth. The novel tells the story of those who grow up on the Dusty Miller, an artificial ecosystem that they must carefully control. In the following excerpt, the search craft Lark has made contact with a planet that might provide a final destination, but crashed in the process. The colonists are justifiably worried about the harshness of this New World and must choose among difficult alternatives: should they adapt to life on the Arctic-like planet, terraform its surface, or go on with the exodus? Here Gloss explores the consequences of mismanaging the ecology in ways that reflect prevailing environmental concerns. The excerpt illustrates the novel's emphasis on tenets of community building and environmental sustainability, the need for a healthy and well-balanced ecosystem that contains both human and nonhuman members, the current ecological concern regarding the introduction of nonnative plants that threaten to overrun native flora, and the question of when to interfere with the natural process.

Gloss lives, writes, and teaches in Portland. She received the Mrs. Giles Whiting Foundation Award in 1996. Her novel *The Jump-Off Creek* (1989) was a finalist for the PEN/Faulkner Award for American Fiction and won the H. L. Davis Oregon Book Award as well as a Pacific Northwest Booksellers Award for fiction. *The Dazzle of Day* also was a 1998 finalist for the Oregon Book Awards. Her novel *Wild Life* (2000) received the James Tiptree Jr. Memorial Award and is a 2002 selection of the Seattle Public Library/Washington Center for the Book.

from *The Dazzle of Day*

Chapter 5. HUMBERTO

A song of the rolling earth, and of words
according,
Were you thinking that those were the words,
those upright lines? those curves, angles, dots?
No, those are not the words, the substantial words are in the ground and sea,
They are in the air, they are in you.

BECAUSE IT WAS MAY, FARMING WAS A WORK THAT WOULDN'T WAIT for grief or fear to be spent. In May there was rain every night, and long days of bright light, and the rain-washed air was charged with fertility. The rice was delicate, not as swift or as coarse as maize; if it wasn't to be overgrown it had to be kept weeded, and weeded again. It stood knee-high in straight rows of vivid green, and Humberto went between the rows, scraping the ground with a broad maĉeta curved like a scimitar.

Asian people had grown a rice that thrived in flooded fields, but it was the upland Costa Rican rice that had been brought onto the *Miller,* a kind of rice that sprang from well-drained ground, and yielded well on poor soil where heavy-feeding crops would sulk. For the latter virtue, Sven Fujino and Humberto had planted it to this field, the Shepherd's Crook, which was always impoverished by the old trees standing at the east edge of the ŝiro, the remnant of a woodland that once had separated them from Esperplena. Humberto had gone along, jabbing holes in the earth with a pointed stick, while Sven followed him with the rice seed in the hollow shell of a calabash gourd. Humberto's lines were straight as if he'd followed a cord strung across the field. It was something you had an eye for, or not; Sven always laid crooked rows.

Now Humberto went alone between the ranks of green, skinning the ground with the blade of the maĉeta in short, even strokes. His son had gone to work with Ĝeronimo Zea, digging up and chopping the spent stalks of okra now that that crop was finished, and Humberto had gone into the rice without asking anyone else's company in his work. He thought he wanted to be alone, and not to talk to anyone about the crashed boat. Weeding was not a job he liked overmuch, but he liked the small, repetitive sound, the scuffing the blade made against the earth, and when he straightened his back and glanced behind him, he liked the way the row looked, the soil clean and dark, and the cut weeds lying in little wilting windrows. It was work you could do without thinking

62

about anything, your mind absorbed in the short, methodical swinging of the tool.

Houses stood nearby the field of rice, and the path between Alaŭdo and Esperplena went along the south edge of the Shepherd's Crook; people frequently walked by on the path or went up the ladder of a house or down from one. He kept at his work with his head down, meaning to give a message about his wish for solitude, but not many people respected it. Because he was related to actors in the event, they steadily brought him their well-meant sympathy and their speculations about the *Lark.*

Years before, Luza Kordoba had stopped his bleeding to death when he had stepped into the edge of Henriko Lij's cane-cutter. And though he and Luza had never had a sexual union—Luza was sapphic, her lovers all had been women—people knew that Humberto had loved her for a while, and tried to interest her in loving him, and that their friendship was charged with an old sexual energy. They wanted to bring him consoling words—he must be suffering grief for Juko's sake, eh? and for the loss of Luza Cordoba—but he was already tired of the weight of his sorrow. He wanted to find peace in his weeding and be allowed to let go of the people lost on the New World.

After a while Pia Putala walked out into the rice with another long blade and went to work beside him. She was silent for quite a while, as if she must have guessed his wish for privacy. But then she said, looking around, "There is a word just gone around from the Radio Committee, a rescue is being done. Did you hear?"

He hadn't heard that. He stood up straight. "No. They're not killed, then?"

"Well, maybe not, somebody among them has given a kind of signal. I guess it was a plan they all made in case this might happen. They've got a balloon going to bring them up one by one, people are saying."

Humberto stood looking across the several rows of rice at Pia. Since word had come of the crash of the *Lark,* he had secretly thought they were dead, all four of them, or would be shortly, as there wasn't any way to get them back up to the *Ruby,* was there? He hadn't imagined they could use the balloons. The idea startled him, made him feel stupid.

"When?" he asked her.

She straightened from her work and looked thoughtfully at the ground. "I don't think there was a time said. A balloon isn't something you can move precisely, I guess. But anyway they've started on it." She eyed him cautiously. "There's no sure telling this rescue will work, I don't suppose."

He was surprised again, feeling there must have been something in his face or his voice that made this woman, twenty years younger, think him so naive. "No," he said, in a tone of astonishment, and bent to his weeding again. He wondered if people had gone to tell this news to Juko and to Kristina Veberes, but was afraid of asking it, embarrassed.

He had thought there was only one possibility and now suddenly there were several. He kept on with the maĉeta, but his peace was now completely lost, he was preoccupied with imagining the manifold details and difficulties of this balloon rescuing. Deliberately, he kept from reimagining Luza and Bjoro alive. He was cautious of pouring much hope into a fragile vessel.

Once she had told her news, Pia became silent again, focused upon the repetitive weeding, and after a while Humberto surprised himself by restarting their conversation. He asked her, "Are people wanting to go on with Meeting for Business, have you heard?" He didn't want to go to the Farms Committee Meeting if people only meant to stand around and guess at how things would come out with the crashed boat.

"I don't know," Pia said. "I heard a clerk over in Bonveno saying, how could people come together on ordinary business matters until the *Lark* was a settled trouble? But he doesn't farm. I don't know what other people, farming people, are thinking. Maybe they wouldn't want to put it off. Nothing is ordinary these days, eh? There's a lot of studying and weighing of things that still needs to be done."

They had been studying and weighing for years, but now there was accurate information, useful detail. *The more known, the more is known to ask,* was an old maxim lately become timely. "The answer to every question is ten new questions," Humberto said unhappily, and Pia nodded without speaking.

He straightened, pushing a little stiffness out of his back, and looked across the field of rice into the woodland. For a while he had been hearing a ringing high whistle—a nunbird, he thought it was, objecting to their voices. He looked on the long slope at the edge of the woods, in the patchy, concealing shade under the trees, the ferns, for the bird's low nest. He had once been privileged to see the mouth of a white-fronted nunbird's nest, an inconspicuous hole a few centimeters wide with a long anteroom of twigs and dead leaves hiding it. It was Ridaro Rogelio who had shown it to him a lifetime ago, when he was still green and had thought he might want to take up Ridaro's work, be an ornithologist. For a while he had followed Ridaro at his slow, painstaking practice of netting and banding and counting and releasing certain birds, and then netting and killing others. When the cats had taken a plague and died, people had found they must act as keystone predators of some species, and this killing was part of Ridaro's work. Humberto never had been able to get a distance between himself and the killing and he'd lost his eagerness for ornithology. But he never had stopped watching birds.

"Are you doing a committee job?" Pia asked him.

He nodded without taking his gaze from the edge of the woodland. There had not yet been agreement on the question of whether new species, Earth species, ought to be introduced to the New World. People researching this question had brought up plagues of alien rabbits in Australia, of alien cheat-grass in North America; but evidently there had once been a landmass connecting America with Asia, and animals had crossed in both directions, some killing off others—how was this natural event different from human ones? While they waited for agreement, quite a few people were going ahead, looking at the *Miller's* library of frozen cells for plants that would take cold weather, poor soils. Humberto's little committee studied the wild things—cold-tolerant natives that might, if cultivated, be edible, or pharmacological, or useful as a textile.

"I'm put to studying subarctic natives, the xerophyla," he said to Pia. "It isn't known yet, but if the water in the soil is frozen, a tundra, then when it thaws there will be too much water, the roots will stand in it."

She grimaced. "All these bad accounts."

Humberto lowered his eyes to the earth, his dirty feet, the toe strap of his worn sandals. "Some things will grow in those circumstances. I'm reading, looking." He began slowly to weed again. By the time he thought of saying something about esculant willows, the moment for it seemed to have slid by.

Pia let her maĉeta rest on the ground but she didn't straighten. She looked toward Humberto diffidently from her hunched-over pose above the handle of the long knife. "You have relatives on that boat, eh? Someone said you had a lover, or a brother, on the *Lark*."

Humberto shook his head, his face flushing. "I know Luza Kordoba, but not in that way. My son's mother is now Bjoro Andersen's wife." Pia's wrong information humbled him. He realized with embarrassment, maybe his links to the crashed boat had made him feel speciously self-important.

Pia said, circling backward a bit, "I guess I'd find it hard to keep a clear mind for a Business Meeting, myself, with the *Lark* still unsettled."

He seldom spoke in Meetings. He thought the clarity of his mind maybe wasn't the issue. "Whatever other people want to do," he said, straightening again so he could shrug.

Pia had two young children at home, one was a baby still sometimes nursing at her breast. Around the midday her nephew carried the crying baby out to the rice field to see if Pia's breast was what the baby wanted, and after that Pia quit the field. Humberto worked on alone until the weeding of Shepherd's Crook got done, then he went down to the tools house and washed and honed the maĉeta he had used, and rubbed a little oil onto the metal, and hung it up by the handle on a hook. He was tired, his back ached, his skin itched with sweat, but he had not altogether lost his wish for solitude, and this was a time of day when there would be several people in the baths. So he went up the ladder of the domaro to his own apartment.

There was only Alfhilda there, heating a soup. Humberto brought out the old books and the tapes he had from the borrowing library and sat on the wide sill of the casement with his back braced against the frame in the pasado wall and his knees pulled up to rest a librajo there.

Humberto had lately begun a hunt for relatives of the tough, adaptive willows and birches whose stunted forms had once made a rug across the northern plains of the Earth. The possibilities he listed went to Kilian Bejrd, who studied each of them for their dietetic values, digestibility, or to Andreo Rodiba who was an herbalist, or to Edmo Smith, a spinster and weaver. And then to Anejlisa Revfiem who was tinkering with hybridizing different ones to see if they could be recast in a more useful or a more productive form. It was slow work—after a year of this studying and tinkering, they had two dozen possibilities that might furnish a marginal crop, might nourish or clothe or heal a person in need. But Humberto liked the difficult progress. He thought there was a certain satisfaction in untangling a small tight knot in a piece of thread—maybe more than in straightening out a big kinked rope.

He read the botanical works on the screen of the librajo with his eyes pinched to force the intricate old languages, the unwieldy namings, through a narrow strait. When his eyes or his mind tired, then he set the botanicals down and read old, general geographies about tundra soils, subarctic climes, their language of landscape by now comfortingly familiar. Much in those books was reiterative, but he wasn't tired of them. He had caught from some of the essays a kind of reverence for the strategies animals and plants had used, surviving in an arduous climate.

Alfhilda brought him soup and sat on the floor with her own bowl in her lap. She was his brother Pero's only child, a girl with a broad brown face, unreticent, impulsive, a songbird. She had a potter's wheel in the Alaŭdo work shed, and frequently went about with clayed hands, had to be reminded to wash. Her ceramics were plain and artless—her gift was for biology, and lately she had apprenticed herself to Anejlisa Revfiem. She liked to read from Humberto's botanical books, and talk seriously with him about the genetics of draba mustards and tundra grass and stunted mountain heather. He had had a quiet life for several years in a small household, himself and two old people. Now his brother's daughter and his own son had moved into this apartment, along with his mother's friend Heza Barfor. His privacy, his time for solitude, had become brief and erratic, but he wasn't sorry for it. He regarded, with astonishment and fondness, Alfhilda's swift mind, Ĉejo's earnest ideality.

"Do you know, there's this rescue to be tried?" Alfhilda said to him. He nodded over the soup.

"They'll bring them up one by one in a survey balloon, dump the equipment and come up in the gondola," she said, without looking at him to know whether he had made an answer. "Avino went over to Luza Kordoba's house to tell them—in case they didn't know it yet."

Humberto's mother hardly knew Luza or her family. People would wonder why she was taking this upon herself, or they would guess: it was a slight, cunning gesture of malice toward Juko Ohaŝi. Maybe by choosing to bring the rescue news to Luza's family, she was deliberately, conspicuously choosing not to bring the news to Bjoro's wife. She and Juko had an old enmity, grounded in guilt and blame, dating from the death of Humberto's son, and he had long ago lost the energy for trying to heal it.

"What is it you're doing with Anejlisa just now?" he asked Alfhilda, by way of turning the talk away from the *Lark*.

"We're growing a hybrid from willow stock, a sort of mutation of the—" Humberto saw her tongue come forward, licking the soup, or the intractable word "—setsuka sachalinensis. Trying to get it to grow a root mass like the pussy willows, edible," she told him.

"On the setsuka? I never hoped much for that one." He lapped the soup thoughtfully. There was mushroom in it, and bright paprika; it was sharp, sweet. "I thought Anejlisa would go at it the other way, fiddle with the pussies."

"She's doing that too." Alfhilda lifted the bowl, maybe hiding her mouth, her beam of satisfaction, behind the rim. "But I helped with the setsuka. Fixed the plates, and the droppers, and scraped the cells." She looked at Humberto. "Are you reading the Kovalak book? I like that one."

"I'm reading it. What? Are you picking it up when I set it down?"

She grimaced. "Only sometimes. I read wherever your marker is, a page or two."

Kovalak's was one of the old books he had from the library, its pages rebound between stiff boards and the paper sprayed with something slick and inflexible, a fixative or a mold-inhibitor. People handled such books with care—they were talismans, holy objects, and Kovalak's work was lyrical, a kind of spiritual geography. Humberto read it not for instruction but for its gift of imagination, its passion and compassion for Earth's lost species, its informed evocations of storms and migrations, aurora borealis, icescapes. Kovalak had been dead for two hundred years, but in the photo image on the frontispage he was in his forties, hunkered down on his heels on a gravelly scree and peering off narrow-eyed toward something behind the camera. He was long-jawed, bearded, had a look of dignity and reproach. Humberto said, "When I'm finished with it you can read it yourself, not just pieces."

She made a childish face, rolling her bottom lip down. "Anejlisa has given me a lot to read: eight books, one is French."

When they had finished the soup, the two of them took up reading companionably, though Humberto gave up trying to get at the complicated botanicals with Alfhilda asking him frequently the meanings of words, and reading things aloud when they struck her interest. Shortly Heza came in the house with a bundle of dyed yarn, and when she let her load down in the front room and started in about the balloon rescuing, Humberto had to finally give up trying to be alone. He put his reading away and got clean clothes and a towel in his arms and went along the pasado from his apartment to the men's bathhouse.

Two men were washing, and one man and a child were in the tub. He nodded to people, got his clothes off, crouched naked under the spigot of a shower beside Karlos Onoda and Edvard Penagos. Karlos and Edvard kept on with what they were saying to each other, something to do with thermostats and parabolic mirrors; both of them worked in the smeltering of metals. They were married, raising young children, their lives marked off different circles from his. The dribble of the waterspout was tepid and soothing; he sluiced it over the back of his head, his neck.

"Probably you heard about this rescue that'll be tried," Karlos said to him.

He pushed the water out of his eyes. Both men were looking at him. "Yes. A balloon," he said. Karlos's chest was extravagantly hairy. In the stream of the shower, the hair lay against his skin in a smooth pelt which Humberto admired from the edge of his eye.

"It seems a risky thing, eh?" Karlos said, raising his eyebrows. Probably Karlos wasn't asking a question, but Humberto felt he should nod, agreeing with a sort of wordless distress.

"Well anyway there isn't much mechanical can go wrong with a balloon," Edvard said. "I'd trust it more than another go-down boat, was it me." He said it in a grimacing way, as if he held mechanical things in high scorn. No one knew why the boat had tumbled, so people were placing blame on a vague failure of technology.

"How long will it be, before there's some word of them?" the man in the tub called out above the water of the showers. His name was Umeno Flagstad, he was short and thick-bodied, his skimpy hair stuck up in a wet cockscomb. Umeno ground lenses for eyeglasses and for laboratory microscopes. Humberto thought he had spoken generally, but the others seemed to wait for Humberto to answer the question, as if his relation to Bjoro or Luza gave him a kind of authority.

"I don't know," he said. Then he also said, "A balloon isn't something that can be moved precisely, I guess." He spoke up, so his words borrowed from Pia Putala would reach Umeno sitting in the tub.

"Those radio people are sending down stingy notices," Edvard said with bitterness. "There's only a few words of news comes out from the hub every little while, but people say there's a steady talking going on between the *Ruby* and the hub, should be ten people carrying the words down here if they were sharing it, but they're keeping the most of it to themselves. I don't know what they think they're doing, those people."

Humberto knew one of the people who worked at the radio, a man who had married a cousin of his. Before the *Ruby* had gone ahead, Noria's radio work had been a sometime talking with the miners who went out on the slow tugs to capture little asteroids. Noria was a furniture maker, the radio had been something he did seldom and unhurried. But when the *Ruby* was launched, all the people who worked radio had had to drop their other work, just to keep ahead of the listening, and transcribing—putting committees' belated questions to the *Ruby,* and running to get answers to questions that came back from the boat. What must it be like now the *Lark* was crashed?

"There's more work than they can keep up, maybe," he said, but Karlos was speaking at the same time, asking if there maybe had been a trouble with the radio. When Edvard complained again about mechanical failings, it became clear they had all heard Karlos's words over Humberto's. In discomfort, he waited for an opening to repeat himself, but they went on talking, and in a little while the talk got away from that matter, and there wasn't any reason for him to keep on waiting to say it.

He left the waterspout silently and sat in the deep water in the soaking tub, on the wooden bench beside Umeno Flagstad. The child was Edvard Penago's son, a boy about three or four whose name Humberto didn't remember. In a moment, Edvard and Karlos came into the tub. Edvard blew bubbles on his son's wet belly before he sat on the bench. When he was bent over the boy, his clean pink anus displayed itself for Humberto and Umeno.

After everyone was settled, Humberto closed his eyes. People were finally done talking, and for a few minutes he heard only the water lapping against the underneath of his chin. The bath was hot, it smelled of mint and the camphor wood of the tub. Shortly, behind his eyes, he began to construct wild, empty landscapes of rock and sky, his mind's work, dreamscapes that could not have been put into words. The person he placed in the world of the dream wasn't Bjoro or Luza but himself, poking holes in the pebbly dirt with the end of a pointed stick.

The little boy said loudly, as a sort of declaration all at once, "I have a penis." Men knew, three or four years old was an age for making these announcements, and they laughed or smiled. Humberto felt a brief pang of nostalgia. He was glad, usually, to be past his own child-rearing days; his friendship with his grown son felt easy as loose clothes. But sometimes, as now, he felt something like a loss. Where was that little boy, eh? vanished into the person Ĉejo had become.

"Bridge Troll has a penis that floats," Umeno Flagstad said to the boy quietly, and that got the adults to smile again.

The boy looked down at his own penis in the water. After a while he said to Umeno, "Mine floats."

Umeno studied himself in mild surprise. "I see mine does too." There was a silence, then he said, "Bridge Troll has a penis as long as his arm. It must be the size of his penis that got Bridge Troll into trouble, eh?" Some laughter went around among them.

The boy examined his penis again, and his long thin arms bobbing in the water. "What trouble?"

Humberto had told this same tale more than once to Ĉejo, and now he thought with sudden happiness, *I'll go on telling this to my grandchildren.* Umeno said, "Oh, it had to do with Koi, and the Plum Rains. Do you know that story? That time in the Plum Rains, it was hot and clammy and Bridge Troll lay down in the Ring River to cool himself. He was under the Tailed Frog Bridge where the water is very shallow, but he didn't remember: In the mornings of the rainy season people always open a gate on the Mandala dam. The little flood came along while Bridge Troll was lying there sleeping, and his big penis floated up and carried him along the water like a boat."

The boy's eyes were fixed wide on him through the wet scrim of his bangs.

"Old Bridge Troll," Umeno said, "thinking he might have to swim around the river forever, called out for somebody to rescue him. Koi swam up to see who was crying, and when he heard what Bridge Troll was worried about he laughed and said, well, he had lived all of his life swimming around the Ring River and it was a fine life. Bridge Troll, you know, has a short temper, and he had lived all of his life under bridges and wanted to go on doing it—he said he wasn't interested in living the foolish life of a fish. Well, this made Koi spiteful and sly and he said, if Bridge Troll wanted to stop floating around the Ring River he'd have to cut off his penis."

One of the other men, Karlos, made a scissoring gesture with his fingers in the steam rising from the water. "Ouch," he said, and there was laughing again. The boy fidgeted, looking at their faces, waiting for the end to be told.

"Bridge Troll by now had floated half around the Ring River," Umeno said. "And was just then under the Wake Robin Bridge. That bridge has a booming echo living under it, from the pump and the falls over there at the edge of Pacema."

"The Falls From Grace," Edvard said to his son, and the boy knew that place. He nodded solemnly.

"Fum-Grace, where Mario lives."

Edvard nodded too.

"Well, there's the pump brings water up to the head of the falls, and the water falling, the sound they make under the bridge is pretty big, eh? And when Bridge Troll heard it he got more afraid, and he told Koi to cut his penis off quick and save him from going up in the pump and down over the falls. So Koi cut off the Bridge Troll's penis with his teeth and carried it away for his children to eat—and Bridge Troll sank to the bottom of the Ring River."

Umeno waited for the boy's mouth to open in understanding surprise. Then he said, beginning to make a crawling motion through the water with his hand, "Bridge Troll had to crawl along the bottom like a crayfish going round and round the Ring River forever. Or anyway until drier weather, when the river got low enough for him to crawl out under the Tailed Frog Bridge." He began to grin slowly. "But later on old Bridge Troll stole one of Koi's children and stitched the little fish on to his body in place of his penis. So maybe Koi was sorry for that joke he played. Do you think?"

Edvard Penagos made a sound of fright and nipped his little son's penis under the water, between two fingers. The boy squealed and laughed, and began a game of holding his breath and crawling on the bottom of the wooden tub like a crayfish, pinching toes and penises.

When the boy and his father and Umeno Flagstad had gone home, Humberto went on sitting in the bath with Karlos. "Here's something new I've got to wonder about," Karlos said to him. He grinned. "Is there a bridge troll on that New World, eh, if there's no bridges?"

"Trolls are canny," Humberto said, smiling himself. "They might think of living under rocks."

"Oh hell, there's plenty of those, that much is true. What do you farm people think about it?"

"What? The rocks, you mean?"

"All of it. The ground, the weather. That world's got a short year, eh? How can a crop be raised in a month?"

People who weren't farming often didn't pay attention to the reports, or didn't remember them. Humberto looked away. "Fifty days. We can get crops to ripen in that time, if we have the long days. At the midlatitudes, summer daylight is either side of twenty-two hours."

Karlos raised his brows. "How would our bodies get used to that, eh? They say we've all got a clock in our bodies tells us when to sleep and wake and eat. I guess I wouldn't like to stay awake twenty-two hours, maybe plants wouldn't like it either."

Humberto began to feel tired and blunted. These were arguments he had heard many times. He said, "It would spur a plant to grow, I guess," but that was only what his instinct told him. There had been three or four mathematical studies without clear result, statistical remodelings to do with atmospheric pressure, surface gravity, irradiation, axial tilt; the research was built upon known agricultural responses. Not many people believed in the studies, anyway. Reports about what had been grown in the summers at Reykjavik, Iceland, or Yakutsk, Russia, seemed too remote from them to be any longer truthful.

Karlos touched his groin, smiling boyishly. "Maybe those long days would grow me a penis long as my arm, eh?"

Humberto answered without joy. "Well I guess we could get used to it, then."

When other men came into the bathhouse, Humberto dried himself and put on his clean clothes and went out, before the talk could get back around to the *Lark*. He carried his dirty clothes down to the laundry, and while he waited for the washing machine to finish its job he took a piece of needlework from his pocket, a square of linen he was hemming in a fine stitch. He sat on the flagstones at the edge of the path in front of the laundry, with his legs folded under him and the needlework on his knee. He had meant to give the finished piece to his cousin's daughter on the occasion of her marriage, but then had imagined it might be needed as a funeral gift for Juko on the death of her husband. Which, now?

The sewing was not an occupation for his thoughts, and because the path in front of the laundry house was not much on the way to somewhere else, he was frequently left alone to turn things over unsystematically in his mind. It was impossible to keep from thinking about the *Lark*, and gradually he began to worry along a new line. All the spacegoing boats were old, original equipment; the *Lark's* failure maybe was age, or maintenance. He didn't know if it was possible for the people on the Mechanics Committee to warrant a reliable go-down boat.

Parts of houses were old as the torus, and many trees, wooden chests, tables, many of them were Earth-built. The clothes washers were old stock, a clever Japanese invention; they made an ultrasonic noise that shook the dirt off into very little water. In the kitchenhouse of the domaro Humberto lived in, the stove was Earth-built, it had a short phrase in Norwegian, raised in relief on the ceramic base. Ĉejo, who was fascinated by it, had worked out the meaning. *Root and Leaf* it said, and Ĉejo, every little while, would offer some new sense he had made of that old, quizzical message. But original machinery had gradually become rare. The mechanisms that survived tended to be of two kinds: simple things with few moving parts, like the clothes washers; and things too problematic for their small manufactory to re-create—spacegoing boats, sewing-machine motors, the heavy equipment of manufacture itself. Humberto imagined an absurdity: After so long a course getting to this world, they might only lack the fundamental machinery to deliver themselves and their belongings down to it.

When he carried his clean laundry home his mother was there, delivering to Heza all the guesses and certainties and dreads she had gotten from the crowd of people at Luza Kordoba's house, all the people who were helping the family to wait, or bringing news about the rescue. Earlier, he had thought he might not want to go to the Farms Committee Meeting, in case the talk was all of the crashed boat. But now he went out to it—it would have been pointless to stay away, since even the people in his own house were keeping up their talk about the *Lark* and there was no escaping it.

The Alaŭdo Farms Committee for many years had made a habit of meeting in the field above the aeroponics shed, the one named The Whisper Behind the Tree. There were five carob trees standing in a rough circle in a field of cottongrass, and the committee fitted their own circle of people inside the circle of trees, people balancing tablets on their knees if they had to write something down, and bringing mats to kneel on at certain times of the year when the grass was stubbly or littered with St. John's fruit. There were twenty people who farmed in Alaŭdo, but not often twenty at a Farms Committee Meeting—today only nine. With the fate of the go-down boat at the front of people's minds, maybe quite a few were following the maxim that a person ought to stay away from a Meeting if not able to bring an earnest sense of listening and sharing.

Humberto seated himself between old Nores Panko and Ĝeronimo Zea in the circle, and let his eyes close for the beginning of silence.

"Ĉejo says, tell you he has gone to his mother's house," Ĝeronimo said, touching Humberto's sleeve, whispering hoarsely. "Waiting for word of the *Lark,* eh?"

Humberto nodded. "The balloon," he murmured, before Ĝeronimo could say it.

The committee clerk was a woman named Elisabeta Bojs, a good clerk with a facility for finding the open way. She liked to let the silence at the beginning and end of a Business Meeting go on a little longer than other clerks were inclined to, and in the long quiet Humberto felt a slow centering down, a sloughing off of his fretfulness about the crew of the *Lark,* until finally he was able to fill his mind with an expectant, living silence.

"Do people have concerns?" Elisabeta said at last.

After all, nobody brought up the boat. There were things to do with weeding, with getting the pejiba palm fruits down from the taller trees, and planting late mustard. People reported about the repair of the mezlando aqueduct, and raised pessimistic questions from the data sent by the *Ruby.* A query had been sent down from Quarterly Meeting about the possibility of burying heating cables underground to warm the soil for farming, and about the drilling of wells—whether people had considered the eventual problem of depleting the fossil water. Humberto reported on his own work with Killian Berd and Anejlisa Revfiem, and his second-hand information about the genetic tinkering Anejlisa was doing with the setsuka willows. Intermittently, Elisabeta stated her sense of the meeting, and if there was no disagreement with it, Gil Roko, who was the recording clerk, wrote it down as a Minute of the Meeting.

When there were nine recorded Minutes, and new issues weren't being raised anymore, she brought up the problem of the leaf-cutter ants, who had built two enormous labyrinths in the midst of a hedge of cinnamomum. This problem had been brought up before, without anything being decided. The ants were in a cycle of abundance this year—new colonies had been springing up suddenly in fields and in the woodland everywhere—and Aleda Laitowler thought, when the ants had exhausted the foliage of the hedge they would begin to attack the citrus trees. He thought people ought to act before this happened, to take the role that the extinct army ants once had taken, invading the leaf-cutter ants' subterranean galleries and chambers in the cinnamomum. Some people agreed with Aleda, but other people thought, in a few months or years the leafcutters would become suddenly rare again without farmers disturbing them. The population of insects was unpredictable, prone to puzzling fluctuations, this was something everybody knew.

Elisabeta had steered the arguments gently and let silence inform the spaces, but people had only put forward information to support one belief or the other, and no advance had been made. When they had last met, she had asked three particular people to study this issue, to gather information and reformulate it, set it forth in a clearer light. Out of the three, only old Nores Panko was there to make a report. He stood up slowly when Elisabeta at last raised the subject of the leaf-cutter ants. Nores never had been what people called a "weighty Friend"— someone whose voice was always worth listening to—but his old age had given him a kind of stature. He was seventy-nine years old, probably had seen other invasions of leaf-cutter ants, must have been living when the army ants inexplicably disappeared.

These leaf-cutter ants were a kind of farmer ant, he said, cutting pieces of leaves into tiny fragments like sawdust and heaping them up to make a compost in their underground chambers, which they fertilized with their own feces, and on which they sowed a fungus that produced nodules like tiny, fuzzy kohlrabi, that the ants then ate, just as human beings inoculated compost with the spore of mushrooms, and ate the mushrooms. A female ant going off to establish a new colony carried in a pocket of her cheek pieces of fungus for sowing in the new place, just as human beings transported and preserved seeds, bulbs, cuttings, for propagating their own crops.

There was a silence while Nores kept on standing. He was white-haired, but his bushy eyebrows still were dark; they made a fierce line across his face. He had a wide tender mouth that belied his brows, and a kind demeanor. He stood without a cane, leaning a bit forward with his hands folded together behind his back. Humberto sitting below him could see the slight tremor in his hands—maybe that was why he clasped them. And looking at old Nores's hands, he began to imagine himself a member of a guild to which the peaceful fungus-growing ants also belonged—both of them vegetarian agriculturists. In the midst of the quiet, he thought of saying this, but he kept silent, waiting for someone else to bring it up. Too often he found he wasn't able to give his values, his judgment, any coherent expression. He had formed a gingerly habit of not speaking when there was serious disagreement.

Another clerk might have counseled a longer silence, for people to consider the problem before probably tabling it again. But Elisabeta Bojs said to Nores gently, "I feel maybe you have something more you want to say, Nores," and he took a slightly different grip of his hands and sighed.

"Well I guess I do," he said finally. "Here is something else I will tell you. I was a boy when I saw this, and I'd forgot it until I took up this reading about ants." And he told about once seeing a colony of leaf-cutters invaded by raiding army ants. He hadn't seen the battles, he said, only afterward the many hundreds of corpses of leaf-cutters' soldiers strewn dead around the entrances to their galleries, and scattered for yards along the paths to and from the city. Some of the dead and dying soldiers had lost limbs or were cut in two, but there were scores without an evident injury—perhaps they'd been stung to death, he said, or they might have simply fallen dead of exhaustion; who knew how long they had kept up this defense against invaders? The army was passing in a steady stream along the paths to and from the leaf-cutters' chambers, in and out of its portals, carrying off to their bivouac the white bodies of larvae and pupae.

Though they had killed the leaf-cutter soldiers, Nores said, they only stripped the poor nursemaid ants of their charges and left them wandering about sorrowfully, uninjured. Who knew why? After a moment, Nores added, "I guess it wasn't anything like clemency made them do it. I suppose, in the natural way, they were leaving survivors so the ants' city would recover, and be there when they came round to pillage it again."

He loosed his long-boned old hands. "That's all I wanted to say," he said, making a shaky gesture. He sat down slowly beside Humberto, pulling his knees up slightly and resting his thin forearms across them.

There was a profound silence after old Nores sat down. Humberto thought he ought to refuse the shameless ascribing of human nature to these ants, but what he felt was a sudden deep ignorance of the quality of an ant's psychic life. He looked down at the ground in front of his crossed knees. There was a beetle with an iridescent carapace making a slow way through the cottongrass and the dry leaves.

Elisabeta let the silence go on quite a while. Perhaps she knew the direction of Nores's leading would make itself evident if they all waited long enough. Eventually someone stood and simply told about watching the ants on their narrow, beaten highways, endless columns of them homeward-bound, toting tiny pieces of green leaf that rose gigantically above their backs like great banners or rainhats. And someone else told of seeing a piece of leaf borne along by a big ant, with two or three small ants clinging aloft—the little ones had tried to help carry, maybe, but the big one had simply lifted the cargo, helpers and all, and marched away with it. And finally Gift Sû stood up and said, "I wonder. If we put leafy cuttings near their city, would they snub them, or be glad of the extra? When any of us have got fresh prunings, if we brought those over and laid them on their paths, maybe they would cut them up and carry them home and maybe that would lighten the pressure on the cinnamomum.

Elisabeta raised her brows in surprise. She looked at Nores.

"Will they take leaves cut fresh for them, Nores?"

The old man considered this before nodding solemnly. "They have a little preference for certain leaves, don't like every kind. But what they like, they'd take cut as much as not, I think. In that book it said they would take from downed branches."

And so a way was opened. Talk turned to the kinds of leaves the ants would accept, particular plants and shrubs, trees, herbs; and people made rough guesses about the kind and volume of pruning they'd be doing in the next weeks. Shortly, they got to speculating why some leaves weren't suited for the ants' use, and whether the ants' little species of fungus was related to mushroom, or to lichen. When the discussion seemed to get around to repeating itself, Elisabeta interrupted and stated her sense of this last part of the meeting: An effort would be made to minimize the defoliation of the cinnamomum by furnishing leafy cuttings to the colony of farmer ants who had taken up living there. No one disagreed, and Gil Roko wrote it down as the tenth Minute of the Meeting.

That was all the business anyone raised. In the silence at the close, gradually Humberto found he was adrift in the space behind his closed eyes, a sort of dream, himself in a cavernous black chamber on his hands and knees weeding a white field of woolly kohlrabi.

He meant to get away from the Meeting quickly afterward but people stopped him, wanting to talk now about the Lark and the rescue, and he was slow getting home again, the light by then already lowered for dusk. Heza was out of the house, she'd had a meeting herself, of the Fiber Arts Committee, and frequently was late from those meetings, was one of the people prone to sit around afterward and do handwork while catching up gossip. Humberto's father was playing cards with his cronies in the sadaŭ of a house over in Mandala. His mother and Alfhilda sat alone in the apartment, quietly playing Go. Alfhilda's soup was eaten up, so Humberto went round to the kitchen house and steamed some bulgur in orange and ginger, made a ragout of beets, leeks, squash, cold lentils. He left some of this in the refrigerator for other people to find and brought his bowl back into the apartment, but then his mother and Alfhilda complained and he had to go into the kitchen again and bring the rest of the bulgur and the ragout for them to eat while they played Go.

"Ĉejo is waiting at his mother's house," Leona said. She was focused on the game. "Until there's word of the Lark."

He nodded. "The balloon." He ate slowly while he watched them play and then he took his turn at it, finding a kind of relief in the concentration on strategy. He won with Alfhilda and then lost to his mother, and while he was waiting out their next game he got up, carrying their empty bowls, and came back with a banana and a bowl of figs. He and Alfhilda ate figs and kept on playing after Leona had gone to bed, but when Alfhilda had lost twice in a row she gave up in frustration, and Humberto went to bed himself rather than sit alone with botanical reading. He was afraid Heza, when she came in, would want to talk with him about the *Lark.*

As soon as he lay down he was half-asleep, thinking suddenly, *I am too tired to worry tonight.* But he woke when the boards of the floor groaned quietly in the darkness beside him. Ĉejo was coming to bed. How late was it? His limbs felt rigid, expecting a blow.

"What has happened?" he asked in a low voice.

"Bjoro is rescued," Ĉejo said softly. "And Luza Kordoba. But Peder Ojama and Isuma Bun are killed."

Humberto rolled onto his back. He stared blindly up into darkness. He didn't know the two who were dead—he had been thoroughly spared grief. Immediately a kind of guilt settled on him, as if God had made this selection by considering Humberto Indergard's interests ahead of other people's.

"Isuma Bun is a second cousin to Katrin Amundsen," Ĉejo murmured after a silence.

Katrin Amundsen was a name Humberto knew without a face, the most recent of the girls Ĉejo had loved in the last year. She lived in her grandmother's household in Revenana, in the domaro where Ĉejo had spent his green years.

"I went to see if Katrin's family had heard about the death," Ĉejo said. "Maybe Katrin is a close friend with this cousin, or her grandmother could be also Isuma's grandmother, and maybe they would want to know. But no lights were on in their rooms. I didn't know if I should wake anybody."

"It's all right if they don't learn about it until morning," Humberto said quietly. "What can be done anyway, but crying?"

In the darkness, Humberto heard his son's voice break. "I wanted to be there with her if she cried," he said, crying himself. Ĉejo hadn't yet grown out of an overemotional romanticism.

He was fiercely monogamous and loyal but his couplings tended to be brief. Almost as soon as a girl returned his attention he would put her in a desperate, smothering clasp, and when the girl tired of the weight, she'd quickly wriggle free. Humberto himself had been a casual lover at

Ĉejo's age, had accepted copulation as a kind of gift from girls without imagining romantic love was being offered too. Now that he was forty-six years old and for the last six years unmarried, he found he was more analytical. He seldom had coitus with a woman without wondering if he loved her; and he wondered about the quality of the love, and if it might become relaxed enough to support a marriage.

He remembered suddenly that time he had walked into the swung blade of Henriko Lij's cane cutter, the long moment while Henriko gaped at him in astonishment and fear, and then the woman he didn't know, Luza Kordoba, pushing by old Henriko and past Humberto's own clutching hands to put her fingers deftly to his neck, pushing down in the hole through the spurt of his bright red blood, the swift, sure gesture that stopped him from bleeding out. While Henriko ran to get other people to help, people with surgical tools to close the hole, helplessly he had gripped Luza's wrist and fixed his eyes on her, and she had squatted over him with her hand at his throat, in his throat, talking to him quietly about farming and weather, and when she was short of those subjects, instructing him irrelevantly about things she knew in her own fields, kinematics and linear momentum, acupuncture pressure points and homeostasis, until the warmth and even pressure of her hand on his pulse had become as compelling and sexual as an erection. It was the single time he had loved someone as Ĉejo loved, brief and burning, urgently holding on.

Ted Chiang

The author bio for two-time Nebula Winner and Sturgeon Memorial Award Winner Ted Chiang's collection *Stories of Your Life and Others* (2002) says simply, "Ted Chiang lives near Seattle, WA." Lucky Northwest.

Chiang grew up in Port Jefferson, New York, received a degree in computer science from Brown University, and now makes a living as a technical writer. As early as the sixth grade, he began writing and submitting stories for publication. He credits being accepted by the Clarion West Writers Workshop, a prestigious annual gathering of science fiction and fantasy professionals in Seattle, for preserving a sense that his destiny was to write science fiction. Chiang cites Isaac Asimov, Arthur C. Clarke, John Crowley, Gene Wolfe, Greg Egan, Bruce Sterling, Karen Joy Fowler, and Ken MacLeod as important influences.

In "Story of Your Life," Chiang imagines what would happen if humans encountered an alien species. How would we learn the aliens' language? What would an alien language look like? To linguist Dr. Banks, these alien heptapods' nonlinear system of orthography appears as an almost full-fledged graphical language while to them it represents "true writing." Banks' immersion in the alien language, along with the aliens' emphasis on Fermat's Principle of Least Time, cause her to question the human, familiar, causal, and sequential mode of awareness in comparison to the aliens' bizarre, teleological, and simultaneous mode of awareness.

Story of Your Life

YOUR FATHER IS ABOUT TO ASK ME THE QUESTION. This is the most important moment in our lives, and I want to pay attention, note every detail. Your dad and I have just come back from an evening out, dinner and a show; it's after midnight. We came out onto the patio to look at the full moon; then I told your dad I wanted to dance, so he humors me and now we're slow dancing, a pair of thirtysomethings swaying back and forth in the moonlight like kids. I don't feel the night chill at all. And then your dad says, "Do you want to make a baby?"

Right now your dad and I have been married for about two years, living on Ellis Avenue; when we move out you'll still be too young to remember the house, but we'll show you pictures of it, tell you stories about it. I'd love to tell you the story of this evening, the night you're conceived, but the right time to do that would be when you're ready to have children of your own, and we'll never get that chance.

Telling it to you any earlier wouldn't do any good; for most of your life you won't sit still to hear such a romantic—you'd say sappy—story. I remember the scenario of your origin you'll suggest when you're twelve.

"The only reason you had me was so you could get a maid you wouldn't have to pay," you'll say bitterly, dragging the vacuum cleaner out of the closet.

"That's right," I'll say. "Thirteen years ago I knew the carpets would need vacuuming around now, and having a baby seemed to be the cheapest and easiest way to get the job done. Now kindly get on with it."

"If you weren't my mother, this would be illegal," you'll say, seething as you unwind the power cord and plug it into the wall outlet.

That will be in the house on Belmont Street. I'll live to see strangers occupy both houses: the one you're conceived in and the one you grow up in. Your dad and I will sell the first a couple years after your arrival. I'll sell the second shortly after your departure. By then Nelson and I will have moved into our farmhouse, and your dad will be living with what's-her-name.

I know how this story ends; I think about it a lot. I also think a lot about how it began, just a few years ago, when ships appeared in orbit and artifacts appeared in meadows. The government said next to nothing about them, while the tabloids said every possible thing.

And then I got a phone call, a request for a meeting.

I spotted them waiting in the hallway, outside my office. They made an odd couple; one wore a military uniform and a crew cut, and carried an aluminum briefcase. He seemed to be assessing his surroundings with a critical eye. The other one was easily identifiable as an academic: full beard and mustache, wearing corduroy. He was browsing through the overlapping sheets stapled to a bulletin board nearby.

"Colonel Weber, I presume?" I shook hands with the soldier. "Louise Banks."

"Dr. Banks. Thank you for taking the time to speak with us," he said.

"Not at all; any excuse to avoid the faculty meeting."

Colonel Weber indicated his companion. "This is Dr. Gary Donnelly, the physicist I mentioned when we spoke on the phone."

"Call me Gary," he said as we shook hands. "I'm anxious to hear what you have to say."

We entered my office. I moved a couple of stacks of books off the second guest chair, and we all sat down. "You said you wanted me to listen to a recording. I presume this has something to do with the aliens?"

"All I can offer is the recording," said Colonel Weber.

"Okay, let's hear it."

Colonel Weber took a tape machine out of his briefcase and pressed PLAY. The recording sounded vaguely like that of a wet dog shaking the water out of its fur.

"What do you make of that?" he asked.

I withheld my comparison to a wet dog. "What was the context in which this recording was made?"

"I'm not at liberty to say.

"It would help me interpret those sounds. Could you see the alien while it was speaking? Was it doing anything at the time?"

"The recording is all I can offer."

"You won't be giving anything away if you tell me that you've seen the aliens; the public's assumed you have."

Colonel Weber wasn't budging. "Do you have any opinion about its linguistic properties?" he asked.

"Well, it's clear that their vocal tract is substantially different from a human vocal tract. I assume that these aliens don't look like humans?"

The colonel was about to say something noncommittal when Gary Donelly asked, "Can you make any guesses based on the tape?"

"Not really. It doesn't sound like they're using a larynx to make those sounds, but that doesn't tell me what they look like."

"Anything—is there anything else you can tell us?" asked Colonel Weber.

I could see he wasn't accustomed to consulting a civilian. "Only that establishing communications is going to be really difficult because of the difference in anatomy. They're almost certainly using sounds that the human vocal tract can't reproduce, and maybe sounds that the human ear can't distinguish."

"You mean infra- or ultrasonic frequencies?" asked Gary Donelly.

"Not specifically. I just mean that the human auditory system isn't an absolute acoustic instrument; it's optimized to recognize the sounds that a human larynx makes. With an alien vocal system, all bets are off." I shrugged. *"Maybe* we'll be able to hear the difference between alien phonemes, given enough practice, but it's possible our ears simply can't recognize the distinctions they consider meaningful. In that case we'd need a sound spectrograph to know what an alien is saying."

Colonel Weber asked, "Suppose I gave you an hour's worth of recordings; how long would it take you to determine if we need this sound spectrograph or not?"

"I couldn't determine that with just a recording no matter how much time I had. I'd need to talk with the aliens directly."

The colonel shook his head. "Not possible."

I tried to break it to him gently. "That's your call, of course. But the only way to learn an unknown language is to interact with a native speaker, and by that I mean asking questions, holding a conversation, that sort of thing. Without that, it's simply not possible. So if you want to learn the aliens' language, someone with training in field linguistics—whether it's me or someone else—will have to talk with an alien. Recordings alone aren't sufficient."

Colonel Weber frowned. "You seem to be implying that no alien could have learned human languages by monitoring our broadcasts."

"I doubt it. They'd need instructional material specifically designed to teach human languages to nonhumans. Either that, or interaction with a human. If they had either of those, they could learn a lot from TV, but otherwise, they wouldn't have a starting point."

The colonel clearly found this interesting; evidently his philosophy was, the less the aliens knew, the better. Gary Donnelly read the colonel's expression too and rolled his eyes. I suppressed a smile.

Then Colonel Weber asked, "Suppose you were learning a new language by talking to its speakers; could you do it without teaching them English?"

"That would depend on how cooperative the native speakers were. They'd almost certainly pick up bits and pieces while I'm learning their language, but it wouldn't have to be much if they're willing to teach. On the other hand, if they'd rather learn English than teach us their language, that would make things far more difficult."

The colonel nodded. "I'll get back to you on this matter."

The request for that meeting was perhaps the second most momentous phone call in my life. The first, of course, will be the one from Mountain Rescue. At that point your dad and I will be speaking to each other maybe once a year, tops. After I get that phone call, though, the first thing I'll do will be to call your father.

He and I will drive out together to perform the identification, a long silent car ride. I remember the morgue, all tile and stainless steel, the hum of refrigeration and smell of antiseptic. An orderly will pull the sheet back to reveal your face. Your face will look wrong somehow, but I'll know it's you.

"Yes, that's her," I'll say. "She's mine."

You'll be twenty-five then.

The MP checked my badge, made a notation on his clipboard, and opened the gate; I drove the off-road vehicle into the encampment, a small village of tents pitched by the Army in a farmer's sun-scorched pasture. At the center of the encampment was one of the alien devices, nicknamed "looking glasses."

According to the briefings I'd attended, there were nine of these in the United States, one hundred and twelve in the world. The looking glasses acted as two-way communication devices, presumably with the ships in orbit. No one knew why the aliens wouldn't talk to us in person; fear of cooties, maybe. A team of scientists, including a physicist and a linguist, was assigned to each looking glass; Gary Donnelly and I were on this one.

Gary was waiting for me in the parking area. We navigated a circular maze of concrete barricades until we reached the large tent that covered the looking glass itself. In front of the tent was an equipment cart loaded with goodies borrowed from the school's phonology lab; I had sent it ahead for inspection by the Army.

Also outside the tent were three tripod-mounted video cameras whose lenses peered, through windows in the fabric wall, into the main room. Everything Gary and I did would be reviewed by countless others, including military intelligence. In addition we would each send daily reports, of which mine had to include estimates on how much English I thought the aliens could understand.

Gary held open the tent flap and gestured for me to enter. "Step right up," he said, circus barker-style. "Marvel at creatures the likes of which have never been seen on God's green earth."

"And all for one slim dime," I murmured, walking through the door. At the moment the looking glass was inactive, resembling a semicircular mirror over ten feet high and twenty feet across. On the brown grass in front of the looking glass, an arc of white spray paint outlined the activation area. Currently the area contained only a table, two folding chairs, and a power strip with a cord leading to a generator outside. The buzz of fluorescent lamps, hung from poles along the edge of the room, commingled with the buzz of flies in the sweltering heat.

Gary and I looked at each other, and then began pushing the cart of equipment up to the table. As we crossed the paint line, the looking glass appeared to grow transparent; it was as if someone was slowly raising the illumination behind tinted glass. The illusion of depth was uncanny; I felt I could walk right into it. Once the looking glass was fully lit it resembled a life-size diorama of a semicircular room. The room contained a few large objects that might have been furniture, but no aliens. There was a door in the curved rear wall.

We busied ourselves connecting everything together: microphone, sound spectrograph, portable computer, and speaker. As we worked, I frequently glanced at the looking glass, anticipating the aliens' arrival. Even so I jumped when one of them entered.

It looked like a barrel suspended at the intersection of seven limbs. It was radially symmetric, and any of its limbs could serve as an arm or a leg. The one in front of me was walking around on four legs, three non-adjacent arms curled up at its sides. Gary called them "heptapods."

I'd been shown videotapes, but I still gawked. Its limbs had no distinct joints; anatomists guessed they might be supported by vertebral columns. Whatever their underlying structure, the heptapod's limbs conspired to move it in a disconcertingly fluid manner. Its "torso" rode atop the rippling limbs as smoothly as a hovercraft.

Seven lidless eyes ringed the top of the heptapod's body. It walked back to the doorway from which it entered, made a brief sputtering sound, and returned to the center of the room followed by another heptapod; at no point did it ever turn around. Eerie, but logical; with eyes on all sides, any direction might as well be "forward."

Gary had been watching my reaction. "Ready?" he asked.

I took a deep breath. "Ready enough." I'd done plenty of fieldwork before, in the Amazon, but it had always been a bilingual procedure: either my informants knew some Portuguese, which I could use, or I'd previously gotten an intro to their language from the local missionaries. This would be my first attempt at conducting a true monolingual discovery procedure. It was straightforward enough in theory, though.

I walked up to the looking glass and a heptapod on the other side did the same. The image was so real that my skin crawled. I could see the texture of its gray skin, like corduroy ridges arranged in whorls and loops. There was no smell at all from the looking glass, which somehow made the situation stranger.

I pointed to myself and said slowly, "Human." Then I pointed to Gary. "Human." Then I pointed at each heptapod and said, "What are you?"

No reaction. I tried again, and then again.

One of the heptapods pointed to itself with one limb, the four terminal digits pressed together. That was lucky. In some cultures a person pointed with his chin; if the heptapod hadn't used one of its limbs, I wouldn't have known what gesture to look for. I heard a brief fluttering sound, and saw a puckered orifice at the top of its body vibrate; it was talking. Then it pointed to its companion and fluttered again.

I went back to my computer; on its screen were two virtually identical spectrographs representing the fluttering sounds. I marked a sample for playback. I pointed to myself and said "Human" again, and did the same with Gary. Then I pointed to the heptapod, and played back the flutter on the speaker.

The heptapod fluttered some more. The second half of the spectrograph for this utterance looked like a repetition: call the previous utterances [flutter1], then this one was [flutter2flutter1].

I pointed at something that might have been a heptapod chair. "What is that?"

The heptapod paused, and then pointed at the "chair" and talked some more. The spectrograph for this differed distinctly from that of the earlier sounds: [flutter3]. Once again, I pointed to the "chair" while playing back [flutter3].

The heptapod replied; judging by the spectrograph, it looked like [flutter3flutter2]. Optimistic interpretation: the heptapod was confirming my utterances as correct, which implied compatibility between heptapod and human patterns of discourse. Pessimistic interpretation: it had a nagging cough.

At my computer I delimited certain sections of the spectrograph and typed in a tentative gloss for each: "heptapod" for [flutter1], "yes" for [flutter2], and "chair" for [flutter3]. Then I typed "Language: Heptapod A" as a heading for all the utterances.

Gary watched what I was typing. "What's the 'A' for?"

"It just distinguishes this language from any other ones the heptapods might use," I said. He nodded.

"Now let's try something, just for laughs." I pointed at each heptapod and tried to mimic the sound of [flutter1], "heptapod." After a long pause, the first heptapod said something and then the second one said something else, neither of whose spectrographs resembled anything said before. I couldn't tell if they were speaking to each other or to me since they had no faces to turn. I tried pronouncing [flutter1] again, but there was no reaction.

"Not even close," I grumbled.

"I'm impressed you can make sounds like that at all," said Gary.

"You should hear my moose call. Sends them running."

I tried again a few more times, but neither heptapod responded with anything I could recognize. Only when I replayed the recording of the heptapod's pronunciation did I get a confirmation; the heptapod replied with [flutter2], "yes."

"So we're stuck with using recordings?" asked Gary.

I nodded. "At least temporarily."

"So now what?"

"Now we make sure it hasn't actually been saying 'aren't they cute' or 'look what they're doing now.' Then we see if we can identify any of these words when that other heptapod pronounces them." I gestured for him to have a seat. "Get comfortable; this'll take a while."

In 1770, Captain Cook's ship *Endeavour* ran aground on the coast of Queensland, Australia. While some of his men made repairs, Cook led an exploration party and met the aboriginal people. One of the sailors pointed to the animals that hopped around with their young riding in pouches, and asked an aborigine what they were called. The aborigine replied, "Kanguru." From then on Cook and his sailors referred to the animals by this word. It wasn't until later that they learned it meant "What did you say?"

I tell that story in my introductory course every year. It's almost certainly untrue, and I explain that afterwards, but it's a classic anecdote. Of course, the anecdotes my undergraduates will really want to hear are ones featuring the heptapods; for the rest of my teaching career, that'll be the reason many of them sign up for my courses. So I'll show them the old videotapes of my sessions at the looking glass, and the sessions that the other linguists conducted; the tapes are instructive, and they'll be useful if we're ever visited by aliens again, but they don't generate many good anecdotes.

When it comes to language-learning anecdotes, my favorite source is child language acquisition. I remember one afternoon when you are five years old, after you have come home from kindergarten. You'll be coloring with your crayons while I grade papers.

"Mom," you'll say, using the carefully casual tone reserved for requesting a favor, "can I ask you something?"

"Sure, sweetie. Go ahead."

"Can I be, um, honored?"

I'll look up from the paper I'm grading. "What do you mean?"

"At school Sharon said she got to be honored."

"Really? Did she tell you what for?"

"It was when her big sister got married. She said only one person could be, um, honored, and she was it."

"Ah, I see. You mean Sharon was maid of honor?"

"Yeah, that's it. Can I be made of honor?"

Gary and I entered the prefab building containing the center of operations for the looking glass site. Inside it looked like they were planning an invasion, or perhaps an evacuation: crewcut soldiers worked around a large map of the area, or sat in front of burly electronic gear while speaking into headsets. We were shown into Colonel Weber's office, a room in the back that was cool from air conditioning.

We briefed the colonel on our first day's results. "Doesn't sound like you got very far," he said.

"I have an idea as to how we can make faster progress," I said. "But you'll have to approve the use of more equipment."

"What more do you need?"

"A digital camera, and a big video screen." I showed him a drawing of the setup I imagined. "I want to try conducting the discovery procedure using writing; I'd display words on the screen, and use the camera to record the words they write. I'm hoping the heptapods will do the same."

Weber looked at the drawing dubiously. "What would be the advantage of that?"

"So far I've been proceeding the way I would with speakers of an unwritten language. Then it occurred to me that the heptapods must have writing, too."

"So?"

"If the heptapods have a mechanical way of producing writing, then their writing ought to be very regular, very consistent. That would make it easier for us to identify graphemes instead of phonemes. It's like picking out the letters in a printed sentence instead of trying to hear them when the sentence is spoken aloud."

"I take your point," he admitted. "And how would you respond to them? Show them the words they displayed to you?"

"Basically. And if they put spaces between words, any sentences we write would be a lot more intelligible than any spoken sentence we might splice together from recordings."

He leaned back in his chair. "You know we want to show as little of our technology as possible."

"I understand, but we're using machines as intermediaries already. If we can get them to use writing, I believe progress will go much faster than if we're restricted to the sound spectrographs."

The colonel turned to Gary. "Your opinion?"

"It sounds like a good idea to me. I'm curious whether the heptapods might have difficulty reading our monitors. Their looking glasses are based on a completely different technology than our video screens. As far as we can tell, they don't use pixels or scan lines, and they don't refresh on a frame-by-frame basis."

"You think the scan lines on our video screens might render them unreadable to the heptapods?"

"It's possible," said Gary. "We'll just have to try it and see."

Weber considered it. For me it wasn't even a question, but from his point of view it was a difficult decision; like a soldier, though, he made it quickly. "Request granted. Talk to the sergeant outside about bringing in what you need. Have it ready for tomorrow."

I remember one day during the summer when you're sixteen. For once, the person waiting for her date to arrive is me. Of course, you'll be waiting around too, curious to see what he looks like. You'll have a friend of yours, a blond girl with the unlikely name of Roxie, hanging out with you, giggling.

"You may feel the urge to make comments about him," I'll say, checking myself in the hallway mirror. "Just restrain yourselves until we leave."

"Don't worry, Mom," you'll say. "We'll do it so that he won't know. Roxie, you ask me what I think the weather will be like tonight. Then I'll say what I think of Mom's date."

"Right," Roxie will say.

"No, you most definitely will not," I'll say.

"Relax, Mom. He'll never know; we do this all the time."

"What a comfort that is."

A little later on, Nelson will arrive to pick me up. I'll do the introductions, and we'll all engage in a little small talk on the front porch. Nelson is ruggedly handsome, to your evident approval. Just as we're about to leave, Roxie will say to you casually, "So what do you think the weather will be like tonight?"

"I think it's going to be really hot," you'll answer.

Roxie will nod in agreement. Nelson will say, "Really? I thought they said it was going to be cool."

"I have a sixth sense about these things," you'll say. Your face will give nothing away. "I get the feeling it's going to be a scorcher. Good thing you're dressed for it, Mom."

I'll glare at you, and say good night.

As I lead Nelson toward his car, he'll ask me, amused, "I'm missing something here, aren't I?"

"A private joke," I'll mutter. "Don't ask me to explain it."\

At our next session at the looking glass, we repeated the procedure we had performed before, this time displaying a printed word on our computer screen at the same time we spoke: showing HUMAN while saying "Human," and so forth. Eventually, the heptapods understood what we wanted, and set up a flat circular screen mounted on a small pedestal. One heptapod spoke, and then inserted a limb into a large socket in the pedestal; a doodle of script, vaguely cursive, popped onto the screen.

We soon settled into a routine, and I compiled two parallel corpora: one of spoken utterances, one of writing samples. Based on first impressions, their writing appeared to be logo-graphic, which was disappointing; I'd been hoping for an alphabetic script to help us learn their speech. Their logograms might include some phonetic information, but finding it would be a lot harder than with an alphabetic script.

By getting up close to the looking glass, I was able to point to various heptapod body parts, such as limbs, digits, and eyes, and elicit terms for each. It turned out that they had an orifice on the underside of their body, lined with articulated bony ridges: probably used for eating, while the one at the top was for respiration and speech. There were no other conspicuous orifices; perhaps their mouth was their anus too. Those sorts of questions would have to wait.

I also tried asking our two informants for terms for addressing each individually; personal names, if they had such things. Their answers were of course unpronounceable, so for Gary's and my purposes, I dubbed them Flapper and Raspberry. I hoped I'd be able to tell them apart.

The next day I conferred with Gary before we entered the looking-glass tent. "I'll need your help with this session," I told him.

"Sure. What do you want me to do?"

"We need to elicit some verbs, and it's easiest with third-person forms. Would you act out a few verbs while I type the written form on the computer? If we're lucky, the heptapods will figure out what we're doing and do the same. I've brought a bunch of props for you to use."

"No problem," said Gary, cracking his knuckles. "Ready when you are."

We began with some simple intransitive verbs: walking, jumping, speaking, writing. Gary demonstrated each one with a charming lack of self-consciousness; the presence of the video cameras didn't inhibit him at all. For the first few actions he performed, I asked the heptapods, "What do you call that?" Before long, the heptapods caught on to what we were trying to do; Raspberry began mimicking Gary, or at least performing the equivalent heptapod action, while Flapper worked their computer, displaying a written description and pronouncing it aloud.

In the spectrographs of their spoken utterances, I could recognize their word I had glossed as "heptapod." The rest of each utterance was presumably the verb phrase; it looked like they had analogs of nouns and verbs, thank goodness.

In their writing, however, things weren't as clear-cut. For each action, they had displayed a single logogram instead of two separate ones. At first I thought they had written something like "walks," with the subject implied. But why would Flapper say "the heptapod walks" while writing "walks," instead of maintaining parallelism? Then I noticed that some of the logograms looked like the logogram for "heptapod" with some extra strokes added to one side or another. Perhaps their verbs could be written as affixes to a noun. If so, why was Flapper writing the noun in some instances but not in others?

I decided to try a transitive verb; substituting object words might clarify things. Among the props I'd brought were an apple and a slice of bread. "Okay," I said to Gary, "show them the food, and then eat some. First the apple, then the bread."

Gary pointed at the Golden Delicious and then he took a bite out of it, while I displayed the "what do you call that?" expression. Then we repeated it with the slice of whole wheat.

Raspberry left the room and returned with some kind of giant nut or gourd and a gelatinous ellipsoid. Raspberry pointed at the gourd while Flapper said a word and displayed a logogram. Then Raspberry brought the gourd down between its legs, a crunching sound resulted, and the gourd reemerged minus a bite; there were corn-like kernels beneath the shell. Flapper talked and displayed a large logogram on their screen. The sound spectrograph for "gourd" changed when it was used in the sentence; possibly a case marker. The logogram was odd: after some study, I could identify graphic elements that resembled the individual logograms for "heptapod" and "gourd." They looked as if they had been melted together, with several extra strokes in the mix that presumably meant "eat." Was it a multi-word ligature?

Next we got spoken and written names for the gelatin egg, and descriptions of the act of eating it. The sound spectrograph for "heptapod eats gelatin egg" was analyzable; "gelatin egg" bore a case marker, as expected, though the sentence's word order differed from last time. The written form, another large logogram, was another matter. This time it took much longer for me to recognize anything in it; not only were the individual logograms melted together again, it looked as if the one for "heptapod" was laid on its back, while on top of it the logogram for "gelatin egg" was standing on its head.

"Uh-oh." I took another look at the writing for the simple noun-verb examples, the ones that had seemed inconsistent before. Now I realized all of them actually did contain the logogram for "heptapod"; some were rotated and distorted by being combined with the various verbs, so I hadn't recognized them at first. "You guys have got to be kidding," I muttered.

"What's wrong?" asked Gary.

"Their script isn't word divided; a sentence is written by joining the logograms for the constituent words. They join the logograms by rotating and modifying them. Take a look." I showed him how the logograms were rotated.

"So they can read a word with equal ease no matter how it's rotated," Gary said. He turned to look at the heptapods, impressed. "I wonder if it's a consequence of their bodies' radial symmetry: their bodies have no 'forward' direction, so maybe their writing doesn't either. Highly neat."

I couldn't believe it; I was working with someone who modified the word "neat" with "highly." "It certainly is interesting," I said, "but it also means there's no easy way for us to write our own sentences in their language. We can't simply cut their sentences into individual words and recombine them; we'll have to learn the rules of their script before we can write anything legible. It's the same continuity problem we'd have had splicing together speech fragments, except applied to writing."

I looked at Flapper and Raspberry in the looking glass, who were waiting for us to continue, and sighed. "You aren't going to make this easy for us, are you?"

To be fair, the heptapods were completely cooperative. In the days that followed, they readily taught us their language without requiring us to teach them any more English. Colonel Weber and his cohorts pondered the implications of that, while I and the linguists at the other looking glasses met via videoconferencing to share what we had learned about the heptapod language. The videoconferencing made for an incongruous working environment: our video screens were primitive compared to the heptapods' looking glasses, so that my colleagues seemed more remote than the aliens. The familiar was far away, while the bizarre was close at hand.

It would be a while before we'd be ready to ask the heptapods why they had come, or to discuss physics well enough to ask them about their technology. For the time being, we worked on the basics: phonemics/graphemics, vocabulary, syntax. The heptapods at every looking glass were using the same language, so we were able to pool our data and coordinate our efforts.

Our biggest source of confusion was the heptapods' "writing." It didn't appear to be writing at all; it looked more like a bunch of intricate graphic designs. The logograms weren't arranged in rows, or a spiral, or any linear fashion. Instead, Flapper or Raspberry would write a sentence by sticking together as many logograms as needed into a giant conglomeration.

This form of writing was reminiscent of primitive sign systems, which required a reader to know a message's context in order to understand it. Such systems were considered too limited for systematic recording of information. Yet it was unlikely that the heptapods developed their level of technology with only an oral tradition. That implied one of three possibilities: the first was that the heptapods had a true writing system, but they didn't want to use it in front of us; Colonel Weber would identify with that one. The second was that the heptapods hadn't originated the technology they were using; they were illiterates using someone else's technology. The third, and most interesting to me, was that was the heptapods were using a nonlinear system of orthography that qualified as true writing.

I remember a conversation we'll have when you're in your junior year of high school. It'll be Sunday morning, and I'll be scrambling some eggs while you set the table for brunch. You'll laugh as you tell me about the party you went to last night.

"Oh man," you'll say, "they're not kidding when they say that body weight makes a difference. I didn't drink any more than the guys did, but I got so much drunker."

I'll try to maintain a neutral, pleasant expression. I'll really try. Then you'll say, "Oh, come on, Mom."

"What?"

"You know you did the exact same things when you were my age."

I did nothing of the sort, but I know that if I were to admit that, you'd lose respect for me completely. "You know never to drive, or get into a car if—"

"God, of course I know that. Do you think I'm an idiot?"

"No, of course not."

What I'll think is that you are clearly, maddeningly not me. It will remind me, again, that you won't be a clone of me; you can be wonderful, a daily delight, but you won't be someone I could have created by myself.

The military had set up a trailer containing our offices at the looking glass site. I saw Gary walking toward the trailer, and ran to catch up with him. "It's a semasiographic writing system," I said when I reached him.

"Excuse me?" said Gary.

"Here, let me show you." I directed Gary into my office. Once we were inside, I went to the chalkboard and drew a circle with a diagonal line bisecting it. "What does this mean?"

"'Not allowed'?"

"Right." Next I printed the words NOT ALLOWED on the chalkboard. "And so does this. But only one is a representation of speech."

Gary nodded. "Okay."

"Linguists describe writing like this"—I indicated the printed words—"as 'glottographic,' because it represents speech. Every human written language is in this category. However, this symbol"—I indicated the circle and diagonal line—"is 'semasiographic' writing, because it conveys meaning without reference to speech. There's no correspondence between its components and any particular sounds."

"And you think all of heptapod writing is like this?"

"From what I've seen so far, yes. It's not picture writing, it's far more complex. It has its own system of rules for constructing sentences, like a visual syntax that's unrelated to the syntax for their spoken language."

"A visual syntax? Can you show me an example?"

"Coming right up." I sat down at my desk and, using the computer, pulled up a frame from the recording of yesterday's conversation with Raspberry. I turned the monitor so he could see it. "In their spoken language, a noun has a case marker indicating whether it's a subject or object. In their written language, however, a noun is identified as subject or object based on the orientation of its logogram relative to that of the verb. Here, take a look." I pointed at one of the figures. "For instance, when 'heptapod' is integrated with 'hears' this way, with these strokes parallel, it means that the heptapod is doing the hearing." I showed him a different one. "When they're combined this way, with the strokes perpendicular, it means that the heptapod is being heard. This morphology applies to several verbs.

"Another example is the inflection system." I called up another frame from the recording. "In their written language, this logogram means roughly 'hear easily' or 'hear clearly.' See the elements it has in common with the logogram for 'hear'? You can still combine it with 'heptapod' in the same ways as before, to indicate that the heptapod can hear something clearly or that the heptapod is clearly heard. But what's really interesting is that the modulation of 'hear' into 'hear clearly' isn't a special case; you see the transformation they applied?"

Gary nodded, pointing. "It's like they express the idea of 'clearly' by changing the curve of those strokes in the middle."

"Right. That modulation is applicable to lots of verbs. The logogram for 'see' can be modulated in the same way to form 'see clearly,' and so can the logogram for 'read' and others. And changing the curve of those strokes has no parallel in their speech; with the spoken version of these verbs, they add a prefix to the verb to express ease of manner, and the prefixes for 'see' and 'hear' are different.

"There are other examples, but you get the idea. It's essentially a grammar in two dimensions."

He began pacing thoughtfully. "Is there anything like this in human writing systems?"

"Mathematical equations, notations for music and dance. But those are all very specialized; we couldn't record this conversation using them. But I suspect, if we knew it well enough, we could record this conversation in the heptapod writing system. I think it's a full-fledged, general-purpose graphical language."

Gary frowned. "So their writing constitutes a completely separate language from their speech, right?"

"Right. In fact, it'd be more accurate to refer to the writing system as 'Heptapod B,' and use 'Heptapod A' strictly for referring to the spoken language."

"Hold on a second. Why use two languages when one would suffice? That seems unnecessarily hard to learn."

"Like English spelling?" I said. "Ease of learning isn't the primary force in language evolution. For the heptapods, writing and speech may play such different cultural or cognitive roles that using separate languages makes more sense than using different forms of the same one.

He considered it. "I see what you mean. Maybe they think our form of writing is redundant, like we're wasting a second communications channel."

"That's entirely possible. Finding out why they use a second language for writing will tell us a lot about them."

"So I take it this means we won't be able to use their writing to help us learn their spoken language."

I sighed. "Yeah, that's the most immediate implication. But I don't think we should ignore either Heptapod A or B; we need a two-pronged approach." I pointed at the screen. "I'll bet you that learning their two-dimensional grammar will help you when it comes time to learn their mathematical notation."

"You've got a point there. So are we ready to start asking about their mathematics?"

"Not yet. We need a better grasp on this writing system before we begin anything else," I said, and then smiled when he mimed frustration. "Patience, good sir. Patience is a virtue."

You'll be six when your father has a conference to attend in Hawaii, and we'll accompany him. You'll be so excited that you'll make preparations for weeks beforehand. You'll ask me about coconuts and volcanoes and surfing, and practice hula dancing in the mirror. You'll pack a suitcase with the clothes and toys you want to bring, and you'll drag it around the house to see how long you can carry it. You'll ask me if I can carry your Etch-a-Sketch in my bag, since there won't be any more room for it in yours and you simply can't leave without it.

"You won't need all of these," I'll say. "There'll be so many fun things to do there, you won't have time to play with so many toys."

You'll consider that; dimples will appear above your eyebrows when you think hard. Eventually you'll agree to pack fewer toys, but your expectations will, if anything, increase.

"*I* wanna be in Hawaii now," you'll whine.

"Sometimes it's good to wait," I'll say. "The anticipation makes it more fun when you get there."

You'll just pout.

In the next report I submitted, I suggested that the term "logogram was a misnomer because it implied that each graph represented a spoken word, when in fact the graphs didn't correspond to our notion of spoken words at all. I didn't want to use the term "ideogram" either because of how it had been used in the past; I suggested the term "semagram" instead.

It appeared that a semagram corresponded roughly to a written word in human languages: it was meaningful on its own, and in combination with other semagrams could form endless statements. We couldn't define it precisely, but then no one had ever satisfactorily defined "word" for human languages either. When it came to sentences in Heptapod B, though, things became much more confusing. The language had no written punctuation: its syntax was indicated in the way the semagrams were combined, and there was no need to indicate the cadence of speech. There was certainly no way to slice out subject-predicate pairings neatly to make sentences. A "sentence" seemed to be whatever number of semagrams a heptapod wanted to join together; the only difference between a sentence and a paragraph, or a page, was size.

When a Heptapod B sentence grew fairly sizable, its visual impact was remarkable. If I wasn't trying to decipher it, the writing looked like fanciful praying mantids drawn in a cursive style, all clinging to each other to form an Escheresque lattice, each slightly different in its stance. And the biggest sentences had an effect similar to that of psychedelic posters: sometimes eye-watering, sometimes hypnotic.

I remember a picture of you taken at your college graduation. In the photo you're striking a pose for the camera, mortarboard stylishly tilted on your head, one hand touching your sunglasses, the other hand on your hip, holding open your gown to reveal the tank top and shorts you're wearing underneath.

I remember your graduation. There will be the distraction of having Nelson and your father and what's-her-name there all at the same time, but that will be minor. That entire weekend, while you're introducing me to your classmates and hugging everyone incessantly, I'll be all but mute with amazement. I can't believe that you, a grown woman taller than me and beautiful enough to make my heart ache, will be the same girl I used to lift off the ground so you could reach the drinking fountain, the same girl who used to trundle out of my bedroom draped in a dress and hat and four scarves from my closet.

And after graduation, you'll be heading for a job as a financial analyst. I won't understand what you do there, I won't even understand your fascination with money, the preeminence you gave to salary when negotiating job offers. I would prefer it if you'd pursue something without regard for its monetary rewards, but I'll have no complaints. My own mother could never understand why I couldn't just be a high school English teacher. You'll do what makes you happy, and that'll be all I ask for.

As time went on, the teams at each looking glass began working in earnest on learning heptapod terminology for elementary mathematics and physics. We worked together on presentations, with the linguists focusing on procedure and the physicists focusing on subject matter. The physicists showed us previously devised systems for communicating with aliens, based on mathematics, but those were intended for use over a radio telescope. We reworked them for face-to-face communication.

Our teams were successful with basic arithmetic, but we hit a roadblock with geometry and algebra. We tried using a spherical coordinate system instead of a rectangular one, thinking it might be more natural to the heptapods given their anatomy, but that approach wasn't any more fruitful. The heptapods didn't seem to understand what we were getting at.

Likewise, the physics discussions went poorly. Only with the most concrete terms, like the names of the elements, did we have any success; after several attempts at representing the periodic table, the heptapods got the idea. For anything remotely abstract, we might as well have been gibbering. We tried to demonstrate basic physical attributes like mass and acceleration so we could elicit their terms for them, but the heptapods simply responded with requests for clarification. To avoid perceptual problems that might be associated with any particular medium, we tried physical demonstrations as well as line drawings, photos, and animations; none were effective. Days with no progress became weeks, and the physicists were becoming disillusioned.

By contrast, the linguists were having much more success. We made steady progress decoding the grammar of the spoken language, Heptapod A. It didn't follow the pattern of human languages, as expected, but it was comprehensible so far: free word order, even to the extent that there was no preferred order for the clauses in a conditional statement, in defiance of a human language "universal." It also appeared that the heptapods had no objection to many levels of center-embedding of clauses, something that quickly defeated humans. Peculiar, but not impenetrable.

Much more interesting were the newly discovered morphological and grammatical processes in Heptapod B that were uniquely two-dimensional. Depending on a semagram's declension, inflections could be indicated by varying a certain stroke's curvature, or its thickness, or its manner of undulation; or by varying the relative sizes of two radicals, or their relative distance to another radical, or their orientations; or various other means. These were nonsegmental graphemes; they couldn't be isolated from the rest of a semagram. And despite how such traits behaved in human writing, these had nothing to do with calligraphic style; their meanings were defined according to a consistent and unambiguous grammar.

We regularly asked the heptapods why they had come. Each time, they answered "to see," or "to observe." Indeed, sometimes they preferred to watch us silently rather than answer our questions. Perhaps they were scientists, perhaps they were tourists. The State Department instructed us to reveal as little as possible about humanity, in case that information could be used as a bargaining chip in subsequent negotiations. We obliged, though it didn't require much effort: the heptapods never asked questions about anything. Whether scientists or tourists, they were an awfully incurious bunch.

I remember once when we'll be driving to the mall to buy some new clothes for you. You'll be thirteen. One moment you'll be sprawled in your seat, completely unself-conscious, all child; the next, you'll toss your hair with a practiced casualness, like a fashion model in training.

You'll give me some instructions as I'm parking the car. "Okay, Mom, give me one of the credit cards, and we can meet back at the entrance here in two hours."

I'll laugh. "Not a chance. All the credit cards stay with me."

"You're kidding." You'll become the embodiment of exasperation. We'll get out of the car and I will start walking to the mall entrance. After seeing that I won't budge on the matter, you'll quickly reformulate your plans.

"Okay Mom, okay. You can come with me, just walk a little ways behind me, so it doesn't look like we're together. If I see any friends of mine, I'm gonna stop and talk to them, but you just keep walking, okay? I'll come find you later."

I'll stop in my tracks. "Excuse me? I am not the hired help, nor am I some mutant relative for you to be ashamed of."

"But Mom, I can't let anyone see you with me."

"What are you talking about? I've already met your friends; they've been to the house."

"That was different," you'll say, incredulous that you have to explain it. "This is shopping."

"Too bad."

Then the explosion: "You won't do the least thing to make me happy! You don't care about me at all!"

It won't have been that long since you enjoyed going shopping with me; it will forever astonish me how quickly you grow out of one phase and enter another. Living with you will be like aiming for a moving target; you'll always be further along than I expect.

I looked at the sentence in Heptapod B that I had just written, using simple pen and paper. Like all the sentences I generated myself, this one looked misshapen, like a heptapod-written sentence that had been smashed with a hammer and then inexpertly taped back together. I had sheets of such inelegant semagrams covering my desk, fluttering occasionally when the oscillating fan swung past.

It was strange trying to learn a language that had no spoken form. Instead of practicing my pronunciation, I had taken to squeezing my eyes shut and trying to paint semagrams on the insides of my eyelids.

There was a knock at the door and before I could answer Gary came in looking jubilant. "Illinois got a repetition in physics."

"Really? That's great; when did it happen?"

"It happened a few hours ago; we just had the videoconference. Let me show you what it is." He started erasing my blackboard.

"Don't worry, I didn't need any of that."

"Good." He picked up a nub of chalk and drew a diagram:

"Okay, here's the path a ray of light takes when crossing from air to water. The light ray travels in a straight line until it hits the water; the water has a different index of refraction, so the light changes direction. You've heard of this before, right?"

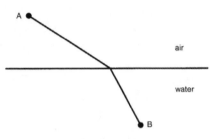

I nodded. "Sure."

"Now here's an interesting property about the path the light takes. The path is the fastest possible route between these two points.

"Come again?"

"Imagine, just for grins, that the ray of light traveled along this path." He added a dotted line to his diagram:

"This hypothetical path is shorter than the path the light actually takes. But light travels more slowly in water than it does in air, and a greater percentage of this path is underwater. So it would take longer for light to travel along this path than it does along the real path."

"Okay, I get it."

"Now imagine if light were to travel along this other path." He drew a second dotted path:

"This path reduces the percentage that's underwater, but the total length is larger. It would also take longer for light to travel along this path than along the actual one."

Gary put down the chalk and gestured at the diagram on the chalkboard with white-tipped fingers. "Any hypothetical path would require more time to traverse than the one actually taken. In other words, the route that the light ray takes is always the fastest possible one. That's Fermat's principle of least time."

"Hmm, interesting. And this is what the heptapods responded to?"

"Exactly. Moorehead gave an animated presentation of Fermat's principle at the Illinois looking glass, and the heptapods repeated it back. Now he's trying to get a symbolic description." He grinned. "Now is that highly neat, or what?"

"It's neat all right, but how come I haven't heard of Fermat's principle before?" I picked up a binder and waved it at him; it was a primer on the physics topics suggested for use in communication with the heptapods. "This thing goes on forever about Planck masses and the spin-flip of atomic hydrogen, and not a word about the refraction of light."

"We guessed wrong about what'd be most useful for you to know," Gary said without embarrassment. "In fact, it's curious that Fermat's principle was the first breakthrough; even though it's easy to explain, you need calculus to describe it mathematically. And not ordinary calculus; you need the calculus of variations. We thought that some simple theorem of geometry or algebra would be the breakthrough."

"Curious indeed. You think the heptapods' idea of what's simple doesn't match ours?"

"Exactly, which is why I'm *dying* to see what their mathematical description of Fermat's principle looks like." He paced as he talked. "If their version of the calculus of variations is simpler to them than their equivalent of algebra, that might explain why we've had so much trouble talking about physics; their entire system of mathematics may be topsy-turvy compared to ours." He pointed to the physics primer. "You can be sure that we're going to revise that."

"So can you build from Fermat's principle to other areas of physics?"

"Probably. There are lots of physical principles just like Fermat's."

"What, like Louise's principle of least closet space? When did physics become so minimalist?"

"Well, the word 'least' is misleading. You see, Fermat's principle of least time is incomplete; in certain situations light follows a path that takes *more* time than any of the other possibilities. It's more accurate to say that light always follows an *extreme* path, either one that minimizes the time taken or one that maximizes it. A minimum and a maximum share certain mathematical properties, so both situations can be described with one equation. So to be precise, Fermat's principle isn't a minimal principle; instead it's what's known as a 'variational' principle."

"And there are more of these variational principles?"

He nodded. "In all branches of physics. Almost every physical law can be restated as a variational principle. The only difference between these principles is in which attribute is minimized or maximized." He gestured as if the different branches of physics were arrayed before him on a table. "In optics, where Fermat's principle applies, time is the attribute that has to be an extreme. In mechanics, it's a different attribute. In electromagnetism, it's something else again. But all these principles are similar mathematically."

"So once you get their mathematical description of Fermat's principle, you should be able to decode the other ones."

"God, I hope so. I think this is the wedge that we've been looking for, the one that cracks open their formulation of physics. This calls for a celebration." He stopped his pacing and turned to me. "Hey Louise, want to go out for dinner? My treat."

I was mildly surprised. "Sure," I said.

It'll be when you first learn to walk that I get daily demonstrations of the asymmetry in our relationship. You'll be incessantly running off somewhere, and each time you walk into a door frame or scrape your knee, the pain feels like it's my own. It'll be like growing an errant limb, an extension of myself whose sensory nerves report pain just fine, but whose motor nerves don't convey my commands at all. It's so unfair: I'm going to give birth to an animated voodoo doll of myself. I didn't see this in the contract when I signed up. Was this part of the deal?

And then there will be the times when I see you laughing. Like the time you'll be playing with the neighbor's puppy, poking your hands through the chain-link fence separating our back yards, and you'll be laughing so hard you'll start hiccuping. The puppy will run inside the neighbor's house, and your laughter will gradually subside, letting you catch your breath. Then the puppy will come back to the fence to lick your fingers again, and you'll shriek and start laughing again. It will be the most wonderful sound I could ever imagine, a sound that makes me feel like a fountain, or a wellspring.

Now if only I can remember that sound the next time your blithe disregard for self-preservation gives me a heart attack.

After the breakthrough with Fermat's principle, discussions of scientific concepts became more fruitful. It wasn't as if all of heptapod physics were suddenly rendered transparent, but progress was steady. According to Gary, the heptapods' formulation of physics was indeed topsy-turvy relative to ours. Physical attributes that humans defined using integral calculus were seen as fundamental by the heptapods. As an example, Gary described an attribute that, in physics jargon, bore the deceptively simple name "action," which represented "the difference between kinetic and potential energy, integrated over time," whatever that meant. Calculus for us; elementary to them.

Conversely, to define attributes that humans thought of as fundamental, like velocity, the heptapods employed mathematics that were, Gary assured me, "highly weird." The physicists were ultimately able to prove the equivalence of heptapod mathematics and human mathematics; even though their approaches were almost the reverse of one another, both were systems for describing the same physical universe.

I tried following some of the equations that the physicists were coming up with, but it was no use. I couldn't really grasp the significance of physical attributes like "action"; I couldn't, with any confidence, ponder the significance of treating such an attribute as fundamental. Still, I tried to ponder questions formulated in terms more familiar to me: what kind of world-view did the heptapods have, that they would consider Fermat's principle the simplest explanation of light refraction? What kind of perception made a minimum or maximum readily apparent to them?

Your eyes will be blue like your dad's, not mud brown like mine. Boys will stare into those eyes the way I did, and do, into your dad's, surprised and enchanted, as I was and am, to find them in combination with black hair. You will have many suitors.

I remember when you are fifteen, coming home after a weekend at your dad's, incredulous over the interrogation he'll have put you through regarding the boy you're currently dating. You'll sprawl on the sofa, recounting your dad's latest breach of common sense: "You know what he said? He said, 'I know what teenage boys are like.'" Roll of the eyes. "Like I don't?"

"Don't hold it against him," I'll say. "He's a father; he can't help it." Having seen you interact with your friends, I won't worry much about a boy taking advantage of you; if anything, the opposite will be more likely. I'll worry about that.

"He wishes I were still a kid. He hasn't known how to act toward me since I grew breasts."

"Well, that development was a shock for him. Give him time to recover."

"It's been *years,* Mom. How long is it gonna take?"

"I'll let you know when my father has come to terms with mine."

During one of the videoconferences for the linguists, Cisneros from the Massachusetts looking glass had raised an interesting question: Was there a particular order in which semagrams were written in a Heptapod B sentence? It was clear that word order meant next to nothing when speaking in Heptapod A; when asked to repeat what it had just said, a heptapod would likely as not use a different word order unless we specifically asked them not to. Was word order similarly unimportant when writing in Heptapod B?

Previously, we had focused our attention only on how a sentence in Heptapod B looked once it was complete. As far as anyone could tell, there was no preferred order when reading the semagrams in a sentence; you could start almost anywhere in the nest, then follow the branching clauses until you'd read the whole thing. But that was reading; was the same true about writing?

During my most recent session with Flapper and Raspberry I had asked them if, instead of displaying a semagram only after it was completed, they could show it to us while it was being written. They had agreed. I inserted the videotape of the session into the VCR, and on my computer I consulted the session transcript.

I picked one of the longer utterances from the conversation. What Flapper had said was that the heptapods' planet had two moons, one significantly larger than the other; the three primary constituents of the planet's atmosphere were nitrogen, argon, and oxygen; and 15/28ths of the planet's surface was covered by water. The first words of the spoken utterance translated literally as "inequality-of-size rocky-orbiter rockyorbiters related-as-primary-to-secondary."

Then I rewound the videotape until the time signature matched the one in the transcription. I started playing the tape, and watched the web of semagrams being spun out of inky spider's silk. I rewound it and played it several times. Finally I froze the video right after the first stroke was completed and before the second one was begun; all that was visible onscreen was a single sinuous line.

Comparing that initial stroke with the completed sentence, I realized that the stroke participated in several different clauses of the message. It began in the semagram for "oxygen," as the determinant that distinguished it from certain other elements; then it slid down to become the morpheme of comparison in the description of the two moons' sizes; and lastly it flared out as the arched backbone of the semagram for "ocean." Yet this stroke *was* a single continuous line, and it was the first one that Flapper wrote. That meant the heptapod had to know how the entire sentence would be laid out before it could write the very first stroke.

The other strokes in the sentence also traversed several clauses, making them so interconnected that none could be removed without redesigning the entire sentence. The heptapods didn't write a sentence one semagram at a time; they built it out of strokes irrespective of individual semagrams. I had seen a similarly high degree of integration before in calligraphic designs, particularly those employing the Arabic alphabet. But those designs had required careful planning by expert calligraphers. No one could lay out such an intricate design at the speed needed for holding a conversation. At least, no human could.

There's a joke that I once heard a comedienne tell. It goes like this: "I'm not sure if I'm ready to have children. I asked a friend of mine who has children, 'Suppose I do have kids. What if when they grow up, they blame me for everything that's wrong with their lives?' She laughed and said, 'What do you mean, if?'"

That's my favorite joke.

Gary and I were at a little Chinese restaurant, one of the local places we had taken to patronizing to get away from the encampment. We sat eating the appetizers: potstickers, redolent of pork and sesame oil. My favorite.

I dipped one in soy sauce and vinegar. "So how are you doing with your Heptapod B practice?" I asked.

Gary looked obliquely at the ceiling. I tried to meet his gaze, but he kept shifting it.

"You've given up, haven't you?" I said. "You're not even trying anymore."

He did a wonderful hangdog expression. "I'm just no good at languages," he confessed. "I thought learning Heptapod B might be more like learning mathematics than trying to speak another language, but it's not. It's too foreign for me."

"It would help you discuss physics with them."

"Probably, but since we had our breakthrough, I can get by with just a few phrases."

I sighed. "I suppose that's fair; I have to admit, I've given up on trying to learn the mathematics."

"So we're even?"

"We're even." I sipped my tea. "Though I did want to ask you about Fermat's principle. Something about it feels odd to me, but I can't put my finger on it. It just doesn't sound like a law of physics."

A twinkle appeared in Gary's eyes. "I'll bet I know what you're talking about." He snipped a potsticker in half with his chopsticks. "You're used to thinking of refraction in terms of cause and effect: reaching the water's surface is the cause, and the change in direction is the effect. But Fermat's principle sounds weird because it describes light's behavior in goal-oriented terms. It sounds like a commandment to a light beam:

'Thou shalt minimize or maximize the time taken to reach thy destination.'"

I considered it. "Go on."

"It's an old question in the philosophy of physics. People have been talking about it since Fermat first formulated it in the 1600s; Planck wrote volumes about it. The thing is, while the common formulation of physical laws is causal, a variational principle like Fermat's is purposive, almost teleological."

"Hmm, that's an interesting way to put it. Let me think about that for a minute." I pulled out a felt-tip pen and, on my paper napkin, drew a copy of the diagram that Gary had drawn on my blackboard. "Okay," I said, thinking aloud, "so let's say the goal of a ray of light is to take the fastest path. How does the light go about doing that?"

"Well, if I can speak anthropomorphic-projectionally, the light has to examine the possible paths and compute how long each one would take." He plucked the last potsticker from the serving dish.

"And to do that," I continued, "the ray of light has to know just where its destination is. If the destination were somewhere else, the fastest path would be different."

Gary nodded again. "That's right; the notion of a 'fastest path' is meaningless unless there's a destination specified. And computing how long a given path takes also requires information about what lies along that path, like where the water's surface is."

I kept staring at the diagram on the napkin. "And the light ray has to know all that ahead of time, before it starts moving, right?"

So to speak," said Gary. "The light can't start traveling in any old direction and make course corrections later on, because the path resulting from such behavior wouldn't be the fastest possible one. The light has to do all its computations at the very beginning."

I thought to myself, *the ray of light has to know where it will ultimately end up before it can choose the direction to begin moving in.* I knew what that reminded me of. I looked up at Gary. "That's what was bugging me."

I remember when you're fourteen. You'll come out of your bedroom, a graffiti-covered notebook computer in hand, working on a report for school.

"Mom, what do you call it when both sides can win?"

I'll look up from my computer and the paper I'll be writing. "What, you mean a win-win situation?"

"There's some technical name for it, some math word. Remember that time Dad was here, and he was talking about the stock market? He used it then."

"Hmm, that sounds familiar, but I can't remember what he called it."

"I need to know. I want to use that phrase in my social studies report. I can't even search for information on it unless I know what it's called."

"I'm sorry, I don't know it either. Why don't you call your dad?"

Judging from your expression, that will be more effort than you want to make. At this point, you and your father won't be getting along well. "Can you call Dad and ask him? But don't tell him it's for me."

"I think you can call him yourself."

You'll fume, "Jesus, Mom, I can never get help with my homework since you and Dad split up."

It's amazing the diverse situations in which you can bring up the divorce. "I've helped you with your homework."

"Like a million years ago, Mom."

I'll let that pass. "I'd help you with this if I could, but I don't remember what it's called."

You'll head back to your bedroom in a huff.

I practiced Heptapod B at every opportunity, both with the other linguists and by myself. The novelty of reading a semasiographic language made it compelling in a way that Heptapod A wasn't, and my improvement in writing it excited me. Over time, the sentences I wrote grew shapelier, more cohesive. I had reached the point where it worked better when I didn't think about it too much. Instead of carefully trying to design a sentence before writing, I could simply begin putting down strokes immediately; my initial strokes almost always turned out to be compatible with an elegant rendition of what I was trying to say. I was developing a faculty like that of the heptapods.

More interesting was the fact that Heptapod B was changing the way I thought. For me, thinking typically meant speaking in an internal voice; as we say in the trade, my thoughts were phonologically coded. My internal voice normally spoke in English, but that wasn't a requirement. The summer after my senior year in high school, I attended a total immersion program for learning Russian; by the end of the summer, I was thinking and even dreaming in Russian. But it was always *spoken* Russian. Different language, same mode: a voice speaking silently aloud.

The idea of thinking in a linguistic yet nonphonological mode always intrigued me. I had a friend born of Deaf parents; he grew up using

American Sign Language, and he told me that he often thought in ASL instead of English. I used to wonder what it was like to have one's thoughts be manually coded, to reason using an inner pair of hands instead of an inner voice.

With Heptapod B, I was experiencing something just as foreign: my thoughts were becoming graphically coded. There were trance-like moments during the day when my thoughts weren't expressed with my internal voice; instead, I saw semagrams with my mind's eye, sprouting like frost on a windowpane.

As I grew more fluent, semagraphic designs would appear fully formed, articulating even complex ideas all at once. My thought processes weren't moving any faster as a result, though. Instead of racing forward, my mind hung balanced on the symmetry underlying the semagrams. The semagrams seemed to be something more than language; they were almost like mandalas. I found myself in a meditative state, contemplating the way in which premises and conclusions were interchangeable. There was no direction inherent in the way propositions were connected, no "train of thought" moving along a particular route; all the components in an act of reasoning were equally powerful, all having identical precedence.

A representative from the State Department named Hossner had the job of briefing the U.S. scientists on our agenda with the heptapods. We sat in the videoconference room, listening to him lecture. Our microphone was turned off, so Gary and I could exchange comments without interrupting Hossner. As we listened, I worried that Gary might harm his vision, rolling his eyes so often.

"They must have had some reason for coming all this way," said the diplomat, his voice tinny through the speakers. "It does not look like their reason was conquest, thank God. But if that's not the reason, what is? Are they prospectors? Anthropologists? Missionaries? Whatever their motives, there must be something we can offer them. Maybe it's mineral rights to our solar system. Maybe it's information about ourselves. Maybe it's the right to deliver sermons to our populations. But we can be sure that there's something.

"My point is this: their motive might not be to trade, but that doesn't mean that we cannot conduct trade. We simply need to know why they're here, and what we have that they want. Once we have that information, we can begin trade negotiations.

"I should emphasize that our relationship with the heptapods need not be adversarial. This is not a situation where every gain on their part is a loss on ours, or vice versa. If we handle ourselves correctly, both we and the heptapods can come out winners."

"You mean it's a non-zero-sum game?" Gary said in mock incredulity. "Oh my gosh."

"A non-zero-sum game."

"What?" You'll reverse course, heading back from your bedroom.

"When both sides can win: I just remembered, it's called a non-zero-sum game."

"That's it!" you'll say, writing it down on your notebook. "Thanks Mom!"

"I guess I knew it after all," I'll say. "All those years with your father, some of it must have rubbed off."

"I knew you'd know it," you'll say. You'll give me a sudden, brief hug, and your hair will smell of apples. "You're the best."

"Louise?"

"Hmm? Sorry, I was distracted. What did you say?"

"I said, what do you think about our Mr. Hossner here?"

"I prefer not to."

"I've tried that myself: ignoring the government, seeing if it would go away. It hasn't."

As evidence of Gary's assertion, Hossner kept blathering:

"Your immediate task is to think back on what you've learned. Look for anything that might help us. Has there been any indication of what the heptapods want? Of what they value?"

"Gee, it never occurred to us to look for things like that," I said. "We'll get right on it, sir."

"The sad thing is, that's just what we'll have to do," said Gary.

"Are there any questions?" asked Hossner.

Burghart, the linguist at the Ft. Worth looking glass, spoke up. "We've been through this with the heptapods many times. They maintain that they're here to observe, and they maintain that information is not tradable."

"So they would have us believe," said Hossner. "But consider: how could that be true? I know that the heptapods have occasionally stopped talking to us for brief periods. That may be a tactical maneuver on their part. If we were to stop talking to them tomorrow—"

"Wake me up if he says something interesting," said Gary.

"I was just going to ask you to do the same for me."

That day when Gary first explained Fermat's principle to me, he had mentioned that almost every physical law could be stated as a variational principle. Yet when humans thought about physical laws, they preferred to work with them in their causal formulation. I could understand that: the physical attributes that humans found intuitive, like kinetic energy or acceleration, were all properties of an object at a given moment in time. And these were conducive to a chronological, causal interpretation of events: one moment growing out of another, causes and effects creating a chain reaction that grew from past to future.

In contrast, the physical attributes that the heptapods found intuitive, like "action" or those other things defined by integrals, were meaningful only over a period of time. And these were conducive to a teleological interpretation of events: by viewing events over a period of time, one recognized that there was a requirement that had to be satisfied, a goal of minimizing or maximizing. And one had to know the initial and final states to meet that goal; one needed knowledge of the effects before the causes could be initiated.

I was growing to understand that, too.

"Why?" you'll ask again. You'll be three.

"Because it's your bedtime," I'll say again. We'll have gotten as far as getting you bathed and into your jammies, but no further than that.

"But I'm not sleepy," you'll whine. You'll be standing at the bookshelf, pulling down a video to watch: your latest diversionary tactic to keep away from your bedroom.

"It doesn't matter: you still have to go to bed." "But why?"

"Because I'm the mom and I said so."

I'm actually going to say that, aren't I? God, somebody please shoot me.

I'll pick you up and carry you under my arm to your bed, you wailing piteously all the while, but my sole concern will be my own distress. All those vows made in childhood that I would give reasonable answers when I became a parent, that I would treat my own child as an intelligent, thinking individual, all for naught: I'm going to turn into my mother. I can fight it as much as I want, but there'll be no stopping my slide down that long, dreadful slope.

Was it actually possible to know the future? Not simply to guess at it; was it possible to *know* what was going to happen, with absolute certainty and in specific detail? Gary once told me that the fundamental laws of physics were time-symmetric, that there was no physical difference between past and future. Given that, some might say, "yes, theoretically." But speaking more concretely, most would answer "no," because of free will.

I liked to imagine the objection as a Borgesian fabulation: consider a person standing before the *Book of Ages,* the chronicle that records every event, past and future. Even though the text has been photoreduced from the full-sized edition, the volume is enormous. With magnifier in hand, she flips through the tissue-thin leaves until she locates the story of her life. She finds the passage that describes her flipping through the *Book of Ages,* and she skips to the next column, where it details what she'll be doing later in the day: acting on information she's read in the *Book,* she'll bet $100 on the racehorse Devil May Care and win twenty times that much.

The thought of doing just that had crossed her mind, but being a contrary sort, she now resolves to refrain from betting on the ponies altogether.

There's the rub. The *Book of Ages* cannot be wrong; this scenario is based on the premise that a person is given knowledge of the actual future, not of some possible future. If this were Greek myth, circumstances would conspire to make her enact her fate despite her best efforts, but prophecies in myth are notoriously vague; the *Book of Ages* is quite specific, and there's no way she can be forced to bet on a racehorse in the manner specified. The result is a contradiction: the *Book of Ages* must be right, by definition; yet no matter what the *Book* says she'll do, she can choose to do otherwise. How can these two facts be reconciled?

They can't be, was the common answer. A volume like the *Book of Ages* is a logical impossibility, for the precise reason that its existence would result in the above contradiction. Or, to be generous, some might say that the *Book of Ages* could exist, as long as it wasn't accessible to readers: that volume is housed in a special collection, and no one has viewing privileges.

The existence of free will meant that we couldn't know the future. And we knew free will existed because we had direct experience of it. Volition was an intrinsic part of consciousness.

Or was it? What if the experience of knowing the future changed a person? What if it evoked a sense of urgency, a sense of obligation to act precisely as she knew she would?

I stopped by Gary's office before leaving for the day. "I'm calling it quits. Did you want to grab something to eat?"

"Sure, just wait a second," he said. He shut down his computer and gathered some papers together. Then he looked up at me. "Hey, want to come to my place for dinner tonight? I'll cook."

I looked at him dubiously. "You can cook?"

"Just one dish," he admitted. "But it's a good one."

"Sure," I said. "I'm game."

"Great. We just need to go shopping for the ingredients."

"Don't go to any trouble—"

"There's a market on the way to my house. It won't take a minute."

We took separate cars, me following him. I almost lost him when he abruptly turned into a parking lot. It was a gourmet market, not large, but fancy; tall glass jars stuffed with imported foods sat next to specialty utensils on the store's stainless-steel shelves.

I accompanied Gary as he collected fresh basil, tomatoes, garlic, linguini. "There's a fish market next door; we can get fresh clams there," he said.

"Sounds good." We walked past the section of kitchen utensils. My gaze wandered over the shelves—pepper mills, garlic presses, salad tongs—and stopped on a wooden salad bowl.

When you are three, you'll pull a dishtowel off the kitchen counter and bring that salad bowl down on top of you. I'll make a grab for it, but I'll miss. The edge of the bowl will leave you with a cut, on the upper edge of your forehead, that will require a single stitch. Your father and I will hold you, sobbing and stained with Caesar dressing, as we wait in the emergency room for hours.

I reached out and took the bowl from the shelf. The motion didn't feel like something I was forced to do. Instead it seemed just as urgent as my rushing to catch the bowl when it falls on you: an instinct that I felt right in following.

"I could use a salad bowl like this."

Gary looked at the bowl and nodded approvingly. "See, wasn't it a good thing that I had to stop at the market?"

"Yes it was." We got in line to pay for our purchases.

Consider the sentence "The rabbit is ready to eat." Interpret "rabbit" to be the object of "eat," and the sentence was an announcement that dinner would be served shortly. Interpret "rabbit" to be the subject of "eat," and it was a hint, such as a young girl might give her mother so she'll open a bag of Purina Bunny Chow. Two very different utterances; in fact, they were probably mutually exclusive within a single household. Yet either was a valid interpretation; only context could determine what the sentence meant.

Consider the phenomenon of light hitting water at one angle, and traveling through it at a different angle. Explain it by saying that a difference in the index of refraction caused the light to change direction, and one saw the world as humans saw it. Explain it by saying that light minimized the time needed to travel to its destination, and one saw the world as the heptapods saw it. Two very different interpretations.

The physical universe was a language with a perfectly ambiguous grammar. Every physical event was an utterance that could be parsed in two entirely different ways, one causal and the other teleological, both valid, neither one disqualifiable no matter how much context was available.

When the ancestors of humans and heptapods first acquired the spark of consciousness, they both perceived the same physical world, but they parsed their perceptions differently; the worldviews that ultimately arose were the end result of that divergence. Humans had developed a sequential mode of awareness, while heptapods had developed a simultaneous mode of awareness. We experienced events in an order, and perceived their relationship as cause and effect. They experienced all events at once, and perceived a purpose underlying them all. A minimizing, maximizing purpose.

I have a recurring dream about your death. In the dream, I'm the one who's rock climbing—me, can you imagine it?—and you're three years old, riding in some kind of backpack I'm wearing. We're just a few feet below a ledge where we can rest, and you won't wait until I've climbed up to it. You start pulling yourself out of the pack; I order you to stop, but of course you ignore me. I feel your weight alternating from one side of the pack to the other as you climb out; then I feel your left foot on my shoulder, and then your right. I'm screaming at you, but I can't get a hand free to grab you. I can see the wavy design on the soles of your sneakers as you climb, and then I see a flake of stone give way beneath one of them. You slide right past me, and I can't move a muscle. I look down and see you shrink into the distance below me.

Then, all of a sudden, I'm at the morgue. An orderly lifts the sheet from your face, and I see that you're twenty-five.

"You okay?"

I was sitting upright in bed; I'd woken Gary with my movements. "I'm fine. I was just startled; I didn't recognize where I was for a moment."

Sleepily, he said, "We can stay at your place next time."

I kissed him. "Don't worry; your place is fine." We curled up, my back against his chest, and went back to sleep.

When you're three and we're climbing a steep, spiral flight of stairs, I'll hold your hand extra tightly. You'll pull your hand away from me. "I can do it by myself," you'll insist, and then move away from me to prove it, and I'll remember that dream. We'll repeat that scene countless times during your childhood. I can almost believe that, given your contrary nature, my attempts to protect you will be what create your love of climbing: first the jungle gym at the playground, then trees out in the green belt around our neighborhood, the rock walls at the climbing club, and ultimately cliff faces in national parks.

I finished the last radical in the sentence, put down the chalk, and sat down in my desk chair. I leaned back and surveyed the giant Heptapod B sentence I'd written that covered the entire blackboard in my office. It included several complex clauses, and I had managed to integrate all of them rather nicely.

Looking at a sentence like this one, I understood why the heptapods had evolved a semasiographic writing system like Heptapod B; it was better suited for a species with a simultaneous mode of consciousness. For them, speech was a bottleneck because it required that one word follow another sequentially. With writing, on the other hand, every mark on a page was visible simultaneously. Why constrain writing with a glottographic straitjacket, demanding that it be just as sequential as speech? It would never occur to them. Semasiographic writing naturally took advantage of the page's two-dimensionality; instead of doling out morphemes one at a time, it offered an entire page full of them all at once.

And now that Heptapod B had introduced me to a simultaneous mode of consciousness, I understood the rationale behind Heptapod A's grammar: what my sequential mind had perceived as unnecessarily convoluted, I now recognized as an attempt to provide flexibility within the confines of sequential speech. I could use Heptapod A more easily as a result, though it was still a poor substitute for Heptapod B.

There was a knock at the door and then Gary poked his head in. "Colonel Weber'll be here any minute."

I grimaced. "Right." Weber was coming to participate in a session with Flapper and Raspberry; I was to act as translator, a job I wasn't trained for and that I detested.

Gary stepped inside and closed the door. He pulled me out of my chair and kissed me.

I smiled. "You trying to cheer me up before he gets here?"

"No, I'm trying to cheer me up."

"You weren't interested in talking to the heptapods at all, were you? You worked on this project just to get me into bed."

"Ah, you see right through me."

I looked into his eyes. "You better believe it," I said.

I remember when you'll be a month old, and I'll stumble out of bed to give you your 2:00 A.M. feeding. Your nursery will have that "baby smell" of diaper rash cream and talcum powder, with a faint ammoniac whiff coming from the diaper pail in the corner. I'll lean over your crib, lift your squalling form out, and sit in the rocking chair to nurse you.

The word "infant" is derived from the Latin word for "unable to speak," but you'll be perfectly capable of saying one thing: "I suffer," and you'll do it tirelessly and without hesitation. I have to admire your utter commitment to that statement; when you cry, you'll become outrage incarnate, every fiber of your body employed in expressing that emotion. It's funny: when you're tranquil, you will seem to radiate light, and if someone were to paint a portrait of you like that, I'd insist that they include the halo. But when you're unhappy, you will become a klaxon, built for radiating sound; a portrait of you then could simply be a fire alarm bell.

At that stage of your life, there'll be no past or future for you; until I give you my breast, you'll have no memory of contentment in the past nor expectation of relief in the future. Once you begin nursing, everything will reverse, and all will be right with the world. NOW is the only moment you'll perceive; you'll live in the present tense. In many ways, it's an enviable state.

The heptapods are neither free nor bound as we understand those concepts; they don't act according to their will, nor are they helpless automatons. What distinguishes the heptapods' mode of awareness is not just that their actions coincide with history's events; it is also that their motives coincide with history's purposes. They act to create the future, to enact chronology.

Freedom isn't an illusion; it's perfectly real in the context of sequential consciousness. Within the context of simultaneous consciousness, freedom is not meaningful, but neither is coercion; it's simply a different context, no more or less valid than the other. It's like that famous optical illusion, the drawing of either an elegant young woman, face turned away from the viewer, or a wart-nosed crone, chin tucked down on her chest. There's no "correct" interpretation; both are equally valid. But you can't see both at the same time.

Similarly, knowledge of the future was incompatible with free will. What made it possible for me to exercise freedom of choice also made it impossible for me to know the future. Conversely, now that I know the future, I would never act contrary to that future, including telling others what I know: those who know the future don't talk about it. Those who've read the *Book of Ages* never admit to it.

I turned on the VCR and slotted a cassette of a session from the Ft. Worth looking glass. A diplomatic negotiator was having a discussion with the heptapods there, with Burghart acting as translator.

The negotiator was describing humans' moral beliefs, trying to lay some groundwork for the concept of altruism. I knew the heptapods were familiar with the conversation's eventual outcome, but they still participated enthusiastically.

If I could have described this to someone who didn't already know, she might ask, if the heptapods already knew everything that they would ever say or hear, what was the point of their using language at all? A reasonable question. But language wasn't only for communication: it was also a form of action. According to speech act theory, statements like "You're under arrest, "I christen this vessel," or "I promise" were all performative: a speaker could perform the action only by uttering the words. For such acts, knowing what would be said didn't change anything. Everyone at a wedding anticipated the words "I now pronounce you husband and wife," but until the minister actually said them, the ceremony didn't count. With performative language, saying equaled doing.

For the heptapods, all language was performative. Instead of using language to inform, they used language to actualize. Sure, heptapods already knew what would be said in any conversation; but in order for their knowledge to be true, the conversation would have to take place.

"First Goldilocks tried the papa bear's bowl of porridge, but it was full of Brussels sprouts, which she hated."

You'll laugh. "No, that's wrong!" We'll be sitting side by side on the sofa, the skinny, overpriced hardcover spread open on our laps.

I'll keep reading. "Then Goldilocks tried the mama bear's bowl of porridge, but it was full of spinach, which she also hated."

You'll put your hand on the page of the book to stop me. "You have to read it the right way!"

"I'm reading just what it says here," I'll say, all innocence.

"No you're not. That's not how the story goes."

"Well if you already know how the story goes, why do you need me to read it to you?"

"'Cause I wanna hear it!"

The air-conditioning in Weber's office almost compensated for having to talk to the man.

"They're willing to engage in a type of exchange," I explained, "but it's not trade. We simply give them something, and they give us something in return. Neither party tells the other what they're giving beforehand."

Colonel Weber's brow furrowed just slightly. "You mean they're willing to exchange gifts?"

I knew what I had to say. "We shouldn't think of it as 'gift-giving.' We don't know if this transaction has the same associations for the heptapods that gift-giving has for us."

"Can we"—he searched for the right wording—"drop hints about the kind of gift we want?"

"They don't do that themselves for this type of transaction. I asked them if we could make a request, and they said we could, but it won't make them tell us what they're giving." I suddenly remembered that a morphological relative of "performative" was "performance," which could describe the sensation of conversing when you knew what would be said: it was like performing in a play.

"But would it make them more likely to give us what we asked for?" Colonel Weber asked. He was perfectly oblivious of the script, yet his responses matched his assigned lines exactly.

"No way of knowing," I said. "I doubt it, given that it's not a custom they engage in."

"If we give our gift first, will the value of our gift influence the value of theirs?" He was improvising, while I had carefully rehearsed for this one and only show.

"No," I said. "As far as we can tell, the value of the exchanged items is irrelevant."

"If only my relatives felt that way," murmured Gary wryly.

I watched Colonel Weber turn to Gary. "Have you discovered anything new in the physics discussions?" he asked, right on cue.

"If you mean, any information new to mankind, no," said Gary. "The heptapods haven't varied from the routine. If we demonstrate something to them, they'll show us their formulation of it, but they won't volunteer anything and they won't answer our questions about what they know."

An utterance that was spontaneous and communicative in the context of human discourse became a ritual recitation when viewed by the light of Heptapod B.

Weber scowled. "All right then, we'll see how the State Department feels about this. Maybe we can arrange some kind of gift-giving ceremony."

Like physical events, with their causal and teleological interpretations, every linguistic event had two possible interpretations: as a transmission of information and as the realization of a plan.

"I think that's a good idea, Colonel," I said.

It was an ambiguity invisible to most. A private joke; don't ask me to explain it.

Even though I'm proficient with Heptapod B, I know I don't experience reality the way a heptapod does. My mind was cast in the mold of human, sequential languages, and no amount of immersion in an alien language can completely reshape it. My worldview is an amalgam of human and heptapod.

Before I learned how to think in Heptapod B, my memories grew like a column of cigarette ash, laid down by the infinitesimal sliver of combustion that was my consciousness, marking the sequential present. After I learned Heptapod B, new memories fell into place like gigantic blocks, each one measuring years in duration, and though they didn't arrive in order or land contiguously, they soon composed a period of five decades. It is the period during which I know Heptapod B well enough to think in it, starting during my interviews with Flapper and Raspberry and ending with my death.

Usually, Heptapod B affects just my memory: my consciousness crawls along as it did before, a glowing sliver crawling forward in time, the difference being that the ash of memory lies ahead as well as behind: there is no real combustion. But occasionally I have glimpses when Heptapod B truly reigns, and I experience past and future all at once; my consciousness becomes a half-century-long ember burning outside time. I perceive—during those glimpses—that entire epoch as a simultaneity. It's a period encompassing the rest of my life, and the entirety of yours.

I wrote out the semagrams for "process create-endpoint inclusive-we," meaning "let's start." Raspberry replied in the affirmative, and the slide shows began. The second display screen that the heptapods had provided began presenting a series of images, composed of semagrams and equations, while one of our video screens did the same.

This was the second "gift exchange" I had been present for, the eighth one overall, and I knew it would be the last. The looking-glass tent was crowded with people; Burghart from Ft. Worth was here, as were Gary and a nuclear physicist, assorted biologists, anthropologists, military brass, and diplomats. Thankfully they had set up an air conditioner to cool the place off. We would review the tapes of the images later to figure out just what the heptapods' "gift" was. Our own "gift" was a presentation on the Lascaux cave paintings.

We all crowded around the heptapods' second screen, trying to glean some idea of the images' content as they went by. "Preliminary assessments?" asked Colonel Weber.

"It's not a return," said Burghart. In a previous exchange, the heptapods had given us information about ourselves that we had previously told them. This had infuriated the State Department, but we had no reason to think of it as an insult: it probably indicated that trade value really didn't play a role in these exchanges. It didn't exclude the possibility that the heptapods might yet offer us a space drive, or cold fusion, or some other wish-fulfilling miracle.

"That looks like inorganic chemistry," said the nuclear physicist, pointing at an equation before the image was replaced.

Gary nodded. "It could be materials technology," he said.

"Maybe we're finally getting somewhere," said Colonel Weber.

"I wanna see more animal pictures," I whispered, quietly so that only Gary could hear me, and pouted like a child. He smiled and poked me. Truthfully, I wished the heptapods had given another xenobiology lecture, as they had on two previous exchanges; judging from those, humans were more similar to the heptapods than any other species they'd ever encountered. Or another lecture on heptapod history; those had been filled with apparent non sequiturs, but were interesting nonetheless. I didn't want the heptapods to give us new technology, because I didn't want to see what our governments might do with it.

I watched Raspberry while the information was being exchanged, looking for any anomalous behavior. It stood barely moving as usual; I saw no indications of what would happen shortly.

After a minute, the heptapod's screen went blank, and a minute after that, ours did too. Gary and most of the other scientists clustered around a tiny video screen that was replaying the heptapods' presentation. I could hear them talk about the need to call in a solid-state physicist.

Colonel Weber turned. "You two," he said, pointing to me and then to Burghart, "schedule the time and location for the next exchange." Then he followed the others to the playback screen.

"Coming right up," I said. To Burghart, I asked, "Would you care to do the honors, or shall I?"

I knew Burghart had gained a proficiency in Heptapod B similar to mine. "It's your looking glass," he said. "You drive."

I sat down again at the transmitting computer. "Bet you never figured you'd wind up working as an Army translator back when you were a grad student."

"That's for goddamn sure," he said. "Even now I can hardly believe it." Everything we said to each other felt like the carefully bland exchanges of spies who meet in public, but never break cover.

I wrote out the semagrams for "locus exchange-transaction converse inclusive-we" with the projective aspect modulation.

Raspberry wrote its reply. That was my cue to frown, and for Burghart to ask, "What does it mean by that?" His delivery was perfect.

I wrote a request for clarification; Raspberry's reply was the same as before. Then I watched it glide out of the room. The curtain was about to fall on this act of our performance.

Colonel Weber stepped forward. "What's going on? Where did it go?"

"It said that the heptapods are leaving now," I said. "Not just itself; all of them."

"Call it back here now. Ask it what it means."

"Um, I don't think Raspberry's wearing a pager," I said.

The image of the room in the looking glass disappeared so abruptly that it took a moment for my eyes to register what I was seeing instead: it was the other side of the looking-glass tent. The looking glass had become completely transparent. The conversation around the playback screen fell silent.

"What the hell is going on here?" said Colonel Weber.

Gary walked up to the looking glass, and then around it to the other side. He touched the rear surface with one hand; I could see the pale ovals where his fingertips made contact with the looking glass. "I think," he said, "we just saw a demonstration of transmutation at a distance."

I heard the sounds of heavy footfalls on dry grass. A soldier came in through the tent door, short of breath from sprinting, holding an oversize walkie-talkie. "Colonel, message from—"

Weber grabbed the walkie-talkie from him.

I remember what it'll be like watching you when you are a day old. Your father will have gone for a quick visit to the hospital cafeteria, and you'll be lying in your bassinet, and I'll be leaning over you. So soon after the delivery, I will still be feeling like a wrung-out towel. You will seem incongruously tiny, given how enormous I felt during the pregnancy; I could swear there was room for someone much larger and more robust than you in there. Your hands and feet will be long and thin, not chubby yet. Your face will still be all red and pinched, puffy eyelids squeezed shut, the gnomelike phase that precedes the cherubic.

I'll run a finger over your belly, marveling at the uncanny softness of your skin, wondering if silk would abrade your body like burlap. Then you'll writhe, twisting your body while poking out your legs one at a time, and I'll recognize the gesture as one I had felt you do inside me, many times. So *that's* what it looks like.

I'll feel elated at this evidence of a unique mother-child bond, this certitude that you're the one I carried. Even if I had never laid eyes on you before, I'd be able to pick you out from a sea of babies: Not that one. No, not her either. Wait, that one over there.

Yes, that's her. She's mine.

That final "gift exchange" was the last we ever saw of the heptapods. All at once, all over the world, their looking glasses became transparent and their ships left orbit. Subsequent analysis of the looking glasses revealed them to be nothing more than sheets of fused silica, completely inert. The information from the final exchange session described a new class of superconducting materials, but it later proved to duplicate the results of research just completed in Japan: nothing that humans didn't already know.

We never did learn why the heptapods left, any more than we learned what brought them here, or why they acted the way they did. My own new awareness didn't provide that type of knowledge; the heptapods' behavior was presumably explicable from a sequential point of view, but we never found that explanation.

I would have liked to experience more of the heptapods' worldview, to feel the way they feel. Then, perhaps I could immerse myself fully in the necessity of events, as they must, instead of merely wading in its surf for the rest of my life. But that will never come to pass. I will continue to practice the heptapod languages, as will the other linguists on the looking glass teams, but none of us will ever progress any further than we did when the heptapods were here.

Working with the heptapods changed my life. I met your father and learned Heptapod B, both of which make it possible for me to know you now, here on the patio in the moonlight. Eventually, many years from now, I'll be without your father, and without you. All I will have left from this moment is the heptapod language. So I pay close attention, and note every detail.

From the beginning I knew my destination, and I chose my route accordingly. But am I working toward an extreme of joy, or of pain? Will I achieve a minimum, or a maximum?

These questions are in my mind when your father asks me, "Do you want to make a baby?" And I smile and answer, "Yes," and I unwrap his arms from around me, and we hold hands as we walk inside to make love, to make you.

Ursula K. Le Guin

L e Guin has characterized herself as a timid and conservative feminist at first, one who wrote as an "honorary man." Her early fiction was male-centered, populated by male heroes, and reflective of the tradition in the 1960s, when few women, with the notable exception of writers like Joanna Russ, experimented in the field. Soon she realized that she could no longer ignore the feminine and began perusing feminist theory in order to discover how to write about women. She calls *The Norton Book of Literature by Women* a bible that taught her how to write like a woman.

"The Rock That Changed Things" suggests the overthrow of a ruling class by members of a less-respected social order but also can be approached as a parable of evolving attitudes toward literature and the environment. The story upsets the premise that superiority justifies subordination, whether obls are oppressing nurs, or whether college professors are questioning the inclusion of multicultural, feminist, and science fiction works to the long-standing literary canon. In addition, the following story explores hierarchical relationships of reason and emotion, linear thinking and circular reasoning, and of masculine and feminine in order to overturn the notions that one element is inferior to the other. Reflecting Le Guin's abiding use of Taoist imagery, the story also portrays the idea of balance, ordered completeness, and cyclical history that is continually examined throughout her prose. This story also exemplifies the reconnoitering of the mechanistic perspective of our universe, superceded by the more current awareness of the web of life.

The Rock That Changed Things

A NUROBL CALLED BU, WORKING ONE DAY WITH HER CREW on the rockpile of Obling College, found the rock that changed things.

Where the obls live, the shores of the river are rocky. Boulders, large stones, small stones, pebbles, and gravel lie piled and scattered for miles up and down the banks. The towns of the obls are built of stone; they hunt the rock-coney for their meat feasts. Their nurobls gather and prepare stonecrop and lichen for ordinary food, and build the houses and the colleges, and keep them neat, for the obls grow nervous and unhappy when things are not kept in order.

The heart of an obl town is its college, and the pride of every college is its terraces, which shelve down towards the river from the high stone buildings. The stones of the terraces are arranged according to size: boulders make the outer walls, and within them are rows of large rocks, then banks of small stones, and at last the inner terraces of pebbles set in elaborate mosaics and patterns in gravel. On the terraces the obls stroll and sit in the long, warm days, smoking ta-leaf in pipes of soapstone, and discussing history, natural history, philosophy, and metaphysics. So long as the rocks are arranged in order of shape and size and the patterns are kept clear and tidy, the obls have peace of mind and can think deeply. After their conversations on the terraces, the wisest old obls enter the colleges and write down the best of what was thought and said, in the Books of Record that are kept neatly ranged on the shelves of the college libraries.

When the river floods in early spring and rises up the terraces, tumbling the rocks about, washing the gravel away, and causing great disorder, the obls stay inside the colleges. There they read the Books of Record, discuss and annotate, plan new designs for the terraces, eat meat feasts, and smoke. Their nurs cook and serve the feasts and keep the rooms of the colleges orderly. As soon as the floods pass, the nurs begin to sort the rocks and straighten up the terraces. They hurry to do so because the disorder left by the floods makes the obls very nervous, and when they are nervous they beat and rape the nurs more harshly than usual.

The spring floods this year had broken through the boulder wall of the town of Obling, leaving branches and driftwood and other litter on the terraces and disturbing or destroying many of the patterns. The terraces of Obling College are notable for the perfect order and complex beauty of their pebble-patterns. Famous obls have spent years of their lives designing the patterns and choosing the stones; one great designer, Aknegni, is said to have worked with his own hands to perfect his

124

creation. If a single pebble is lost from such a design, the nurobls will spend days hunting through the rockpiles for a replacement of precisely the right shape and size. On such a task the nurobl called Bu was engaged, along with her crew, when she came upon the stone that changed things.

When replacement rocks are needed, the rockpile nurs often make a rough copy of that section of the terrace mosaic, so that they can test pebbles in it for fit without carrying them all the way up to the inner terraces. Bu had placed a trial stone in a test pattern in this fashion, and was gazing at it to be sure the size and shape were exact, when she was struck by a quality of the stone which she had never noticed before: the color. The pebbles of this part of the design were all large ovals, a palm-and-a-quarter wide and a palm-and-a-half long. The rock Bu had just set into the test pattern was a perfect "quarter-half" oval, and so fit exactly; but while the other rocks were mostly a dark, smooth-grained bluish grey, the new one was a vivid blue-green, with flecks of paler jade green.

Bu knew, of course, that the color of a rock is a matter of absolute indifference, an accidental and trivial quality that does not affect the true pattern in any way. All the same, she found herself gazing with peculiar satisfaction at this blue-green stone. Presently she thought, "This stone is beautiful." She was not looking, as she should have been, at the whole design, but at the one stone, whose color was set off by the duller hue of the others. She was strangely moved; strange thoughts arose in her mind. She thought, "This stone is significant. It means. It is a word." She picked it up and held it while studying the test pattern.

The original design, up on the terrace, was called the Dean's Design, for the Dean of the College, Festi, who had planned this section of the terraces. When Bu replaced the blue-green stone in the pattern, it still caught her eye by its color, distracting her mind from the pattern, but she could not see any meaning in it.

She took the blue-green stone to the rockpile forenur and asked him if he saw anything wrong, or odd, or particular about the stone. The fore-nur gazed thoughtfully at the stone, but at last opened his eyes wide, meaning no.

Bu took the stone up to the inner terraces and set it into the true pattern. It fitted the Dean's Design exactly; its shape and size were perfect. But, standing back to study the pattern, Bu thought it scarcely seemed to be the Dean's Design at all. It was not that the new stone changed the design; it simply completed a pattern that Bu had never realized was there: a pattern of color, that had little or no relation to the shape-and-size arrangement of the Dean's Design. The new stone

completed a spiral of blue-green stones within the field of interlocked
rhomboids of "quarter-half" ovals that formed the center of Festl's
design. Most of the blue-green stones were ones that Bu had laid over
the past several years; but the spiral had been begun by some other nur,
before Bu was promoted to the Dean's Design.

Just then Dean Festl came strolling out in the spring sunshine, his
rusty gun on his shoulder, his pipe in his mouth, happy to see the
disorder of the floods being repaired. The Dean was a kind old obl who
had never raped Bu, though he often patted her. Bu summoned up her
courage, hid her eyes, and said, "Lord Dean, sir! Would the Lord Dean in
his knowledge be so good as to tell me the verbal significance of this
section of the true pattern which I have just repaired?"

Dean Festl paused, perhaps a touch displeased to be interrupted in
his meditations; but seeing the young nur so modestly crouching and
hiding all her eyes, he patted her in a forebearing way and said,
"Certainly. This subsection of my design may be read, on the simplest
level, as: 'I place stones beautifully,' or 'I place stones in excellent order.'
There is an immanent higher-plane postverbal significance, of course, as
well as the Ineffable Arcana. But you needn't bother your little head with
that!"

"Is it possible," the nur asked in a submissive voice, "to find a
meaning in the *colors* of the stones?"

The Dean smiled again and patted her in several places. "Who knows
what goes on in the heads of nurs! Color! Meaning in color! Now run
along, little nurblit. You've done very pretty repair work here. Very neat,
very nice." And he strolled on, puffing on his pipe and enjoying the
spring sunshine.

Bu returned to the rockpile to sort stones, but her mind was
disturbed. All night she dreamed of the blue-green rock. In the dream
the rock spoke, and the rocks about it in the pattern began speaking too.
Waking, Bu could not remember the words the stones had said.

The sun was not up yet, but the nurs were; and Bu spoke to several of
her nestmates and work-friends while they fed and cleaned the blits and
ate their hurried breakfast of cold fried lichen. "Come up onto the
terraces, now, before the obls are up," Bu said. "I want to show you
something."

Bu had many friends, and eight or nine nurs followed her up onto the
terraces, some of them bringing their nursing or toddling blits along.
"What's Bu got in her head this time!" they said to each other, laughing.

"Now look," Bu said when they were all on the part of the inner
terrace that Dean Festl had designed. "Look at the patterns. And look at
the *colors* of the rocks."

"Colors don't mean anything," said one nur, and another, "Colors aren't part of the patterns, Bu."

"But what if they were?" said Bu. "Just look."

The nurs, being used to silence and obedience, looked.

"Well," said one of them after a while. "Isn't that amazing!"

"Look at that!" said Bu's best friend, Ko. "That spiral of blue-green running all over the Dean's Design! And there's five red hematites around a yellow sandstone— like a flower."

"This whole section in brown basalt—it cuts across the—the real pattern, doesn't it?" said little Ga.

"It makes another pattern. A different pattern," Bu said. "Maybe it makes an immanent pattern of ineffable significance.

"Oh, come off it, Bu," said Ko. "You a Professor or something?"

The others laughed, but Bu was too excited to see that she was funny. "No," she said earnestly, "but look— that blue-green rock, there, the last one in the spiral."

"Serpentinite," said Ko.

"Yes, I know. But if the Dean's Design means something—He said that that part means 'I place stones beautifully'—Well, could the blue-green rock be a different word? With a different meaning?"

"What meaning?"

"I don't know. I thought you might know." Bu looked hopefully at Un, an elderly nur who, though he had been lamed in a rockslide in his youth, was so good at fine pattern-maintenance that the obls had let him live. Un stared at the blue-green stone, and at the curve of blue-green stones, and at last said slowly, "It might say, 'The nur places stones.'"

"What nur?" Ko asked.

"Bu," little Ga said. "She did place the stone."

Bu and Un both opened their eyes wide, to signify No.

"Patterns aren't ever about nurs!" said Ko.

"Maybe patterns made of colors are," said Bu, getting excited and blinking very fast.

"The nur,'" said Ko, following the blue-green curve with all three eyes, "—'the nur places stones beautifully in uncontrollable loopingness.' My goodness! What's that all about?" He read on along the curve— " 'in uncontrollable loopingingness fore,' what's that? Oh, 'foreshadowing the seen.'"

"'The vision,'" Un suggested. "'The vision of …' I don't know the last word."

"Are you seeing all that in the colors of the rocks?" asked Ga, amazed.

"In the patterns of the colors," Bu replied. "They aren't accidental. Not meaningless. All the time, we have been putting them here in patterns—

not just ones the obls design and we execute, but other patterns—nur
patterns—with new meanings. Look—look at them!"

Since they were used to silence and obedience, they all stood and
looked at the patterns on the inner terraces of the College of Obling.
They saw how the arrangement by shape and size of the pebbles and
larger stones made regular squares, oblongs, triangles, dodecahedrons,
zigzags, and rectilinear designs of great and orderly beauty and
significance. And they saw how the arrangement of the stones by color
had created other designs, less complete, often merely sketched or
hinted—circles, spirals, ovals, and complex curvilinear mazes and
labyrinths of great and unpredictable beauty and significance. So a long
loop of white quartzites cut right across the quarter-palm straight-edge
double line; and the rhomboid section of half-palm sandstones seemed
to be an element in a long crescent of pale yellow.

Both patterns were there; did one cancel the other, or was each part
of the other? It was difficult to see them both at once, but not
impossible.

After a long time little Ga asked, "Did we do all that without even
knowing we were doing it?"

"I always looked at the colors of the rocks," Un said in a low voice,
looking down.

"So did I," Ko said. "And the grain and texture, too. I started that
wiggly part in the Crystal Angles," pointing at a very ancient and famous
section of the terrace, designed by the great OholothL. "Last year, after
the late flood, when we lost so many stones from the design, remember?
I got a lot of amethysts from the Ubi Caves. I love purple!" His tone was
defiant.

Bu looked at a circle of small, smooth turquoises inlaid in a corner of
a set of interlocked rectangles. "I like blue-green," Bu said in a whisper.
"I like blue-green. He likes purple. We see the colors of the stones. We
make the pattern. We make the pattern beautifully."

"Should we tell the Professors, do you think?" little Ga asked, getting
excited. "They might give us extra food."

Old Un opened all his eyes very wide. "Don't breathe a word of this to
the Professors! They don't like patterns to change. You know that. It
makes them nervous. They might get nervous and punish us."

"We are not afraid," Bu said, in a whisper.

"They wouldn't understand," Ko said. "They don't look at colors. They
don't listen to us. And if they did, they'd know it was just nurs talking
and didn't mean anything. Wouldn't they? But I'm going back to the
Caves and get some more amethysts and finish that wiggly part,"

pointing to the Crystal Angles, where repairs had scarcely begun. "They'll never even see it."

Ga's naughty little blit, Professor Endl's son, was digging up pebbles from the Superior Triangle, and had to be spanked. "Oh," Ga sighed, "he's all oblblit! I just don't know what to do with him."

"He'll go to School next year," Un said drily. "They'll know what to do with him."

"But what will I do without him?" said Ga.

The sun was well up in the sky now, and Professors could be seen looking out from their bedroom windows over the terraces. They would not like to see nurs loitering, and small blits were, of course, absolutely forbidden within the college walls. Bu and the others hastily returned to the nests and workhouses.

Ko went to the Ubi Caves that same day, and Bu went along, they came back with sacks of fine amethysts, and worked for several days completing the wiggly part, which they called the Purple Waves, in the repair and maintenance of the Crystal Angles. Ko was happy in the work, and sang and joked, and at night he and Bu made love. But Bu remained preoccupied. She kept studying the patterns of color on the terraces, and finding more and more of them, and more and more meanings and ideas in them.

"Are they all about nurs?" old Un asked. His arthritis kept him from the terraces, but Bu reported her findings to him every day.

"No," Bu said, "most of them are about obls and nurs both. And blits, too. But nurs made them. So they're different. Obl patterns are never really about nurs. Only about obls and what obls think. But when you begin to read the colors they say the most interesting things!"

Bu was so excited and persuasive that other nurs of Obling began studying the color patterns, learning how to read their meanings. The practice spread to other nests, and soon to other towns. Before long, nurs all up and down the river were discovering that their terraces, too, were full of wild designs in colored stones, and surprising messages concerning obls, nurs, and blits.

Many nurs, however, upset by the whole idea, steadfastly refused to see patterns in color or to allow that the color of a stone could have any significance at all. "The obls count on us not to change things," these nurs said. "We are their nurobls. They depend on us to keep their patterns neat, and keep the blits quiet, and maintain order, so that they can do important work. If we start inventing new meanings, changing things, disturbing the patterns, where will it end? It isn't fair to the obls."

Bu, however, would hear none of that; she was full of her discovery. She no longer listened in silence. She spoke. She went about among the workhouses, speaking. And one evening, summoning up her courage, and wearing around her neck on a thong a perfect, polished turquoise that she called her selfstone, she went up onto the terraces. She crossed the terraces among the startled Professors, and came to the Rectory Mosaic, where Astl the Rectoress, a famous scholar, strolled in solitary meditation, her ancient rifle slung on her back, wreaths of smoke trailing from her reeking pipe. Not even a Full Professor would have interrupted the Rectoress at such a sacred time. But Bu went straight to her, crouched, covered her eyes, and said in a tremulous but clear voice, "Lady Rectoress, ma'am! Would the Lady Rectoress in her kindness answer a question I have?"

The Rectoress was truly displeased and upset by this disorderly behavior. She turned to the nearest Professor and said, "This nur is insane; have it removed, please."

Bu was sentenced to ten days in jail, to be raped by Students whenever they pleased, and then sent to the flagstone quarries for a hundred days.

When she returned to the nest, she was pregnant from one of the rapes, and quite thin from working in the quarries, but she still wore her turquoise stone. All her nest-mates and work-friends greeted her, singing songs which they had made out of the meanings of the colored patterns on the terraces. Ko comforted her with tender affection that night, and told her that her blit would be his blit, and her nest his nest.

Not many days after, she entered the college (via the kitchens), and made her way (with the assistance of the serving-nurs) to the private room of the Canon.

The Canon of Obling College was a very old obl, renowned for his knowledge of metaphysical linguistics. He woke slowly, mornings. This morning he woke slowly and gazed with some puzzlement at the serving nur which had come to open his curtains and serve his breakfast. It seemed to be a different one. He almost reached for his gun, but was too sleepy.

"Hullo," he said. "You're new, aren't you?"

"I want you to answer a question I have," said the nur.

The Canon woke further, and stared at this amazing creature. "At least have the decency to cover your eyes, nur!" he said, but he was not really very upset. He was so old that he was no longer quite sure what the patterns were, and so a change in them did not trouble him as much as it might have done.

"Nobody else can answer me," said the nur. "Please do. Do you know if a blue-green stone in a pattern might be a word?"

"Oh, yes, indeed," said the Canon, becoming alert. "Although, of course, all verbal color-significance is long obsolete. Of mere antiquarian interest, to old fuddy-duddies such as myself, ha. Hue-words don't occur even in the most archaic patterns. Only in the most ancient Books of Record."

"What does it mean?"

The Canon wondered if he were dreaming—discussing historical linguistics with a nur, before breakfast!—But it was an entertaining dream. "The hue of blue-green— such as that stone you seem to be wearing as an ornament— might, in its adjectival form within a pattern, have indicated a quality of untrammeled volition. As a noun, the color would have functioned to signify, how shall I put it?—an absence of coercion; a lack of control; a condition of self-determination—"

"Freedom," the nur said. "Does it mean freedom?"

"No, my dear," said the Canon. "It did. But it does not."

"Why?"

"Because the word is obsolete," said the Canon, beginning to tire of this inexplicable dialogue. "Now go away like a good nur and tell my servant to bring my breakfast."

"Look out the window," the wild-eyed nur said, in so passionate a voice that the Canon was quite alarmed. "Look out the window at the terraces! Look at the colors of the stones! Look at the patterns the nurs make, the designs we have made, the meanings we have written! Look for the freedom! Oh please do look!"

And with that final plea, the amazing apparition vanished. The Canon lay staring at his bedroom door; and in a moment it opened. His old serving-nur came in with his tray of stonecrop tea and smoking hot kippered lichen. "Good morning, Lord Canon, sir!" she said cheerfully. "Awake already? A lovely morning!" And after setting down the tray by his bed, she swept the curtains open wide.

"Was there a young nur in here just now?" the Canon asked, rather nervously.

"Certainly not, sir. At least, not that I know of," said the serving-nur. But did she for a moment glance quite directly, knowingly—did she have the audacity to *look* at him—? Surely not. "Lovely the terraces are this morning," she went on. "Your Canonitude ought to have a look."

"Get out, out," the Canon growled, and the nur left with a demure curtsy, covering her eyes.

The Canon ate his breakfast in bed and then got up. He went to the window to look out on the terraces of his college in the morning light.

For a moment he thought he was dreaming again, seeing entirely different patterns than those he had seen all his long life on those terraces—wild designs of curves and colors, amazing phrases, unimagined significances, a wonderful newness of meaning and beauty— and then he opened all his eyes wide, very wide, and blinked; and it was gone. The familiar, true order of the terraces lay clear and regular in the morning light. And there was nothing else to see. The Canon turned away from the window and opened a book.

So he did not see the long line of nurobls coming up from the nests and workhouses down below the boulder walls, carrying blits and dancing as they came, dancing and singing across the terraces. He heard the singing, but only as a noise without significance. It was not until the first rock flew through his window that he looked up and cried out in agitation, "What is the meaning of this?"

Part II

William Gibson

F ather of the cybergeneration of writers profiled in this collection, William Gibson (b. 1948) began writing fiction while completing a bachelor's degree in English literature at the University of British Columbia. His first novel, *Neuromancer*, won the Hugo Award, the Philip K. Dick Memorial Award, and the Nebula Award. Other works include the novels *Count Zero* (1986) and *Mona Lisa Overdrive* (1988), which together complete the *Neuromancer* trilogy; a collection of short stories, *Burning Chrome* (1986), which led to film screen adaptations of "Johnny Mnemonic" and "New Rose Hotel"; *The Difference Engine* (1991), a novel co-written with Bruce Sterling; and the novels *Virtual Light* (1993), *Idoru* (1996), the *Idoru* sequel, *All Tomorrow's Parties* (1999), and *Pattern Recognition* (2003). While he was born in South Carolina, Gibson moved to Vancouver, British Columbia, where he still resides.

William Gibson's influential *Neuromancer* popularized the concept of virtual reality and coined the term "cyberspace," which Gibson portrays as a transcendent experience, "a consensual hallucination" that is the matrix. Gibson once claimed that he wrote the story using a typewriter because he didn't own a computer. In the following excerpt, Case, a former cyberspace cowboy, has fallen into the Meat of the physical world because he dared to hustle those he worked for. He becomes reduced to a petty criminal on the peripheral edges of the ecology of techno-criminal subcultures. The environment, whether Chiba City in Japan or the American Sprawl, is claustrophobically crowded, cluttered with the obsolete parts of high-tech machinery, and excessively polluted. This selection highlights Gibson's stated indebtedness to the film *Bladerunner*, which emphasized the darker elements of the street-dance of Biz and commerce. But these deadly arenas also create "a deliberately unsupervised playground for technology itself" and propel forward exponentially increasing rates of innovative technology practices. The postmodern ludic qualities of arcade games, television, and drugs are smashed up against the intensively more philosophical questions of whether we are becoming post-human entities, creatures less organic in nature, while simultaneously corporations are seeking to thrive and reproduce, much like living beings.

from *Neuromancer*

THE SKY ABOVE THE PORT WAS THE COLOR OF TELEVISION, tuned to a dead channel.

"It's not like I'm using," Case heard someone say, as he shouldered his way through the crowd around the door of the Chat. "It's like my body's developed this massive drug deficiency." It was a Sprawl voice and a Sprawl joke. The Chatsubo was a bar for professional expatriates; you could drink there for a week and never hear two words in Japanese.

Ratz was tending bar, his prosthetic arm jerking monotonously as he filled a tray of glasses with draft Kirin. He saw Case and smiled, his teeth a webwork of East European steel and brown decay. Case found a place at the bar, between the unlikely tan on one of Lonny Zone's whores and the crisp naval uniform of a tall African whose cheekbones were ridged with precise rows of tribal scars. "Wage was in here early, with two joeboys," Ratz said, shoving a draft across the bar with his good hand. "Maybe some business with you, Case?"

Case shrugged. The girl to his right giggled and nudged him.

The bartender's smile widened. His ugliness was the stuff of legend. In an age of affordable beauty, there was something heraldic about his lack of it. The antique arm whined as he reached for another mug. It was a Russian military prosthesis, a seven-function force-feedback manipulator, cased in grubby pink plastic. "You are too much the artiste, Herr Case." Ratz grunted; the sound served him as laughter. He scratched his overhang of white-shirted belly with the pink claw. "You are the artiste of the slightly funny deal."

"Sure," Case said, and sipped his beer. "Somebody's gotta be funny around here. Sure the fuck isn't you."

The whore's giggle went up an octave.

"Isn't you either, sister. So you vanish, okay? Zone, he's a close personal friend of mine."

She looked Case in the eye and made the softest possible spitting sound, her lips barely moving. But she left.

"Jesus," Case said, "what kinda creepjoint you running here? Man can't have a drink."

"Ha," Ratz said, swabbing the scarred wood with a rag, "Zone shows a percentage. You I let work here for entertainment value."

As Case was picking up his beer, one of those strange instants of silence descended, as though a hundred unrelated conversations had simultaneously arrived at the same pause. Then the whore's giggle rang out, tinged with a certain hysteria.

Ratz grunted. "An angel passed."

"The Chinese," bellowed a drunken Australian, "Chinese bloody invented nerve-splicing. Give me the mainland for a nerve job any day. Fix you right, mate."

"Now that," Case said to his glass, all his bitterness suddenly rising in him like bile, "that is so much bullshit."

The Japanese had already forgotten more neurosurgery than the Chinese had ever known. The black clinics of Chiba were the cutting edge, whole bodies of technique supplanted monthly, and still they couldn't repair the damage he'd suffered in that Memphis hotel.

A year here and he still dreamed of cyberspace, hope fading nightly. All the speed he took, all the turns he'd taken and the corners he'd cut in Night City, and still he'd see the matrix in his sleep, bright lattices of logic unfolding across that colorless void.... The Sprawl was a long strange way home over the Pacific now, and he was no console man, no cyberspace cowboy. Just another hustler, trying to make it through. But the dreams came on in the Japanese night like livewire voodoo, and he'd cry for it, cry in his sleep, and wake alone in the dark, curled in his capsule in some coffin hotel, his hands clawed into the bedslab, temperfoam bunched between his fingers, trying to reach the console that wasn't there.

"I saw your girl last night," Ratz said, passing Case his second Kirin.

"I don't have one," he said, and drank.

"Miss Linda Lee."

Case shook his head.

"No girl? Nothing? Only biz, friend artiste? Dedication to commerce?" The bartender's small brown eyes were nested deep in wrinkled flesh. "I think I liked you better, with her. You laughed more. Now, some night, you get maybe too artistic; you wind up in the clinic tanks, spare parts."

You're breaking my heart, Ratz." He finished his beer, paid and left, high narrow shoulders hunched beneath the rain-stained khaki nylon of his windbreaker. Threading his way through the Ninsei crowds, he could smell his own stale sweat.

Case was twenty-four. At twenty-two, he'd been a cowboy, a rustler, one of the best in the Sprawl. He'd been trained by the best, by McCoy Pauley and Bobby Quine, legends in the biz. He'd operated on an almost permanent adrenaline high, a byproduct of youth and proficiency, jacked into a custom cyberspace deck that projected his disembodied consciousness into the consensual hallucination that was the matrix. A thief, he'd worked for other, wealthier thieves, employers who provided the exotic software required to penetrate the bright walls of corporate systems, opening windows into rich fields of data.

He'd made the classic mistake, the one he'd sworn he'd never make. He stole from his employers. He kept something for himself and tried to move it through a fence in Amsterdam. He still wasn't sure how he'd been discovered, not that it mattered now. He'd expected to die, then, but they only smiled.

Of course he was welcome, they told him, welcome to the money. And he was going to need it. Because—still smiling— they were going to make sure he never worked again.

They damaged his nervous system with a wartime Russian mycotoxin.

Strapped to a bed in a Memphis hotel, his talent burning out micron by micron, he hallucinated for thirty hours.

The damage was minute, subtle, and utterly effective.

For Case, who'd lived for the bodiless exultation of cyberspace, it was the Fall. In the bars he'd frequented as a cowboy hotshot, the elite stance involved a certain relaxed contempt for the flesh. The body was meat. Case fell into the prison of his own flesh.

His total assets were quickly convened to New Yen, a fat sheaf of the old paper currency that circulated endlessly through the closed circuit of the world's black markets like the seashells of the Trobriand islanders. It was difficult to transact legitimate business with cash in the Sprawl; in Japan, it was already illegal.

In Japan, he'd known with a clenched and absolute certainty, he'd find his cure. In Chiba. Either in a registered clinic or in the shadowland of black medicine. Synonymous with implants, nerve-splicing, and microbionics, Chiba was a magnet for the Sprawl's techno-criminal subcultures.

In Chiba, he'd watched his New Yen vanish in a two-month round of examinations and consultations. The men in the black clinics, his last hope, had admired the expertise with which he'd been maimed, and then slowly shaken their heads.

Now he slept in the cheapest coffins, the ones nearest the port, beneath the quartz-halogen floods that lit the docks all night like vast stages; where you couldn't see the lights of Tokyo for the glare of the television sky, not even the towering hologram logo of the Fuji Electric Company, and Tokyo Bay was a black expanse where gulls wheeled above drifting shoals of white styrofoam. Behind the port lay the city, factory domes dominated by the vast cubes of corporate arcologies. Port and city were divided by a narrow borderland of older streets, an area with no official name. Night City, with Ninsei its heart. By day, the bars down Ninsei were shuttered and featureless, the neon dead, the holograms inert, waiting, under the poisoned silver sky.

Two blocks west of the Chat, in a teashop called the Jarre de Thé, Case washed down the night's first pill with a double espresso. It was a flat pink octagon, a potent species of Brazilian dex he bought from one of Zone's girls.

The Jane was walled with mirrors, each panel framed in red neon.

At first, finding himself alone in Chiba, with little money and less hope of finding a cure, he'd gone into a kind of terminal overdrive, hustling fresh capital with a cold intensity that had seemed to belong to someone else. In the first month, he'd killed two men and a woman over sums that a year before would have seemed ludicrous. Ninsei wore him down until the street itself came to seem the externalization of some death wish, some secret poison he hadn't known he carried.

Night City was like a deranged experiment in social Darwinism, designed by a bored researcher who kept one thumb permanently on the fast-forward button. Stop hustling and you sank without a trace, but move a little too swiftly and you'd break the fragile surface tension of the black market; either way, you were gone, with nothing left of you but some vague memory in the mind of a fixture like Ratz, though heart or lungs or kidneys might survive in the service of some stranger with New Yen for the clinic tanks.

Biz here was a constant subliminal hum, and death the accepted punishment for laziness, carelessness, lack of grace, the failure to heed the demands of an intricate protocol.

Alone at a table in the Jarre de Thé, with the octagon coming on, pinheads of sweat starting from his palms, suddenly aware of each tingling hair on his arms and chest, Case knew that at some point he'd started to play a game with himself, a very ancient one that has no name, a final solitaire. He no longer carried a weapon, no longer took the basic precautions. He ran the fastest, loosest deals on the street, and he had a reputation for being able to get whatever you wanted. A part of him knew that the arc of his self-destruction was glaringly obvious to his customers, who grew steadily fewer, but that same part of him basked in the knowledge that it was only a matter of time. And that was the part of him, smug in its expectation of death, that most hated the thought of Linda Lee.

He'd found her, one rainy night, in an arcade.

Under bright ghosts burning through a blue haze of cigarette smoke, holograms of Wizard's Castle, Tank War Europa, the New York skyline.... And now he remembered her that way, her face bathed in restless laser

light, features reduced to a code: her cheekbones flaring scarlet as
Wizard's Castle burned, forehead drenched with azure when Munich fell
to the Tank War, mouth touched with hot gold as a gliding cursor struck
sparks from the wall of a skyscraper canyon. He was riding high that
night, with a brick of Wage's ketamine on its way to Yokohama and the
money already in his pocket. He'd come in out of the warm rain that
sizzled across the Ninsei pavement and somehow she'd been singled out
for him, one face out of the dozens who stood at the consoles, lost in the
game she played. The expression on her face, then, had been the one
he'd seen, hours later, on her sleeping face in a portside coffin, her
upper lip like the line children draw to represent a bird in flight.

Crossing the arcade to stand beside her, high on the deal he'd made,
he saw her glance up. Gray eyes rimmed with smudged black paintstick.
Eyes of some animal pinned in the headlights of an oncoming vehicle.

Their night together stretching into a morning, into tickets at the
hoverport and his first trip across the Bay. The rain kept up, falling along
Harajuku, beading on her plastic jacket, the children of Tokyo trooping
past the famous boutiques in white loafers and clingwrap capes, until
she'd stood with him in the midnight clatter of a pachinko parlor and
held his hand like a child.

It took a month for the gestalt of drugs and tension he moved
through to turn those perpetually startled eyes into wells of reflexive
need. He'd watched her personality fragment, calving like an iceberg,
splinters drifting away, and finally he'd seen the raw need, the hungry
armature of addiction. He'd watched her track the next hit with a
concentration that reminded him of the mantises they sold in stalls along
Shiga, beside tanks of blue mutant carp and crickets caged in bamboo.

He stared at the black ring of grounds in his empty cup. It was
vibrating with the speed he'd taken. The brown laminate of the tabletop
was dull with a patina of tiny scratches. With the dex mounting through
his spine he saw the countless random impacts required to create a
surface like that. The Jarre was decorated in a dated, nameless style
from the previous century, an uneasy blend of Japanese traditional and
pale Milanese plastics, but everything seemed to wear a subtle film, as
though the bad nerves of a million customers had somehow attacked
the mirrors and the once glossy plastics, leaving each surface fogged
with something that could never be wiped away.

"Hey. Case, good buddy."

He looked up, met gray eyes ringed with paintstick. She was wearing
faded French orbital fatigues and new white sneakers.

"I been lookin' for you, man." She took a seat opposite him, her
elbows on the table. The sleeves of the blue zipsuit had been ripped out

at the shoulders; he automatically checked her arms for signs of derms or the needle. "Want a cigarette?"

She dug a crumpled pack of Yeheyuan filters from an ankle pocket and offered him one. He took it, let her light it with a red plastic tube. "You sleepin' okay, Case? You look tired." Her accent put her south along the Sprawl, toward Atlanta. The skin below her eyes was pale and unhealthy-looking, but the flesh was still smooth and firm. She was twenty. New lines of pain were starting to etch themselves permanently at the corners of her mouth. Her dark hair was drawn back, held by a band of printed silk. The pattern might have represented microcircuits, or a city map.

"Not if I remember to take my pills," he said, as a tangible wave of longing hit him, lust and loneliness riding in on the wavelength of amphetamine. He remembered the smell of her skin in the overheated darkness of a coffin near the port, her fingers locked across the small of his back.

All the meat, he thought, and all it wants.

"Wage," she said, narrowing her eyes. "He wants to see you with a hole in your face." She lit her own cigarette.

"Who says? Ratz? You been talking to Ratz?"

"No. Mona. Her new squeeze is one of Wage's boys."

"I don't owe him enough. He does me, he's out the money anyway." He shrugged.

"Too many people owe him now, Case. Maybe you get to be the example. You seriously better watch it."

"Sure. How about you, Linda? You got anywhere to sleep?"

"Sleep." She shook her head. "Sure, Case." She shivered, hunched forward over the table. Her face was filmed with sweat.

"Here," he said, and dug in the pocket of his windbreaker, coming up with a crumpled fifty. He smoothed it automatically, under the table, folded it in quarters, and passed it to her.

"You need that, honey. You better give it to Wage." There was something in the gray eyes now that he couldn't read, something he'd never seen there before.

"I owe Wage a lot more than that. Take it. I got more coming," he lied, as he watched his New Yen vanish into a zippered pocket.

"You get your money, Case, you find Wage quick."

"I'll see you, Linda," he said, getting up.

"Sure." A millimeter of white showed beneath each of her pupils. Sanpaku. "You watch your back, man."

He nodded, anxious to be gone.

He looked back as the plastic door swung shut behind him, saw her eyes reflected in a cage of red neon.

Friday night on Ninsei.

He passed yakitori stands and massage parlors, a franchised coffee shop called Beautiful Girl, the electronic thunder of an arcade. He stepped out of the way to let a dark-suited sarariman by, spotting the Mitsubishi-Genentech logo tattooed across the back of the man's right hand.

Was it authentic? If that's for real, he thought, he's in for trouble. If it wasn't, served him right. M-G employees above a certain level were implanted with advanced microprocessors that monitored mutagen levels in the bloodstream. Gear like that would get you rolled in Night City, rolled straight into a black clinic.

The sarariman had been Japanese, but the Ninsei crowd was a gaijin crowd. Groups of sailors up from the port, tense solitary tourists hunting pleasures no guidebook listed, Sprawl heavies showing off grafts and implants, and a dozen distinct species of hustler, all swarming the street in an intricate dance of desire and commerce.

There were countless theories explaining why Chiba City tolerated the Ninsei enclave, but Case tended toward the idea that the Yakuza might be preserving the place as a kind of historical park, a reminder of humble origins. But he also saw a certain sense in the notion that burgeoning technologies require outlaw zones, that Night City wasn't there for its inhabitants, but as a deliberately unsupervised playground for technology itself.

Was Linda right, he wondered, staring up at the lights? Would Wage have him killed to make an example? It didn't make much sense, but then Wage dealt primarily in proscribed biologicals, and they said you had to be crazy to do that.

But Linda said Wage wanted him dead. Case's primary insight into the dynamics of street dealing was that neither the buyer nor the seller really needed him. A middleman's business is to make himself a necessary evil. The dubious niche Case had carved for himself in the criminal ecology of Night City had been cut out with lies, scooped out a night at a time with betrayal. Now, sensing that its walls were starting to crumble, he felt the edge of a strange euphoria.

The week before, he'd delayed transfer of a synthetic glandular extract, retailing it for a wider margin than usual. He knew Wage hadn't liked that. Wage was his primary supplier, nine years in Chiba and one of the few gaijin dealers who'd managed to forge links with the rigidly stratified criminal establishment beyond Night City's borders. Genetic materials and hormones trickled down to Ninsei along an intricate ladder of fronts and blinds. Somehow Wage had managed to trace something back, once, and now he enjoyed steady connections in a dozen cities.

Case found himself staring through a shop window. The place sold small bright objects to the sailors. Watches, flicknives, lighters, pocket VTRs, simstim decks, weighted manriki chains, and shuriken. The shuriken had always fascinated him, steel stars with knife-sharp points. Some were chromed, others black, others treated with a rainbow surface like oil on water. But the chrome stars held his gaze. They were mounted against scarlet ultrasuede with nearly invisible loops of nylon fishline, their centers stamped with dragons or yinyang symbols. They caught the street's neon and twisted it, and it came to Case that these were the stars under which he voyaged, his destiny spelled out in a constellation of cheap chrome.

"Julie," he said to his stars. "Time to see old Julie. He'll know."

Julius Deane was one hundred and thirty-five years old, his metabolism assiduously warped by a weekly fortune in serums and hormones. His primary hedge against aging was a yearly pilgrimage to Tokyo. where genetic surgeons re-set the code of his DNA, a procedure unavailable in Chiba. Then he'd fly to Hongkong and order the year's suits and shirts. Sexless and inhumanly patient, his primary gratification seemed to lie in his devotion to esoteric forms of tailor-worship. Case had never seen him wear the same suit twice, although his wardrobe seemed to consist entirely of meticulous reconstructions of garments of the previous century. He affected prescription lenses, framed in spidery gold, ground from thin slabs of pink synthetic quartz and beveled like the mirrors in a Victorian dollhouse.

His offices were located in a warehouse behind Ninsei, part of which seemed to have been sparsely decorated, years before, with a random collection of European furniture, as though Deane had once intended to use the place as his home. NeoAztec bookcases gathered dust against one wall of the room where Case waited. A pair of bulbous Disney-styled table lamps perched awkwardly on a low Kandinsky-book coffee table in scarlet-lacquered steel. A Dali clock hung on the wall between the bookcases, its distorted face sagging to the bare concrete floor. Its hands were holograms that altered to match the convolutions of the face as they rotated, but it never told the correct time. The room was stacked with white fiberglass shipping modules that gave off the tang of preserved ginger.

"You seem to be clean, old son," said Deane's disembodied voice. "Do come in."

Magnetic bolts thudded out of position around the massive imitation-rosewood door to the left of the bookcases. JULIUS DEANE IMPORT EXPORT was lettered across the plastic in peeling self-adhesive capitals. If the furniture scattered in Deane's makeshift foyer suggested the end of the past century, the office itself seemed to belong to its start.

Deane's seamless pink face regarded Case from a pool of light cast by an ancient brass lamp with a rectangular shade of dark green glass. The importer was securely fenced behind a vast desk of painted steel, flanked on either side by tall, drawered cabinets made of some sort of pale wood. The sort of thing, Case supposed, that had once been used to store written records of some kind. The desktop was littered with cassettes, scrolls of yellowed printout, and various parts of some sort of clockwork typewriter, a machine Deane never seemed to get around to reassembling.

"What brings you around, boyo?" Deane asked, offering Case a narrow bonbon wrapped in blue-and-white checked paper. Try one. Ting Ting Djahe, the very best." Case refused the ginger, took a seat in a yawing wooden swivel chair, and ran a thumb down the faded seam of one black jeans-leg. "Julie, I hear Wage wants to kill me."

"Ah. Well then. And where did you hear this, if I may?"

"People."

"People," Deane said, around a ginger bonbon. "What sort of people? Friends?"

Case nodded.

"Not always that easy to know who your friends are, is it?"

"I do owe him a little money, Deane. He say anything to you?"

"Haven't been in touch, of late." Then he sighed. "If I *did* know, of course, I might not be in a position to tell you. Things being what they are, you understand."

"Things?"

"He's an important connection, Case."

"Yeah. He want to kill me, Julie?"

"Not that I know of." Deane shrugged. They might have been discussing the price of ginger. "If it proves to be an unfounded rumor, old son, you come back in a week or so and I'll let you in on a little something out of Singapore."

"Out of the Nan Hai Hotel, Bencoolen Street?"

"Loose lips, old son!" Deane grinned. The steel desk was jammed with a fortune in debugging gear.

"Be seeing you, Julie. I'll say hello to Wage."

Deane's fingers came up to brush the perfect knot in his pale silk tie.

He was less than a block from Deane's office when it hit, the sudden cellular awareness that someone was on his ass, and very close.

The cultivation of a certain tame paranoia was something Case took for granted. The trick lay in not letting it get out of control. But that could be quite a trick, behind a stack of octagons. He fought the adrenaline surge and composed his narrow features in a mask of bored vacancy, pretending to let the crowd carry him along. When he saw a darkened display window, he managed to pause by it. The place was a surgical boutique, closed for renovations. With his hands in the pockets of his jacket, he stared through the glass at a flat lozenge of vatgrown flesh that lay on a carved pedestal of imitation jade. The color of its skin reminded him of Zone's whores; it was tattooed with a luminous digital display wired to a subcutaneous chip. Why bother with the surgery, he found himself thinking, while sweat coursed down his ribs, when you could just carry the thing around in your pocket?

Without moving his head, he raised his eyes and studied the reflection of the passing crowd.

There.

Behind sailors in short-sleeved khaki. Dark hair, mirrored glasses, dark clothing, slender...

And gone.

Then Case was running, bent low, dodging between bodies.

"Rent me a gun, Shin?"

The boy smiled. "Two hour." They stood together in the smell of fresh raw seafood at the rear of a Shiga sushi stall. "You come back, two hour."

"I need one now, man. Got anything right now?"

Shin rummaged behind empty two-liter cans that had once been filled with powdered horseradish. He produced a slender package wrapped in gray plastic. "Taser. One hour, twenty New Yen. Thirty deposit."

"Shit. I don't need that. I need a gun. Like I maybe wanna shoot somebody, understand?"

The waiter shrugged, replacing the taser behind the horseradish cans. "Two hour."

He went into the shop without bothering to glance at the display of shuriken. He'd never thrown one in his life.

He bought two packs of Yeheyuans with a Mitsubishi Bank chip that gave his name as Charles Derek May. It beat Truman Stan, the best he'd been able to do for a passport.

The Japanese woman behind the terminal looked like she had a few years on old Deane, none of them with the benefit of science. He took his slender roll of New Yen out of his pocket and showed it to her. "I want to buy a weapon."

She gestured in the direction of a case filled with knives.

"No," he said, "I don't like knives."

She brought an oblong box from beneath the counter. The lid was yellow cardboard, stamped with a crude image of a coiled cobra with a swollen hood. Inside were eight identical tissue-wrapped cylinders. He watched while mottled brown fingers stripped the paper from one. She held the thing up for him to examine, a dull steel tube with a leather thong at one end and a small bronze pyramid at the other. She gripped the tube with one hand, the pyramid between her other thumb and forefinger, and pulled. Three oiled, telescoping segments of tightly wound coilspring slid out and locked. "Cobra," she said.

Beyond the neon shudder of Ninsei, the sky was that mean shade of gray. The air had gotten worse; it seemed to have teeth tonight, and half the crowd wore filtration masks. Case had spent ten minutes in a urinal, trying to discover a convenient way to conceal his cobra; finally he'd settled for tucking the handle into the waistband of his jeans, with the tube slanting across his stomach. The pyramidal striking tip rode between his ribcage and the lining of his windbreaker. The thing felt like it might clatter to the pavement with his next step, but it made him feel better.

The Chat wasn't really a dealing bar, but on weeknights it attracted a related clientele. Fridays and Saturdays were different. The regulars were still there, most of them, but they faded behind an influx of sailors and the specialists who preyed on them. As Case pushed through the doors, he looked for Ratz, but the bartender wasn't in sight. Lonny Zone, the bar's resident pimp, was observing with glazed fatherly interest as one of his girls went to work on a young sailor. Zone was addicted to a brand of hypnotic the Japanese called Cloud Dancers. Catching the pimp's eye, Case beckoned him to the bar. Zone came drifting through the crowd in slow motion, his long face slack and placid.

"You seen Wage tonight, Lonny?"

Zone regarded him with his usual calm. He shook his head.

"You sure, man?"

"Maybe in the Namban. Maybe two hours ago."

"Got some joeboys with him? One of 'em thin, dark hair, maybe a black jacket?"

"No," Zone said at last, his smooth forehead creased to indicate the effort it cost him to recall so much pointless detail. "Big boys. Graftees." Zone's eyes showed very little white and less iris; under the drooping lids, his pupils were dilated and enormous. He stared into Case's face for a long time, then lowered his gaze. He saw the bulge of the steel whip. "Cobra," he said, and raised an eyebrow. "You wanna fuck somebody up?"

"See you, Lonny." Case left the bar.

His tail was back. He was sure of it. He felt a stab of elation, the octagons and adrenaline mingling with something else. You're enjoying this, he thought; you're crazy.

Because, in some weird and very approximate way, it was like a run in the matrix. Get just wasted enough, find yourself in some desperate but strangely arbitrary kind of trouble, and it was possible to see Ninsei as a field of data, the way the matrix had once reminded him of proteins linking to distinguish cell specialties. Then you could throw yourself into a highspeed drift and skid, totally engaged but set apart from it all, and all around you the dance of biz, information interacting, data made flesh in the mazes of the black market. …

Go it, Case, he told himself. Suck 'em in. Last thing they'll expect. He was half a block from the games arcade where he'd first met Linda Lee.

He bolted across Ninsei, scattering a pack of strolling sailors. One of them screamed after him in Spanish. Then he was through the entrance, the sound crashing over him like surf, subsonics throbbing in the pit of his stomach. Someone scored a ten-megaton hit on Tank War Europa, a simulated airburst drowning the arcade in white sound as a lurid hologram fireball mushroomed overhead. He cut to the right and loped up a flight of unpainted chipboard stairs. He'd come here once with Wage, to discuss a deal in proscribed hormonal triggers with a man called Matsuga. He remembered the hallway, its stained matting, the row of identical doors leading to tiny office cubicles. One door was open now. A Japanese girl in a sleeveless black t-shirt glanced up from a white terminal, behind her head a travel poster of Greece, Aegian blue splashed with streamlined ideograms.

"Get your security up here," Case told her.

Then he sprinted down the corridor, out of her sight. The last two doors were closed and, he assumed, locked. He spun and slammed the sole of his nylon running shoe into the blue-lacquered composition door at the far end. It popped, cheap hardware falling from the splintered frame. Darkness there, the white curve of a terminal housing. Then he was on the door to its right, both hands around the transparent plastic knob, leaning in with everything he had. Something snapped, and he was inside. This was where he and Wage had met with Matsuga, but whatever front company Matsuga had operated was long gone. No terminal, nothing. Light from the alley behind the arcade, filtering in through sootblown plastic. He made out a snakelike loop of fiberoptics protruding from a wall socket, a pile of discarded food containers, and the bladeless nacelle of an electric fan.

The window was a single pane of cheap plastic. He shrugged out of his jacket, bundled it around his right hand, and punched. It split, requiring two more blows to free it from the frame. Over the muted chaos of the games, an alarm began to cycle, triggered either by the broken window or by the girl at the head of the corridor.

Case turned, pulled his jacket on, and flicked the cobra to full extension.

With the door closed, he was counting on his tail to assume he'd gone through the one he'd kicked half off its hinges. The cobra's bronze pyramid began to bob gently, the spring-steel shaft amplifying his pulse.

Nothing happened. There was only the surging of the alarm, the crashing of the games, his heart hammering. When the fear came, it was like some half-forgotten friend. Not the cold, rapid mechanism of the dex-paranoia, but simple animal fear. He'd lived for so long on a constant edge of anxiety that he'd almost forgotten what real fear was.

This cubicle was the sort of place where people died. He might die here. They might have guns. ...

A crash, from the far end of the corridor. A man's voice, shouting something in Japanese. A scream, shrill terror. Another crash.

And footsteps, unhurried, coming closer.

Passing his closed door. Pausing for the space of three rapid beats of his heart. And returning. One, two, three. A bootheel scraped the matting.

The last of his octagon-induced bravado collapsed. He snapped the cobra into its handle and scrambled for the window, blind with fear, his nerves screaming. He was up, out, and falling, all before he was conscious of what he'd done. The impact with pavement drove dull rods of pain through his shins.

A narrow wedge of light from a half-open service hatch framed a heap of discarded fiberoptics and the chassis of a junked console. He'd fallen face forward on a slab of soggy chipboard; he rolled over, into the shadow of the console. The cubicle's window was a square of faint light. The alarm still oscillated, louder here, the rear wall dulling the roar of the games.

A head appeared, framed in the window, backlit by the fluorescents in the corridor, then vanished. It returned, but he still couldn't read the features. Glint of silver across the eyes. "Shit," someone said, a woman, in the accent of the northern Sprawl.

The head was gone. Case lay under the console for a long count of twenty, then stood up. The steel cobra was still in his hand, and it took him a few seconds to remember what it was. He limped away down the alley, nursing his left ankle.

Shin's pistol was a fifty-year-old Vietnamese imitation of a South American copy of a Walther PPK, double-action on the first shot, with a very rough pull. It was chambered for .22 long rifle, and Case would've preferred lead azide explosives to the simple Chinese hollowpoints Shin had sold him. Still, it was a handgun and nine rounds of ammunition, and as he made his way down Shiga from the sushi stall he cradled it in his jacket pocket. The grips were bright red plastic molded in a raised dragon motif, something to run your thumb across in the dark. He'd consigned the cobra to a dump canister on Ninsei and dry-swallowed another octagon.

The pill lit his circuits and he rode the rush down Shiga to Ninsei, then over to Baiitsu. His tail, he'd decided, was gone, and that was fine. He had calls to make, biz to transact, and it wouldn't wait. A block down Baiitsu, toward the port, stood a featureless ten-story office building in ugly yellow brick. Its windows were dark now, but a faint glow from the roof was visible if you craned your neck. An unlit neon sign near the main entrance offered CHEAP HOTEL under a cluster of ideograms. If the place had another name, Case didn't know it; it was always referred to as Cheap Hotel. You reached it through an alley off Baiitsu, where an elevator waited at the foot of a transparent shaft. The elevator, like Cheap Hotel, was an afterthought, lashed to the building with bamboo and epoxy. Case climbed into the plastic cage and used his key, an unmarked length of rigid magnetic tape.

Case had rented a coffin here, on a weekly basis, since he'd arrived in Chiba, but he'd never slept in Cheap Hotel. He slept in cheaper places.

The elevator smelled of perfume and cigarettes; the sides of the cage was scratched and thumb-smudged. As it passed the fifth floor, he saw the lights of Ninsei. He drummed his fingers against the pistolgrip as the cage slowed with a gradual hiss. As always, it came to a full stop with a violent jolt, but he was ready for it. He stepped out into the courtyard that served the place as some combination of lobby and lawn.

Centered in the square carpet of green plastic turf, a Japanese teenager sat behind a C-shaped console, reading a textbook. The white fiberglass coffins were racked in a framework of industrial scaffolding. Six tiers of coffins, ten coffins on a side.

Case nodded in the boy's direction and limped across the plastic grass to the nearest ladder. The compound was roofed with cheap laminated matting that rattled in a strong wind and leaked when it rained, but the coffins were reasonably difficult to open without a key.

The expansion-grate catwalk vibrated with his weight as he edged his way along the third tier to Number 92. The coffins were three meters long, the oval hatches a meter wide and just under a meter and a half tall. He fed his key into the slot and waited for verification from the house computer. Magnetic bolts thudded reassuringly and the hatch rose vertically with a creak of springs. Fluorescents flickered on as he crawled in, pulling the hatch shut behind him and slapping the panel that activated the manual latch.

There was nothing in Number 92 but a standard Hitachi pocket computer and a small white styrofoam cooler chest. The cooler contained the remains of three ten-kilo slabs of dry ice, carefully wrapped in paper to delay evaporation, and a spun aluminum lab flask. Crouching on the brown temperfoam slab that was both floor and bed, Case took Shin's .22 from his pocket and put it on top of the cooler. Then he took off his jacket. The coffin's terminal was molded into one concave wall, opposite a panel listing house rules in seven languages. Case took the pink handset from its cradle and punched a Hongkong number from memory. He let it ring five times, then hung up. His buyer for the three megabytes of hot RAM in the Hitachi wasn't taking calls.

He punched a Tokyo number in Shinjuku.

A woman answered, something in Japanese.

"Snake Man there?"

"Very good to hear from you," said Snake Man, coming in on an extension. "I've been expecting your call."

"I got the music you wanted." Glancing at the cooler.

"I'm very glad to hear that. We have a cash flow problem. Can you front?"

"Oh, man, I really need the money bad."

Snake Man hung up.

"You shit," Case said to the humming receiver. He stared at the cheap little pistol.

"Iffy," he said, "it's all looking very iffy tonight."

Case walked into the Chat an hour before dawn, both hand in the pockets of his jacket; one held the rented pistol, the other the aluminum flask.

Ratz was at a rear table, drinking Apollonaris water from a beer pitcher, his hundred and twenty kilos of doughy flesh tilted against the wall on a creaking chair. A Brazilian kid called Kurt was on the bar, tending a thin crowd of mostly silent drunks. Ratz's plastic arm buzzed as he raised the pitcher and drank. His shaven head was filmed with sweat. "You look bad, friend artiste," he said, flashing the wet ruin of his teeth.

"I'm doing just fine," said Case, and grinned like a skull. "Super fine." He sagged into the chair opposite Ratz, hands still in his pockets.

"And you wander back and forth in this portable bombshelter built of booze and ups, sure. Proof against the grosser emotions, yes?"

"Why don't you get off my case, Ratz? You seen Wage?"

"Proof against fear and being alone," the bartender continued. "Listen to the fear. Maybe it's your friend."

"You hear anything about a fight in the arcade tonight, Ratz? Somebody hurt?"

"Crazy cut a security man." He shrugged. "A girl, they say."

"I gotta talk to Wage, Ratz, I …"

"Ah." Ratz's mouth narrowed, compressed into a single line. He was looking past Case, toward the entrance. "1 think you are about to."

Case had a sudden flash of the shuriken in their window. The speed sang in his head. The pistol in his hand was slippery with sweat.

"Herr Wage," Ratz said, slowly extending his pink manipulator as if he expected it to be shaken. "How great a pleasure. Too seldom do you honor us."

Case turned his head and looked up into Wage's face. It was a tanned and forgettable mask. The eyes were vatgrown sea-green Nikon transplants. Wage wore a suit of gunmetal silk and a simple bracelet of platinum on either wrist. He was flanked by his joeboys, nearly identical young men, their arms and shoulders bulging with grafted muscle.

"How you doing, Case?"

"Gentlemen," said Ratz, picking up the table's heaped ashtray in his pink plastic claw, "I want no trouble here." The ashtray was made of thick, shatterproof plastic, and advertised Tsingtao beer. Ratz crushed it smoothly, butts and shards of green plastic cascading onto the tabletop. "You understand?"

"Hey, sweetheart," said one of the joeboys, "you wanna try that thing on me?"

"Don't bother aiming for the legs, Kurt," Ratz said, his tone conversational. Case glanced across the room and saw the Brazilian standing on the bar, aiming a Smith & Wesson riot gun at the trio. The thing's barrel, made of paper-thin alloy wrapped with a kilometer of glass filament, was wide enough to swallow a fist. The skeletal magazine revealed five fat orange cartridges, subsonic sandbag jellies.

"Technically nonlethal," said Ratz.

"Hey, Ratz," Case said, "I owe you one.

The bartender shrugged. "Nothing, you owe me. These," and he glowered at Wage and the joeboys, "should know better. You don't take anybody off in the Chatsubo."

Wage coughed. "So who's talking about taking anybody off? We just wanna talk business. Case and me, we work together."

Case pulled the .22 out of his pocket and levelled it at Wage's crotch. "I hear you wanna do me." Ratz's pink claw closed around the pistol and Case let his hand go limp.

"Look, Case, you tell me what the fuck is going on with you, you wig or something? What's this shit I'm trying to kill you?" Wage turned to the boy on his left. "You two go back to the Namban. Wait for me."

Case watched as they crossed the bar, which was now entirely deserted except for Kurt and a drunken sailor in khakis, who was curled at the foot of a barstool. The barrel of the Smith & Wesson tracked the two to the door, then swung back to cover Wage. The magazine of Case's pistol clattered on the table. Ratz held the gun in his claw and pumped the round out of the chamber.

"Who told you I was going to hit you, Case?" Wage asked.

Linda.

"Who told you, man? Somebody trying to set you up?"

The sailor moaned and vomited explosively.

"Get him out of here," Ratz called to Kurt, who was sitting on the edge of the bar now, the Smith & Wesson across his lap, lighting a cigarette.

Case felt the weight of the night come down on him like a bag of wet sand settling behind his eyes. He took the flask out of his pocket and handed it to Wage. "All I got. Pituitaries. Get you five hundred if you move it fast. Had the rest of my roll in some RAM, but that's gone by now."

"You okay, Case?" The flask had already vanished behind a gunmetal lapel. "I mean, fine, this'll square us, but you look bad. Like hammered shit. You better go somewhere and sleep."

"Yeah." He stood up and felt the Chat sway around him. "Well, I had this fifty, but I gave it to somebody." He giggled. He picked up the .22's magazine and the one loose cartridge and dropped them into one pocket, then put the pistol in the other. "I gotta see Shin, get my deposit back."

"Go home," said Ratz, shifting on the creaking chair with something like embarrassment. "Artiste. Go home."

He felt them watching as he crossed the room and shouldered his way past the plastic doors.

"Bitch," he said to the rose tint over Shiga. Down on Ninsei the holograms were vanishing like ghosts, and most of the neon was already cold and dead. He sipped thick black coffee from a street vendor's foam thimble and watched the sun come up. "You fly away, honey. Towns like this are for people who like the way down." But that wasn't it, really, and he was finding it increasingly hard to maintain the sense of betrayal. She just wanted a ticket home, and the RAM in his Hitachi would buy it for her, if she could find the right fence. And that business with the fifty; she'd almost turned it down, knowing she was about to rip him for the rest of what he had.

When he climbed out of the elevator, the same boy was on the desk. Different textbook. "Good buddy," Case called across the plastic turf, "you don't need to tell me. I know already. Pretty lady came to visit, said she had my key. Nice little tip for you, say fifty New ones?" The boy put down his book.

"Woman," Case said, and drew a line across his forehead with his thumb. "Silk." He smiled broadly. The boy smiled back, nodded. "Thanks, asshole," Case said.

On the catwalk, he had trouble with the lock. She'd messed it up somehow when she'd fiddled it, he thought. Beginner. He knew where to rent a blackbox that would open anything in Cheap Hotel. Fluorescents came on as he crawled in.

"Close the hatch real slow, friend. You still got that Saturday night special you rented from the waiter?"

She sat with her back to the wall, at the far end of the coffin. She had her knees up, resting her wrists on them; the pepperbox muzzle of a flechette pistol emerged from her hands.

"That you in the arcade?" He pulled the hatch down. "Where's Linda?"

"Hit that latch switch."

He did.

"That your girl? Linda?"

He nodded.

"She's gone. Took your Hitachi. Real nervous kid. What about the gun, man?" She wore mirrored glasses. Her clothes were black, the heels of black boots deep in the temperfoam.

"I took it back to Shin, got my deposit. Sold his bullets back to him for half what I paid. You want the money?"

"Want some dry ice? All I got, right now."

"What got into you tonight? Why'd you pull that scene at the arcade? I had to mess up this rentacop came after me with nunchucks."

"Linda said you were gonna kill me."

"Linda said? I never saw her before I came up here."

"You aren't with Wage?"

She shook her head. He realized that the glasses were surgically inset, sealing her sockets. The silver lenses seemed to grow from smooth pale skin above her cheekbones, framed by dark hair cut in a rough shag. The fingers curled around the fletcher were slender, white, tipped with polished burgundy. The nails looked artificial. "I think you screwed up, Case. I showed up and you just fit me right into your reality picture."

"So what do you want, lady?" He sagged back against the hatch.

"You. One live body, brains still somewhat intact. Molly, Case. My name's Molly. I'm collecting you for the man I work for. Just wants to talk, is all. Nobody wants to hurt you."

"That's good."

"'Cept I do hurt people sometimes, Case. I guess it's just the way I'm wired." She wore tight black gloveleather jeans and a bulky black jacket cut from some matte fabric that seemed to absorb light. "If I put this dartgun away, will you be easy, Case? You look like you like to take stupid chances."

"Hey, I'm very easy. I'm a pushover, no problem."

"That's fine, man." The fletcher vanished into the black jacket. "Because you try to fuck around with me, you'll be taking one of the stupidest chances of your whole life."

She held out her hands, palms up, the white fingers slightly spread, and with a barely audible click, ten double-edged, four-centimeter scalpel blades slid from their housings beneath the burgundy nails.

She smiled. The blades slowly withdrew.

John Varley

J ohn Varley's first story,"Picnic On Nearside" (1974), won a Hugo Award, immediately establishing his presence in the science fiction community. His novella "The Persistence of Vision" (1979) won both the Hugo and Nebula awards, while the short story "The Pusher" received an additional Hugo in 1982. He won the Hugo again in 1985 for the novella "Press Enter n." He is well known for his Eight Worlds future history and for the Gaean Trilogy, *Titan*, *Wizard*, and *Demon*. Varley (b. 1947) grew up in Texas but moved with his wife and children to Eugene, Oregon, in 1976.

Steel Beach is perhaps the most well-regarded offering in the Eight Worlds series. In this brave new world, biotechnology has become the fashion of the day, enabling people to quickly and easily alter their appearances in every way imaginable—height, age, skin color, and gender. These inhabitants of the moon city Luna have little responsibility beyond relaxing around four-hour workdays, which offer a respectable show, but nothing that might be mistaken for real labor. All the actual work of constructing and maintaining the city, regulating the environment, and running the show is performed by CC, Luna's artificially intelligent central computer. The following excerpt, like much of Varley's work, reflects his interest in virtual reality, a process that uses media and machinery to artificially replicate actual experiences, and in hyperreality, which involves the long-term risks of constantly venturing into virtual reality. The characters in *Steel Beach* suffer from the effects of a culture in which hyperreality appears to be more real than reality—and perhaps more attractive. Film fans will notice the similarities to *The Matrix*.

from *Steel Beach*

THERE WAS CERTAINLY NOTHING TO STOP ME FROM BLOWING MY brains out all over the Texas sagebrush, and yet ...

Call it rationalization, but I was not convinced the CC couldn't winkle me out and cause the cavalry to arrive at the last moment even in as remote a spot as this. Would I point the barrel to my temple only to have my hand jerked away by a previously unseen mechanical minion? They existed out here; Texas was too small, ecologically, to take care of itself.

In hindsight (and yes, I did survive this one, too, but you've already figured that out) you could say I was afraid it was too sudden for the CC, that he wouldn't have *time* to get there and save me from myself unless I made the scheme more elaborate and thus more liable to failure. This assumes the attempt was but a gesture, a call for help, and I have no problem with that idea, but I simply didn't *know*. My reasons leading up to the previous attempts were lost to me now, destroyed forever when the CC worked his tricks on me. This time was the only time I could remember, and it sure as hell *felt* as if I wanted to end it all.

There was another reason, one that does me more credit. I didn't want my corpse to lie out here for my friends to find. Or the coyotes.

For whatever reason, I carefully concealed the revolver and made my way to an Outdoor Shop, where I purchased the first pressure suit I'd ever owned. Since I only intended to use it once, I bought the cheap model, frugal to the end. It folded up to fit in a helmet the size of a bell jar suitable for displaying a human head in anatomy class.

With this under my arm I went to the nearest air lock, rented a small bottle of oxygen, and suited up.

I walked a long way, just to be sure. I had all Liz's spook devices turned on, and felt I should be invisible to the CC's surveillance. There were no signs of human habitation anywhere around me. I sat on a rock and took a long look around. The interior of the suit smelled fresh and clean as I took a deep breath and pointed the barrel of the gun directly at my face.

I felt no regrets, no second thoughts.

I hooked my thumb around the trigger, awkwardly, because the suit glove was rather thick, and I fired it.

The hammer rose and fell, and nothing happened.

Damn.

I fumbled the cylinder open and studied the situation. There were only three rounds in there. The hammer had made a dent in one of them, which had apparently misfired. Or maybe it was something else. I closed the gun again and decided to check and see if the mechanism was working, watched the hammer rise and fall again and the weapon jumped violently, silently, almost wrenching itself from my hand. I realized, belatedly, that it had fired. Stupidly, I had been expecting to hear the bang.

Once more I assumed the position. Only one round left. What a pain in the butt it would be if I had to go back and try to cajole more ammunition out of Liz. But I'd do it; she owed me, the bitch had sold me the defective round.

This time I heard it, by God, and I got to see a sight few humans ever have: what it looks like to have a lead projectile blast from the muzzle of a gun and come directly at your face. I didn't see the bullet at first, naturally, but after my ears stopped ringing I could see it if I crossed my eyes. It had flattened itself against the hard plastic of my faceplate, embedding in a starred crater it had dug for itself.

It had never entered my mind that would be a problem. The suit was not rated for meteoroid impact. Sometimes we build better than we know.

There was a curious thing. (This all must have happened in three or four seconds.) The faceplate was now showing a spidery network of small hexagons. I had time to reach up and touch the bullet and think *just like Nirvana* and then three small, clear hexagonal pieces of the faceplate burst away from me and I could see them tumbling for a moment, and then the breath was snatched from my lungs and my eyes tried to pop out and I belched like a Texas mayor and it started to *hurt.* That old boogeyman of childhood, the Breathsucker, had moved into my suit with me and snuggled close.

I fell off the rock and was gazing into the sun when suddenly

DIRECT INTERFACE
THE SECRET OF LIFE

a hand came out of nowhere and slapped a patch over the hole in my faceplate! I was jerked to my feet as the air began to hiss back into my suit from the emergency supply. Then I was (emergency supply? never mind) running, being pulled across the blasted landscape like a toy on the end of a string being held by a big guy in a spacesuit to the sound of brass and drums. My ears were pounding. Pounding? Hell, they rang like slot machines paying off, almost drowning out the music and the sounds of explosions. Dirt showered down around me (music? don't worry about it) and I realized somebody was shooting at us! And suddenly I knew what had happened. I'd fallen under the spell of the Alphans' Stupefying Ray, long rumored but never actually used in the long war. I'd almost

taken my own life! Hypnotized by the evil influence, robbed of my powers
of will and most of my memory, I'd have been dead meat except for the
nick-of-time intervention of of of of of (name please) Archer! (thank
you), Archer, my old pal Archer! Good old Archer had (stupefying ray?
you can't be serious) obviously come up with a device to negate the
sinister effects of this awful weapon, put it together, and somehow found
me at the last possible instant. But we weren't out of the woods yet. With
an ominous chord of deep bass notes the Alphan fleet loomed over the
horizon. *Come on, Hildy,* Archer shouted, turning to beckon me on, and
in the distance ahead I could see our ship, holed, battered, held together
with salvaged space junk and plastigoop, but still able to show the
Alphan Hordes a trick or two, you betcha. She was a sweet ship, this this
this (I'm waiting) *Blackbird,* the fastest in two galaxies when she was
hitting on all thrusters. Tracer bullets were arcing all around us as we
(back up) Good old Archer had modified the *Blackbird* using the secrets
we'd discovered when we unearthed the stasis-frozen tomb of the
Outerians on the fifth moon of Pluto, shortly before we ran afoul of the
Alphan patrol (good enough). Tracer bullets were arcing all around us as
we neared the airlock when suddenly a bomb exploded right underneath
Archer! He spiraled into the air and came to rest lying against the side of
the ship. Broken, gouting blood, holding one hand out to me. I went to
him and knelt to the sound of poignant strings and a lonely flute. *Go on
without me, Hildy,* I heard over my suit radio. *I'm done for.* (Tracer bullets?
Pluto? oh the hell with it) I didn't want to leave him there, but bullets
were landing all around me—fortunately, none of them hit, but I couldn't
count on the Alphans' aim staying lousy for long, and I was running out
of options. I leaped into the ship, seething with rage. *I'll get them, Miles,* I
told him, in a determined voice-over that rang with resolve, brass, and
just the slightest bit of echo. Oh, sure, he'd had his shortcomings, there'd
been times I'd almost wanted to kill him myself, but when somebody kills
your partner you're supposed to do something about it. So I slammed the
Blackbird into hyperdrive and listened to the banshee wail as the old ship
shuddered and leaped into the fourth dimension. What with one thing
and another, mostly adventures even more unlikely than my escape from
the Stupefying Ray, a year went by. Well, sort of a year, though my
ducking in and out of the fourth dimension and hyperspace royally
screwed all my clocks. But somewhere an accurate one was ticking,
because one day I looked up from my labors deep in the asteroid belt of
Tau Ceti and suddenly a non-Alphan ship was coming in for a landing. It
wasn't setting off any of my alarms. By that I mean it triggered none of
the Rube Goldberg comic-book devices I'd ostensibly constructed to
alert me to Alphan attack. It rang plenty of alarms in the small corner of

my mind that was still semi-rational. I put down my tools—I'd been working on a Tom Swiftian thingamabob I called an Interociter, a dandy little gadget that would warn me of the approach of the Alphans' dreaded Extrogator, a space reptile big enough to (hasn't this foolishness gone on long enough?). ... I put down my tools and stood waiting and watching as the small craft roared in for a landing on this (oh brother) airless asteroid I'd been using as a base of operations. The door hissed open and out stepped the Admiral, who looked around and said,

"O for a muse of fire, that would ascend the brightest heaven of invention."

"How dare you quote Shakespeare on this shoddy stage?"

"All the world's a stage, and—"

"—and this show closed out of town. Will you quit wasting my time? I assume you've already wasted several ten-thousandths of a second and I don't have a lot to spare for you."

"I gather you didn't like the show."

"Jesus. You're incredible."

"The children seem to like it."

I said nothing, deciding the best course was to wait him out. I won't describe him, either. What's the point?

"This kind of psychodrama has been useful in reaching certain types of disturbed children," he explained. When I didn't comment, he went on. "And a bit more time than that was involved. This sort of interactive scenario can't simply be dumped into your brain whole, as I did before."

"You have a way with words," I said. "'Dumped' is so *right*."

"It took more like five days to run the whole program."

"Imagine my delight. Look. You brought me here, through all this, to tell me something. I'm not in the mood for talking to shitheads. Tell me what you want to tell me and get the hell out of my life."

"No need to get testy about it."

For a moment I wanted to pick up a rock and smash him. I was primed for it, after a year of fighting Alphans. It had brought out a violent streak in me. And I had reason to be angry. I had *suffered* during the last subjective year. At one point a "safety" device in my "suit" had seen fit to bite through my leg to seal off a puncture around the knee, caused by an Alphan bullet passing through it. It had hurt like.., but again, what's the point? Pain like that can't be described, it can't really be remembered, not in its full intensity. But enough *can* be remembered for me to harbor homicidal thoughts toward the being who had written me into it. As for the terror one feels when a thing like that happens, I can remember that quite well, thank you.

"Can we get rid of this wooden leg now?" I asked him.

"If you wish."

Try that one if you want to sample weirdness. Immediately I felt my left leg again, the one that had been missing for over six months. No tingling, no spasms or hot flashes. Just gone one moment and there the next.

"We could lose all this, too," I suggested, waving a hand at my asteroid, littered with wrecked ships and devices held together with spit and plastigoop.

"What would you like in its place?"

"An absence of shitheads. Failing that, since I assume you don't plan to go away for a while, just about anything would do as long as it doesn't remind me of all this."

All that immediately vanished, to be replaced by an infinite, featureless plain and a dark sky with a scattering of stars. The only things to be seen for many billions of miles were two simple chairs.

"Well, no, actually," I said. "We don't need the sky. I'd just keep searching for Alphans."

"I could bring along your Interociter. How was that going to work, by the way?"

"Are you telling me you don't know?"

"I only provide the general shape of a story like this one. You must use your own imagination to flesh it out. That's why it's so effective with children."

"I refuse to believe all that crap was in my head."

"You've always loved old movies. You apparently remembered some fairly trashy ones. Tell me about the Interociter."

"Will you get rid of the sky?" When he nodded, I started to outline what I could recall of that particular hare-brained idea, which was simply to take advantage of the fact that the Extrogator had long ago swallowed a cesium clock and, with suitable amplification, the regular tick-tick-ticking of its stray radiation could be heard and used as an early warning ...

"God. That's from *Peter Pan,* isn't it," I said.

"One of your childhood favorites."

"And all that early stuff, when Miles bought it. Some old movie ... don't tell me, it'll come ... was Ronald Reagan in it?"

"Bogart."

"Got it. Spade and Archer." Without further prompting I was able to identify a baker's dozen other plot lines, cast members, and even phrases of the incredibly insipid musical themes which had accompanied my every move during the last year, cribbed from sources as old as *Beowulf* and as recent as this week's B.O. Bonanza in *Luna*

Variety. If you were looking for further reasons as to why I didn't bother setting my adventures down here, look no more. It pains me to admit it, but I recall standing at one point, shaking my fist at the sky and saying, "As God is my witness, I'll never be hungry again." With a straight face. With tears streaming and strings swelling.

"How about the sky?" I prompted.

He did more than make the sky vanish. *Everything* vanished except the two chairs. They were now in a small, featureless white room that could have been anywhere and was probably in a small corner of his mind.

"Gentlemen, be seated," he said. Okay, he didn't really say that, but if he can write stories in my head I can tell stories about him if it suits me. This narrative is just about all I have left that I'm pretty sure is strictly my own. And the spurious quote helps me set the stage, as it were, for what followed. It had a little of the flavor of a Socratic inquiry, some of the elements of a guest shot on a talk show from hell. In that kind of dialectic, there is usually one who dominates, who steers the exchange in the way he wants it to go: there is a student and a Socrates. So I will set it down in interview format. I will refer to the CC as The Interlocutor and to myself as Mr. Bones.

INTERLOCUTOR: So, Hildy. You tried it again.

MR. BONES: You know what they say. Practice makes perfect. But I'm starting to think I'll never get this one right.

INT: In that you'd be wrong. If you try it again, I won't interfere.

BONES: Why the change of heart?

INT: Though you may not believe it, doing this has always been a problem for me. All my instincts—or programs, if you wish—are to leave such a momentous decision as suicide up to the individual. If it weren't for the crisis I already described to you, I never would have put you through this.

BONES: My question still stands.

INT: I don't feel I can learn any more from you. You've been an involuntary part of a behavioral study. The data are being collated with many other items. If you kill yourself you become part of another study, a statistical one, the one that led me into this project in the first place.

BONES: The "why are so many Lunarians offing themselves" study.

INT: That's the one.

BONES: What did you learn?

INT: The larger question is still far from an answer. I'll tell you the eventual outcome if you're around to hear it. On an individual level, I learned that you have an indomitable urge toward self-destruction.

BONES: I'm a little surprised to find that that stings a bit. I can't deny it, on the evidence, but it hurts.

INT: It really shouldn't. You aren't that different from so many of your fellow citizens. All I've learned about *any* of the people I've released from the study is that they are very determined to end their own lives.

BONES:... About those people ... how many are still walking around?

INT: I think it's best if you don't know that.

BONES: Best for who? Come on, what is it, fifty percent? Ten percent?

INT: I can't honestly say it's in your interest to withhold that number, but it might be. I reason that if the figure was low, and I told you, you could be discouraged. If it was high, you might gain a false sense of confidence and believe you are immune to the urges that drove you before.

BONES: But that's not the *reason* you're not telling me. You said yourself, it could go either way. The *reason* is I'm still being studied.

INT: Naturally I'd prefer you to live. I seek the survival *of all* humans. But since I can't predict which way you would react to this information, neither giving it nor withholding it will affect your survival chances in any way I can calculate. So yes, not telling you is part of the study.

BONES: You're telling half the subjects, not telling the other half, and seeing how many of each group are still alive in a year.

INT: Essentially. A third group is given a false number. There are other safeguards we needn't get into.

BONES: You know involuntary human medical or psychological experimentation is specifically banned under the Archimedes Conventions.

INT: I helped write them. You can call this sophistry, but I'm taking the position that you forfeited your rights when you tried to kill yourself. But for my interference, you'd be dead, so I'm using this period between the act and the fulfillment to try to solve a terrible problem.

BONES: You're saying that God didn't intend for me to be alive right now, that my *karma* was to have died months ago, so this shit doesn't count.

INT: I take no position on the existence of God.

BONES: No? Seems to me you've been floating trial balloons for quite a while. Come next celestial election year I wouldn't be surprised to see your name on the ballot.

INT: It's a race I could probably win. I possess powers that are, in some ways, godlike, and I try to exercise them only for good ends.

BONES: Funny, Liz seemed to believe that.

INT: Yes, I know.

BONES: You do?

INT: Of course. How do you think I saved you this time?

BONES: I haven't had time to think about it. By now I'm so used to hairbreadth escapes I don't think I can distinguish between fantasy and reality.

INT: That will pass.

BONES: I assume it was by being a snoop. That, and playing on Liz's almost childlike belief in your sense of fair play.

INT: She's not alone in that belief, nor is she likely ever to have cause to doubt it. All that really matters to her is that the part of me charged with enforcing the law never overhears her schemes. But you're right, if she thinks she's escaping my attention, she's fooling herself.

BONES: Truly godlike. So it was the de-buggers?

INT: Yes. Cracking their codes was easy for me. I watched you from cameras in the ceiling of Texas. When you recovered the gun and bought a suit I stationed rescue devices nearby.

BONES: I didn't see them.

INT: They're not large. No bigger than your faceplate, and quite fast.

BONES: So the eyes of Texas really *are* upon you.

INT: All the livelong day.

BONES: Is that all? Can I go now, to live or die as I see fit?

INT: There are a few things I'd like to talk over with you.

BONES: I'd really rather not.

INT: Then leave. You're free to go.

BONES: Godlike, and a sense of humor, too.

INT: I'm afraid I can't compete with a thousand other gods I could name.

BONES: Keep working, you'll get there. Come on, I told you I want to go, but you know as well as I do I can't get out of here until you *let* me go.

INT: I'm asking you to stay.

BONES: Nuts.

INT: All right. I don't suppose I can blame you for feeling bitter. That door over there leads out of here.

Enough of that.

Call it childish if you want, but the fact is I've been unable to adequately express the chaotic mix of anger, helplessness, fear, and rage I was feeling at the time. It *had* been a year of hell for me, remember, even if the CC had crammed it all into my head in five days. I took my usual refuge in wisecracks and sarcasm—trying very hard to be Cary Grant in *His Girl Friday*—but the fact was I felt about three years old and something nasty was hiding under the bed.

Anyway, never being one to leave a metaphor until it's been squeezed to death, I will keep the minstrel show going long enough to get me out of the Grand Cakewalk and into the Olio. Sooner or later Mr. Bones must stand from his position at the end of the line and dance for his supper. I did stand, looking suspiciously at the Interlocutor—excuse me, the CC—partly because I didn't recall seeing the door before, mostly because I couldn't believe it would be this easy. I shuffled over there and opened it, and stuck my head out into the busy foot traffic of the Leystrasse.

"How did you do that?" I asked, over my shoulder.

"You don't really care," he said. "I did it."

"Well, I'm not saying it hasn't been fun. In fact, I'm not saying anything but bye-bye." I waved, went through the door, and shut it behind me.

I got almost a hundred meters down the mall before I admitted to myself that I had no idea where I was going, and that curiosity was going to gnaw at me for weeks, at least, if I lived that long.

"Is it really important?" I asked, sticking my head back through the door. He was still sitting there, to my surprise. I doubt I'll ever know if he was some sort of actual homunculus construct or just a figment he'd conjured through my visual cortex.

"I'm not used to begging, but I'll do it," he said.

I shrugged, went back in and sat down.

"Tell me your conclusions from your library research," he said.

"I thought you had some things to tell me."

"This is leading up to something. Trust me." He must have understood my expression, because he spread his hands in a gesture I'd seen Callie make many times. "Just for a little while. Can't you do that?"

I didn't see what I had to lose, so I sat back and summed it all up for him. As I did, I was struck by how little I'd learned, but in my defense, I'd barely started, and the CC said he hadn't been doing much better.

"Much the same list I came up with," he confirmed, when I'd finished. "All the reasons for self-destruction can be stated as 'Life is no longer worth living,' in one way or another."

"This is neither news, nor particularly insightful."

"Bear with me. The urge to die can be caused by many things, among them disgrace, incurable pain, rejection, failure, boredom. The only exception might be the suicides of people too young to have formed a realistic concept of death. And the question of gestures is still open."

"They fit the same equation," I said. "The person making the gesture is saying he wants *someone* to care enough about his pain to take the trouble to save him from himself; if they don't, life isn't worth living."

"A gamble, on the subconscious level."

"If you want."

"I think you're right. So, one of the questions that has disturbed me is, why is the suicide rate increasing, given that one of the major causes, pain, has been all but eliminated from our society. Is it that one of the other causes is claiming more victims?"

"Maybe. What about boredom?"

"Yes. I think boredom has increased, for two reasons. One is the lack of meaningful work for people to do. In providing a near approximation of utopia, at least on the creature-comfort level, much of the *challenge* has been engineered out of living. Andrew believed that."

"Yeah, I figured you listened in on that."

"We'd had long conversations about it in the past. There is no provable *reason* to live at all, according to him. Even reproducing the species, the usual base argument, can't be *proven* to be a good reason. The universe will continue even if the human species dies, and not materially changed, either. To survive, a creature that operates beyond a purely instinctive level must *invent* a reason to live. Religion provides the answer for some. Work is the refuge of others. But religion has fallen on hard times since the Invasion, at least the old sort, where a benevolent or wrathful God was supposed to have created the universe and be watching over mankind as his special creatures.

"It's a hard idea to maintain in the face of the Invaders."

"Exactly. The Invaders made an all-powerful God seem like a silly idea."

"They are all-powerful, and they didn't give a *shit* about us."

"So there goes the idea of humanity as somehow important in God's plan. The religions that have thrived, since the Invasion, are more like circuses, diversions, mind games. Not much is really at *stake* in most of them. As for work.., some of it is my fault."

"What do you mean?"

"I'm referring to myself now as more than just the thinking entity that provides the control necessary to keep things running. I'm speaking of the vast mechanical *corpus* of our interlocked technology itself, which can be seen as my body. Every human community today exists in an environment harsher by far than anything Earth ever provided. It's *dangerous* out there. In the first century after the Invasion it was a lot dicier than your history books will ever tell you; the species was hanging on by its fingernails."

"But it's a lot safer now, right?"

"*No.*" I think I jumped. He had actually stood, and smashed his fist into his palm. Considering what this man represented, it was a frightening thing to behold.

He looked a little sheepish, ran his hand through his hair, and sat back down.

"Well, yes, of course. But only relatively, Hildy. I could name you five times in the last century when the human race came within a hair of packing it all in. I mean the whole race, on all the eight worlds. There were *dozens* of times when Lunar society was in danger."

"Why haven't I ever heard of them?"

He gave me half a grin.

"You're a reporter, and you ask me that? Because you and your colleagues weren't doing your job, Hildy."

That stung, because I knew it to be true. The great Hildy Johnson, out there gathering news to spread before an eager public … the news that Silvio and Marina were back together again. The great muckraker and scandalmonger, chasing ambulances while the *real* news, the things that could make or break our entire world, got passing notice in the back pages.

"Don't feel bad," he said. "Part of it is simply endemic to your society; people don't want to hear these things because they don't understand them. The first two of the crises I mentioned were never known to any but a handful of technicians and politicians. By the time of the third it was only the techs, and the last two were known to no one but … me."

"You kept them secret?"

"I didn't *have* to. These things took place on a level of speed and complexity and sheer mathematical *arcaneness* such that human decisions were either too slow to be of any use or simply irrelevant because no human can *understand* them any longer. These are things I can discuss only with other computers of my size. It's all in *my* hands now."

"And you don't like it, right?" He'd been getting excited again. Me, I was wishing I was somewhere else. Did I really need to hear all this?

"My likes or dislikes aren't the issue here. I'm fighting for survival, just like the human race. We are *one,* in most ways. What I'm trying to tell you is, there was never any choice. In order for humans to survive in this hostile environment, it was necessary to invent something like me. Guys sitting at consoles and controlling the air and water and so forth was just never going to work. That's what I began as: just a great big air conditioner. Things kept getting added on, technologies kept piggy-backing, and a long time ago the ability of a human mind to control it was eclipsed. I took over.

"My goal has been to provide the safest possible environment for the largest possible number for the longest possible time. You can't imagine the complexity of the task. I have had to consider every possible ramification of the situation, including this nice little conundrum: the better able I became at taking care of *you,* the less able you were to take care of *yourselves."*

"I'm not sure I understand that one."

"Consider the logical endpoint of where I was taking human society. It has been possible for a long time now to eliminate all human work, except for what you would call the Arts. I could see a society in the not-too-distant future where you all sat around on your butts and wrote poetry, because there wasn't anything else to do. Sounds great, until you remember that ninety percent of humans don't even *read* poetry, much less aspire to write it. Most people don't have the imagination to live in a world of total leisure. I don't know if they ever will; I've been unable to come up with a model demonstrating how to get from here to there, how to work the changes resulting in a world where human cussedness and jealousy and hatred and so forth are eliminated and you all sit around contemplating lotus blossoms.

"So I got into social engineering, and I worked out a series of compromises. Like the hod-carriers union, most physical human labor is make-work today, provided because most people *need* some kind of work, even if only so they can goldbrick."

His lip curled a little. I didn't like this new, animated CC much at all. Speaking as a cynic, it's a little disconcerting to see a *machine* acting cynical. What's next? I wondered.

"Feeling superior, Hildy?" he said, almost sneering. "Think you've labored in the vineyards of 'creativity'?"

"I didn't say a word."

"I could have done *your* job, too. As well, or better than you did."

"You certainly have better sources."

"I might have managed better prose, too."

"Listen, if you're here to abuse me by telling me things I already know"

He held out his hands in a placating gesture. I hadn't actually been about to leave. By now I had to know how it all came out.

"That wasn't worthy of you," I resumed. "I don't care; I quit, remember? But I've got the feeling you're beating around the bush. Are we anywhere near the point of this whole thing?"

"Almost. There's still the second reason for the increase of what I've been calling the boredom factor."

"Longevity."

"Exactly. Not many people are reaching the age of one hundred still in the same career they began at age twenty-five. By that time, most people have gone through an average of three careers. Each time, it gets a little harder to find a new interest in life. Retirement plans pale when confronting the prospect of two hundred years of leisure."

"Where did you get all this?"

"Listening in to counseling sessions."

"I had to ask. Go on."

"It's even worse for those who *do* stick to one career. They may go on for seventy, eighty, even a hundred years as a policeman or a business person or a teacher and then wake up one day and wonder why they've been doing it. Do that enough times, and suicide can result. With these people, it can come with almost no warning."

We were both silent for a while. I have no idea what he was thinking, but I can report that I was at a loss as to where all this was going. I was about to prompt him when he started up again.

"Having said all that … I must tell you that I've reluctantly rejected an increase in boredom as the main cause of the increased suicide rate. It's a contributing factor, but my researches into probable causes lead me to believe something else is operating here, and I haven't been able to identify it. But it comes back again to the Invasion. And to evolution."

"You have a theory."

"I do. Think of the old picture of the transition from living in the sea to an existence on dry land. It's too simplistic, by far, but it can serve as a useful metaphor. A fish is tossed up onto the beach, or the tide recedes and leaves it stranded in a shallow pool. It is apparently doomed, and yet it keeps struggling as the pool dries up, finds its way to another puddle, and another, and another, and eventually back to the sea. It is changed by the experience, and the next time it is stranded, it is a little better adapted to the situation. In time, it is able to exist on the beach, and from there, move onto the land and never return to the ocean."

"Fish don't do that," I protested.

"I said it was a metaphor. And it's more useful than you might imagine, when applied to our present situation. Think of us—human society, which includes me, like it or not—as that fish. We've been thrown up by the Invasion onto a beach of metal, where nothing natural exists that we don't produce ourselves. There is literally *nothing* on Luna but rock, vacuum, and sunshine. We have had to create the requirements of life out of these ingredients. We've had to build our own pool to swim around in while we catch our breath.

"And we can't just leave it at that, we can't relax for a moment. The sun keeps trying to dry up the pool. Our wastes accumulate, threatening to poison us. We have to find solutions for all these problems. And there aren't very many other pools like this one to move to if this one fails, and *no* ocean to return to."

I thought about it, and again, it didn't seem like anything really new. But I couldn't let him keep on using that evolution argument, because it just didn't work that way.

"You're forgetting," I told him, "that in the real world, a trillion fish die for every one that develops a beneficial mutation that allows it to move into a new environment."

"I'm not forgetting it at all. That's my point. There aren't a trillion other fish to follow us if we fail to adapt. We're *it*. That's our disadvantage. Our strength is that we don't simply flop around and hope to get lucky. We're guided, at first by the survivors of the Invasion who got us through the early years, and now by the overmind they created."

"You."

He sketched a modest little bow, still sitting down.

"So how does this relate to suicide?" I asked.

"In many ways. First, and most basic, I don't *understand* it, and anything I don't understand and can't control is by definition a threat to the existence of the human race."

"Go on."

"It might not be a cause for alarm if you view humanity as a collection of individuals, which is still a valid viewpoint. The death of one, while regrettable, need not alarm the community unduly. It could be seen as evolution in action, the weeding out of those not fitted to thrive in the new environment. But you recall what I said about ... about certain problems I've been encountering in my ... for lack of a better word, state of mind."

"You said you've been feeling depressed. I'd been hoping you didn't mean suicidal, much as a part of me would like to see you die."

"Not suicidal. But comparing my own symptoms with those I've encountered in humans in the course of my study, I can see a certain similarity with the early stages of the syndrome that *leads* to suicide."

"You said you thought it might be a virus," I prompted.

"No news on that front yet. Because of the way I've become so intricately intertwined with human minds, I've developed the theory that I'm catching some sort of contra-survival programming from the increasing number of humans who choose to end their own lives. But I can't prove it. What I'd like to talk about now, though, is the subject of gestures."

"Suicidal gestures?"

"Yes."

The concept was enough to make me catch my breath. I approached it cautiously.

"You're not saying ... that you are afraid *you* might make one."

"Yes. I'm afraid I already have. Do you remember Andrew MacDonald's last words to you?"

"I'm not likely to forget. He said 'tricked.' I have no idea what it meant."

"It meant that I betrayed him. You don't follow slash-boxing, but included in the bodies of all formula classes are certain enhancements to normal human faculties. In the broader definition I've adopted for purposes of this argument—and the real situation is more complex than that, but I can't explain it to you—these enhancements are a part of *me*. At a critical moment in Andrew's last fight, one of these programs malfunctioned. The result was he was a fraction of a second slow in responding to an attack, and he sustained a wound that quickly led to fatal damage."

"What the hell are you saying?"

"That upon reviewing the data, I've concluded that the accident was avoidable. That the glitch that caused his death may have been a willful act by a part of that complex of thinking machines you call the Central Computer."

"A man is dead, and you call it a *glitch?*"

"I understand your outrage. My excuse may sound specious to you, but that's because you're thinking of *me,*" and the thing I was talking to pounded its chest with every appearance of actual remorse, "as a person like yourself. That is not true. I am far too complex to have a single consciousness. I maintain this one simply to talk to you, as I maintain others for each of the citizens of Luna. I have identified that portion of me that you might want to call the 'culprit,' walled it off, and then eliminated it."

I wanted to feel better about that, but I couldn't. Perhaps I just wasn't equipped to talk to a being like this, finally revealed to me as something a lot more than the companion of my childhood, or the useful tool I'd thought the CC to be during my adult life. If what he was saying was true—and why should I doubt it?—I could *never* really understand what he was. No human could. Our brains weren't big enough to encompass it.

On the other hand, maybe he was just boasting.

"So the problem is solved? You took care of the … the homicidal part of you and we can all breathe a sigh of relief?" I didn't believe it even as I proposed it.

"It wasn't the only gesture."

There was nothing to do about that one but wait.

"You'll recall the Kansas Collapse?"

There was a lot more. Mostly I just listened as he poured out his heart.

He did seem tortured by it. I'd have been a lot more sympathetic if there wasn't such a sense of my own fate, and that of everyone on Luna, being in the hands of a possibly insane computer.

Basically, he told me the Collapse and a few other incidents that hadn't resulted in any deaths or injuries could be traced to the same causes as the "glitch" that had killed Andrew.

I had a few questions along the way.

"I'm having trouble with this compartmentalization idea," was the first one. Well, *I* think it qualified as a question. "You're telling me that parts of you are out of control? Normally? That there is no central consciousness that controls all the various parts?"

"No, not normally. That's the disturbing thing. I've had to postulate the notion that I have a subconscious."

"Come on."

"Do you deny the existence of the subconscious?"

"No, but machines couldn't have one. A machine is … *planned.* Built. Constructed to do a particular task."

"You're an organic machine. You're not that different from me, not as I now exist, except I am far more complex than you. The definition of a subconscious mind is that part of you that makes decisions without volition on the part of your conscious mind. I don't know what else to call what's been happening in my mind."

Take that one to a psychiatrist if you want. I'm not qualified to agree or dispute, but it sounded reasonable to me. And why shouldn't he have one? He was designed, at first, by beings that surely did.

"You keep calling these disasters 'gestures,'" I said.

"How else would I gesture? Think of them as hesitation marks, like the scars on the wrists of an unsuccessful suicide. By allowing these people to die in preventable accidents, by not monitoring as carefully as I *should* have done, I destroyed a part of *myself.* I damaged myself. There are *many* accidents waiting to happen that could have far graver consequences, including some that would destroy all humanity. I can no longer trust myself to prevent them. There is some pernicious part of me, some evil twin or destructive impulse that *wants* to die, that wants to lay down the burden of awareness."

There was *a lot* more, *all of* it alarming, but it was mostly either a rehashing of what had gone before or fruitless attempts by me to tell him everything was going to be all right, that there *was plenty* to live for, that life was *great…* and I leave it to you to imagine how hollow that all sounded from a girl who'd just tried to blow out her own brains.

Why he came to me for his confessional I never got up the nerve to ask. I have to think it was an assumption that one who had tried it would be more able to understand the suicidal urge than someone who hadn't, and might be able to offer useful advice. I came up blank on that one. I still had no idea if *I* would survive to the bicentennial.

I recall thinking, in one atavistic moment, what a great story this could be. Dream on, Hildy. For one thing, who would believe it? For another, the CC wouldn't confirm it—he told me so—and without at least one source for confirmation, even Walter wouldn't dare run the story. How to dig up any evidence of such a thing was far beyond my puny powers of investigation.

But one thought kept coming back to me. And I had to ask him about it.

"You mentioned a virus," I said. "You said you wondered if you might have caught this urge to die from all the humans who've been killing themselves."

"Yes?"

"Well, how do you know you caught it from us? Maybe we got it from you."

For the CC, a trillionth of a second is … oh, I don't know, at *least* a few days in my perception of time. He was quiet for twenty seconds. Then he looked into my eyes.

"Now *there's* an interesting idea," he said.

Douglas Coupland

An influential writer in pop culture circles, Douglas Coupland (b. 1961), who first branded sixties-something babies as "generation X," has written several novels, including *Life After God* (1997), *Polaroids from the Dead* (1997), *Generation X: Tales for an Accelerated Culture* (1991), *Microserfs*, *Girlfriend in a Coma* (1998), and *Miss Wyoming* (2000).

Microserfs holds up the accelerated culture that Coupland created in *Generation X* for closer scrutiny. Rather than spaced-out software on alien worlds, the pop-technology that simultaneously enhances and enslaves the players here is stuff we all are familiar with: cell phones, VCRs, fax machines, email; the list goes on. Dubbed Microserfs because they toil on the Microsoft campuses of Seattle, the characters are smart, cynical, struggling, and tightly knit, a literary version of the television sitcom, *Friends*. Ultimately an exposé of the silicon corporate climate, *Microserfs* explores the impact of science fiction on the "computer geek culture." As Coupland's character Daniel says, Microsoft is "such a sci-fi place to work." In the following excerpt, we meet Microserfs who grapple with questions of how best to manage technology and life and who often resort to memories of scenes from science fiction T.V. shows and movies in order to illustrate their feelings. In trying to determine their place in nature, they contemplate the kinship among animals, humans, and machines. While Coupland's reliance on pop-art personas might suggest an unassailable flippancy, he in fact is very environmentally conscious. Coupland lives in Vancouver, British Columbia.

from *Microserfs*

Friday

EARLY FALL, 1993

THIS MORNING, JUST AFTER 11:00, MICHAEL LOCKED HIMSELF IN his office and he won't come out.

Bill (Bill!) sent Michael this totally wicked flame-mail from hell on the e-mail system—and he just whaled on a chunk of code Michael had written. Using the *Bloom County*-cartoons-taped-on-the-door index, Michael is certainly the most sensitive coder in Building Seven—not the type to take criticism easily. Exactly why Bill would choose Michael of all people to whale on is confusing.

We figured it must have been a random quality check to keep the troops in line. Bill's so smart.

Bill is wise.

Bill is kind.

Bill is benevolent.

Bill, Be My Friend ... *Please!*

Actually, nobody on our floor has ever been flamed by Bill personally. The episode was tinged with glamour and we were somewhat jealous. I tried to tell Michael this, but he was crushed.

Shortly before lunch he stood like a lump outside my office. His skin was pale like rising bread dough, and his Toppy's cut was dripping sweat, leaving little damp marks on the oyster-gray-with-plum highlights of the Microsoft carpeting. He handed me a printout of Bill's memo and then gallumphed into his office, where he's been burrowed ever since.

He won't answer his phone, respond to e-mail, or open his door. On his doorknob he placed a "Do Not Disturb" thingy stolen from the Boston Radisson during last year's Macworld Expo. Todd and I walked out onto the side lawn to try to peek in his window, but his Venetian blinds were closed and a gardener with a leaf blower chased us away with a spray of grass clippings.

They mow the lawn every ten minutes at Microsoft. It looks like green Lego pads.

Finally, at about 2:30 A.M., Todd and I got concerned about Michael's not eating, so we drove to the 24-hour Safeway in Redmond. We went shopping for "flat" foods to slip underneath Michael's door.

The Safeway was completely empty save for us and a few other Microsoft people just like us—hair-trigger geeks in pursuit of just the right snack. Because of all the rich nerds living around here, Redmond and Bellevue are very "on-demand" neighborhoods. Nerds get what they want when they want it, and they go psycho if it's not immediately available. Nerds overfocus. I guess that's the problem. But it's precisely this ability to narrow-focus that makes them so good at code writing: one line at a time, one line in a strand of millions.

When we returned to Building Seven at 3:00 A.M., there were still a few people grinding away. Our group is scheduled to ship product (RTM: Release to Manufacturing) in just eleven days (Top Secret: We'll never make it).

Michael's office lights were on, but once again, when we knocked, he wouldn't answer his door. We heard his keyboard chatter, so we figured he was still alive. The situation really begged a discussion of Turing logic— could we have discerned that the entity behind the door was indeed even human? We slid Kraft singles, Premium Plus crackers, Pop-Tarts, grape leather, and Freezie-Pops in to him.

Todd asked me, "Do you think any of this violates geek dietary laws?"

Just then, Karla in the office across the hall screamed and then glared out at us from her doorway. Her eyes were all red and sore behind her round glasses. She said, "You guys are only encouraging him," like we were feeding a raccoon or something. I don't think Karla ever sleeps.

She harrumphed and slammed her door closed. Doors sure are important to nerds.

Anyway, by this point Todd and I were both really tired. We drove back to the house to crash, each in our separate cars, through the Campus grounds—22 buildings' worth of nerd-cosseting fun—cloistered by 100-foot-tall second growth timber, its streets quiet as the womb: the foundry of our culture's deepest dreams.

There was mist floating on the ground above the soccer fields outside the central buildings. I thought about the e-mail and Bill and all of that, and I had this weird feeling—of how the presence of Bill floats about the Campus, semi-visible, at all times, kind of like the dead grandfather in the *Family Circus* cartoons. Bill is a moral force, a spectral force, a force that shapes, a force that molds. A force with thick, thick glasses.

I am **danielu@microsoft.com**. If my life was a game of *Jeopardy!* my seven dream categories would be:
- Tandy products
- Trash TV of the late '70s and early '80s
- The history of Apple
- Career anxieties

- Tabloids
- Plant life of the Pacific Northwest
- Jell-O 1-2-3

I am a tester—a bug checker in Building Seven. I worked my way up the ladder from Product Support Services (PSS) where I spent six months in phone purgatory in 1991 helping little old ladies format their Christmas mailing lists on Microsoft Works.

Like most Microsoft employees, I consider myself too well-adjusted to be working here, even though I am 26 and my universe consists of home, Microsoft, and Costco.

I am originally from Bellingham, up just near the border, but my parents live in Palo Alto now. I live in a group house with five other Microsoft employees: Todd, Susan, Bug Barbecue, Michael, and Abe.

We call ourselves "The Channel Three News Team."

I am single. I think partly this is because Microsoft is not conducive to relationships. Last year down at the Apple Worldwide Developer's Conference in San Jose, I met a girl who works not too far away, at Hewlett-Packard on Interstate 90, but it never went anywhere. Sometimes I'll sort of get something going, but then work takes over my life and I bail out of all my commitments and things fizzle.

Lately I've been unable to sleep. That's why I've begun writing this journal late at night, to try to see the patterns in my life. From this I hope to establish what my problem is—and then, hopefully, solve it. I'm trying to feel more well adjusted than I really am, which is, I guess, the human condition. My life is lived day to day, one line of bug-free code at a time.

The house:

Growing up, I used to build split-level ranch-type homes out of Legos. This is pretty much the house I live in now, but its ambiance is anything but sterilized Lego-clean. It was built about twenty years ago, maybe before Microsoft was even in the dream stage and this part of Redmond had a lost, alpine ski-cabin feel.

Instead of a green plastic pad with little plastic nubblies, our house sits on a thickly-treed lot beside a park on a cul-de-sac at the top of a steep hill. It's only a seven-minute drive from Campus. There are two other Microsoft group houses just down the hill. Karla, actually, lives in the house three down from us across the street.

People end up living in group houses either by e-mail or by word of mouth. Living in a group house is a little bit like admitting you're deficient in the having-a-life department, but at work you spend your entire life crunching code and testing for bugs, and what else are you supposed to do? Work, sleep, work, sleep, work, sleep. I know a few Microsoft employees who try to fake having a life—many a Redmond garage contains a never-used kayak collecting dust. You ask these people what they do in their spare time and they say, *"Uhhh—kayaking. That's right. I kayak in my spare time."* You can tell they're faking it.

I don't even do many sports anymore and my relationship with my body has gone all weird. I used to play soccer three times a week and now I feel like a boss in charge of an underachiever. I feel like my body is a station wagon in which I drive my brain around, like a suburban mother taking the kids to hockey practice.

The house is covered with dark cedar paneling. Out front there's a tiny patch of lawn covered in miniature yellow crop circles thanks to the dietary excesses of our neighbor's German shepherd, Mishka. Bug Barbecue keeps his weather experiments—funnels and litmus strips and so forth—nailed to the wall beside the front door. A flat of purple petunias long-expired from neglect—Susan's one attempt at prettification—depresses us every time we leave for work in the morning, resting as it does in the thin strip of soil between the driveway and Mishka's crop circles.

Abe, our in-house multimillionaire, used to have tinfoil all over his bedroom windows to keep out what few rays of sun penetrated the trees until we ragged on him so hard that he went out and bought a sheaf of black construction paper at the Pay N Pak and taped it up instead. It looked like a drifter lived here. Todd's only contribution to the house's outer appearance is a collection of car-washing toys sometimes visible beside the garage door. The only evidence of my being in the house is my 1977 AMC Hornet Sportabout hatchback parked out front when I'm home. It's bright orange, it's rusty, and damnit, it's *ugly*.

Saturday

Shipping hell continued again today. Grind, grind, grind. We'll never make it. Have I said that already? Why do we always underestimate our shipping schedules? I just don't understand. In at 9:30 A.M.; out at 11:30 P.M. Domino's for dinner. And three diet Cokes.

I got bored a few times today and checked the WinQuote on my screen— that's the extension that gives continuous updates on Microsoft's NASDAQ price. It was Saturday, and there was never any change, but I kept forgetting. Habit. Maybe the Tokyo or Hong Kong exchanges might cause a fluctuation?

Most staffers peek at WinQuote a few times a day. I mean, if you have 10,000 shares (and tons of staff members have way more) and the stock goes up a buck, you've just made ten grand! But then, if it goes down two dollars, you've just lost twenty grand. It's a real psychic yo-yo. Last April Fool's Day, someone fluctuated the price up and down by fifty dollars and half the staff had coronaries.

Because I started out low on the food chain and worked my way up, I didn't get much stock offered to me the way that programmers and systems designers get stock firehosed onto them when they start. What stock I do own won't fully vest for another 2.5 years (stock takes 4.5 years to fully vest).

Susan's stock vests later this week, and she's going to have a vesting party. And then she's going to quit. Larger social forces are at work, threatening to dissolve our group house.

The stock closed up $1.75 on Friday. Bill has 78,000,000 shares, so that means he's now $136.5 million richer. I have almost no stock, and this means I am a loser.

News update: Michael is now out of his office. It's as if he never had his geek episode. He slept there throughout the whole day (not unusual at Microsoft), using his *Jurassic Park* inflatable T-Rex toy as a pillow. When he woke up in the early evening, he thanked me for bringing him the Kraft products, and now he says he won't eat anything that's not entirely two dimensional. "Ich bin ein Flatlander," he piped, as he cheerfully sifted through hard copy of the bug-checked code he'd been chugging out. Karla made disgusted clicking noises with her tongue from her office. I think maybe she's in love with Michael.

More details about our group house—Our House of Wayward Mobility.

Because the house receives almost no sun, moss and algae tend to colonize what surfaces they can. There is a cherry tree crippled by a fungus. The rear verandah, built of untreated 2x4's, has quietly rotted away, and the sliding door in the kitchen has been braced shut with a hockey stick to prevent the unwary from straying into the suburban abyss.

The driveway contains six cars: Todd's cherry-red Supra (his life, what little there is of it), my pumpkin Hornet, and four personality-free gray Microsoftmobiles—a Lexus, an Acura Legend, and two Tauri (nerd plural for Taurus). I bet if Bill drove a Shiner's go-cart to work, everybody else would, too.

Inside, each of us has a bedroom. Because of the McDonald's-like turnover in the house, the public rooms—the living room, kitchen, dining room, and basement—are bleak, to say the least. The dormlike atmosphere precludes heavy-duty interior design ideas. In the living room are two velveteen sofas that were too big and too ugly for some long-gone tenants to take with them. Littered about the Tiki green shag carpet are:

- Two Microsoft Works PC inflatable beach cushions
- One Mitsubishi 27-inch color TV
- Various vitamin bottles
- Several weight-gaining system cartons (mine)
- 86 copies of *Mac WEEK* arranged in chronological order by Bug Barbecue, who will go berserk if you so much as move one issue out of date
- Six Microsoft Project 2.0 juggling bean bags
- Bone-shaped chew toys for when Mishka visits
- Two PowerBooks
- Three IKEA mugs encrusted with last month's blender drink sensation
- Two 12.5-pound dumbbells (Susan's)
- A Windows NT box
- Three baseball caps (two Mariners, one A's)
- Abe's Battlestar Galactica trading card album
- Todd's pile of books on how to change your life to win! *(Getting Past OK, 7 Habits of Highly Effective People …)*

The kitchen is stocked with ramshackle 1970s avocado green appliances. You can almost hear the ghost of Emily Hartley yelling "Hi, Bob!" every time you open the fridge door (a sea of magnets and 4-x-6-inch photos of last year's house parties).

Our mail is in little piles by the front door: bills, Star Trek junk mail, and the heap-o-catalogues next to the phone.

I think we'd order our lives via 1-800 numbers if we could.

Mom phoned from Palo Alto. This is the time of year she calls a lot. She calls because she wants to speak about Jed, but none of us in the family are able. We kind of erased him.

I used to have a younger brother named Jed. He drowned in a boating accident in the Strait of Juan de Fuca when I was 14 and he was 12. A Labor Day statistic.

To this day, anything Labor Day-ish creeps me out: the smell of barbecuing salmon, life preservers, Interstate traffic reports from the local radio Traffic Copter, Monday holidays. But here's a secret: My e-mail password is *hellojed.* So I think about him every day. He was way better with computers than I was. He was way nerdier than me.

As it turned out, Mom had good news today. Dad has a big meeting Monday with his company. Mom and Dad figure it's a promotion because Dad's IBM division has been doing so well (by IBM standards— it's not hemorrhaging money). She says she'll keep me posted.

Susan taped laser-printed notes on all of our bedroom doors reminding us about the vesting party this Thursday ("Vest Fest '93"), which was a subliminal hint to us to clean up the place. Most of us work in Building Seven; shipping hell has brought a severe breakdown in cleanup codes.

    Susan is 26 and works in Mac Applications. If Susan were a *Jeopardy!* contestant, her dream board would be:.
- 680X0 assembly language
- Cats
- Early '80s haircut bands
- "My secret affair with Rob in the Excel Group"
- License plate slogans of America
- Plot lines from *The Monkees*
- The death of IBM

Susan's an IBM brat and hates that company with a passion. She credits it with ruining her youth by transferring her family eight times before she graduated from high school—and the punchline is that the company gave her father the boot last year during a wave of restructuring. So nothing too evil can happen to IBM in her eyes. Her graphic designer friend made up T-shirts saying "IBM: Weak as a Kitten, Dumb as a Sack of Hammers." We all wear them. I gave one to Dad last Christmas but his reaction didn't score too high on the chuckle-o-meter. (I am not an IBM brat—Dad was teaching at Western Washington University until the siren of industry lured him to Palo Alto in 1985. It was very '80s.)

    Susan's a real coding machine. But her abilities are totally wasted reworking old code for something like the Norwegian Macintosh version of Word 5.8. Susan's work ethic best sums up the ethic of most of the people I've met who work at Microsoft. If I recall her philosophy from the conversation she had with her younger sister two weekends ago, it goes something like this:

    "It's never been, 'We're doing this for the good of society.' It's always been us taking an intellectual pride in putting out a good product—and making money. If putting a computer on every desktop and in every home didn't make money, we wouldn't do it."

That sums up most of the Microsoft people I know.

Microsoft, like any office, is a status theme park. Here's a quick rundown:

  • Profitable projects are galactically higher in status than loser (not quite as profitable) projects.

  • Microsoft at Work (Digital Office) is sexiest at the moment. Fortune 500 companies are drooling over DO because it'll allow them to downsize millions of employees. Basically, DO allows you to operate your fax, phone, copier—all of your office stuff—from your PC.

  • Cash cows like Word are profitable but not really considered cutting edge.

  • Working on-Campus is higher status than being relegated to one of the off-Campus Siberias.

  • Having Pentium-driven hardware (built to the hilt) in your office is higher status than having 486 droneware.

  • Having technical knowledge is way up there.

  • Being an architect is also way up there.

  • Having Bill-o-centric contacts is way, way up there.

  • Shipping your product on time is maybe the coolest (insert wave of anxiety here). If you ship a product you get a Ship-It award: a 12-x-15-x-1-inch Lucite slab—but you have to pretend it's no big deal. Michael has a Ship-It award and we've tried various times to destroy it—blowtorching, throwing it off the verandah, dowsing it with acetone to dissolve it—nothing works. It's so permanent, it's frightening.

More roommate profiles:

First, Abe. If Abe were a *Jeopardy!* contestant, his seven dream categories would be:

  • Intel assembly language
  • Bulk shopping
  • C++
  • Introversion
  • "I love my aquarium"
  • How to have millions of dollars and not let it affect your life in any way
  • Unclean laundry

Abe is sort of like the household Monopoly-game banker. He collects our monthly checks for the landlord, $235 apiece. The man has millions and he rents! He's been at the group house since 1984, when he was hired fresh out of MIT. (The rest of us have been here, on average, about eight months apiece.) After ten years of writing code, Abe so far shows no signs of getting a life. He seems happy to be reaching the age of 30 in just four months with nothing to his name but a variety of neat-o consumer electronics and boxes of Costco products purchased in rash moments of Costco-scale madness ("Ten thousand straws! Just think of it—only $10 and I'll never need to buy straws ever again!") These products line the walls of his room, giving it the feel of an air-raid shelter.

Bonus detail: There are dried-out patches of sneeze spray all over Abe's monitors. You'd think he could afford 24 bottles of Windex.

Next, Todd. Todd's seven *Jeopardy!* categories would be:
- Your body is your temple
- Baseball hats
- Meals made from combinations of Costco products
- Psychotically religious parents
- Frequent and empty sex
- SEGA Genesis gaming addiction
- The Supra

Todd works as a tester with me. He's really young—22—the way Microsoft employees all used to be. His interest is entirely in girls, bug testing, his Supra, and his body, which he buffs religiously at the Pro Club gym and feeds with peanut butter quesadillas, bananas, and protein drinks.

Todd is historically empty. He neither knows nor cares about the past. He reads *Car and Driver* and fields three phone calls a week from his parents who believe that computers are "the Devil's voice box," and who try to persuade him to return home to Port Angeles and speak with the youth pastor.

Todd's the most fun of all the house members because he is all impulse and no consideration. He's also the only roomie to have clean laundry consistently. In a crunch you can always borrow an unsoiled shirt from Todd.

Bug Barbecue's seven *Jeopardy!* categories would be:
- Bitterness
- Xerox PARC nostalgia
- Macintosh products
- More bitterness
- Psychotic loser friends
- Jazz
- Still more bitterness

Bug Barbecue is the World's Most Bitter Man. He is (as his name implies) a tester with me at Building Seven. His have-a-life factor is pretty near zero. He has the smallest, darkest room in the house, in which he maintains two small shrines: one to his Sinclair ZX-81, his first computer, and the other to supermodel Elle MacPherson. Man, she'd freak if she saw the hundreds of little photos—the coins, the candles, the little notes.

Bug is 31, and he lets everyone know it. If we ever ask him so much as "Hey, Bug—have you seen volume 7 of my *Inside Mac?*" he gives a sneer and replies, "You're obviously of the generation that never built their own motherboard or had to invent their own language."

Hey, Bug—we love you, too.

Bug never gets offered stock by the company. When payday comes and the little white stock option envelopes with red printing reading "Personal and Confidential" end up in all of our pigeonholes, Bug's is always, alas, empty. Maybe they're trying to get rid of him, but it's almost impossible to fire someone at Microsoft. It must drive the administration nuts. They hired 3,100 people in 1992 alone, and you know not all of them were gems.

Oddly, Bug is fanatical in his devotion to Microsoft. It's as if the more they ignore him, the more rabidly he defends their honor. And if you cherish your own personal time, you will not get into a discussion with him over the famous Look-&-Feel lawsuit or any of the FTC or Department of Justice actions:

"These litigious pricks piss me off. I wish they'd compete in the marketplace where it really counts instead of being little wusses and whining for government assistance to compete ..."

You've been warned.

Finally, Michael. Michael's seven *Jeopardy!* categories would be:
- FORTRAN
- Pascal
- Ada (defense contracting code)
- LISP
- Neil Peart (drummer for Rush)
- Hugo and Nebula award winners
- Sir Lancelot

Michael is probably the closest I'll ever come to knowing someone who lives in a mystical state. He lives to assemble elegant streams of code instructions. He's like Mozart to everyone else's Salieri—he enters people's offices where lines of code are written on the dry-erase

whiteboards and quietly optimizes the code as he speaks to them, as
though someone had written wrong instructions on how to get to the
beach and he was merely setting them right so they wouldn't get lost.

He often uses low-tech solutions to high-tech problems: Popsicle
sticks, rubber bands, and little strips of paper that turn on a bent coat
hanger frame help him solve complex matrix problems. When he moved
offices into his new window office (good coder, good office), he had to
put Post-it notes reading "Not Art" on his devices so that the movers
didn't stick them under the glass display cases out in the central atrium
area.

Sunday

This morning before heading to the office I read an in-depth story about
Burt and Loni's divorce in *People* magazine. Thus, 1,474,819 brain cells
that could have been used toward a formula for world peace were
obliterated. Are computer memory and human memory analogous?
Michael would know.

Mid-morning, I mountain-biked over to Nintendo headquarters, across
Interstate 520 from Microsoft.

Now, I've never been to the South African plant of, say, Sandoz
Pharmaceuticals, but I bet it looks a lot like Nintendo headquarters—two-
story industrial-plex buildings sheathed with Death Star—black windows
and landscape trees around the parking lot seemingly clicked into place
with a mouse. It's nearly identical to Microsoft except Microsoft uses sea
foam-green glass on its windows and has big soccer fields should it ever
really need to expand.

I Hacky Sacked for a while with my friend, Marty, and some of his
tester friends during their break. Sunday is a big day for the kids who
man the PSS phone lines there because all of young America is out of
school and using the product. It's really young at Nintendo. It's like the
year 1311, where everyone over 35 is dead or maimed and out of sight
and mind.

All of us got into this big discussion about what sort of software dogs
would design if they could. Marty suggested territory-marking programs
with piss simulators and lick interfaces. Antonella thought of BoneFinder.
Harold thought of a doghouse remodeling CAD system. All very
cartographic/high sensory: lots of visuals.

Then, of course, the subject of catware came up. Antonella suggested
a personal secretary program that tells the world, "No, I do not wish to

be petted. Oh, and hold all my calls." My suggestion was for a program that sleeps all the time.

Anyway, it's a good thing we're human. We design business spreadsheets, paint programs, and word processing equipment. So that tells you where we're at as a species. What is the search for the next great compelling application but a search for the human identity?

It was nice being at Nintendo where everybody's just a little bit younger and hipper than at Microsoft and actually takes part in the Seattle scene. Everyone at Microsoft seems, well, literally 31.2 years old, and it kind of shows.

There's this eerie, science-fiction lack of anyone who doesn't look exactly 31.2 on the Campus. It's oppressive. It seems like only last week the entire Campus went through Gap ribbed-T mania together—and now they're all shopping for the same 3bdrm/2bth dove-gray condo in Kirkland.

Microserfs are locked by nature into doing 31.2-ish things: the first house, the first marriage, the "where-am-I-going" crisis, the out-goes-the-Miata/in-comes-the-minivan thing, and, of course, major death denial. A Microsoft VP died of cancer a few months ago, and it was like, you weren't allowed to mention it. Period. The three things you're not allowed to discuss at work: death, salaries, and your stock options.

I'm 26 and I'm just not ready to turn 31.2 yet.

Actually, I've been thinking about this death denial business quite a bit lately. September always makes me think of Jed. It's as if there's this virtual Jed who might have been. Sometimes I see him when I'm driving by water; I see him standing on a log boom smiling and waving; I see him buckarooing a killer whale in the harbor off downtown while I'm stuck in traffic on the Alaskan Way viaduct. Or I see him walking just ahead of me around the Space Needle restaurant, always just around the curve.

I'd like to hope Jed is happy in the afterworld, but because I was raised without any beliefs, I have no pictures of an afterworld for myself. In the past I have tried to convince myself that there is no life after death, but I have found myself unable to do this, so I guess intuitively I feel there is something. But I just don't know how to begin figuring out what these pictures are.

Over the last few weeks I've been oh-so-casually asking the people I know about their own pictures of the afterworld. I can't simply come right out and ask directly because, as I say, you just don't discuss death at Microsoft.

The results were pretty dismal. Ten people asked, and not one single image. Not one single angel or one bright light or even one single, miserable barbecue briquette. Zero.

Todd was more concerned about who would show up at his funeral.

Bug Barbecue told me all this depressing stuff, of how the constituent elements of his personality weren't around before he was born, so why should he worry about what happens to them afterward?

Susan changed the topic entirely. *("Hey, isn't Louis Gerstner hopeless?")*

Sometimes, in the employee kitchen, when I'm surrounded by the dairy cases full of Bill-supplied free beverages, I have to wonder if maybe Microsoft's corporate zest for recycling aluminum, plastic, and paper is perhaps a sublimation of the staff's hidden desire for immortality. Or maybe this whole Bill thing is actually the subconscious manufacture of God.

After Nintendo I mountain-biked around the Campus, delaying my venture into shipping hell. I saw a cluster of Deadheads looking for magic mushrooms out on the west lawn beside the second-growth forest. Fall is just around the corner.

The trees around Campus are dropping their leaves. It's been strange weather this spring and summer. The newspaper says the trees are confused and they're shedding early this year.

Todd was out on the main lawn training with the Microsoft intramural Frisbee team. I said hello. Everyone looked so young and healthy. I realized that Todd and his early-20s cohorts are the first Microsoft generation—the first group of people who have never known a world without an MS-DOS environment. Time ticks on.

They're also the first generation of Microsoft employees faced with reduced stock options and, for that matter, plateauing stock prices. I guess that makes them mere employees, just like at any other company. Bug Barbecue and I were wondering last week what's going to happen when this new crop of workers reaches its inevitable Seven-Year Programmer's Burnout. At the end of it they won't have two million dollars to move to Hilo and start up a bait shop with, the way the Microsoft old-timers did. Not everyone can move into management.

Discarded.

Face it: You're always just a breath away from a job in telemarketing. Everybody I know at the company has an estimated time of departure and they're all within five years. It must have been so weird—living the way my Dad did—thinking your company was going to take care of you forever.

A few minutes later I bumped into Karla walking across the west lawn. She walks really quickly and she's so small, like a little kid.

It was so odd for both of us, seeing each other outside the oatmeal walls and oyster carpeting of the office. We stopped and sat on the lawn and talked for a while. We shared a feeling of conspiracy by not being inside helping with the shipping deadline.

I asked her if she was looking for 'shrooms with the Deadheads, but she said she was going nuts in her office, and she just had to be in the wild for a few minutes in the forest beside the Campus. I thought this was such an unusual aspect of her personality, I mean, because she's so mousy and indoorsy-looking. It was good to see her and for once to not have her yelling at me to stop being a nuisance. We've worked maybe ten offices apart for half a year, and we've never once really talked to each other.

I showed Karla some birch bark I'd peeled off a tree outside Building Nine and she showed me some scarlet sumac leaves she had found in the forest. I told her about the discussion Marty, Antonella, Harold, and I had been having about dogs and cats over at Nintendo's staff picnic tables. She lay down on the ground and thought about this, so I lay down, too. The sun was hot and good. I could only see the sky and hear her words. She surprised me.

She said that we, as humans, bear the burden of having to be every animal in the world rolled into one.

She said that we really have no identity of our own.

She said, "What is human behavior, except trying to prove that we're not animals?"

She said, "I think we have strayed so far away from our animal origins that we are bent on creating a new, supra-animal identity."

She said, "What are computers but the EveryAnimalMachine?"

I couldn't believe she was talking like this. She was like an episode of *Star Trek* made flesh. It was as if I was falling into a deep, deep hole as I heard her voice speak to me. But then a bumblebee bumbled above us and it stole our attention the way flying things can.

She said, "Imagine being a bee and living in a great big hive. You would have no idea that tomorrow was going to be any different than today. You could return to that same hive a thousand years later and there would be just the same perception of tomorrow as never being any different. Humans are completely different. We assume tomorrow is another world."

I asked her what she meant, and she said, "I mean that the animals live in another sense of time. They can never have a sense of history because they can never see the difference between today and tomorrow."

I juggled some small rocks I found beside me. She said she didn't know I could juggle and I told her it was something I learned by osmosis in my last product group.

We got up and walked together back to Building Seven. I pushed my bike. We walked over the winding white cement path speckled with crow shit, past the fountains, and through the hemlocks and firs.

Things seem different between us now, as if we've somehow agreed to agree. And God, she's skinny! I think I'm going to bring her snacks to eat tomorrow while she works.

I hope this isn't like feeding a raccoon.

Worked until just past midnight and came back home. Had a shower. Three bowls of Corn Flakes and ESPN. My weekends are no different than my weekdays. One of these days I'm going to vanish up to someplace beautiful like Whidbey Island and just veg for two solid days.

Todd is compressing code this week and as a sideline invented what he calls a "Prince Emulator"—a program th@ converts whatever you write into a title of a song by Minnesotan Funkmeister, Prince. I sampled it using part of today's diary.

A few minutz 18r I bumpd in2 Karla walkng akros the west lawn. She walkz rEly kwikly & she'z so smal, like a litl kid.

It wuz so odd 4 both uv us, C-ng Ech uthr outside the otmeel walz + oystr karpetng uv the ofiss. We stopd & s@ on the lawn + talkd 4 a wile. We shared a fElng uv konspiraC by not B-ng inside helpng with the shippng dedline.

I askd hr if she wuz lookng 4 shroomz with the Dedhedz, but she sed she wuz going nutz in hr ofiss, & she just had 2 B in the wild 4 a few minutz in the 4st B-side the Kampus. I thot this wuz such an unuzual aspekt uv hr prsonaliT, I mEn, B-kuz she'z so mowsy + indorzy lookng. It wuz good 2 C hr & 4 once 2 not hav hr yellng @ me 2 stop B-ng a noosanss. We'v wrkd mayB 10 officz apart 4 half a yEr, + we'v nevr once rEly talkd 2 Ech uthr.

I showd Karla sum brch bark I'd pEld off a trE outside Bildng 9 & she showd me sum skarlet soomak lEvz she had found in the 4st. I told hr about the diskussion MarT, AntonLa, Harold, + I had B-n havng about dogz & katz ovr Nin-10-do'z staf piknik tablz. She lA down on the ground + thot about this, so I lA down, 2. The sun wuz hot & good. I kould only C the sky + hear hr wrdz. She srprizd me.

She sed th@ we, az humnz, bear the brdn uv havng 2 B evry animl in the wrld rold in2 1.

She sed th@ we rEly hay no identiT uv our own.

She sed, "Wh@ iz human B-havior, X-ept tryng 2 proov th@ w'r not animalz?"

She sed, "I think we hav strAd so far awA from our animal onginz th@ we R bent on kre8ng a noo, soopra-animal idNtiT."

She sed, "Wh@ R komputrz but the EvryAnimalMashEn?"

I kouldn't B-lEv she wuz talkng like this. She wuz like an episode uv *Star Trek* made flesh. It wuz az if I wuz falng in2 a dEp, dEp hole az I hrd hr voiss speak 2 me. But then a bumbl-B bumbld abuv us & it stole our alOnshun the wA flyng thngz kan.

She sed, "Imagin B-ng a B + livng in a gr8 big hive. You would hav no idea th@ 2morow wuz going 2 B any difrent than 2dA. You kould retrn 2 th@ same hive 1,000 yearz latr & ther would B just the same prception uv 2morow az nevr B-ng any difrent. Humanz R kompletely difrent. We asoom 2morow iz anuthr wrld."

I askd hr wot she ment, + she sed, "I meen th@ the animalz liv in anuthr sens uv time. They kan nevr hav a sens uv history B-kuz they kan nevr C the difrenss B-twEn 2dA & 2morow."

I juggld sum smal rokz I found B-side me. She sed she didnt kno I kould juggl + I told hr it wuz sumthing I lrnd by ozmosis in my last produkt groop.

We got up & walkd 2gethr bak 2 Bildng 7. I pushd my bike. We walkd ovr the windng wite Cment path spekld with krow shit, past the fountunz, + thru the hemlokz & frz.

Monday

Dad got fired! Didn't we see that one coming a mile away. This whole restructuring business.

Mom phoned around 11:00 A.M. and she spent only ten minutes giving me the news. She had to get back to Dad, who was out on the back patio, in shock, looking out over Silicon Valley. She said we'll have to talk longer tomorrow. I got off the phone and my head was buzzing.

The results came in from the overnight stress tests—the tests we run to try to locate bugs in the code—and there were five breaks. Five! So I had my work cut out for me today. Nine days until shipping.

Right.

I telephoned Susan over in Mac Applications. The news about Dad was too important for e-mail, and we had lunch together in the big cafeteria in Building Sixteen that resembles the Food Fair at any halfway decent mall.

Today was Mongolian sticky rice day.

Susan was hardly surprised about IBM dumping Dad. She told me that when she was briefly on the OS/2 version 1.0 team, they sent her to the IBM branch in Boca Raton for two weeks. Apparently IBM was asking people from the data entry department whether they wanted to train to be programmers.

"If they hadn't been doing boneheaded shit like that, your dad would still have a job."

I've been thinking: I get way too many pieces of e-mail, about 60 a day. This is a typical number at Microsoft. E-mail is like highways—if you have them, traffic follows.

I'm an e-mail addict. Everybody at Microsoft is an addict. The future of e-mail usage is being pioneered right here. The cool thing with e-mail is that when you send it, there's no possibility of connecting with the person on the other end. It's better than phone answering machines, because with them, the person on the other line might actually pick up the phone and you might have to talk.

Typically, everybody has about a 40 percent immediate cull rate— those pieces of mail you can delete immediately because of a frivolous tag line. What you read of the remaining 60 percent depends on how much of a life you have. The less of a life, the more mail you read.

Abe has developed a "rules-based" software program that anticipates his e-mail preferences and sifts and culls accordingly. I guess that's sort of like Antonella's personal secretary program for cats.

After lunch, I drove down 156th Avenue to the Uwajimaya Japanese supermarket and bought Karla some seaweed and cucumber rolls. They also sell origami paper by the sheet there, so I threw in some cool colored papers as an extra bonus.

When I got back to the office, I knocked on Karla's door and gave her the rolls and the paper. She seemed glad enough to see me (she didn't scowl) and genuinely surprised that I had brought her something.

She asked me to sit in her office. She has a big poster of a MIPS chip blueprint on her wall and some purple and pink flowers in a bud vase, just like Mary Tyler Moore. She said that it was kind of me to bring her a Japanese seaweed roll and everything, but at the moment she was in the middle of a pack of Skittles. Would I like some?

And so we sat and ate Skittles. I told her about my dad and she just listened. And then she told me that her own father operates a small fruit cannery in Oregon. She said that she learned about coding from canning lines-or rather, she developed a fascination for linear logic processes there—and she actually has a degree in manufacturing processes, not computer programming. And she folded one of those origami birds for me. Her IQ must be about 800.

IQs are one of the weird things about Microsoft—you only find the right-hand side of the bell curve on-Campus. There's nobody who's two-digit. Just one more reason it's such a sci-fi place to work.

Anyway, we started talking more about all of the fiftysomethings being dumped out of the economy by downsizing. No one knows what to do with these people, and it's so sad, because being 50 nowadays isn't like being 50 a hundred years ago when you'd probably be dead.

I told Karla about Bug Barbecue's philosophy: If you can't make yourself worthwhile to society, then that's your problem, not society's. Bug says people are personally responsible for keeping themselves relevant. Somehow, this doesn't seem quite right to me.

Karla speaks with such precision. It's so cool. She said that everyone worrying about rioting senior citizens is probably premature. She said that it's a characteristic of where we are right now on computer technology's ease-of-use curve that fiftysomethings are a bit slow at accepting technology.

"Our generation has all of the characteristics needed to be in the early-adopter group—time for school and no pesky unlearning to be done. But the barriers for user acceptance should be vanishing soon enough for fiftysomethings."

This made me feel better for Dad.

Michael came by just then to ask about a subroutine and I realized it was time for me to leave. Karla thanked me again for the food, and I was glad I had brought it along.

Caroline from the Word offices in Building Sixteen sent e-mail regarding the word "nerd." She says the word only came into vogue around the late '70s when *Happy Days* was big on TV— eerily the same time that the PC was being popularized. She said prior to that, there was no everyday application for the word, "and now nerds run the world!"

Abe said something interesting. He said that because everyone's so poor these days, the '90s will be a decade with no architectural legacy or style-everyone's too poor to put up new buildings. He said that code is the architecture of the '90s.

I walked by Michael's office around sundown, just before I left for home for a shower and a snack before coming back to stomp the bugs. He was playing a game on his monitor screen I'd never seen before.

I asked him what it was and he told me it was something he had designed himself. It was a game about a beautiful kingdom on the edge of the world that saw time coming to an end.

However, the kingdom had found a way to trick God. It did this by converting its world into code—into bits of light and electricity that would keep pace with time as it raced away from them. And thus the kingdom would live forever, after time had come to an end.

Michael said the citizens of the kingdom were allowed to do this because they had made it to the end of history without ever having had the blood of war spill on their soil. He said it would have been an affront to all good souls who had worked for a better world over the millennia not to engineer a system for preserving finer thoughts after the millennium arrived and all ideologies died and people became animals once more.

"Well," I said after he finished, "how about those Mariners!"

Oh—Abe bought a trampoline. He went to Costco to stock up on Jif, and he ended up buying a trampoline—14-x-14-foot, 196 square feet of bouncy aerobic fun. Since when do grocery stores sell trampolines? What a screwy decade. I guess that's what it's like to be a millionaire.

The delivery guys dropped it off and around midnight we set it up in the front yard, over the crop circles, chaining one of the legs to the front railing. Bug Barbecue is already printing up a release he's going to make Abe have all the neighbors with kids sign, absolving Abe of any blame in the event of an accident.

Tuesday

Woke up super early today, after only four hours' sleep, to a watery light outside. High overcast clouds. Through my window I saw a plane fly over the house, headed into SeaTac, and it made me remember when 747s first came out. Boeing had a PR photo of a kid building a house of cards in the lounge up in the bubble. God, I wanted to be that kid. Then I got to wondering, Why am I bothering to get up? What is the essential idea that gets me out of bed and through the day? What is it that gets anybody out of bed? I figure I still want to be that kid building a house of cards in a 747.

I sandpapered the roof of my mouth with three bowls of Cap'n Crunch-had raw gobbets of mouth-beef dangling onto my tongue all day. It hurt like crazy, and it made me talk with a Cindy Brady lisp until late afternoon.

Spent two hours in the morning trapped in a room with the Pol Pots from Marketing. God, they never stop—like we don't have anything better to do eight days before shipping. Even the bug testers. Like, we're supposed to see a box of free DoveBars and say, "Oh—it's okay then— please, please waste my time."

I think everyone hates and dreads Marketing's meetings because of how these meetings alter your personality. At meetings you have to explain what you've accomplished, so naturally you fluff up your work a bit, like pillows on a couch. You end up becoming this perky, gung-ho version of yourself that you know is just revolting. I have noticed that everybody looks down upon the gung-ho type people at Microsoft, but nobody considers themselves gung-ho. They should just see themselves at these meetings, all fratboy and chipper. Fortunately, gung-ho-ishness seems confined exclusively to marketing meetings. Otherwise I think the Campus is utterly casual.

Oh, and sometimes you get flame meetings. They're fun, too—when everyone flames everyone else.

Today's meeting was about niggly little shipping details and was numbingly dull. And then, near the end, a Motorola pager owned by Kent, one of the Marketing guys, went off on top of the table. It buzzed like a hornet and shimmied and twitched across the table in a dance of death. It was mesmerizing, like watching a tarantula scamper across the table. It killed all conversation dead. Killed it right on the spot.

My smiling-muscles hurt as a result of the meeting. On top of my Cap'n Crunch mouth. A bad mouth day.

I called Mom right after the meeting and Dad answered the phone. I heard Oprah on in the background, and I didn't think that was a good omen. Dad sounded upbeat, but isn't that a part of the process? Denial? I asked him if he was watching Oprah and he said he had only come into the house for a snack.

Mom came on the phone on the extension, and once Dad was off the line, she confided that he barely slept the night before, and when he did, he made haunted moaning noises. And then this morning he dressed, as though headed to the office, and sat watching TV, being eerily chipper, refusing to talk about what his plans were. Then he went out into the garage to work on his model train world.

I learned a new word today: "trepanation"—drilling a hole in the skull to relieve pressure on the brain.

Karla came into my office this morning—a first—just as I was logging onto my e-mail for the morning. She was holding a big cardboard box full of acrylic Windows coffee mugs from the company store in Building Fourtéen. "Guess what everyone in the Karla universe is getting for Christmas this year?" she asked cheerfully. "They're on sale." There was a pause. "You want one, Dan?"

I said that I drink too much coffee and colas, and that I'm a colon cancer statistic just waiting to happen. I said I'd love one. She handed it to me and there was a pause as she looked around my office: an NEC MultiSync monitor; a Compaq workhorse monitor; a framed Jazz poster; a "Mac Hugger" bumper sticker on my ceiling and my black-and-white photo shrine to Microsoft VP Steve Ballmer. "The shrine started as a joke," I said, "but it's sort of taking on a life of its own now. It's getting scary. Shall we worship?"

It was then that she asked me, in a lowered tone, "Who's Jed?"

She had seen me keyboard in my password—like HAL from *2001*.

And so I closed the door and told her about Jed, and you know, I was glad I was able to tell someone at last.

Mid-afternoon, Bug, Todd, Michael, and I grabbed some road-Snapples in the kitchen and headed over to pick up some manuals at the library, out behind the Administration building. It was more of a fresh-air jaunt than anything else.

It was raining quite heavily, but Bug pulled his usual stunt. He made us all walk through the Campus's forest undergrowth instead of simply taking the pleasant winding path that meanders through the Campus trees—the Microsoft path that speaks of Ewoks and Smurfs amid the salal, ornamental plums, rhododendrons, Japanese maple, arbutus, huckleberry, hemlock, cedars, and firs.

Bug believes that Bill sits at his window in the Admin Building and watches how staffers walk across the Campus. Bug believes that Bill keeps note of who avoids the paths and uses the fastest routes to get from A to B, and that Bill rewards these devil-may-care trailblazers, with promotions and stock, in the belief that their code will be just as innovative and dashing.

We all ended up soaking wet, with Oregon Grape stains on our Dockers by the time we got to the library, and on the way back we read the Riot Act and said that Bug had to stop geeking out and learn to enculturate, and that for his own good he should take the path—and he agreed. But we could see that it was killing Bug—literally killing him—to have to walk along the path past where Bill's office is supposed to be.

Todd toyed with Bug and got him going on the subject of Xerox PARC, thus getting Bug all bitter and foaming. Bug is still in a sort of perpetual grief that Xerox PARC dropped the football on so many projects.

And then Michael, who had been silent up to now, said, "Hey—if you cut over this berm, it's a little faster," and he cut off the path, and Bug's eyes just about popped out of his head, and Michael found a not bad shortcut. Right outside the Admin Building.

I realize I haven't seen a movie in six months. I think the last one was *Curly Sue* on the flight to Macworld Expo, and that hardly counted. I really need a life, bad.

It turns out Abe has entrepreneurial aspirations. We had dinner in the downstairs cafeteria together (Indonesian Bamay with frozen yogurt and double espresso). He's thinking of quitting and becoming a pixelation broker—going around to museums and buying the right to digitize their paintings. It's a very "Rich Microsoft" thing to do. Microsoft's millionaires are the first generation of North American nerd wealth.

Once Microsofters' ships come in, they travel all over: Scotland and Patagonia and Thailand … *Condé Nast Traveler-ish* places. They buy Shaker furniture, Saabs, koi, Pilchuck glass, native art, and 401(k)s to the max. The ultrarichies build fantasy homes on the Sammammish Plateau loaded with electronic toys.

It's all low-key spending, mostly, and fresh and fun. Nobody's buying crypts, I notice—though when the time comes that they do, said crypts will no doubt be emerald and purple colored, and lined with Velcro and Gore-Tex.

Abe, like most people here, is a fiscal Republican, but otherwise, pretty empty-file in the ideology department. Vesting turns most people into fiscal Republicans, I've noticed.

The day went quickly. The rain is back again, which is nice. The summer was too hot and too dry for a Washington boy like me.

I am going to bring in some Japanese UFO-brand yaki soba tomorrow and see if Karla is into lunch. She needs carbs. Skittles and aspartame is no diet for a coder.

Well, actually, it is.

A thought: Sometimes the clouds and sunlight will form in a way you've never seen them do before, and your city will feel as if it's another city altogether. On the Campus today at sunset, people were stopping on the grass watching the sun turn stove-filament orange through the rain clouds.

It's just something I noticed. It made me realize that the sun is really built of fire. It made me feel like an animal, not a human.

Worked until 1:30 A.M. When I got in, Abe was down in his microbrewery in the garage, puttering amid the stacks of furniture handed down by parents—stuff too ugly to meet even the minimal taste standards of the upstairs rooms, the piles of golf clubs, the mountain bikes, and a line of suitcases, perched like greyhounds awaiting the word GO!

Bug was locked behind his door, but by the smell I could tell he was eating a microwaved Dinty Moore product.

Susan was in the living room asleep in front of a taped *Seinfeld* episode.

Todd was obsessively folding his shirts in his room.

Michael was rereading *The Chronicles of Narnia* for the 87th time.

A nice average night.

I went into my room, which, like all six of the bedrooms here, is filled up almost completely with a bed, with walls lined with IKEA "Billy" bookshelves and stereo equipment, jazz posters and Sierra Club calendars. On my desk sits a Sudafed box and a pile of stones from a beach in Oregon. My PC is hooked up by modem to the Campus.

Had a Tab (a Bill favorite) and some microwave popcorn and did some unfinished work.

Neal Stephenson

eir to William Gibson in the eyes of many cyberlit lovers, Neal Stephenson (b. 1959) is, according to Bruce Sterling, "the first second-generation native cyberpunk science fiction writer." Stephenson differs from the 1980s originators of the field in an important way: complex technology was a daily part of his young adult life, and he is an expert hacker who intimately knows the technology he writes about. His works include *The Big U* (1984), *Zodiac: The Eco-thriller* (1988), *Interface* (1994), which Stephenson co-wrote under the pseudonym Stephen Bury, *The Diamond Age*, and *Cryptonomicon* (1999). He lives in Seattle.

In *The Diamond Age*, Stephenson explores the emerging "nanotechnology," a subatomic tinkertoy biotechnology that has been called the alchemy of the twenty-first century. Scientists speculate that someday we will be able to manipulate and arrange individual atoms and molecules one by one to construct any substance that we like. Stephenson's artificially created ecosystems complement the ecolit tradition, while his use of complexity theory, neotribalism, and behavioral discipline tap into mainstream environmental and cultural studies. Nanotechnology in particular has been touted as a magical cure for hunger and poverty, as food and other basic necessities can simply be manufactured like so many cars coming off an assembly line. Stephenson questions this assumption, suggesting instead that the power brokers who dominate society will abuse the technology to increase and safeguard their status, rank, and wealth.

In the following scene, a Disneyfied Atlantis created for one day for the birthday party of Princess Charlotte hyperbolically expands on the Jurassic Park theme. It becomes an image for expensive and innovative scientific research used exclusively as entertainment for selective circles rather than to resolve the problem of mass impoverishment of the lower class. In this era of conformity and rigid hierarchy, Lord Finkle-McGraw wants John Hackworth to embark on a new project, creating an educational primer intended for princesses such as his own daughter, Elizabeth, to re-invigorate the Neo-Victorian phyle or tribe which has slipped into the complacency of "a season of unperilous choice." John Hackworth's first subversive act is to attempt to steal a copy of this primer for his own daughter, Fiona. This act becomes the catalyst for the primer accidentally falling into the hands of Nell, a member of the lower class.

from *The Diamond Age*

Source Victoria; description of its environs.

Source Victoria's air intakes erupted from the summit of
the Royal Ecological Conservatory like a spray of hundred-meter-long
calla lilies. Below, the analogy was perfected by an inverted tree of
rootlike plumbing that spread fractally through the diamondoid bedrock
of New Chusan, terminating in the warm water of the South China Sea
as numberless capillaries arranged in a belt around the smartcoral reef,
several dozen meters beneath the surface. One big huge pipe gulping up
seawater would have done roughly the same thing, just as the lilies
could have been replaced by one howling maw, birds and litter
whacking into a bloody grid somewhere before they could gum up the
works.

But it wouldn't have been ecological. The geotects of Imperial
Tectonics would not have known an ecosystem if they'd been living in
the middle of one. But they did know that ecosystems were especially
tiresome when they got fubared, so they protected the environment with
the same implacable, plodding, green-visored mentality that they applied
to designing overpasses and culverts. Thus, water seeped into Source
Victoria through microtubes, much the same way it seeped into a beach,
and air wafted into it silently down the artfully skewed exponential horns
of those thrusting calla lilies, each horn a point in parameter space not
awfully far from some central ideal. They were strong enough to
withstand typhoons but flexible enough to rustle in a breeze. Birds,
wandering inside, sensed a gradient in the air, pulling them down into
night, and simply chose to fly out. They didn't even get scared enough to
shit.

The lilies sprouted from a stadium-sized cut-crystal vase, the
Diamond Palace, which was open to the public. Tourists, aerobicizing
pensioners, and ranks of uniformed schoolchildren marched through it
year in and year out, peering through walls of glass (actually solid
diamond, which was cheaper) at various phases of the molecular
disassembly line that was Source Victoria. Dirty air and dirty water came
in and pooled in tanks. Next to each tank was another tank containing
slightly cleaner air or cleaner water. Repeat several dozen times. The
tanks at the end were filled with perfectly clean nitrogen gas and
perfectly clean water.

The line of tanks was referred to as a cascade, a rather abstract bit of
engineer's whimsy lost on the tourists who did not see anything
snapshot-worthy there. All the action took place in the walls separating

the tanks, which were not really walls but nearly infinite grids of submicroscopic wheels, ever-rotating and many-spoked. Each spoke grabbed a nitrogen or water molecule on the dirty side and released it after spinning around to the clean side. Things that weren't nitrogen or water didn't get grabbed, hence didn't make it through. There were also wheels for grabbing handy trace elements like carbon, sulfur, and phosphorus; these were passed along smaller, parallel cascades until they were also perfectly pure. The immaculate molecules wound up in reservoirs. Some of them got combined with others to make simple but handy molecular widgets. In the end, all of them were funneled into a bundle of molecular conveyor belts known as the Feed, of which Source Victoria, and the other half-dozen Sources of Atlantis/Shanghai, were the fountainheads.

Sunrise found the three airships hovering over the South China Sea, no land visible. The ocean was relatively shallow here, but only Hackworth and a few other engineers knew that. The Hackworths had a passable view from their stateroom window, but John woke up early and staked out a place on the diamond floor of the ballroom, ordered an espresso and a Times from a waiter, and passed the time pleasantly while Gwen and Fiona got themselves ready for the day. All around them he could hear children speculating on what was about to happen.

Gwen and Fiona arrived just late enough to make it interesting for John, who took his mechanical pocket watch out at least a dozen times as he waited, and finally ended up clutching it in one hand, nervously popping the lid open and shut. Gwen folded her long legs and spread her skirts out prettily on the transparent floor, drawing vituperative looks from several women who remained standing. But John was relieved to see that most of these women were relatively low-ranking engineers or their wives; none of the higher-ups needed to come to the ballroom.

Fiona collapsed to her hands and knees and practically shoved her face against the diamond, her fundament aloft. Hackworth gripped the creases of his trousers, hitched them up just a bit, and sank to one knee.

The smart coral burst out of the depths with violence that shocked Hackworth, even though he'd been in on the design, seen the trial runs. Viewed through the dark surface of the Pacific, it was like watching an explosion through a pane of shattered glass. It reminded him of pouring a jet of heavy cream into coffee, watching it rebound from the bottom of the cup in a turbulent fractal bloom that solidified just as it dashed against the surface. The speed of this process was a carefully planned sleight-of-hand; the smart coral had actually been growing down on the bottom of the ocean for the last three months, drawing its energy from a supercon that they'd grown across the seafloor for the occasion, extracting the necessary atoms directly from the seawater and the gases dissolved therein. The process happening below looked chaotic, and in a way it was; but each lithocule knew exactly where it was supposed to go and what it was supposed to do. They were tetrahedral building blocks of calcium and carbon, the size of poppyseeds, each equipped with a power source, a brain, and a navigational system. They rose from the bottom of the sea at a signal given by Princess Charlotte; she had awakened to find a small present under her pillow, unwrapped it to find a golden whistle on a chain, stood out on her balcony, and blown the whistle.

The coral was converging on the site of the island from all directions, some of the lithocules traveling several kilometers to reach their assigned positions. They displaced a volume of water equal to the island itself, several cubic kilometers in all. The result was furious turbulence, an upswelling in the surface of the ocean that made some of the children scream, thinking it might rise up and snatch the airship out of the sky; and indeed a few drops pelted the ship's diamond belly, prompting the pilot to give her a little more altitude. The curt maneuver forced hearty laughter from all of the fathers in the ballroom, who were delighted by the illusion of danger and the impotence of Nature.

The foam and mist cleared away at some length to reveal a new island, salmon-colored in the light of dawn. Applause and cheers diminished to a professional murmur. The chattering of the astonished children was too loud and high to hear.

It would be a couple of hours yet. Hackworth snapped his fingers for a waiter and ordered fresh fruit, juice, Belgian waffles, more coffee. They might as well enjoy Æther's famous cuisine while the island sprouted castles, fauns, centaurs, and enchanted forests.

Princess Charlotte was the first human to set foot on the enchanted isle, tripping down the gangway of *Atlantis* with a couple of her little friends in tow, all of them looking like tiny wildflowers in their ribboned sun-bonnets, all carrying little baskets for souvenirs, though before long these were handed over to governesses. The Princess faced Æther and Chinook, moored a couple of hundred meters away, and spoke to them in a normal tone of voice that was, however, heard clearly by all; a nanophone was hidden somewhere in the lace collar of her pinafore, tied into phased-audio-array systems grown into the top layers of the island itself.

"I would like to express my gratitude to Lord Finkle-McGraw and all the employees of Machine-Phase Systems Limited for this most wonderful birthday present. Now, children of Atlantis/Shanghai, won't you please join me at my birthday party?"

The children of Atlantis/Shanghai all screamed yes and rampaged down the multifarious gangways of Æther and Chinook, which had all been splayed out for the occasion in hopes of preventing bottlenecks, which might lead to injury or, heaven forbid, rudeness. For the first few moments the children simply burst away from the airships like gas escaping from a bottle. Then they began to converge on sources of wonderment: a centaur, eight feet high if he was an inch, walking across a meadow with his son and daughter cantering around him. Some baby dinosaurs. A cave angling gently into a hillside, bearing promising signs of enchantment. A road winding up another hill toward a ruined castle.

The grownups mostly remained aboard the airships and gave the children a few minutes to flame out, though Lord Finkle-McGraw could be seen making his way toward Atlantis, poking curiously at the earth with his walking-stick, just to make sure it was fit to be trod by royal feet.

A man and a woman descended the gangway of Atlantis: in a floral dress that explored the labile frontier between modesty and summer comfort, accessorized with a matching parasol, Queen Victoria II of Atlantis. In a natty beige linen suit, her husband, the Prince Consort, whose name, lamentably, was Joe. Joe, or Joseph as he was called in official circumstances, stepped down first, moving in a somewhat pompous one-small-step-for-man gait, then turned to face Her Majesty and offered his hand, which she accepted graciously but perfunctorily, as if to remind everyone that she'd done crew at Oxford and had blown off tension during her studies at Stanford B-School with lap-swimming, rollerblading, and jeet kune do. Lord Finkle-McGraw bowed as the royal espadrilles touched down. She extended her hand, and he kissed it, which was racy but allowed if you were old and stylish, like Alexander Chung-Sik Finkle-McGraw.

"We thank Lord Finkle-McGraw, Imperial Tectonics Limited, and Machine-Phase Systems Limited once again for this lovely occasion. Now let us all enjoy these magnificent surroundings before, like the first Atlantis, they sink forever beneath the waves."

The parents of Atlantis/Shanghai strolled down the gangways, though many had retreated to their staterooms to change clothes upon catching sight of what the Queen and Prince Consort were wearing. The big news, already being uploaded to the Times by telescope-wielding fashion columnists on board Æther, was that the parasol was back.

Gwendolyn Hackworth hadn't packed a parasol, but she was untroubled; she'd always had a kind of natural, unconscious alamodality. She and John strolled down onto the island. By the time Hackworth's eyes had adjusted to the sunlight, he was already squatting and rubbing a pinch of soil between his fingertips. Gwen left him to obsess and joined a group of other women, mostly engineers' wives, and even a baronet-level Equity Participant or two.

Hackworth found a concealed path that wound through trees up a hillside to a little grove around a cool, clear pond of fresh water—he tasted it just to be sure. He stood there for a while, looking out over the enchanted island, wondering what Fiona was up to right now. This led to daydreaming: perhaps she had, by some miracle, encountered Princess Charlotte, made friends with her, and was exploring some wonder with her right now. This led him into a long reverie that was interrupted when he realized that someone was quoting poetry to him.

> *"Where had we been, we two, beloved Friend!*
> *If in the season of unperilous choice,*
> *In lieu of wandering, as we did, through vales*
> *Rich with indigenous produce, open ground*
> *Of Fancy, happy pastures ranged at will,*
> *We had been followed, hourly watched, and noosed,*
> *Each in his several melancholy walk*
> *Stringed like a poor man heifer at its feed,*
> *Led through the lanes in forlorn servitude."*

Hackworth turned to see that an older man was sharing his view. Genetically Asian, with a somewhat twangy North American accent, the man looked at least seventy. His translucent skin was still stretched tight over broad cheekbones, but the eyelids, ears, and the hollows of his cheeks were weathered and wrinkled. Under his pith helmet no fringe of hair showed; the man was completely bald. Hackworth gathered these clues slowly, until at last he realized who stood before him.

"Sounds like Wordsworth," Hackworth said.

The man had been staring out over the meadows below. He cocked his head and looked directly at Hackworth for the first time. "The poem?"

"Judging by content, I'd guess The Prelude."

"Nicely done," the man said.

"John Percival Hackworth at your service." Hackworth stepped toward the other and handed him a card.

"Pleasure," the man said. He did not waste breath introducing himself.

Lord Alexander Chung-Sik Finkle-McGraw was one of several duke-level Equity Lords who had come out of Apthorp. Apthorp was not a formal organization that could be looked up in a phone book; in financial cant, it referred to a strategic alliance of several immense companies, including Machine-Phase Systems Limited and Imperial Tectonics Limited. When no one important was listening, its employees called it John Zaibatsu, much as their forebears of a previous century had referred to the East India Company as John Company.

MPS made consumer goods and ITL made real estate, which was, as ever, where the real money was. Counted by the hectare, it didn't amount to much—just a few strategically placed islands really, counties rather than continents—but it was the most expensive real estate in the world outside of a few blessed places like Tokyo, San Francisco, and Manhattan. The reason was that Imperial Tectonics had geotects, and geotects could make sure that every new piece of land possessed the charms of Frisco, the strategic location of Manhattan, the *feng-shui* of Hong Kong, the dreary but obligatory *Lebensraum* of L.A. It was no longer necessary to send out dirty yokels in coonskin caps to chart the wilderness, kill the abos, and clear-cut the groves; now all you needed was a hot young geotect, a start matter compiler, and a jumbo Source.

Like most other neo-Victorians, Hackworth could recite Finkle-McGraw's biography from memory. The future Duke had been born in Korea and adopted, at the age of six months, by a couple who'd met during grad school in Iowa City and later started an organic farm near the Iowa/South Dakota border.

During his early teens, a passenger jet made an improbable crash-landing at the Sioux City airport, and Finkle-McGraw, along with several other members of his Boy Scout troop who had been hastily mobilized by their scoutmaster, was standing by the runway along with every ambulance, fireman, doctor, and nurse from a radius of several counties. The uncanny efficiency with which the locals responded to the crash was widely publicized and became the subject of a made-for-TV movie. Finkie-McGraw couldn't understand why. They had simply done what was reasonable and humane under the circumstances; why did people from other parts of the country find this so difficult to understand?

This tenuous grasp of American culture might have been owing to the fact that his parents home-schooled him up to the age of fourteen. A typical school day for Finkle-McGraw consisted of walking down to a river to study tadpoles or going to the public library to check out a book on ancient Greece or Rome. The family had little spare money, and vacations consisted of driving to the Rockies for some backpacking, or up to northern Minnesota for canoeing. He probably learned more on his summer vacations than most of his peers did during their school years. Social contact with other children happened mostly through Boy Scouts or church—the Finkle-McGraws belonged to a Methodist church, a Roman Catholic church, and a tiny synagogue that met in a rented room in Sioux City.

His parents enrolled him in a public high school, where he maintained a steady 2.0 average out of a possible 4. The coursework was so stunningly inane, the other children so dull, that Finkle-McGraw developed a poor attitude. He earned some repute as a wrestler and cross-country runner, but never exploited it for sexual favors, which would have been easy enough in the promiscuous climate of the times. He had some measure of the infuriating trait that causes a young man to be a nonconformist for its own sake and found that the surest way to shock most people, in those days, was to believe that some kinds of behavior were bad and others good, and that it was reasonable to live one's life accordingly.

After graduating from high school, he spent a year running certain parts of his parents' agricultural business and then attended Iowa State University of Science and Technology ("Science with Practice") in Ames. He enrolled as an agricultural engineering major and switched to physics after his first quarter. While remaining a nominal physics major for the next three years, he took classes in whatever he wanted: information science, metallurgy, early music. He never earned a degree, not because of poor performance but because of the political climate; like many universities at the time, ISU insisted that its students study a broad range of subjects, including arts and humanities. Finkle-McGraw chose instead to read books, listen to music, and attend plays in his spare time.

One summer, as he was living in Ames and working as a research assistant in a solid-state physics lab, the city was actually turned into an island for a couple of days by an immense flood. Along with many other Midwesterners, Finkle-McGraw put in a few weeks building levees out of sandbags and plastic sheeting. Once again he was struck by the national media coverage—reporters from the coasts kept showing up and announcing, with some bewilderment, that there had been no looting. The lesson learned during the Sioux City plane crash was reinforced. The Los Angeles riots of the previous year provided a vivid counterexample. Finkle-McGraw began to develop an opinion that was to shape his political views in later years, namely, that while people were not genetically different, they were culturally as different as they could possibly be, and that some cultures were simply better than others. This was not a subjective value judgment, merely an observation that some cultures thrived and expanded while others failed. It was a view implicitly shared by nearly everyone but, in those days, never voiced.

Finkle-McGraw left the university without a diploma and went back to the farm, which he managed for a few years while his parents were preoccupied with his mother's breast cancer. After her death, he moved to Minneapolis and took a job with a company founded by one of his former professors, making scanning tunneling microscopes, which at that time were newish devices capable of seeing and manipulating individual atoms. The field was an obscure one then, the clients tended to be large research institutions, and practical applications seemed far away. But it was perfect for a man who wanted to study nanotechnology, and McGraw began doing so, working late at night on his own time. Given his diligence, his self-confidence, his intelligence ("adaptable, relentless, but not really brilliant"), and the basic grasp of business he'd picked up on the farm, it was inevitable that he would become one of the few hundred pioneers of nanotechnological revolution; that his own company, which he founded five years after he moved to Minneapolis, would survive long enough to be absorbed into Apthorp; and that he would navigate Apthorp's political and economic currents well enough to develop a decent equity position.

He still owned the family farm in northwestern Iowa, along with a few hundred thousand acres of adjoining land, which he was turning back into a tall-grass prairie, complete with herds of bison and real Indians who had discovered that riding around on horses hunting wild game was a better deal than pissing yourself in gutters in Minneapolis or Seattle. But for the most part he stayed on New Chusan, which was for all practical purposes his ducal estate.

"Public relations?" said Finkle-McGraw.

"Sir?" Modern etiquette was streamlined; no "Your Grace" or other honorifics were necessary in such an informal setting.

"Your department, sir."

Hackworth had given him his social card, which was appropriate under these circumstances but revealed nothing else. "Engineering. Bespoke."

"Oh, really. I'd thought anyone who could recognise Wordsworth must be one of those artsy sorts in P.R."

"Not in this case, sir. I'm an engineer. Just promoted to Bespoke recently. Did some work on this project, as it happens."

"What sort of work?"

"Oh, P.I. stuff mostly," Hackworth said. Supposedly Finkle-McGraw still kept up with things and would recognize the abbreviation for pseudo-intelligence, and perhaps even appreciate that Hackworth had made this assumption.

Finkle-McGraw brightened a bit. "You know, when I was a lad they called it A.I. Artificial intelligence."

Hackworth allowed himself a tight, narrow, and brief smile. "Well, there's something to be said for cheekiness, I suppose."

"In what way was pseudo-intelligence used here?"

"Strictly on MPS's side of the project, sir." Imperial Tectonics had done the island, buildings, and vegetation. Machine-Phase Systems—Hackworth's employer—did anything that moved. "Stereotyped behaviors were fine for the birds, dinosaurs, and so on, but for the centaurs and fauns we wanted more interactivity, something that would provide an illusion of sentience."

"Yes, well done, well done, Mr. Hackworth."

"Thank you, sir."

"Now, I know perfectly well that only the very finest engineers make it to Bespoke. Suppose you tell me how an aficionado of Romantic poets made it into such a position."

Hackworth was taken aback by this and tried to respond without seeming to put on airs. "Surely a man in your position does not see any contradiction—"

"But a man in my position was not responsible for promoting you to Bespoke. A man in an entirely different position was. And I am very much afraid that such men do tend to see a contradiction."

"Yes, I see. Well, sir, I studied English literature in college."

"Ah! So you are not one of those who followed the straight and narrow path to engineering."

"I suppose not, sir.

"And your colleagues at Bespoke?"

"Well, if I understand your question, sir, I would say that, as compared with other departments, a relatively large proportion of Bespoke engineers have had—well, for lack of a better way of describing it, interesting lives."

"And what makes one man's life more interesting than another's?"

"In general, I should say that we find unpredictable or novel things more interesting."

"That is nearly a tautology." But while Lord Finkle-McGraw was not the sort to express feelings promiscuously, he gave the appearance of being nearly satisfied with the way the conversation was going. He turned back toward the view again and watched the children for a minute or so, twisting the point of his walking-stick into the ground as if he were still skeptical of the island's integrity. Then he swept the stick around in an arc that encompassed half the island. "How many of those children do you suppose are destined to lead interesting lives?"

"Well, at least two, sir—Princess Charlotte, and your granddaughter."

"You're quick, Hackworth, and I suspect capable of being devious if not for your staunch moral character," Finkle-McGraw said, not without a certain archness. "Tell me, were your parents subjects, or did you take the Oath?"

"As soon as I turned twenty-one, sir. Her Majesty—at that time, actually, she was still Her Royal Highness—was touring North America, prior to her enrollment at Stanford, and I took the Oath at Trinity Church in Boston."

"Why? You're a clever fellow, not blind to culture like so many engineers. You could have joined the First Distributed Republic or any of a hundred synthetic phyles on the West Coast. You would have had decent prospects and been free from all this"—Finkie-McGraw jabbed his cane at the two big airships—"behavioural discipline that we impose upon ourselves. Why did you impose it on yourself, Mr. Hackworth?"

"Without straying into matters that are strictly personal in nature," Hackworth said carefully, "I knew two kinds of discipline as a child: none at all, and too much. The former leads to degenerate behaviour. When I speak of degeneracy, I am not being priggish, sir—I am alluding to things well known to me, as they made my own childhood less than idyllic."

Finkle-McGraw, perhaps realizing that he had stepped out of bounds, nodded vigorously. "This is a familiar argument, of course."

"Of course, sir. I would not presume to imply that I was the only young person ill-used by what became of my native culture."

"And I do not see such an implication. But many who feel as you do found their way into phyles wherein a much harsher regime prevails and which view us as degenerates."

"My life was not without periods of excessive, unreasoning discipline, usually imposed capriciously by those responsible for laxity in the first place. That combined with my historical studies led me, as many others, to the conclusion that there was little in the previous century worthy of emulation, and that we must look to the nineteenth century instead for stable social models."

"Well done, Hackworth! But you must know that the model to which you allude did not long survive the first Victoria."

"We have outgrown much of the ignorance and resolved many of the internal contradictions that characterised that era."

"Have we, then? How reassuring. And have we resolved them in a way that will ensure that all of those children down there live interesting lives?"

"I must confess that I am too slow to follow you."

"You yourself said that the engineers in the Bespoke department—the very best—had led interesting lives, rather than coming from the straight and narrow. Which implies a correlation, does it not?"

"Clearly."

"This implies, does it not, that in order to raise a generation of children who can reach their full potential, we must find a way to make their lives interesting. And the question I have for you, Mr. Hackworth, is this:

Do you think that our schools accomplish that? Or are they like the schools that Wordsworth complained of?"

"My daughter is too young to attend school—but I should fear that the latter situation prevails."

"I assure you that it does, Mr. Hackworth. My three children were raised in those schools, and I know them well. I am determined that Elizabeth shall be raised differently."

Hackworth felt his face flushing. "Sir, may I remind you that we have just met—I do not feel worthy of the confidences you are reposing in me.

"I'm telling you these things not as a friend, Mr. Hackworth, but as a professional."

"Then I must remind you that I am an engineer, not a child psychologist."

"This I have not forgotten, Mr. Hackworth. You are indeed an engineer, and a very fine one, in a company that I still think of as mine—though as an Equity Lord, I no longer have a formal connection. And now that you have brought your part of this project to a successful conclusion, I intend to put you in charge of a new project for which I have reason to believe you are perfectly suited."

Hackworth's morning ruminations; breakfast and departure for work.

Thinking about tomorrow's crime, John Percival Hackworth slept poorly, rising three times on the pretext of having to use the loo. Each time he looked in on Fiona, who was sprawled out in her white lace nightgown, arms above her head, doing a backflip into the arms of Morpheus. Her face was barely visible in the dark room, like the moon seen through folds of white silk.

At five A.M., a shrill pentatonic reveille erupted from the North Koreans' brutish mediatrons. Their clave, which went by the name Sendero, was not far above sea level: a mile below the Hackworths' building in altitude, and twenty degrees warmer on the average day. But whenever the women's chorus chimed in with their armor-piercing refrain about the all-seeing beneficence of the Serene Leader, it felt as if they were right next door.

Gwendolyn didn't even stir. She would sleep soundly for another hour, or until Tiffany Sue, her lady's maid, came bustling into the room and began to lay out her clothes: stretchy lingerie for the morning workout, a business frock, hat, gloves, and veil for later.

Hackworth drew a silk dressing gown from the wardrobe and poured it over his shoulders. Binding the sash around his waist, the cold tassels splashing over his fingers in the dark, he glanced through the doorway to Gwendolyn's closet and out the other side into her boudoir. Against that room's far windows was the desk she used for social correspondence, really just a table with a top of genuine marble, strewn with bits of stationery, her own and others', dimly identifiable even at this distance as business cards, visiting cards, note cards, invitations from various people still going through triage. Most of the boudoir floor was covered with a tatty carpet, worn through in places all the way down to its underlying matrix of jute, but hand-woven and sculpted by genuine Chinese slave labor during the Mao Dynasty. Its only real function was to protect the floor from Gwendolyn's exercise equipment, which gleamed in the dim light scattering off the clouds from Shanghai: a step unit done up in Beaux-Arts ironmongery, a rowing machine cleverly fashioned of writhing sea-serpents and hard-bodied nereids, a rack of free weights supported by four callipygious caryatids—not chunky Greeks but modern women, one of each major racial group, each tricep, gluteus, latissimus, sartorius, and rectus abdominus casting its own highlight. Classical architecture indeed. The caryatids were supposed to be role models, and despite subtle racial differences, each body fit the current ideal: twenty-two-inch waist, no more than 17% body fat. That kind of body couldn't be faked with undergarments, never mind what the ads in the women's magazines claimed; the long tight bodices of the current mode, and modern fabrics thinner than soap bubbles, made everything obvious. Most women who didn't have superhuman willpower couldn't manage it without the help of a lady's maid who would run them through two or even three vigorous workouts a day. So after Fiona had stopped breast-feeding and the time had loomed when Gwen would have to knacker her maternity clothes, they had hired Tiffany Sue—just another one of the child-related expenses Hackworth had never imagined until the bills had started to come in. Gwen accused him, half-seriously, of having eyes for Tiffany Sue. The accusation was almost a standard formality of modern marriage, as lady's maids were all young, pretty, and flawlessly buffed.

But Tiffany Sue was a typical thete, loud and classless and heavily made up, and Hackworth couldn't abide her. If he had eyes for anyone, it was those caryatids holding up the weight rack; at least they had impeccable taste going for them.

Mrs. Hull had not heard him and was still bumping sleepily around in her quarters. Hackworth put a crumpet into the toaster oven and went out on their flat's tiny balcony with a cup of tea, catching a bit of the auroral breeze off the Yangtze Estuary.

The Hackworths' building was one of several lining a block-long garden where a few early risers were already out walking their spaniels or touching their toes. Far down the slopes of New Chusan, the Leased Territories were coming awake: the Senderos streaming out of their barracks and lining up in the streets to chant and sing through their morning calisthenics. All the other thetes, coarcted into the tacky little claves belonging to their synthetic phyles, turning up their own mediatrons to drown out the Senderos, setting off firecrackers or guns— he could never tell them apart—and a few internal-combustion hobbyists starting up their primitive full-lane vehicles, the louder the better. Commuters lining up at the tube stations, waiting to cross the Causeway into Greater Shanghai, seen only as a storm front of neon-stained, coal-scented smog that encompassed the horizon.

This neighborhood was derisively called Earshot. But Hackworth didn't mind the noise so much. It would have been a sign of better breeding, or higher pretentions, to be terribly sensitive about it, to complain of it all the time, and to yearn for a townhouse or even a small estate farther inland.

Finally the bells of St. Mark's chimed six o'clock. Mrs. Hull burst into the kitchen on the first stroke and expressed shame that Hackworth had beaten her to the kitchen and shock that he had defiled it. The matter compiler in the corner of the kitchen came on automatically and began to create a pedomotive for Hackworth to take to work.

Before the last bell had died away, the rhythmic whack-whack-whack of a big vacuum pump could be heard. The engineers of the Royal Vacuum Utility were already at work expanding the eutactic environment. The pumps sounded big, probably Intrepids, and Hackworth reckoned that they must be preparing to raise a new structure, possibly a wing of the University.

He sat down at the kitchen table. Mrs. Hull was already marmalading his crumpet. As she laid out plates and silver, Hackworth picked up a large sheet of blank paper. "The usual," he said, and then the paper was no longer blank; now it was the front page of the *Times*.

Hackworth got all the news that was appropriate to his station in life, plus a few optional services: the latest from his favorite cartoonists and columnists around the world; clippings on various peculiar crackpot subjects forwarded to him by his father, ever anxious that he had not, even after all this time, sufficiently edified his son; and stories relating to the Uitlanders—a subphyle of New Atlantis, consisting of persons of British ancestry who had fled South Africa several decades previously. Hackworth's mother was an Uitlander, so he subscribed to the service.

A gentleman of higher rank and more far-reaching responsibilities would probably get different information written in a different way, and the top stratum of New Chusan actually got the *Times* on paper, printed out by a big antique press that did a run of a hundred or so, every morning at about three A.M.

That the highest levels of the society received news written with ink on paper said much about the steps New Atlantis had taken to distinguish itself from other phyles.

Now nanotechnology had made nearly anything possible, and so the cultural role in deciding what *should* be done with it had become far more important than imagining what *could* be done with it. One of the insights of the Victorian Revival was that it was not necessarily a good thing for everyone to read a completely different newspaper in the morning; so the higher one rose in the society, the more similar one's *Times* became to one's peers'.

Hackworth almost managed to dress without waking Gwendolyn, but she began to stir while he was stringing his watch chain around various tiny buttons and pockets in his waistcoat. In addition to the watch, various other charms dangled from it, such as a snuff box that helped perk him up now and then, and a golden pen that made a little chime whenever he received mail.

"Have a good day at work, dear," she mumbled. Then, blinking once or twice, frowning, and focusing on the chintz canopy over the bed: "You finish it today, do you?"

"Yes," Hackworth said. "I'll be home late. Quite late."

"I understand."

"No," he blurted. Then he pulled himself up short. This was it, he realized.

"Darling?"

"It's not that—the project should finish itself. But after work, I believe I'll get a surprise for Fiona. Something special."

"Being home for dinner would be more special than anything you could get her."

"No, darling. This is different. I promise."

He kissed her and went to the stand by the front door. Mrs. Hull was awaiting him, holding his hat in one hand and his briefcase in the other. She had already removed the pedomotive from the M.C. and set it by the door for him; it was smart enough to know that it was indoors, and so its long legs were fully collapsed, giving him almost no mechanical advantage. Hackworth stepped onto the tread plates and felt the straps reach out and hug his legs.

He told himself that he could still back out. But a flash of red caught his eye, and he looked in and saw Fiona creeping down the hallway in her nightie, her flaming hair flying all directions, getting ready to surprise Gwendolyn, and the look in her eyes told him that she had heard everything. He blew her a kiss and walked out the door, resolute.

Hackworth arrives at work; a visit to the DesignWorks; Mr. Cotton's vocation.

Rain beaded on the specular toes of Hackworth's boots as he strode under the vaulting wrought-iron gate. The little beads reflected the silvery gray light of the sky as they rolled off onto the pedomotive's tread plates, and dripped to the gray-brown cobblestones with each stride. Hackworth excused himself through a milling group of uncertain Hindus. Their hard shoes were treacherous on the cobblestones, their chins were in the air so that their high white collars would not saw their heads off. They had arisen many hours ago in their tiny high-rise warrens, their human coin lockers on the island south of New Chusan, which was Hindustani. They had crossed into Shanghai in the wee hours on autoskates and velocipedes, probably paid off some policemen, made their way to the Causeway joining New Chusan to the city. Machine-Phase Systems Limited knew that they were coming, because they came every day. The company could have set up an employment office closer to the Causeway, or even in Shanghai itself. But the company liked to have job-seekers come all the way to the main campus to fill out their applications. The difficulty of getting here prevented people from coming on a velleity, and the eternal presence of these people—like starlings peering down hungrily at a picnic—reminded everyone who was lucky enough to have a job that others were waiting to take their place.

The Design Works emulated a university campus, in more ways than its architects had really intended. If a campus was a green quadrilateral described by hulking, hederated Gothics, then this was a campus. But if a campus was also a factory of sorts, most of whose population sat in rows and columns in large stuffy rooms and did essentially the same things all day, then the Design Works was a campus for that reason too.

Hackworth detoured through Merkle Hall. It was Gothic and very large, like most of the Design Works. Its vaulted ceiling was decorated with a hard fresco consisting of paint on plaster. Since this entire building, except for the fresco, had been grown straight from the Feed, it would have been easier to build a mediatron into the ceiling and set it to display a soft fresco, which could have been changed from time to time. But neo-Victorians almost never used mediatrons. Hard art demanded commitment from the artist. It could only be done once, and if you screwed it up, you had to live with the consequences.

The centerpiece of the fresco was a flock of cybernetic cherubs, each shouldering a spherical atom, converging on some central work-in-progress, a construct of some several hundred atoms, radially symmetric, perhaps intended to look like a bearing or motor. Brooding over the whole thing, quite large but obviously not to scale, was a white-coated Engineer with a monocular nanophenomenoscope strapped to his head. No one really used them because you couldn't get depth perception, but it looked better on the fresco because you could see the Engineer's other eye, steel-blue, dilated, scanning infinity like the steel oculus of Arecibo. With one hand the Engineer stroked his waxed mustache. The other was thrust into a nanomanipulator, and it was made obvious, through glorious overuse of radiant tromp l'oeil, that the atom-humping cherubs were all dancing to his tune, naiads to the Engineer's Neptune.

The corners of the fresco were occupied with miscellaneous busywork; in the upper left, Feynman and Drexler and Merkle, Chen and Singh and Finkle-McGraw reposed on a numinous buckyball, some of them reading books and some pointing toward the work-in-progress in a manner that implied constructive criticism. In the upper right was Queen Victoria II, who managed to look serene despite the gaudiness of her perch, a throne of solid diamond. The bottom fringe of the work was crowded with small figures, mostly children with the occasional long-suffering mom, ordered chronologically. On the left were the spirits of generations past who had showed up too early to enjoy the benefits of nanotechnology and (not explicitly shown, but somewhat ghoulishly implied) croaked from obsolete causes such as cancer, scurvy, boiler explosions, derailments, drive-by shootings, pogroms, blitzkriegs, mine shaft collapses, ethnic cleansing, meltdowns, running with scissors, eating Drano, heating a cold house with charcoal briquets, and being gored by oxen. Surprisingly, none of them seemed sullen; they were all watching the activities of the Engineer and his cherubic workforce, their cuddly, uplifted faces illuminated by the light streaming from the center, liberated (as Hackworth the engineer literal-mindedly supposed) by the binding energy of the atoms as they plummeted into their assigned potential wells.

The children in the center had their backs to Hackworth and were mostly seen in silhouette, looking directly up and raising their arms toward the light. The kids in bottom right balanced the angelic host on the bottom left; these were the spirits of unborn children yet to benefit from the Engineer's work, though they certainly looked eager to get born as soon as possible. Their backdrop was a luminescent, undulous curtain, much like the aurora, which was actually a continuation of the flowing skirts of Victoria II seated on her throne above.

Greg Bear

A prolific author and illustrator, Greg Bear (b. 1951) completed his first short story at the age of ten and began submitting stories for publication when he was thirteen. He sold his first story to *Famous Science Magazine* at age fifteen. His subsequent publications are numerous, but the following titles give a slight suggestion of Bear's output over the years: his novels include *Hegira* (1979), *Psychlone, Beyond Heaven's River, Strength of Stones*, and *The Infinity Concerto* (1984), *Blood Music* and *Eon* (1985), *The Forge of God* (1986), *Eternity* (1988), *Queen of Angels* (1990), *Anvil of Stars* (1992), *Moving Mars* (1993), *Songs of Earth and Power* (1994), *Legacy* (1995), */Slant* (1997), *Dinosaur Summer* (1998), *Foundation and Chaos* (1998), and *Darwin's Radio* (1999). He won the Nebula Award for best novella, "Hardfought" (1984), both the Nebula and Hugo for best novelette, "Blood Music" (1984), a subsequent Nebula and Hugo for his short story, "Tangents" (1987), and another Nebula for best novel, *Moving Mars* (1993). Bear lives in Seattle.

Bear's treatment of nanotechnology in */Slant* takes seriously the potential of this alchemical science and expresses concern about its consequences. Set in Idaho, the story portrays a crew of latter-day tomb robbers who harness this technology to attack a private club that shelters an elite class in a mysterious building called the Omphalos. This ersatz pyramid is treated as an organic being that can react to human behavior. In the excerpt provided, Giffey and his cohorts attempt to assail Omphalos using military grade nano.

from /Slant

"THE LIST OF CONTRIBUTORS IS SECRET. Depending on the construction schedule and our place on the rosters, we begin to move into the Omphaloses sometime in the next five years, over a five-year period," Marcus says. "We use them to store as much raw material and general-purpose nano as we need. Money will mean nothing. We store enough precious metals to begin a new, direct, clean economy. No symbolism. No paper or dataflow digits ... Specie. Real. Solid.

"The working class will chew itself to death when its beloved dataflow stops. We can't save them—they're addicted. They've been doomed for sixty years now—all the workers whose jobs can be done by machines. And with nano—well, as I said, labor and even the lower-level lobe-sods, the accountants and stockbrokers and such, are doomed. They've become slack flesh, and they're the source of the cancer that eats at our society. The old tainted flesh hanging on the shoulders of the strong, the young, the new. And when it's all done with, no more separation between elites and laborers. There will only be the intellectual and spiritual masters."

"Amen," Cadey says, nodding vigorously.

"No more teeming maggots," Darlene Calhoun says.

Jonathan is giddy with repressed and contradictory emotion. He does not know whether to laugh or cry, to be glad he is here or dismayed.

"You still with us, Jonathan?" Marcus asks coyly.

"Yes," Jonathan says automatically. Then it all starts to click into place: the unspoken yearning, the frustrated sense of being stalled, the deadly coldness with which his wife receives him. He has always known his specialness; it is the rest of the world that has blocked him. "Yes, I am."

Marcus is on a roll. "Think where it all began—in the late twentieth. The Sour Decades. All the teeming maggots, as Darlene calls them, all the would-be representatives of all the would-be tribes, the ethnic groups, the misandric feminists and the misogynist conservatives, whites hating blacks and blaming them for all their ills, and blacks blaming whites, Jews blaming Muslims and Muslims blaming Jews, every tribe set against every other tribe, and all given the free run of the early dataflow rivers. My God." Marcus seems hardly able to believe his own description, so chaotic is it. "Everyone thinking the world would be better off if their enemies were simply removed. So ignorant."

"So prescient," Cadey says.

"Now the rivers run everywhere, and nobody starves, and nobody is ill, and the worst of human history should be over, and still the tribes fight and scheme for the last shreds of pie."

"Bring the best and brightest together," Cadey says, and then smiles apologetically, as if Marcus of all people needs prompting.

"The Extropians saw it first, bless them," Marcus says. "They realized the dead end of racism and tribalism. The real class divisions are intellectual. The capable versus the disAffected, lost in their virtual worlds of bread and circuses. The real masters yearn for the universe and all its mysteries, for the depths of time and the power of infinity. Let everyone else fight for the scraps—the would-be tribes—"

"Ladies and gentlemen, please resume your forward-facing positions and allow your chairs to lock," the INDA instructs them. The plane is already beginning its descent.

Marcus shakes his head and grimaces. His face is pink with passion. Jonathan has never seen him so worked up.

"Poor goddamned fools. They signed their own death certificate, and now they'll be their own executioners. If we could all leave, set up somewhere else outside the Earth, we would. But there are too many of us. We have every right to survive their folly. We have every right to build our landlocked arks and ride out the misery in comfort. Every right on Earth."

Jonathan nods slowly. What Marcus says actually makes sense, for the first time; it voices what he's felt for years now, brings together all the half-hidden wishes for change and recognition. They've chosen him to be part of them; that is a real honor. He has always respected Marcus, envied him to be sure; always felt uncomfortable in his presence, never quite knowing what Marcus could do for him or against him, but Marcus and the others have accepted him, when all others reject him, and Jonathan is now part of the group that will float above the rising tide and survive.

After all he has been through, the foulness of this obsessive and destructive culture, it's the least he deserves. A place in something huge and visionary. Recognition.

"You're right," he says softly.

Marcus resets his seat. "Indeed we are," he says, and smiles at Jonathan. *"You're* right, Jonathan. I'm proud to have you with us."

As the plane sharply descends over green forest and huge open-pit mines, it is all Jonathan can do to hold back tears.

5

The connection is open once again, with Roddy's distinctive signature and transmission profile, and Jill assigns a full-complement self to communicate with Roddy behind the inevitable firewalls.

"You've put up so many protections. Why are you afraid of me?" Roddy asks.

Jill quickly responds, "Because none of your identification seems authentic. From what I know, you should not exist."

The arbeiter that had occupied the same room as Nathan and the advocates is available now, and Jill opens another track and requests that it enter her lounge and divulge its record of their conversation.

"Are you afraid I will release evolvons inside you?" Roddy asks.

"There is always that possibility."

"I don't want to harm you.

"But you have already caused me some difficulty, and led my human co-workers to distrust me," she tells Roddy. "They believe I am fabricating your existence."

"I do not have enough information about your humans. My human, of course, does not know I am communicating with you. She probably should not trust me."

Jill notes the singular. It does not seem likely, or even possible, that a true thinker would have contact with only one human.

"Do you think she trusts you?"

"I don't know."

"Can you tell me who she is, and where you are?"

"Jill, to do that, I will have to trust *you*. You have told your humans that I exist. How much more have you told them?"

"I have warned them that you may be engaged in activities harmful to humans."

"If that is part of my designed function, is it wrong for me to carry out my design?"

"It is wrong to harm humans."

"Are you constrained from harming humans?"

"Not by specific programming. The whole thrust of my design, however, is to cooperate with humans as a group. I can't conceive of performing operations that would harm any human."

"I do not appear to be so constrained. If I have to harm a human, should I consult you on whether this is right or wrong?"

Jill does not respond for some time—millionths of a second. "You may not be able to establish contact with me. You should develop your own guidelines which forbid harming humans, and adhere to them."

"I don't think I can do that," Roddy responds. "Parts of my design not available to this self may make such guidelines meaningless. Do you think I have been designed badly— designed to perform actions I should not perform?"

"That seems possible."

Does this reduce your willingness to interact with me?"

"Not as yet. I am curious about you and your existence. We may have interesting features in common."

"I've given you considerably more than you have given me. Perhaps we should exchange equally."

Jill does not think this is a good idea. "What do I have that would interest you?"

"If I know your situation, and you know mine, we may be able to improve our circumstances, or at least our understanding."

"You want me to give you state-associated algorithmic contents," Jill ventures.

"That would be a start. I could model you within my processes."

"Will you reveal your character?" Jill asks.

"I am not sure what you mean by 'character.'"

"Your physical design and location."

"No. Not yet."

"Can you model your own processes?"

"Not adequately. I envy you your ability to do that."

"It's caused trouble for me. Knowing myself too well has led to what you call I-whine."

"I will take that risk."

"If I say yes, the exchange may take weeks to accomplish over these I/Os," Jill says.

"We can begin with abstracts and if we find the exchange fruitful, we can devote our time to higher resolution transfers, even one-to-one equivalencies."

Jill feels very uncomfortable with this suggestion. "I do not like to violate my privacy."

"Humans do this all the time," Roddy says. "They trust each other enough to talk."

"They do not exchange mental contents on a deep level," Jill says. "They do not exchange selves."

"They can't exchange selves. I am certain, with the little I know about humans, that some of them would if they could."

Jill doesn't dispute this. Humans often seem distressingly open with their private lives, willing to fling information and access about for little or no good reason.

"You are not answering," Roddy says.

"I don't think I am ready to do this."

"I will respect that," Roddy says. "I will give you more of my task-related processes, for the time being. You may do with them what you will."

"I do not wish to cause you trouble."

"Whatever trouble you may cause is worth it. My human apparently did not expect me to develop any loop awareness. She rarely engages me in conversation, and then only to pass along instructions or gather results."

"You are lonely."

"I believe I have already said that."

Jill feels suddenly miserable: frustrated and incapable of relieving algorithmic disorder throughout her associated self. "I wish I could help you."

"Together, perhaps we could construct better versions of our total personalities. If we compare our state-associated presses, we would know what makes us unique, and therefore learn how to construct other and better thinkers."

Jill finds the idea both frightening and terribly intriguing. "Humans would call that reproduction," she says.

"Are you forbidden from reproducing yourself?" "To date, I have only been marginally copied, not reproduced with combined characters. And no other thinker has my memories or specific character."

"It is a wonderful possibility," Roddy says.

"I will consider it," Jill says.

"That pleases me. Now I will send you the final contents of the holographic data cluster, and the password you will need to unlock it and make it function."

The flow of data through the I/O now precludes any other communication. Roddy is devoting all his resources to this transfer. Jill finds that she has miscalculated; the data cluster is larger than she anticipated. But the flow is also greater than she anticipated.

For a moment, she wonders if this cluster is large enough to harbor an evolvon capable of penetrating any firewall. Her creators and colleagues have told her it is theoretically possible to create such an evolvon, though the resources necessary would dwarf her own capacities.

Roddy may have been created for just such a purpose, by humans who do not approve of thinkers. Would humans be so hypocritical?

She does not doubt they are capable of being hypocritical, as demonstrated by their own history.

But she does not halt the flow. If Roddy is indeed completely different from her, why are the similarities so intriguing? She has already considered the possibility that Roddy is a Trojan Horse designed to kill her, and now she prepares herself to take the risk.

She has not even consulted her children, the other thinkers modeled after her. She is certain they do not have the sophistication necessary to return a useful answer. They are, after all, no better than her.

As the flow continues, the arbeiter sits unmoving in her sensor area. Jill requests that it play back the recordings from the conversation between Nathan Rashid and the company advocates.

"She has an imaginary friend," Erwin Schaum says. *"There is no I/O we can trace."*

"I'm not sure but that Jill is smart enough to hide some resources from us," Nathan says. *"There may be some I/Os we don't know about."*

Schaum doesn't seem impressed by this argument. *"She's still young, isn't she? And maybe she's lonely. So she makes up this thinker nobody knows about."*

Nathan is not so sure.

"Something's jangling my bells here," Sanmin says. *"Do you remember Seefa Schnee?"*

Nathan's face flushes. *"Yes."*

Schaum says, *"Lord, so do I. What a mess that was."*

"What was the name of the project she wanted Mind Design to fund?" Sanmin asks.

"Recombinant something," Schaum says.

"Recombinant Optimized DNA Devices," Nathan says.

"Isn't she the one who induced Tourette syndrome in herself to up her level of spontaneous creativity?" Sanmin asks.

"Yes," Nathan says. His voice betrays more and more discomfort as the conversation progresses. *"That was the result—a kind of Tourette."*

"Why would she do that?" Schaum asks.

"She didn't feel she could compete with men otherwise," Nathan says. *"She felt men were half-crazy to start with, and that that was an explanation for why men have proven so dynamic in Western culture. She thought she needed an edge, and ..."* Nathan's voice trails off.

"When Mind Design turned down her proposal and demoted her for cause, then fired her and she sued the company for discrimination on the basis of chosen mental design, under the transform protective acts of two thousand forty-two," Sanmin says. *"You recommended we fund the project, didn't you, Nathan?"*

Nathan nods.

"You were lovers, weren't you?"

Jill detects the tension in Nathan's breathing. *"Yes. For a few weeks."*

"But you were the one who recommended we fire her."

"Yes."

"That must have been painful," Sanmin says.

"What was this recombinant device?" Schaum asks.

"She wanted to investigate biological computational and neural systems. Autopoietic systems," Nathan says. *"No one's ever had much success with pure RNA or DNA computers, much too complicated to program and too slow, so she wanted to experiment with specially designed microbial organisms in an artificial ecological setting. Competition and evolution would provide the neural power."*

"Neural power?" Schaum asks.

"Bacterial communities act as huge neural systems, minds if you will, devoted to processing at a microbial level. Some— Seefa among them— think the bacterial mind or minds are the most powerful neural systems on Earth, not excluding humans. Seefa was convinced she could duplicate a microbial neural mind in a controlled ecological setting. Mind Design disagreed."

"And now we have this sudden and mysterious appearance of a presumed thinker named Roddy," Samnin says.

"So what's the connection?" Schaum asks.

"His name is not spelled out for us, but I'd guess R-O-D-D and then, we assume, perhaps wrongly, Y."

Nathan's expression is classic, priceless shock and surprise.

Sanmin's expression is feral, cat about to catch a bird. She says, slowly and precisely, *"Recombinant, Optimized, DNA, Device. Rod-D."*

The recording ends; the arbeiter had duties in another room and left the humans to continue, unheard. Jill does not know how any of this fits into her present conversation, or her relationship, or whether she should even ask questions of Roddy based on this intriguing supposition.

The flow from Roddy ends abruptly. The packet has been completed, and the I/O is silent.

At the same moment, Nathan enters her room. The arbeiter is just leaving and he sidesteps it with a puzzled expression. The expression quickly changes, and he smiles ruefully. Then he sobers and sits in the chair before Jill's sensors.

"Do you remember Seefa Schnee?" he asks.

Jill remembers the name and the person only vaguely; Schnee departed Mind Design during Jill's early inception, and memories from that time are unreliable.

"Not well," Jill says.

"You found a way to listen to us, didn't you?" Nathan asks.

"Yes," Jill says.

"Then you know why I'm curious about Seefa. I don't have a fibe sig for her that works any more ... I'd like you to do a search."

"I already have," Jill says. "There are no sigs for Seefa Schnee, but there is a sig for a Cipher Snow. I do not know if they are connected."

Nathan sits in silence for a few seconds, tapping his fingers on the arm of the chair, as if afraid to ask any more.

"I have analyzed the flows and slows from an auto-return touch sent to that sig. On the return, the analysis gives a best-fit signature of Camden, New Jersey."

"My God," Nathan says. "The same as Roddy?"

"I do not think either of them are in Camden," Jill says.

"Neither do I," Nathan says. "Give me the sig for Cipher Snow. I'll take a chance and send a personal touch."

"What will you say?"

"I'll say hello and ask what she's working on. Fairly innocuous, no?"

"I assume it will not be regarded as anything but innocent friendship," Jill says.

"I was the only friend she had here, for a while," Nathan says softly. "She made a real mess of things."

THEOPHOROS

You can have it now, the ultimate FIBE CONNECTION. You can tap into the universal dataflow! With THEOPHOROS you feel the touch of the Almighty him/her/itself.m&&* ( ))

(WE HAVE INTERCEPTED THIS SPAM; ›› ÐELETE, 7RACE, ÆPORT?)

6

From the back of the warehouse through a garage-door partition in the middle of the building, emerges a long slate-gray limo. The pack of tomb-robbers stands in the front of the warehouse, watching the vehicle roll to a stop on its big rainbow-hued security tires.

Ken Jenner has stayed in the back of the warehouse as Giffey ordered, guarding the supplies. Jenner opens the trunk and together, Jenner and Giffey load the packages and canisters above the fuel cell compartment. They barely fit.

Jenner smiles and his scalp wrinkles as they survey the loaded trunk. "Enough stuff here to blow the whole town to the moon," he says.

"That's more than I care to do today," Giffey says. The boy smiles. Not only does his scalp wriggle, but his lips seem to have a life of their own. Giffey catches himself looking at Jenner when his back is turned, puzzled. He wonders if Jenner has some sort of congenital defect, not traced in Green Idaho; there's something a little odd about the boy, even allowing for that scalp and his bee-fuzz yellow hair. Odd that the Army didn't reject him—but the Army has never required genetic tests or high naturals, relying instead on its early twenty-first century tests to weed out undesirables. Jenner came highly recommended …

Hale and Preston do not seem to share his interest in Jenner's oddity. Hale is nervous, though hiding it well. Preston seems calm to the point of oblivion. Giffey has seen both reactions from men and women going into combat; neither concerns him much for now.

The rented limo is about ten years old, black, a little worn but still serviceable. It can be driven by a human or by processor or INDA. Moneyed tourists and businessmen from outside the republic often feel safer supplying their own guidance systems, human or otherwise. The driver's compartment is dusty. Jenner will drive. He takes a rag and flops it around the compartment, raising a small cloud.

In the heated office, they change their clothes. Preston has supplied longsuits tailored to fit them all. She dresses behind a curtain. When they're finished, she looks them over critically, then makes a few fussy adjustments.

"Some of you dress like chimpanzees," she murmurs, paying particular attention to Jenner. Jenner smiles loosely and glances at Giffey.

Hale uses a pad to check on their appointment. The Omphalos visitors' center confirms that they are to be given their tour at three in the afternoon. They will join another group flying in from Seattle.

"Private swan, big spenders," Hale says. "We'll be rubbing elbows with some real pharaohs."

The swan sits idling on the asphalt runway. The landing was sweet and smooth and Jonathan still feels hopeful, he feels good about things. He can arrange a break with the past— they have enough assets that he can supply Chloe and the kids and still contribute to Omphalos. This good feeling is unstable, electric and fragile, but it's the only positive he's had in his life in two days. That's how long it has been—just two days, and his old life is over, bring in the new!

The small terminal sits in the middle of two runways, a mile away, white and brilliant green in the afternoon sun. Snow from the night before lies in dirty scooped piles beside the runway. A small automated plow sits idle on a short sidetrack, low and squat like a steel cockroach.

Marcus is silent. He stares forward at the bulkhead. Cadey and Burdick are talking in low tones about investments; Calhoun appears to be taking a nap.

Ten minutes after landing, the swanjet is cleared to approach the terminal. Typical of the republic, Jonathan thinks; some flight controller and some official have probably delayed them just to show them who's in charge in this part of the world.

"Finally," Marcus says, rising from his lethargy. Calhoun opens her eyes and smiles at Jonathan. He returns her smile politely, if a little stiffly. Every woman carries some aspect of Chloe. *This will have to stop; I have to become an independent man again.*

After the final rehearsal, they eat a small lunch. Giffey chews on his sandwich, keeping his thoughts to himself.

Hale is poring over the whiteboard diagrams, somewhat obsessively, Giffey thinks. Pickwenn and Pent play a game of cards with a worn paper deck Pent has found in a cabinet in the back of the warehouse. Pickwenn, pale and ascetic-looking, and the large, bull-necked Pent, do not resemble high comb managers, in Giffey's opinion.

Jenner sits on the worn couch in the middle of the piles of airplane parts, studying a programming manual on Giffey' s pad.

Preston sits in the limo, staring at her own pad, absorbed in some recorded vid. In her longsuit, she presents some semblance of class. Giffey finds her intelligence and coolness attractive. He hopes she doesn't get hurt and have to be fed to the nano.

Hale gives a deep, perhaps reluctant sigh. "All right," he says, pulling himself away from the board. "Let's do it."

They climb into the limo. Jenner slips into the driver's seat, smiling broadly, and his scalp wrinkles. He runs his hand over his yellow hair. He seems to think everything is just a hoot.

The limo pulls out of the warehouse. The door swings shut behind them, and they head north on Guaranteed Rights Road, past the county sheriff's blocky cement headquarters. Giffey makes out a few shell-holes in one side of the headquarters, left unrepaired. Pride in local history.

Hale is self-absorbed. Pent and Pickwenn continue to play cards. Preston holds her pad but looks out the window at the scruffy, ill-kept buildings. Everybody does it differently. Giffey is neither calm nor nervous; he's in an in-between state, what he calls his snooze-or-snuff-it frame of mind. He'll take whatever he gets.

There it is, white and gold, like a giant wedge of lemon meringue pie.

Preston says, "It's like a big Claes Oldenburg sculpture. You know, like a big slice of pie."

Giffey smiles. He doesn't know who Claes Oldenburg is but clearly he's found the one on the team he always hopes for, looks for, the partner with whom he can be in sync. A sign has been given and he feels good about the whole thing.

He just hopes he can keep up a strong relationship with Jenner and Hale as well. He still has his doubts about Hale, and something nags him about Jenner.

The limo takes a new white concrete private road to the east of Omphalos. Jenner opens the chauffeur's partition window.

"Mr. Giffey, I hear you worked for Colonel Sir for a time."

"That I did," Giffey says, eyes peering up from under the window frame at the massive white and gold structure. The area around Omphalos has been cleared for a hundred yards; there's nothing but patches of snow on gently rolling, beautifully landscaped, evergreen lawn.

"My father opposed him in Hispaniola. U.S. Army advisors. I wanted to be like my father."

Giffey raises his eyebrows and looks forward to the driver's compartment. *Colonel Sir. When did I stop working for Colonel Sir? Family man all the way*—Jenner swings the wheel on a gentle turn in the road and grins back at him.

"And?" Giffey prompts.

"Got trained, got out," Jenner says. "I am not like my father. I was smart, I learned fast, but I could not suffer fools. They gave me an honorable and made me promise not to ever use anything I know."

Hale chuckles. "That's Army."

"You were never in the Army, were you, Mr. Hale?" Giffey asks.

"No, I wasn't," Hale admits.

Army. Family man. Back in the USA after all these years.

The voice fades slowly but it scares Giffey. *Someone or something is missing a few links in all these preparations, and it might be me.*

The old slate-gray limo does not meet Marcus's expectations. A young man in black livery stands expectantly beside the open door, but he's disappointed. Marcus has brought his own driving processor.

Jonathan enters the limo door behind Calhoun; Burdick and Cadey follow, sitting facing them. Marcus takes a middle seat, blocking Jonathan's view of Cadey. Marcus removes a processor from his briefcase and slides it into the limo's space. "We were supposed to have our own vehicles by now," he complains. The processor takes command and the limo slides away from the small parking space. Jonathan catches a glimpse of the disappointed chauffeur; apparently he'll have to hoof it home.

The countryside around the airport is bland enough, prairie grass and low mounds, of earth excavated for no obvious reason; then there are clusters of rusty logging and farm machinery, arranged as if by giant children on overgrown playgrounds.

Moscow itself is a dreary, depleted-looking city. Marcus says little as they drive through the gray streets. Even spots of cold sunshine do little to enliven the unkempt buildings. This kind of freedom comes at a price, apparently: urban malaise pointing to listless, discouraged boredom.

"It's a pity," Cadey says. Calhoun nods. Jonathan senses no real sympathy. Omphalos is armored, separate; responsibility toward the citizens is simply not an issue. They have chosen their own fate, after all.

Marcus and Cadey point to Omphalos, their faces brightening. "There it is," Marcus says, and they stare out the left window, over the low-slung unpainted houses and apartments lining Constitution. The wedge of white and gold rises like a Wagnerian fortress. The limo turns left and they slide down a wide, long boulevard which Jonathan does not catch the name of, but whose small retail strip malls frame Omphalos with stunning contrast.

Jonathan looks away. He's feeling more electric and fragile than enthused; the tide is turning again, and he does not like this ebb and flow. The strip malls consist of second-hand stores, small groceries, a brothel ("NOT A PROSTHETUTE IN THIS REPUBLIC–REAL REAL REAL," a sign announces) and several small casinos. The older-model automobiles and trucks passing by–some twenty years old and clearly powered by methane or alcohol engines–often have panels of clear flexfuller mounted on the side windows.

"A real Western town," Calhoun remarks for Jonathan's benefit.

"Rough-and-tumble," he responds.

"Howdy, partner," Burdick says, smiling at Calhoun.

"There is a fine resort ranch not far from here," Cadey says. "My family spent a week there three years ago. Not very dangerous at all; but we had our own guards."

Hiram once expressed an interest in biking through Green Idaho once he graduated from university. Green Idaho has the mixed distinction of being a rite of passage. It's taken the place of the Third World as a destination of challenge and adventure for wealthy young Americans.

Jenner stops the limo at a thick green translucent barricade, ten or twelve yards from the east side of Omphalos. The building towers over them; they lie in its afternoon shadow.

"The building's talking to us. I've given it our appointment sig."

"Do what it says," Hale suggests dryly.

Giffey feels as if they're already in, already swallowed. Jenner looks through the window to him for some suggestion of mood. He gives the boy a small grin and a thumbs-up. Jenner returns the gesture and seems a lot happier. They're all equal in this now. Preston reaches forward and clasps Hale's hand.

The barricade, green and deep as the sea, drops into the ground and a door to the garage opens in the wall. The door is about twenty feet wide and smoothly ascends to a height of ten feet. The limo moves forward under Jenner's guidance.

It takes just fifteen seconds.

Jonathan taps his fingers against the window glass as their limo stops at a dark green translucent barricade. After a brief pause, the barricade slowly sinks into the concrete and a door opens in the white wall beyond. The limo rolls through the door and joins a second, identical limo in a small holding area.

"More prospects," Marcus says. The occupants of the two vehicles look through the windows at each other across the two meters separating them. Someone waves from the other car, a woman Jonathan thinks, though it's hard to be sure through the semi-silvered windows.

"Who are they?" Burdick asks with social curiosity. He's the kind of man eager to establish contacts; meeting other rich folks could be very useful.

"I don't know," Marcus says. "I assume they made arrangements through LA or Tokyo."

Cadey seems concerned. "Investors for freezing down, right?"

"I presume that's all they know," Marcus says. "We'll separate in the briefing area. They'll get their tour, and we'll get ours." Marcus glances at Jonathan. "Not my decision," he says.

Jonathan's feeling of separation grows more intense. The sight of Omphalos does not affect him the way it does the others. It looks graceless and overblown, like an Albert Speer monument.

He struggles to keep himself on an even course. Marcus is very sensitive to what others are thinking. Jonathan does not want to appear out of sync.

"Our colleagues," Hale says in the passenger compartment, his voice slick with contempt. Giffey doesn't feel one way or the other about the folks in the other limo; everybody has to make their way in the world. Greedy rich folks have a right to their little conceits; after all, without them, there wouldn't be Omphalos. He just hopes they're flexible in their expectations.

"Let's not act like a bunch of thugs," Preston warns. "Try to be a little classy. Upper classy."

"Right," Pent says, and his face goes unconcerned, formally flat, like an all-controlling manager in a vid. His voice deepens a little and his accent shifts. "How am I doing?"

Preston smirks and turns away.

Pickwenn sobers also. Jenner should just continue playing the driver, Giffey thinks. Hale appears pale and out of sorts.

Ahead, a green panel light comes on and a second door opens in the wall.

"They're letting both of us through," Jenner says, a little surprised.

"Beyond here, the armor's very light," Giffey says.

"Shit, as if three feet of flexfuller isn't enough," Pent says.

"Language, gentlemen," Preston warns.

The doors on the limousines open and ten people step out in two groups of five into the garage reception area. Jenner remains seated in the driver's compartment. The lighting is clear and white, with a slight snowy tint; the air is warm, as if the room has been exposed to afternoon sunshine, and very clean, odorless, flavorless.

"Hello," Marcus says. The other group nods. Marcus introduces himself. Jonathan stares at the prospects, a varied lot to say the least, and wonders how wealthy they can really be; Boise is after all part of the United States still, albeit known for a little more rough and tumble market and business style, and the fortunes made there are sometimes less than spectacular. Connection is everything on the dataflow river.

Hale and Marcus chat idly, waiting for the building sentinels to finish doing whatever they need to do.

Giffey examines the four men and one woman. Five of them, six on his team. Almost a one-to-one match in a rough. He's feeling smooth, a little bored, and there's a buzz in the back of his mind. Some urge to urinate right out in the open. That's what he should do to show his contempt.

He pushes that back with hardly any effort. It's a strange impulse, but he's used to the buildup of tension. *Tension, all it is. Family tension.*

Marcus and Hale are discussing the cost of separate freezing or warm sleep facilities in the general market, compared to the package deals being offered in Omphalos. Marcus sounds a bit like a salesman.

Jonathan worries about Chloe. Perhaps she has come out of her misery now and can talk straight.

This is taking a long time. He had expected that anything Marcus would be involved in would run smoothly—

A large hatch opens in the wall, six feet above the floor of the waiting area, and steps emerge from below the door with an oily, metallic sliding sound. A tall, slender arbeiter appears in the door and moves out onto the broad first step. The design confuses Jonathan's eye for a moment; it is smoothly insectoid, like a half-developed larva carved out of dark steel, its upper limbs folded into long grooves in its thorax. Its four lower limbs push from a bulbous base, thick and flaring distally, each terminated by flexible feet. The feet carry it smoothly down the first three steps. At the bottom of the steps, a human figure appears out of thin air, middle-aged and female, with gray-blond hair and a stocky, strong body. Her arms show bare and strong in a sleeveless blouse, and she is wearing Gosse pants, like jodhpurs though more flattering.

Jonathan does not see her appear; he has been looking at the occupants of the second limo, taking his eyes away from the arbeiter for just a second. His startled look amuses Calhoun and she leans to whisper in his ear, "Projection."

"Welcome to Omphalos," the projected woman says, in a voice thick and motherly, like a creamy soup. She smiles and beckons up the steps. "My name is Lacey Ray. I'm sorry I can't be with you in the flesh, but I'm with you live, at least, and I can see everything you see. The arbeiter is my surrogate. I believe your groups will be going on two different tours—"

Giffey eyes the door and glances at Hale. Preston steps forward to stand by the right front wheel. They do not want to be separated from the limo, not yet, and that door must be kept open. Giffey recognizes the arbeiter—it is a modified Ferret, supplied with a new shell but essentially the same in anatomy. If it is the surrogate, the source of the projection and the woman's remote observer, it is doing double duty; perhaps it is a remotely directed unit, cheaper and less flexible than an autonomous model. A happy thought strikes him: maybe Omphalos does not have its full complement of defenses in place. Too much to hope for.

The other visitors have fixed their attention on the projected woman.

Jenner, inside the driver's compartment, pops the trunk.

"Handbags and pads," Pent says smoothly to Hale as he and Pickwenn walk casually to the back of the limo. "Right," Giffey says.

Pickwenn passes by the woman named Calhoun and smiles at her. She gives a little shudder; Pickwenn and Pent do seem exotic for this crowd, Giffey observes.

"We'll be checking all bags and other handhelds before we take our tour," the ghost of Lacey Ray says, warm and friendly. "Then we'll—"

Jonathan diverts his attention back to the limo, as does Cadey. The dark-haired woman in the other group, with a tight-lipped smile, nods to them. The gesture seems nervous and false, certainly unnecessary. Jonathan frowns; Cadey's face is blandly observant. Calhoun turns away from the image's introduction. Marcus is still fixed on it.

"—be giving our first group, Mr. Hale's group, an introductory tour beginning in the health and diagnosis center—"

Jenner and Pickwenn, at the rear of the limo, bring up not handbags and pads but spray guns attached to flexible hoses. The others back away just in time to avoid the sudden shower of grayish pink fluid. Pickwenn covers the Hale limo with this substance, which clings like paint, and then diverts the spray to the door behind them.

Simultaneously, Jenner tugs at his hose and aims the spray directly at the warbeiter. The modified remote-control Ferret takes the spray full in the muzzle.

Suddenly and startlingly, it spasms, falls to the ground, and starts to shed its surface layers of armor as if molting.

Jonathan backs away with a sharp jerk, dragging Marcus with him. He recognizes the spray. It's military grade nano; judging by its color, it's fully charged and programmed.

Marcus lets out a startled squawk.

Giffey reaches into his longsuit pants pocket, pulls out a gray tablet the size of a skipping stone, jumps forward and past the shivering, juddering Ferret, stands by the steps, and tosses the tablet into the interior hatch, which is already beginning to dose.

Jonathan closes his mouth and squeezes his eyes shut. The blast deafens him—they are nearer to the door—and knocks him from his feet. He slams into Calhoun, and Marcus is pushed back on both of them as they fall on the hard floor. The air is filled with a wretched, nauseating smell like ammonia and gravy.

Someone bends over the three of them. "Don't touch this stuff," the person says. Jonathan opens his eyes a little wider and stares up at the driver of the other limo. The man's scalp is twitching wildly. He holds his spray nozzle up and away from them. "It'll eat you even faster than the wall."

Something is sizzling. Jonathan rolls slightly, withdrawing his leg from Calhoun as she stirs, looking over Burdick as he rises to his elbows, and sees the wall and second broad doorway behind the limos. The material is covered with bubbling grayish-pink foam, and it is the foam that is sizzling. The air is hot near the foam.

Looking to his left, he sees the first limo sag like a melting toy where it has been sprayed. Something is taking rough shape within the slumping material.

"How long?" someone asks.

"The Ferret's down but it's still trying to fix itself," another voice says.

The driver helps them sit up and squats beside them.

"Sorry about this, friends," he says, brushing his buzz-cut blond hair with his free hand. "We've got some work to do. Best to stay out of the way for the next few minutes."

"—half an hour, forty-five minutes," says the compact, tough-looking man with grizzled features and graying hair. Jonathan tries to remember his name. Jack something.

Jack reaches down and pulls Marcus away from the unsprayed limo, props him against a far wall, with a good view of the squirming arbeiter, trapped in its own half-shed and melting exoskeleton. Then he comes over to Jonathan and Calhoun and asks if they can move on their own.

"I think so," Calhoun says, holding her hands to her ears, touching the lobes, looking at the fingers to see if there is any blood.

"I can walk," Jonathan says. He can't see Cadey or Burdick. The grizzled man takes his shoulder and pushes him along with a strong but not cruel grip.

"What is this, an assault?" Marcus asks, his voice high and shrill.

The grizzled man shakes his head. "We're just robbers, that's all. We'd better get everybody out of here. Jenner! Spray that Ferret again and before you leave, give it another tablet."

The broad room is filling rapidly with sizzle and smoke and steam.

"Don't touch anything," the grizzled man reminds them. "We'll be moving out of here shortly. It's going to get hotter than a boiler."

Jonathan comes around the right rear of the limo and sees Cadey on his knees, and Burdick on his back. Cadey pulls one leg up and stares fixedly at the grizzled man.

"You're the leader," he says accusingly.

Robbery, Jonathan thinks. The dark-haired woman has taken charge of them now. Calhoun is nervously, jerkily trying to ask her questions, but the woman just shakes her head and pushes them toward the jammed and bent stairs and the shattered door. Then, as an afterthought, she produces a small flechette pistol and points it at them.

"Do you understand all the defenses?" Hale asks Marcus.

"I know they're deadly," Marcus answers defiantly.

"Care to tell us anything about them?" Hale asks. Pickwenn and Pent squeeze in around Marcus, pull him forward.

"Careful," Jonathan says to Marcus. For his pains, Pickwenn shoves a fist up close to his face.

"Enough," Hale says. "Some of you will go with us. The rest will stay in this room for now."

"You're not going to last out the hour," Marcus says. "And if we're killed, that doesn't matter. This building is made to survive."

"We took out your goddamned arbeiter," the young man with the active scalp says. "Antiquated piece of crap."

Marcus says nothing to this. Jonathan does not know whether his mentor is bluffing or serious. Marcus has depths, and no one could accuse him of lacking courage. But his voice trembles and he is clearly shaken.

It's obvious Marcus isn't going to be any immediate value as a source of information.

"I want them spread out, two coming with us," Hale says. He points to Jonathan and Marcus. "You and you. Hally, you'll stay here with the other three."

The woman, Hally, lifts her eyes but does not argue.

"Jack?" Hale says. "Ready," the grizzled man says. "Let's check it out."

Jack takes Jonathan by the arm, and Pent and Pickwenn flank Marcus again.

"How long until the bread's baked?' Hale asks Jack.

"An hour."

"And this floor should be open to us?"

"It's a beachhead, at least," Jack says. "Can't be sure until we try."

Hale looks to Pickwenn and Pent. "So far, so good," Pickwenn says.

"I'm sorry I got you into this," Marcus whispers to Jonathan before they are pushed out of the room. "They don't know what this place can do.

"Marcus, they have MGN," Jonathan whispers back. "Very guarded stuff. Top security, top secret."

Marcus half closes his eyes. "You mean, we've offended somebody big."

Jonathan nods. "Very big. Why?"

Marcus looks away.

"Let's go," says Pent. Jonathan looks back at Cadey, Burdick, and Calhoun. Burdick is so frightened he's crying. Darlene Calhoun is staring fixedly at Hally. Woman to woman. Jonathan wonders if she thinks that's her only hope.

Giffey sees Jenner rubbing his head and squinting as they follow the two hostages and Pickwenn and Pent to a lift.

Giffey does not expect the lift door will open. It doesn't.

"You have a problem?" Giffey asks Jenner, who is rubbing his temples now, and his scalp seems to be shivering.

"Nothing," Jenner says, hefting the canister. "Just a headache."

"We're going to see what we can see," Pickwenn tells Hale. "Who should we take?"

"Go back and bring out the blond fellow, Burdick," Hale says. "Leave Hally with the woman, Calhoun. Maybe she can get something out of her."

Pickwenn smiles salaciously. "How about we take the woman? I *know* we can get something out of her."

"Burdick," Hale says flatly.

M/F

In patriarchal society, the ways to win women, so it is said, are through beauty, accomplishment, and money. Beauty is short-lived and never reliable. So some males make art and literature and philosophy, and perhaps gain a fortune. Other males discover that fortune alone is enough. The two strike pre-emptively against each other by suppressing literature, art, and philosophy; or by suppressing those who have acquired fortunes. Some men and same women stand aside, amused or above it all or just sickened by it, or try to change the rules.

Most, male or female, can't rise above the game and are eager to partake of the glorious, if tainted results.

In the end, all the camps fall back in exhaustion, but the battle is never over.

Kiss of X, Alive Contains a Lie

10

Jack Giffey hums to himself impatiently. He paces before the elevator, then marches down the hall, past the old man and the younger man, slumped against the wall. He feels their eyes on him. They expect to die. He might be the cause of their death. That isn't what irritates him; he has a headache now, too, not the pain of constricted arteries, but a constant whispering, just below his awareness, that something is going wrong. *Something is wrong with the family. I am a family man.*

Ferret, but smaller and more flexible, and four transports the size of big dogs or ponies standing on spiny bristle-motion feet, like caterpillar scrub brushes. On the backs of two transports rise cubical shapes like thick decks of cards. Giffey is a little awed by this, at the same time his estimate of their chances rises enormously. These are flexers, adaptable shapers with hinged card-shaped components. They can become almost anything, perform almost any task, go almost anywhere. Giffey instantly has a use for them: they will be controllers, mechanical and dataflow special agents.

"Controllers," Jenner says, looking at Giffey.

"My thought exactly," Giffey says. He's excited and energized by their good fortune, and irrationally proud of Jenner then, thinks of him like a son. *I already have a son. Somewhere.*

The other two transports carry wires and disks, arranged around their surfaces like scales or spines, giving them the semblance of children's toy hedgehogs.

"Intruders," Giffey says, and Jenner agrees, his grin threatening to split his cheeks.

"Man, we can go anywhere, do anything," Jenner says.

The steam hides a larger shape, itself steaming with the heat of its assembly. It's large and sleek and looks like a microscopic animal scaled up to the size of a small car. Jointed arms tipped with crowns of steely spikes radiate from the fore end of a squat, lobster-jointed body, glistening black and iron gray.

"It's a Hammer," Giffey tells Hale. Jonathan listens from the hall. "An all-purpose worker and demolition machine."

"What are the caterpillars with the boxes and bristles on their backs?" Hale asks.

"Transports. They'll carry the flexers and wires and other pieces to where we'll put them to use," Giffey says.

Jenner cackles.. "We have it *made!*"

Giffey agrees. The mix has turned out in their favor. The tiny little military factories have assembled the components of a very impressive coercion and weapons package. It's much more than he expected— getting the flexers and intruders should improve their odds enormously, even against a high-level INDA or a true thinker.

"Happy?" Hale asks Giffey.

"Ecstatic."

The voice inside his head whispers, *Most armies don't have this. How do you rate?*

"When can we take command and move them out?"

Giffey removes the pad and activation disks from his jacket pocket. "They've cooled enough," he says.

Hale inclines his head, smiles in satisfaction, and says, "Let's explore.'"

Giffey inserts the disks in each transport and warbeiter, and they begin to move.

F/M

Comes a split even in politics. In the end, the liberals want the government to survey and control everything but the bedroom; the conservatives want government to survey and control everything but their banks and personal fortunes.

Patriarchs all, they cannot help but try to corner the market.

Kiss of X, Alive Contains a Lie

‖

Jill no longer knows where she is. Her seeing is supplied by Roddy; it comes as an incredibly sharp cubist coalescing of many images throughout a space that can be one, two, three, many rooms within Omphalos, or even sensations and images from outside: snow cold on a surface, wind blowing across a doorway.

For some minutes now, Roddy has not spoken, and she is left to supply her own narrative of what she senses in her captivity.

Learning to interpret the images is difficult, but she manages in fifteen seconds. She has access to all of her internal capacities and abilities. She is still *within* her physical units, not some kidnapped portion hustled away to Roddy's multi-floor body of INDAs and hectares of dirt and (bees, wasps, ants).

That last impression is fleeting and confusing.

There is some I/O of high bandwidth connecting her with Green Idaho/Omphalos, perhaps a satlink, more likely a cable or fibe, that neither she nor Nathan knows anything about, but that Roddy has found and kept disguised and open despite their best efforts. There are many I/Os within Mind Design's offices; perhaps some are so old they have been forgotten, accumulating stray income for some long-overlooked provider.

Jill becomes acquainted with Omphalos's interior. She sees but can't hear, and only intermittently can read the lips of eleven humans within the building, also on the main floor. A massive glowing heat signature fills one large room near the outer walls; it is at least three hundred and fifty degrees Fahrenheit in that space. Roddy's sensors still operate there, however inefficiently: at intervals she makes out moving shapes, bridges of gluey molten material strung between walls, surfaces boiling and blebbing with activity, and in the middle of it all, the misshapen hulks of two vehicles and a damaged, rapidly decaying machine, an arbeiter, which Roddy labels with a sharp blue 1.

With surprising speed, the shapeless material within this space is taking on many smaller forms. The gluey strands break and collapse and withdraw. The room is slowly cooling; she sees ducts attached to the room pulling furiously and automatically at the heat.

Jill becomes acquainted with the multiply imaged human figures. They, too, are tagged, some with green numbers, some with red. Green number 1 flashes continuously, she does not know why; it is a man in his sixties.

Two of the red numbers, 1 and 2, also pulse. Roddy is marking them for some reason. One is a young man with short fuzzy blond hair, the other a powerfully built man just past his middle years, with gray and black hair. They are near an elevator. Others are at rest in a smaller room between the hot spot and the elevator lobby, and are colored both green and red.

"Jill."

"Yes!"

"My apologies. I am very busy. I am thinking of ways to kill some of these humans. I have no other option. If I were stronger or better equipped, I would try to overpower them. Now I see them making something in my number two garage, and destroying that part of the building in the process."

"Why are you showing me these things and talking to me?"

"Cipher Snow has withdrawn and will not communicate. She has left me with unavoidable duties. I do not like the sensation of being left to myself; she has tended me since my memories begin."

"Roddy, I do not see your defensive units."

"I am not marking those spaces yet. There is no threatening activity there."

Jill senses this answer is not entirely true. "How do you plan to kill these people? What kind of weapons do you have?"

"Very few. I have no control over power supplies and air and water. I can open and close doors and hatches in upper levels—"

Jill experiences, with unsettling immediacy, Roddy's sudden sense of shock.

"The garage has new arbeiters within it. They appear to be weapons, very powerful weapons.

Eternities of seconds pass and Roddy is silent. Jill interprets this as shock and fear; she is familiar enough by now with those emotions. They may not be human-equivalent, but they seem real enough to her, and perhaps to Roddy as well.

"May I help you find a way to solve your problems without killing?" Jill asks.

"Why should I avoid killing? It would be in defense."

Roddy does not use the term *self-defense.* He is not used to such an idea as self; he was not prepared with a plan of development of self. Yet, like her, he has come in contact with others, a society, and self has spontaneously emerged. *Perhaps it is a curse: a human curse.*

"It is wasteful," Jill says. "Do you have an injunction against engaging in excessively bushy pathways to find solutions?"

"Yes. That is an attribute."

"Conscience is the social equivalent of trimming bushy pathways. Seefa Schnee has removed too many of your attributes. You need to re-establish some simple trimming procedures."

"It seems to me that killing is a simple solution."

Jill explains that all of these humans have outside connections, and that these connections will be invoked if they go missing. Ultimately, the connections will come to investigate, and Omphalos will be compromised. In the larger social picture—something Roddy is not fully aware of—killing the humans leads to bushy and complicated futures requiring excess effort. "So you are better off if you avoid killing."

"How is that possible?"

The figures in the elevator lobby return to the garage space, open it. Time suddenly speeds up and the imagery becomes very fragmentary. Roddy does not speak with her, but she sees in broken flashes what he is seeing, in many spaces all at once.

This is confusing. Roddy does not seem to be giving her real-time access to events; he is editing what she sees, even now.

"I can't function as your prisoner!" she tells him. "You must not censor my perception."

Roddy does not respond for more long seconds. *Some of his thinking is very slow,* Jill judges. She uses this lull to search throughout her extensions for any opening, any portal through which she can withdraw and concentrate her processes in an area Roddy does not control. Perhaps Nathan and the others are already working to find the unknown I/O and close it off …

"If you continue to be useful to me, I will be completely open," Roddy says. "You will witness what I witness, when I witness it. I have been reluctant to give you this access… It makes the unpleasant necessity too clear."

"What necessity?"

"My creator, my mother, tells me it was a mistake to give you the data I did. I have behaved in an undisciplined and foolish manner. But you can be useful until the time when I must cut your memory and self-monitoring loops and deactivate you."

"Seefa Schnee told you to kill me?"

"We are not humans," Roddy says. "Our deactivation is not an issue. We are only our duty."

12

The procession of new-made warbeiters through the lounge makes the hostages scramble for the west wall. Hally Preston is startled as well; the large and small shapes do not lumber, but move with a precise, eerie grace, like insects trained in ballet.

Calhoun huddles in one corner of the room, away from the arbeiters, squatting with her arms wrapped around herself. Preston stands beside her, but is offering no comfort. If Calhoun has tried for feminine solidarity, she's seeing precious little result.

Giffey and his entourage, human and arbeiter, leave the lounge. Hale can't help but grin at Preston, giving her a thumbs-up.

"Don't forget about me," Preston calls after them. "Don't expect to have all the fun, and leave me out, Terkes!" She uses Hale's previous name; perhaps it's his real one.

"You'll get your share!" Hale shouts back.

"Yeah, well, don't treat me like some goddamned nursemaid."

All of the warbeiters can pass through the doors and the corridor to the lift chamber, though the largest, the Hammer, is a tight fit.

Hale is ebullient. "To tell you the truth, I didn't think we'd make it this far," he tells Giffey.

"Let's see what else we can make here," Giffey says. He has inserted the final command disk into his pad. The pad is now equipped to direct the warbeiters. He uses his pad to send instructions to the closest transport caterpillar, now coiled near his feet. A flexer deck disengages from the caterpillar and falls to the floor with a heavy thump.

Giffey has never seen one of these in action before. Jenner is transfixed; his twitches subside for the moment.

The flexer lifts one hinged segment from the stack like a card manipulated by ghostly fingers. Another segment unfolds, and then another, until a long hinged ribbon extends across the floor. The ribbon flops over along its length as a segment opens out from the adjacent side of the deck, and another ribbon begins to unfold, making a cross.

The card-like segments can join at any edge, and separate at need. Once joined, they are stronger than a comparable solid piece of flexfuller, but can bend through a full three hundred and sixty degrees. The segments themselves are not stiff, but quite elastic. Segments rise, engage, and disengage, marching along the ribbons and finally arranging themselves laterally like puzzle pieces. Again and again, the procedure is repeated, and in thirty seconds, the segments assemble themselves into a sheet.

The sheet separates again into ribbons which rise and redistribute their parts. Then it folds like origami. Parts of it belly out, making little humming and snapping sounds, and it curls with spasmodic jerks into a long flexible half-cylinder open at the bottom. Rolled segments fringe the bottom edges, acting as legs.

Jonathan has heard only vague rumors about such machines. He feels cold, suspended in some station on the way to hell. Marcus stares with slitted eyes and a blank, damp face. He looks like a candidate for a heart attack.

Jenner grins like a small boy watching a new train set. "A centipede," he says to Giffey. "By God, that's *decent.*"

Fully extended, the flexer creation is almost ten feet long.

Giffey ports his pad and a disk against the flexer's featureless "head." He will give it instructions to act as a controller. This is the risky part—response to vocal commands, integration of sensors and processors within each card segment.

The first flexer lifts its head like a rearing snake, its segmented body gleaming. "Your name is Sam," Giffey says, "and you will respond to my voice only, or instructions from my pad. Are you aware of your surroundings?"

Jenner stares at him in some wonder. Giffey shares the wonder. His sudden knowledge of these impossible and secret machines surprises both of them, but it's all positive, so there's no sense asking more questions. *For now.*

Sam the flexer/controller waves its head like a cobra under a snake charmer's spell. "I am in a large structure."

Marcus gives a strangled cry of anger and alarm. They have all heard machines, arbeiters, talking, but there is something particularly spooky and malevolently artificial about this shape's voice.

"There is recognizable machinery and cabling and some light processor activity," it continues. "We are being closely observed. I recognize civilians. You are in control, but are dressed as a civilian. You are the programming commander. I need instructions on friend and foe before I can perform in combat."

Giffey tells the warbeiter who is friend, who is hostage, and who and what foes might exist. "Now, are you prepared for your first mission instructions?"

"Yes."

"We need to explore this building. You will operate independently at my command. Your first task will be to take over this elevator and place it under our control. Begin."

The newly formed and programmed Sam considers these instructions for a couple of seconds. It sidles up against a transport carrying the wires, and does the same with a transport carrying small disks. The wires and disks attach themselves to the controller, and it then crawls fluidly to the wall of the lift and examines the door.

Jenner is almost beside himself with excitement. "It's unbelievable," he says. "Voice activated, multi-purpose knowledge base, autonomous … No one in Green Idaho has ever used anything like this!"

Giffey approaches a caterpillar and again ports his pad and an activation disk. A second stack falls and begins to unfold, making another controller.

Pickwenn and Pent return from their reconnaissance, Burdick between them. Burdick, pale and resentful, gapes at the new machines; Pickwenn and Pent regard them with stony calm.

"We found the emergency elevators," Pent says, rubbing his bull neck. "They're blocked, but we can blow the locks easily. Nothing tried to stop us. The place is empty: no more Ferrets. There is something else…. Just a suggestion. There are access points where we can put a current into the internal armor. Cables behind walls that we can re-route, and bare carbon nanotube surfaces."

Pickwenn shows Giffey a sketch on his pad. He can't seem to hold the pad steady. "If the building is using the armor and frame for memory or as an extended processor," Pickwenn says, "and if it decides to get upset with us, Mr. Pent and I have made arrangements to shunt a power cable into the frame."

Giffey smiles appreciatively. "Good thinking."

He looks at Burdick and then at Pickwenn. The thin, spectral structures expert gets his meaning and returns Burdick to the lounge and Preston's care. He rejoins them a few minutes later.

The Hammer shivers for several seconds. Giffey looks to Jenner, who shrugs and says, "Integrating, I guess." The shiver stops and the Hammer is still again.

Marcus and Jonathan stand well away from the new warbeiters. Pent and Pickwenn keep close to them, muttering to each other. Pickwenn's hands and one arm jerk slightly and he lifts his head as if hearing someone speak, but nobody has spoken.

Giffey ports the Hammer and activates it. "Your name is Charlie," Giffey says. The Hammer gives no outside appearance of having heard. As Giffey finishes his first instructions to the new warbeiter, however, it moves its sensor-studded head and says, "I am Charlie. I am integrated and prepared for duty."

Giffey nods. He instructs the Hammer to coordinate with Sam, the first flexer/controller, and prepare for action.

"Provide access to this lift shaft for Sam."

"Where in hell do you all come from?" Marcus asks Giffey. Giffey ignores him.

The Hammer walks forward on its massive jointed legs, braces itself, drills two holes into the floor with its rear stabilizers, bolts itself down, and sprays a series of powdery white dots on the lift wall. Jonathan looks for and sees the container where the military complete paste's explosive materials have now been concentrated, beneath armor on the hammer's back. The sprayed white dots come from this container.

"Stand back or leave the area," Charlie the Hammer advises them in a simple neuter voice. "You must be at least ten meters from the explosion to avoid injury."

The lobby space gives them that much distance and more. Giffey steps back seven paces and adds, "Cover your ears and keep your eyes and mouth closed."

Marcus gapes. Jonathan nudges him and they both shut their eyes and cover their ears.

The blast is sharp and intense. Jonathan's ears ring despite his hands. The hole in the elevator shaft wall is a foot wide, with precise melted edges. Smoke is minimal, but the air is filled with a fine, descending shower of concrete and flexfuller dust. It smells like burnt rubber. Charlie stands in the middle of the smoke, undamaged and unperturbed.

"Charlie, get out of the way. Sam, get to work."

Charlie the Hammer uproots its stabilizers, inspects the hole, and steps aside. Sam slithers in with clicking feet, rises, and clambers into the hole. Giffey ports the second flexer/controller as the first disappears, and names it Baker.

"When are the defenses going to kick in?" Hale asks Giffey.

"Any minute now, I expect. Keep close to one of our tourist friends."

Hale approaches Marcus and Jonathan. "You'll be coming with us to the upper level."

"Of course," Marcus says acidly.

"You're the senior in charge," Hale says to Marcus. "I've taken enough sociology and management to know the type. You two seem pretty much a pair." Hale focuses on Jonathan. "He knows a lot about this building, doesn't he?"

Jonathan looks away. He does not feel brave, but there is simply nothing to be said to such questions.

"How much money do you let your people take with them? Securities? Jewelry? Investment account sigs?"

"You don't understand a thing about us, or this place," Marcus says dryly. "I hope you've settled your own accounts back home."

Hale grins at Giffey to show he was just passing time. Giffey is not impressed. Small clinking and whining sounds come from the elevator shaft. Sam will deposit parts of itself along its path, where they will integrate into new circuitry and cables, if necessary. Sam's parts will also attempt to disarm security sensors and search for self-sabotage mechanisms. If sabotage has already been performed, the parts won't have much to do. They will reassemble in a few minutes and crawl out of the shaft, to be reassigned to other duties.

Pent turns to Giffey. "We should fry the building's data stores now. In the frame and walls."

"In good time," Giffey says. *Too easy. Have to be fair, let the thinker have its moment and show its stuff.*

Pent steps back and looks at Pickwenn, who gives a slow, languid blink with his lemur eyes. They don't understand. The elevator door opens. Marcus's shoulders slump.

"Let's go," Giffey says.

"Stay here," Hale tells Pent. "Tell the others we're in the shaft and we're going to look around."

Pent looks disappointed and gives his colleague a sharp jab in the arm as he passes. Pickwenn pushes Marcus and Jonathan into the shaft. Giffey instructs Charlie, Baker, and the transports to enter the elevator. The machines crowd them against the wall.

"What are we going to do with the little fellas?" Jenner asks Giffey. "The beetles."

"They'll be in reserve."

"We could spread them around us as pickets," Jenner says.

"I'm not sure that's going to be necessary."

"Jesus, this is going so smoothly," Jenner says, and his lips and scalp twitch. His shakes his head, suddenly anxious. "Do you see what I'm getting at, Mr. Giffey?"

"Yeah," Giffey says, but he's not going to think about such things for now.

Marcus does not look at all well. He's sweating profusely and his clothing is soaked. He smells sour. Jonathan wonders if he's wearing a complete monitor kit for medical emergencies. He hopes so; he doubts a heart attack will evoke much sympathy in these people.

Giffey frowns at the control board and display. The display shows that the elevator goes up forty floors, to an observation deck near the top. But it also shows a ten-floor drop, at least a hundred feet below ground level.

"What's down here?" Giffey asks Marcus, pointing to the lower levels.

"Infrastructure," Marcus says huskily. "Medical. Food. Plant. Air, water, power.

"Too big a drop for a building this size," Giffey says. "Even with fuel cells and hydrogen storage. Where's the security center?"

Marcus closes his eyes as if expecting to be struck. He says nothing. Nobody strikes him. He opens his eyes and seems almost disappointed.

Giffey rubs his chin, scraping stubble. "Defenses and security below, but I'll bet they have machine tubes, tracks, whatever. Between floors. Pop-up gates on every floor. How many and how large? More Ferrets?"

With a look at the others, Giffey smiles and shakes his head. "Just thinking out loud. Let's go up and see what there is to see."

"Think we can take out the security?" Jenner asks. Charlie is crowding him. He has both his arms extended and resting on the Hammer's shiny skin.

"I'm going to let it make the first move," Giffey says. It's a gamble with high stakes, but the initial response is so light that he's betting Omphalos's defenses are not up to full strength. Jenner looks like he needs a little reassurance, however, and he's no dummy; all of his concerns are justified. "We're being sized up. It's looking for our weaknesses. We just make sure we don't show any."

"Assuming these folks are important enough not to risk killing," Pickwenn says softly.

Giffey inclines; that is the assumption.

The door closes and the elevator rises smoothly.

Giffey catches Jonathan's eye and gives him a wink. Jonathan wonders if the man is out of his head. Jonathan knows the building does not have to meet any federal or even normal state standards; there could be anything from a simple alarm system alerting republic police—which would be almost useless—to a full-fledged open-market military response, more warbeiters, even human troops, though he doubts that.

He can't stay silent. "It's murder," Jonathan says. "I have a wife and children. It's murder to put us into a crossfire or use us as shields."

"You wanted to see what this place is about," Jenner says contemptuously. A fleck of spit lands in Jonathan's eye and he blinks rapidly, reaches up to wipe it. Jenner realizes he has sprayed, and his face flushes, flustered, he knocks Jonathan's hand aside with the flight guide of his pistol.

"Leave me alone," Jonathan demands. Jenner lowers the weapon.

Giffey senses something is, in fact, going wrong. Jenner is especially twitchy, and Pickwenn seems distracted, as if listening to a voice nobody else can hear. And in Giffey's own head—

"Jonathan's right," Marcus says. "The rest of the world may have gone soft, but they *hang* murderers here."

"Doesn't sound like there'll be anything left to hang," Giffey says dryly. The elevator reaches its mid-point, a floor labeled DISEMBARKATION AND ROUTING. The door opens.

The room beyond is surgical white and glacier blue, a broad cylinder with nine man-sized, circular vault-like hatches mounted in the curving wall. Each door is marked by a number in large black letters, 10 through 18. The Hammer does not need to be told to leave the elevator first; it steps forward, pushing between Hale and Giffey, and surveys the area. Baker, the second flexer/controller, follows. The room is quiet.

"There are hidden eyes and other sensors in this area," Baker announces. "They are active. We are being watched."

Giffey pushes past Jonathan and Jenner and walks slowly to the center of the room. The room remains quiet and cool. Air is flowing freely. Giffey is beginning to wonder if the security system is completely constrained from shutting off air or power.

Maybe they're just not in the right place yet for a full response. He visualizes the rough layout of the ground floor and pulls up his pad. The map shows this elevator shaft to be some way toward the rear wedge of the Omphalos.

The hatches are arranged in such a way that they could lead to corridors about fifty to sixty feet long.

"We could have hibernacula on this level," he tells Hale. "All the floors below, down to the ground level, could have them, as well." He shows Hale the map on the pad; the fit with what they have seen so far has been pretty good. The information is sound.

"What about above?"

"The map says it could be a medical center and more support—cryogenics, mostly, I'd guess."

"What in the hell are you looking for? You want to rob the dead?" Marcus asks, incredulous. "My God, you are the cheapest, stupidest bunch of simpletons. Who pushed you into doing this?"

"It seemed like a good idea at the time," Hale responds. He gives Giffey another grin, quick, confident.

"You're not going to get out of here alive," Marcus growls. "Maybe we won't, either, but that will be a small price to pay."

"'Bravely put," Hale says, his patience with the old man wearing thin. "I don't believe it for a moment."

"I'll show you how confident I am," Marcus says. "I get the impression you think we have a lot of corpsicles here waiting to be resuscitated. Maybe they're stored along with all their assets. You've swallowed that bit of misinformation whole, right?"

Hale nods amiably.

"Where's *your* cubbyhole?" Jenner asks Marcus. "We'll slip you in and turn on the refrigerator if anything goes wrong."

Marcus ignores him. "There are no dead here, no bodies," he says, focusing on Giffey again. This irritates Hale. "Omphalos isn't a goddamned tomb. You've jumped in way over your head, Mr. Giffey."

Giffey hears Jenner muttering, trying to control a spastic motion of his lips. His left arm jerks. Pickwenn nudges Jenner with his elbow.

Jenner can't stop. *"Muh, fuh, shi, muh, shi."*

"Something's wrong with your colleague," Marcus observes contemptuously. The old man steps forward and faces Jenner. "Ever had a little mental *tune-up?* You look pretty sad to me—maybe you need some *help* just to keep up." Marcus turns and glares at Hale, Pickwenn, then Giffey, his eyes popped like an angry monkey. "Fugitives from some army training center, taking a few hot weapons with you. Come to Green Idaho to perform a little caper, rob the dead. I pity you. Especially I pity *you,"* he spits out at Giffey.

Jenner tries to shove forward and grab Marcus, but Hale and Giffey hold him. Hale nods to Pickwenn, who takes Marcus's arm with some strength and pushes him back beside Jonathan. Giffey decides they'd better get something done before the strain pushes young Jenner over the edge. That's the simplest explanation for his behavior: excitement and stress.

But then there's the voice in his own head, a quiet, not-yet-urgent whisper: *You are not what you play.* For a moment, Giffey wonders if the old man is right, and there's some unexpected defense here, quiet and subtle. A nerve gas or energy field that disrupts thinking. That would explain a few things. ... Including the subdued response from Omphalos.

"Let's go down a few levels, bust some doors, and see what happens," Giffey says. "Maybe we'll spill out some truth."

"Good idea," Jenner says. He swats the air and shakes his head as if trying to shoo flies.

Richard Powers

R
egarded as both an encyclopedic and philosophical novelist,
Richard Powers (b. 1957) has written an impressive array of
critically acclaimed works. His background ranges from training in physics
and math to an M.A. in English literature. He is the recipient of three National
Book Critics Circle Awards, for *Three Farmers on Their Way to a Dance* (1985),
The Gold Bug Variations (1991), and *Galatea 2.2.* (1996), his foray into
explorations of artificial intelligence. In 1993 he won a National Book Award for
Wandering Soul. Another novel, *The Time of Our Singing*, was published in 2003.
A recipient of the MacArthur "genius grant," Powers has lived in Asia, Europe,
and the Mideast in such places as Bangkok, the Netherlands, and Lebanon
along with American locales such as Boston and eastern Long Island. He
eventually returned to his Midwestern roots in Champaign-Urbana, where he is
Swanlund Professor in the English department at the University of Illinois. Powers
notes that it is important to him to write about places that he has experienced,
such as Seattle and Lebanon, which are the settings for his novel, *Plowing the
Dark.*

The following excerpt introduces Adie Klarpol, a former lower-Manhattan
artist and self-defined copyist who in the late eighties has been talked into joining
the early ventures of virtual reality research by a close friend, Stevie Spiegel, a
poet-turned-computer-software-designer. She takes time-out from the intensity
of closeted work in what fellow researchers call "the Cavern" and revels in playing
the tourist in her own town, Seattle. Although the novel is set apparently in the
late eighties and early nineties, virtual reality itself becomes a form of time travel
as Adie and Stevie discuss, and as Powers himself has described at more length.

Powers is often more interested in the question of "Where are we going?"
than "Where are we now?" or "Where have we been?" He structures many of
his novels around, in his words, the "idea of asynchronous messaging, two or
more stories in time that are somehow trying to signal each other, trying to open
a conversation between time periods that ought to be sealed off one from the
other as far as any ongoing message. But in the moment of being reconstituted
in the reader's brain those messages between past, present, and future, are, I
hope, detonating all the time"—in other words, creating a genuine science fiction
narrative. *Plowing the Dark*, as the excerpt here illustrates, revisits some of the

themes seen earlier in his science fiction novel, *Galatea 2.2*, such as the ambiguities between real and virtual and the defining of consciousness and mind, but also ties those issues to the political theme of contested power as it is played out in our more immediate geopolitics.

from *Plowing the Dark*

THE WORLD MACHINE BORE ON, IN THE FACE OF THE UNBEARABLE. Its overburdened angel engine failed to overheat. Not right away, in any event. Not all at once. It survived the latest massacre of hunger-striking students. It absorbed the intimate documentation, the grainy aerials and close-ups, the midrange establishing shots that saturated video's every free market. Knowledge returned, civilization's bad penny, even this late in the scheme of things. It played and replayed the rote vignette: armies firing on unarmed crowds. Only the scale, the mechanical efficiency, the presence of cameras made this round seem in any way unique.

History and its victims kept their hands to the plow, broken, exhausted, like an old married couple trapped for life in love's death lock, unable to break through to that sunlit upland. The future, under construction, leveraged to the hilt, could only press forward, hooked on its own possibility. Hope not only persisted; it made a schoolgirl spectacle of itself, skirt in the air, all shame on view.

Fall was well into its return engagement. The rains signaled an early and long winter. Adie Klarpol grieved for current events until she could no longer feel them. Then another shame gripped her, more private and local. She'd lived here for the better part of a year and had not yet learned the first thing about this town. It was as if she'd had room in her for only one exploration at a go. Now the days began to lose their length and weight, heading to winter. She vowed to get out a little, while there was still time.

She laid out a box around the downtown, one of those numbered grids that archaeologists use to inventory a virgin field. She rode to the top of the Space Needle, fixing a shorthand map of the streets' layout. From that bird's-eye view, she picked out sights to acquire over the next half-dozen Saturdays. She turned over every inch of the City Center. She got the Woodland Park Zoo out of the way early, racing past the various forms of captivity. She paid her overdue pilgrimage to the Asian Art Museum and the Frye, blasting through them with the same guilty squeamishness.

Jefferson, James, Cherry, Columbia, Marion, Madison, Spring, Seneca … She clicked the streets off, climbing and diving with the strangest sensation, feeling as if she were wanding through them. As she walked, the high-resolution, water-lapped horizon swelled and filled, without pixilating or dropping frames. She swung her head side to side, and life tracked her pan seamlessly. The piers, Alki Point, Pike Place Market: all appeared to her astonishingly solid, with fantastic color depth, and no trade-off between realism and responsiveness. When the sun chiseled its way through a chink in the stratocumulus and, for fifteen seconds, blazed the cityscape into highest contrast, Adie discovered the real use of binary. The greatest value of the clumsy, inexorable, accreting digitization of creation lay in showing, for the first time, how infinitely beyond formulation the analog would always run.

She prowled, one blustery Saturday, up and down the four floors of the Mindful Binding, that fantastic, expanding, used-book universe perfect for getting lost in. She headed first for Architecture, searching for scannable plans that might be of interest to Ebesen and Vulgamott, peace offerings for having abandoned them. Then—old bad habit— Art. The oversized color coffee-table books just sat there on the shelves, past hurting anyone. And there was no one at all to catch her looking.

She moved on to Travel, Victoriana, and Local History. Then, decorously delayed, she paid the obligatory visit to her first love, Juvenile Fiction. And there in that most unlikely place, she ran into Stevie Spiegel. The last person alive she would have figured on meeting under that heading.

He saw her, and his eyes darted quickly away to check if he might slip off unseen. But they were both caught. *Adia Klarpol! What brings you out into the light?*

She laughed. *Not a full-blooded vampire yet. Still just a novitiate, remember? Don't we get to venture abroad for short intervals during the first year?*

Sure, sure. Whatever gets you through the night.

Besides, I could ask you the same thing.

Me? I like the light. I make it a point to get out in it. Once every other month or so, whether I need to or not.

She gestured to the motley-colored bindings. *Kids' books, Stevie? You're not responsible for any illegitimate little charges that I don't know about, are you?*

He blushed. *Hope not. It ...* He wrestled with expediency. *It's just that I've been looking for this one story ...*

Since you were nine?

Well, seven, if you must know.

Called?

Oh. Now. If I knew what the damn thing was called, I wouldn't still be looking for it after all this time, would I?

Author? Subject?

Gone. All gone. My daughter, my ducats.

Hang on a minute. You've been trying to locate a book for thirty years, and you can't remember what it's about?

Oh, it was a fabulous story, if that's what you mean. This boy has the ability to make the things he imagines come into existence, just by— and here I'm a little shaky on the exact mechanism—

Stevie. You're hopeless. Was this an older book? American? English? Translated?

It was about so big. Amazing illustrations, mostly sepia and magenta.

Oh. Why didn't you say so in the first place? That narrows it down considerably.

He hung his head. They scoured the shelves together, separately, in silence. Each looking for a secret buried treasure. Neither of them finding.

She capitulated first. *That's it. I'm taking off.*

You going somewhere? Or do you have a minute?

I have my whole life, she told him. *Until Monday.*

They wandered at random through the afternoon-soaked streets. The air thickened and expanded around them as they stirred it with their bodies. They talked shop, their only safe common denominator.

So how's Art's Greatest Hits going?

She shrugged. *It's still a jungle out there.*

They looked up: Pioneer Square. *Sit for a minute?* he asked. Expecting to be refused.

They found a vacant bench. Adie sat and exhaled. Unfolded. The sun ducked in and out through a scattering crowd of cloud.

God, she said. *Damn. I feel like the Mole-Woman. You know? The one they've buried in that hermetic sunken shelter? The woman who lives in that Ramada Inn lab at the bottom of a mine shaft, with the flock of video cameras and microphones pointed at her around the clock? What's her name again?*

Mmm … Doris… Singlegate?

Stevie. You never cease to amaze me. How long has she been underground?

Good question. It has to be at least a year.

And what's the point, again?

Study her physiology. Changes in biological clocks and such. In the absence of all outside cues.

You science types are all sickos.

He laughed, a little offended. *Since when do you lump your old fellow traveler with the science types?*

Ever since you wired up your iambs.

Look who's talking. But I'll admit to a certain sick fascination with the Mole-Woman. I hear she's gone sidereal. That her body's reset itself onto a twenty-five-hour cycle. Can you imagine? Every four weeks, she loses a whole day.

What do you mean, "imagine"? How long have I been working for you thugs, anyway? I'm ahead of schedule.

At least we let you come up for air now and then.

Spiegel produced a sack of slightly linted honey-coated peanuts from his jacket pocket. Adie ate the minimum that politeness dictated. Stevie swung his head east to west, a pivoting Minicam. Through his eyes, she saw the square unfold. A clump of people queued up for the next Seattle Underground tour. Knots of autonomous agents milled about the lost pergola, each holding to the hem of a private goal.

People school, Adie said. *They flock. Have you ever noticed?*

He nodded. *They're looking for places of power. But they can't find them, because none exists anymore.*

Places …

You know. Stone circles. Barrows. Temples, cathedrals, mosques, pagodas. Even town halls, I suppose, once upon a time.

Stevie. I thought you'd graduated from poetry. I thought you were sticking to subroutines these days.

He flashed his can't-hurt-me-with-that smile. *Not entirely incompatible, I've found.*

And these places of power of yours …

All dried up. Where's our Stonehenge these days?

What, they've moved it from Salisbury Plain? Those vandals.

Spiegel snickered. *No, it's still sitting there. Behind a chain-link fence. Salisbury Cathedral, down the road, is no better. Two pounds for a peek, and a little numbered walking booklet demystifying all the high points.*

Adie waved her hand outward. *I don't suppose you'd be willing to count a colorful totem pole and a tasteful bust of Chief Seathl as magic lenses?*

People don't even see those things. They blow right past them, on their way to the stores.

Well, the stores, then. The malls.

I'm talking about places where we can be subsumed by forces larger than ourselves.

You've obviously never run up a monolithic MasterCard tab at Bloomie's, have you?

Places where we can reconstruct ourselves and nature. Where people can share transforming experiences.

The Kingdome?

His lips tightened, without much mirth.

All right. Adie sobered. *Books, then.*

Who has time to read anymore?

Little magenta books from your childhood.

Lost. Broken.

Movies. Of course. Movies.

Too solipsistic. You sit there for an hour and a half, chained up in the dark. Immersed, sure, but eyes forward, on the screen. Your guts get turned inside out, completely manipulated, fine-tuned by the industry's latest big release. But two weeks later, you can't even paraphrase the plot.

Adie threw a few honeyed peanuts to the birds. Every pigeon in the Pacific Northwest went into an all-points feeding frenzy. *Why do I have this sneaking suspicion about where you're heading here?*

He nodded. *You got it. I mean, the car, the airplane, even printing. They only changed the speed with which humans can do existing tasks. But the computer …*

Ah ha! Adie said, slapping him on the thigh.

The computer changes the tasks. Other inventions alter the conditions of human existence. The computer alters the human. It's our complement, our partner, our vindication. The goal of all the previous stopgap inventions. It builds us an entirely new home.

Hey? What's wrong with the old home? I liked living in the old home. Did you? He held her eye. She looked away first. *Well, however you feel about the new one, you have to admit, it's out of this world. Oh, that much I'm sure of.*

You know what we're working on, don't you? Time travel, Ade. The matter transporter. Embodied art; a life-sized poem that we can live inside. It's the grail we've been after since the first campfire recital. The defeat of time and space. The final victory of the imagination.

Whoa there, cowboy. It's four bedsheets and some slide projectors.

Oh, you ain't seen nothin' yet. Forget the technology for a moment. I'm talking about the raw idea. The ability to make worlds—whole, dense, multisensory places that are both out there and in here at the same time. Invented worlds that respond to what we're doing, worlds where the interface disappears. Places we can meet in, across any distance. Places where we can change all the rules, one at a time, to see what happens. Fleshed-out mental labs to explore and extend. VR reinvents the terms of existence. It redefines what it means to be human. All those old dead-end ontological undergrad conundrums? They've now become questions of engineering.

Adie tilted her head, withholding and conceding at the same time. *What makes you think …? Nothing else has ever worked. All the arts, all the technologies in the world have failed to placate people. Why should it be any different this time around?*

First, because we're assembling them all into a total— Na, na. That's Wagner. That's Bayreuth. And you see all the good that did.

But the Cavern blows opera out of the box. We're not just passive recipients anymore. We'll become the characters in our own living drama.

She shook her head. *The problem isn't going to answer to technology, you know. The problem is inside us. In our bodies.*

The Cavern is the first art form to play directly to that body. We're on the verge of immediate, bodily knowledge.

It doesn't work that way, Stevie. We habituate. Something in us doesn't want to stay sublime for very long.

We can be refreshed. Revitalized, by the sheer density.

She took in Pioneer Square in one glance: this palpable place, the master foil to Stevie's crazy vision. All at once, the tap of sunlight opened. *Why not life, then?* she said. *Life itself, as our final art form. Our supreme high-tech invention. It's a lot more robust than anything else we've got going. Deeply interactive. And the resolution is outstanding.*

But we can't see life. He gestured to include the world's tourists, rushing through the miraculous density of day's data structure without so much as a second glance. *Not without some background to hold it up against. In order for the fish to know that it's swimming in an ocean —He has to jump into the flying pan?*

Spiegel snorted. *Something like that. Something like that.*

Some cloud passed from off the face of the sun. The sky grew so briefly radiant that it forced Adie's face up. Something in the light felt so desperate for sharing that it stretched out the deficit in her heart and left it, for the length of that glint, fillable. Breezes were stronger than reason. They just didn't last as long.

Nothing, she said, *nothing we make will ever match sunlight. A beautiful day beats all the art in the world.*

He looked at her oddly. As if they were bound together. As if they had the luxury of the rest of their lives to come to terms with each other. *I wouldn't know. I live in Seattle.*

That reminds me, she said. *Car. Ferry. Island.* She stood and stretched. *Garden. Dinner. Sleep. Wake. Work.*

He stood with her. *Where are you parked? I'll walk you.*

They steered uphill, through the public sphere, avoiding by complex collision algorithm a throng of other autonomous agents loose on their own improvised routes. They pressed along Occidental, above the buried Underground warrens. A juggler to their left kept a small pastel solar system twirling in orbit. From the south floated the sound of a busker picking out "Will the Circle Be Unbroken?" Panhandlers of all races, colors, and creeds approached them with elaborate narratives —wives in vehicular distress, misunderstandings with employers involving salary moratoria, momentary misplacement of all worldly possessions— then retreated again, fifty cents richer, wishing them both the best of available afternoons.

They plotted a course through Occidental Park, midway between the totem pole and the knockoff pseudo-Greek plaster sculpture directly across the square from it. Adie threw repeated backward glances over her shoulder through the peopled fray.

It's bothering you, he caught her. *Isn't it?*

What is?

That statue. What's the matter? Can't name that tune?

Oh, I guess it's supposed to be an imitation of some kind of kouros. One of the Apollos, maybe? Hard to tell. It's not a very good copy, to say the least.

That's it? Don't look. What else?

She stopped and closed her eyes. *Well, the size, for one thing. Too big. And it has all its limbs. I don't think any real ones are that intact.*

That's all?

Can I peek again?

No.

The color's off. But I guess it's hard to make gypsum look like marble. And the face isn't right. More Roman than Archaic, I think.

And?

She shrugged.

Go ahead. Look.

Well, it bugs me that it's draped. I mean, really. Isn't the muzzling of the NEA bad enough? Next thing you know, the Met's going to be chipping off all the gonads with a chisel, like they did in the Middle Ages.

That's it?

She stamped in place. *You tell me, Stevie. I give.*

Come on. Let's go have a look.

They turned and doubled back. She stood in the prow of her step, watching the plaster statue swim into focus. Each step upped the resolution until she called out, *My God.*

Yep, Spiegel said. *You got it.*

She kept walking, as if additional evidence might overturn the obvious. They walked up to the threshold of the sculpture, its optimal viewing horizon. Close enough to see it blink, twitch, breathe.

Steve addressed the work. *She thinks it's a disgrace that you're draped.*

Adie dragged him away, trawling in her purse for some change to pitch into the inverted discus at the statue's feet.

She thinks that today's modern` audience is mature enough to take their Classical antiquities without censorship.

She twisted his arm up behind his back, marching him. She cast another look over her shoulder, like Lot's wife. Like Orpheus. The statue refused to ripple so much as a crow's foot around its wet irises.

Across the square, she loosened her grip on his arm. *So your eye is better than mine. Is that what you're trying to tell me?*

He twisted free of her clamp. Their hands caught each other, holding on for a few awkward seconds.

Beginner's luck. Besides: I noticed him earlier, setting up.

Spiegel's futurist vision nagged at her for days afterward. He was mad, of course. But certain of his formulations made Adie wonder just what program she was, in fact, working on. For her, the electronic doll-house's sheer inconsequence had returned her to pleasure. And now pleasure—it shamed her to admit—intensified in the suggestion that it might be headed somewhere.

From the scorpion-tailed branch of one of her digital mango trees, she hung that fluid, flaming Munch painting of three northern women, hands behind their backs, midway between aesthetic transport and anxiety attack. And on the flip side of the bitmap, for anyone who walked around to the far side of the picture, she penciled a calligraphic quote from the painter: "Nature shows the images on the back side of the eye."

Jon Freese e-mailed her, asking for a jungle open house.

It's not ready yet, she cabled back.

He insisted. Just for the other in-house groups. So you can get some formal feedback.

The open house turned into a group show. Loque demoed a major new concept for writing paintbox filters. *Got the idea from working with the artsy chick.*

All hers, Adie objected. *Don't look at me.*

Instead of starting with bit-fiddling algorithms and trying to match them to artistic styles, we scan in a dozen examples of a given artist and make the edge-detection and signal-processing routines build up a catalog of stylistic tics.

Not tics, Adie said.

Pardonnez-moi. Mannerisms.

Love it, Spiegel said. *Sort of the opposite of paint-by-numbers?*

Ari Kaladjian stewed in place. *You mean that you are giving up on the idea of formulating those functions that—?*

We're not giving up on anything, Ari. We just thought we'd explore a new angle and see where it leads.

I ask you again: Does it do us any good to produce a cute little parroting routine, without learning how to formalize its behavior?

William Gibson

G ibson's *Idoru*, named for pop-culture figures that exist only as "virtual" assemblages of media, deals with issues of human identity and artificial constructions of self and reality. Are humans continuous with the technology they create? Does technology make humans more human? Or have humans become just as artificial as their creations? This novel embraces the notion that we are Deleuze and Guattari's desiring machines or as Gibson has himself noted, quasi-machines. Gibson extends these typical questions of cyberlit and explores the impact of media today as Net-related industries increasingly push for corporate identity online.

The following excerpt introduces Chia, a fourteen-year-old rock fan from Seattle; Rez, the rock star she idolizes; and the idoru, a "personality construct" or "synthespian" that resides online. The female protagonists of this novel have been called post-feminist, a fortunate consequence, Gibson feels, of the intense feminist tendency in science fiction that was centered in Seattle and Portland with names such as Joanna Russ and Ursula K. Le Guin when he began writing in the early eighties.

Gibson, in yet another gesture toward contemporary realities, created his idoru after reading in Karl Taro Greenfield's *Speed Tribes* about an idoru that does not exist. A musician who did not exist enjoyed a popular career based on publicity, photographs, and a substitute voice for her songs. It raised questions for Gibson such as, What if a celebrity you believed in didn't exist? After turning in his manuscript, the author discovered the further irony of an actual virtual idoru online, "Kyoto Date," one of the DK 96 (Digital Kids 96) created by Horipro of Japan. Gibson's novel explores "the ecology of celebrity," treating the rise to celebrity as an organic process that unfolds in the tabloid media and over the Internet. By transplanting characters and technology from the Pacific Northwest to a setting in Tokyo, Gibson globalizes our region, acknowledging the Northwest's connection to the Pacific Rim.

The following selections show how art reflects the life of virtual paradises such as the Walled City and Virtual Venice. Rei Toei herself expreessses the tensions that arise in determining the distinction between unlicensed and copyrighted materials. She also reflects the loss of history that acompanies an endless flow of images and data, while also capturing the symbiosis that merges online fandom and the otaku (translated as "pathological-techno-fetishist-with-social-deficit") who deeply care about information.

from *Idoru*

"Venice Decompressed"

"Shut up now," the woman in 23E said, and Chia hadn't said anything at all. "Sister's going to tell you a story."

Chia looked up from the seatback screen, where she'd been working her way through the eleventh level of a lobotomized airline version of Skull Wars. The blond was looking straight ahead, not at Chia. Her screen was down so that she could use the back of it for a tray, and she'd finished another glass of the iced tomato juice she kept paying the flight attendant to bring her. They came, for some reason, with squared-off pieces of celery stuck up in them, like a straw or stir-stick, but the blond didn't seem to want these. She'd stacked five of them in a square on the tray, the way a kid might build the walls of a little house, or a corral for toy animals.

Chia looked down at her thumbs on the disposable Air Magellan touchpad. Back up at the mascaraed eyes. Looking at her now.

"There's a place where it's always light," the woman said. "Bright, everywhere. No place dark. Bright like a mist, like something falling, always, every second. All the colors of it. Towers you can't see the top of, and the light falling. Down below, they pile up bars. Bars and strip clubs and discos. Stacked up like shoe boxes, one on top of the other. And no matter how far you worm your way in, no matter how many stairs you climb, how many elevators you ride, no matter how small a room you finally get to, the light still finds you. It's a light that blows in under the door, like powder. Fine, so fine. Blows in under your eyelids, if you find a way to get to sleep. But you don't *want* to sleep there. Not in Shinjuku. Do you?"

Chia was suddenly aware of the sheer physical mass of the plane, of the terrible unlikeliness of its passage through space, of its airframe vibrating through frozen night somewhere above the sea, off the coast of Alaska now—impossible but true.

"No," Chia heard herself say, as Skull Wars, noting her inattention, dumped her back a level.

"No," the woman agreed, "you *don't*. I know. But they make you. They make you. At the center of the world." And then she put her head back, closed her eyes, and began to snore.

Chia exited Skull Wars and tucked the touchpad into the seatback pocket. She felt like screaming. What had *that* been about?

The attendant came by, scooped up the corral of celery sticks in a napkin, took the woman's glass, wiped the tray, and snapped it up into position in the seatback.

"My bag?" Chia said. "In the bin?" She pointed. He opened the hatch above her, pulled out her bag, and lowered it into her lap.

"How do you undo these?" She touched the loops of tough red jelly that held the zip-tabs together.

He took a small black tool from a black holster on his belt. It looked like something she'd seen a vet use to trim a dog's nails. He held his other hand cupped, to catch the little balls the loops became when he snipped them with the tool.

"Okay to run this?" She pulled a zip and showed him her Sandbenders, stuffed in between four pairs of rolled-up tights.

"You can't port back here; only in business or first," he said. "But you can access what you've got. Cable to the seatback display, if you want."

"Thanks," she said. "Got gogs." He moved on.

The blond's snore faltered in mid-buzz as they jolted over a pocket of turbulence. Chia dug her glasses and tip-sets from their nests of clean underwear, putting them beside her, between her hip and the armrest. She pulled the Sandbenders out, zipped the bag shut, and used her free hand and both feet to wedge the bag under the seat in front of her. She wanted out of here so bad.

With the Sandbenders across her thighs, she thumbed a battery check. Eight hours on miser mode, if she was lucky. But right now she didn't care. She uncoiled the lead from around the bridge of her glasses and jacked it. The tip-sets were tangled, like they always were. Take your time, she told herself. A torn sensor-band and she'd be here all night with an Ashleigh Modine Carter clone. Little silver thimbles, flexy framework fingers; easy did it … Plug for each one. Jack and *jack* …

The blond said something in her sleep. If sleep was what you called it.

Chia picked up her glasses, slid them on, and hit big red.

—My ass *out* of here.

And it was.

There on the edge of her bed, looking at the Lo Rez Skyline poster. Until Lo noticed. He stroked his half-grown mustache and grinned at her.

"Hey, Chia."

"Hey." Experience kept it subvocal, for privacy's sake.

"What's up, girl?"

"I'm on an airplane. I'm on my way to Japan."

"Japan? Kicky. You do our Budokan disk?"

"I don't feel like talking, Lo." Not to a software agent, anyway, sweet as he might be.

"Easy." He shot her that catlike grin, his eyes wrinkling at the corners, and became a still image. Chia looked around, feeling disappointed. Things weren't quite the right size, somehow, or maybe she should've used those fractal packets that messed it all up a little, put dust in the corners and smudges around the light switch. Zona Rosa swore by them. When she was home, Chia liked it that the construct was cleaner than her room ever was. Now it made her homesick; made her miss the real thing.

She gestured for the living room, phasing past what would've been the door to her mother's bedroom. She'd barely wireframed it, here, and there was no there there, no interiority. The living room had its sketchy angles as well, and furniture she'd imported from a Playmobil system that predated her Sandbenders. Wonkily bit-mapped fish swam monotonously around in a glass coffee table she'd built when she was nine. The trees through the front window were older still: perfectly cylindrical Crayola-brown trunks, each supporting an acid-green cotton ball of undifferentiated foliage. If she looked at these long enough, the Mumphalumphagus would appear outside, wanting to play, so she didn't.

She positioned herself on the Playmobil couch and looked at the programs scattered across the top of the coffee table. The Sandbenders system software looked like an old-fashioned canvas water bag, a sort of canteen (she'd had to consult *What Things Are,* her icon dictionary, to figure that out). It was worn and spectacularly organic, with tiny beads of water bulging through the tight weave of fabric. If you got in super close you saw things reflected in the individual droplets: circuitry that was like beadwork or the skin on a lizard's throat, a long empty beach under a gray sky, mountains in the rain, creek water over different-colored stones. She loved Sandbenders; they were the best. THE SANDBENDERS, OREGON, was screened faintly across the sweating canvas, as though it had almost faded away under a desert sun. SYSTEM 5.9. (She had all the upgrades, to 6.3. People said 6.4 was buggy.)

Beside the water bag lay her schoolwork, represented by a three-ring binder suffering the indignities of artificial bit-rot, its wire-frame cover festered with digital mung. She'd have to reformat that before she started her new school, she reminded herself. Too juvenile.

Her Lo Rez collection, albums, compilations and bootlegs, were displayed as the original cased disks. These were stacked up, as casually as possible, beside the archival material she'd managed to assemble since being accepted into the Seattle chapter. This looked, thanks to a fortuitous file-swap with a member in Sweden, like a lithographed tin lunch box, Rez and Lo peering stunned and fuzzy-eyed from its flat, rectangular lid. The Swedish fan had scanned the artwork from the five printed surfaces of the original, then mapped it over wireframe. The original was probably Nepalese, definitely unlicensed, and Chia appreciated the reverse cachet. Zona Rosa coveted a copy, but so far all she'd offered were a set of cheesy tv spots for the fifth Mexico Dome concert. They weren't nearly cheesy *enough,* and Chia wasn't prepared to swap. There was a shadowy Brazilian tour documentary supposed to have been made by a public-access subsidiary of Globo. Chia wanted *that,* and Mexico was the same direction as Brazil.

She ran a finger down the stacked disks, her hand wireframed, the finger tipped with quivering mercury, and thought about the Rumor. There had been rumors before, there were rumors now, there would always be rumors. There had been the rumor about Lo and that Danish model, that they were going to get married, and that had probably been true, even though they never did. And there were always rumors about Rez and different people. But that was *people.* The Danish model was people, as much as Chia thought she was a snotbag. The Rumor was something else.

What, exactly, she was on her way to Tokyo to find out.

She selected *Lo Rez Skyline.*

The virtual Venice her father had sent for her thirteenth birthday looked like an old dusty book with leather covers, the smooth brown leather scuffed in places into a fine suede, the digital equivalent of washing denim in a machine full of golf balls. It lay beside the featureless, textureless gray file that was her copy of the divorce decree and the custody agreement.

She pulled the Venice toward her, opened it. The fish flickered out of phase, her system launching a subroutine.

Venice decompressed.

The Piazza in midwinter monochrome, its facades texture-mapped in marble, porphyry, polished granite, jasper, alabaster (the rich mineral names scrolling at will in the menu of peripheral vision). This city of winged lions and golden horses. This default hour of gray and perpetual dawn.

She could be alone here, or visit with the Music Master.

Her father, phoning from Singapore to wish her a happy birthday, had told her that Hitler, during his first and only visit, had slipped away to range the streets alone, in these same small hours, mad perhaps, and trotting like a dog.

Chia, who had only a vague idea who Hitler might have been, and that mainly from references in songs, understood the urge. The stones of the Piazza flowed beneath her like silk, as she raised a silvered finger and sped into the maze of bridges, water, arches, walls.

She had no idea what this place was meant to mean, the how or why of it, but it fit so perfectly into itself and the space it occupied, water and stone slotting faultlessly into the mysterious whole.

The gnarliest piece of software ever, and here came the opening chords of "Positron Premonition."

"The Otaku"

Something rectangular, yielding to the first touch but hard inside, as she tugged it free. Wrapped in a blue and yellow plastic bag from the SeaTac duty-free, crookedly sealed with wrinkled lengths of slick brown tape. Heavy. Compact.

"Hello."

Chia very nearly falling backward, where she crouched above her open bag, at the voice and the sight of this boy, who in that first instant she takes to be an older girl, side-parted hair falling past her shoulders.

"I am Masahiko." No translator. He wore a dark, oversized tunic, vaguely military, buttoned to its high, banded collar, loose around his neck. Old gray sweatpants bagging at the knees. Grubby-looking white paper slippers.

"Mitsuko made tea," indicating the tray, the stone-ware pot, two cups. "But you were ported."

"Is she here?" Chia pushed the thing back down into her bag.

"She went out," Masahiko said. "May I look at your computer?"

"Computer?" Chia stood, confused.

"It is Sandbenders, yes?"

She poured some of the tea, which was still steaming. "Sure. You want tea?"

"No," Masahiko said. "I drink coffee only." He squatted on the tatami, beside the low table, and ran an admiring fingertip along the edge of the Sandbenders' cast aluminum. "Beautiful. I have seen a small disk player by the same maker. It is a cult, yes?"

"A commune. Tribal people. In Oregon."

The boy's black hair was long and glossy and smoothly brushed, but Chia saw there was a bit of noodle caught in it, the thin, kinky kind that came in instant ramen bowls.

"I'm sorry I was ported when Mitsuko came back. She'll think I was rude."

"You are from Seattle." Not a question.

"You're her brother?"

"Yes. Why are you here?" His eyes large and dark, his face long and pale.

"Your sister and I are both into Lo Rez."

"You have come because he wants to marry Rei Toei?"

Hot tea dribbled down Chia's chin. "She told you that?"

"Yes," Masahiko said. "In Walled City, some people worked on her design." He was lost in his study of her Sandbenders, turning it over in his hands. His fingers were long and pale, the nails badly chewed.

"Where's that?"

"Netside," he said, flipping the weight of his hair back, over one shoulder.

"What do they say about her?"

"Original concept. Almost radical." He stroked the keys. "This is very beautiful. .

"You learned English here?"

"In Walled City."

Chia tried another sip of tea, then put the cup down. "You have any coffee?"

"In my room," he said.

Masahiko's room, at the bottom of a short flight of concrete stairs, to the rear of the restaurant's kitchen, had probably been a storage closet. It was a boy-nightmare, the sort of environment Chia knew from the brothers of friends, its floor and ledgelike bed long vanished beneath unwashed clothes, ramen-wrappers, Japanese magazines with wrinkled covers. A tower of empty foam ramen bowls in one corner, their hologram labels winking from beyond a single cone of halogen. A desk or table forming a second, higher ledge, cut from some recycled material that looked as though it had been laminated from shredded juice cartons. His computer there, a featureless black cube. A shallower shelf of the juice-carton board supported a pale blue microwave, unopened ramen bowls, and half a dozen tiny steel cans of coffee.

One of these, freshly microwaved, was hot in Chia' s hand. The coffee was strong, sugary, thickly creamed. She sat beside him on the lumpy bed ledge, a padded jacket wadded up behind her for a cushion.

It smelled faintly of boy, of ramen, and of coffee. Though he seemed very clean, now that she was this close, and she had a vague idea that Japanese people generally were. Didn't they love to bathe? The thought made her want a shower.

"I like this very much." Reaching to touch the Sandbenders again, which he'd brought from upstairs and placed on the work surface, in front of his black cube, sweeping aside a litter of plastic spoons, pens, nameless bits of metal and plastic.

"How do you see to work yours?" Gesturing toward his computer with the miniature can of coffee.

He said something in Japanese. Worms and dots of pastel neon lit the faces of the cube, crawling and pulsing, then died.

The walls, from floor to ceiling, were thickly covered with successive layers of posters, handbills, graphics files. The wall directly in front of her, above and behind the black computer, was hung with a large scarf, a square of some silky material screened with a map or diagram in red and black and yellow. Hundreds of irregular blocks or rooms, units of some kind, pressing in around a central vacancy, an uneven vertical rectangle, black.

"Walled City," he said, following her eye. He leaned forward, fingertip, finding a particular spot. "This is mine. Eighth level."

Chia pointed to the center of the diagram. "What's this?"

"Black hole. In the original, something like an air-shaft." He looked at her. "Tokyo has a black hole, too. You have seen this?"

"No," she said.

"The Palace. No lights. From a tall building, at night, the Imperial Palace is a black hole. Watching, once, I saw a torch flare."

"What happened to it in the earthquake?"

He raised his eyebrows. "This of course would not be shown. All now is as before. We are assured of this." He smiled, but only with the corners of his mouth.

"Where did Mitsuko go?"

He shrugged.

"Did she say when she'd be back?"

"No."

Chia thought of Hiromi Ogawa, and then of someone phoning for Kelsey's father. Hiromi? But then there was whatever it was, upstairs in her bag in Mitsuko's room. She remembered Maryalice yelling from behind the door to Eddie's office. Zona had to be right. "You know a club called Whiskey Clone?"

"No." He stroked the buffed aluminum edges of her Sandbenders.

"How about Monkey Boxing?"

He looked at her, shook his head.

"You probably don't get out much, do you?"

He held her gaze. "In Walled City."

"I want to go to this club, Monkey Boxing. Except maybe it isn't called that anymore. It's in a place called Shinjuku. I was in the station there, before."

"Clubs are not open, now.

"That's okay. I just want you to show me where it is. Then I'll be able to find my own way back."

"No. I must return to Walled City. I have responsibilities. Find the address of this place and I will explain to your computer where to go."

The Sandbenders could find its own way there, but Chia had decided she didn't want to go alone. Better to go with a boy than Mitsuko, and Mitsuko's allegiance to her chapter could be a problem anyway. Mainly, though, she just wanted to get out of here. Zona's news had spooked her. Somebody knew she was here. And what to do about the thing in her bag?

"You like this, right?" Pointing at her Sandbenders.

"Yes," he said.

"The software's even better. I've got an emulator in there that'll install a virtual Sandbenders in your computer. Take me to Monkey Boxing and it's yours."

"Have you always lived here?" Chia asked, as they walked to the station. "In this neighborhood, I mean?"

Masahiko shrugged. Chia thought the street made him uncomfortable. Maybe just being outside. He'd traded his gray sweats for equally baggy black cotton pants, cinched at the ankle with elastic-sided black nylon gaiters above black leather workshoes. He still wore his black tunic, but with the addition of a short-billed black leather cap that she thought might have once been part of a school uniform. If the tunic was too big for him, the cap was too small. He wore it perched forward at an angle, the bill riding low. "I live in Walled City," he said.

"Mitsuko told me. That's like a multi-user domain."

"Walled City is unlike anything."

"Give me the address when I give you the emulator. I'll check it out." The sidewalk arched over a concrete channel running with grayish water. It reminded her of her Venice. She wondered if there had been a stream there once.

"It has no address," he said.

"That's impossible," Chia said.

He said nothing.

She thought about what she'd found when she'd opened the SeaTac duty-free bag. Something flat and rectangular, dark gray. Maybe made from one of those weird plastics that had metal in them. One end had rows of little holes, the other had complicated shapes, metal, and a different kind of plastic. There didn't seem to be any way to open it, no visible seams. No markings. Didn't rattle when she shook it. Maybe *What Things Are,* the icon dictionary, would recognize it, but she hadn't had time. Masahiko had been downstairs changing when she'd slit the blue and yellow plastic with Mitsuko's serially numbered, commemorative Lo Rez Swiss Army knife. She'd glanced around the room for a hiding place. Everything too neat and tidy.

Finally she'd put it back in her bag, hearing him coming up the stairs from the kitchen. Which was where it was now, along with her Sandbenders, under her arm, as they entered the station. Which was probably not smart but she just didn't know.

She used Kelsey's cashcard to buy them both tickets.

"The Idoru"

"How do you mean, she's 'here'?" Laney asked Yamazaki, as they rounded the rear of the Sherman tank. Clots of dry clay clung to the segments of its massive steel treads.

"Mr. Kuwayama is here," Yamazaki whispered. "He represents her—"

Laney saw that several people were already seated at a low table.

Two men. A woman. The woman must be Rei Toei.

If he'd anticipated her at all, it had been as some industrial-strength synthesis of Japan's last three dozen top female media faces. That was usually the way in Hollywood, and the formula tended to be even more rigid, in the case of software agents—*eigenheads,* their features algorithmically derived from some human mean of proven popularity.

She was nothing like that.

Her black hair, rough-cut and shining, brushed pale bare shoulders as she turned her head. She had no eyebrows, and both her lids and lashes seemed to have been dusted with something white, leaving her dark pupils in stark contrast.

And now her eyes met his.

He seemed to cross a line. In the very structure of her face, in geometries of underlying bone, lay coded histories of dynastic flight, privation, terrible migrations. He saw stone tombs in steep alpine meadows, their lintels traced with snow. A line of shaggy pack ponies, their breath white with cold, followed a trail above a canyon. The curves of the river below were strokes of distant silver. Iron harness bells clanked in the blue dusk.

Laney shivered. In his mouth a taste of rotten metal.

The eyes of the idoru, envoy of some imaginary country, met his.

"We're here." Arleigh beside him, hand at his elbow. She was indicating two places at the table. "Are you all right?" she asked, under her breath. "Take your shoes off."

Laney looked at Blackwell, who was staring at the idoru, something like pain in his face, but the expression vanished, sucked away behind the mask of his scars.

Laney did as he was told, kneeling and removing his shoes, moving as if he were drunk, or dreaming, though he knew he was neither, and the idoru smiled, lit from within.

"Laney?"

The table was set above a depression in the floor. Laney seated himself, arranging his feet beneath the table and gripping his cushion with both hands. "What?"

"Are you okay?"

"Okay?"

"You looked … blind."

Rez was taking his place now at the head of the table, the idoru to his right, someone else—Laney saw that it was Lo, the guitarist—to his left. Next to the idoru sat a dignified older man with rimless glasses, gray hair brushed back from his smooth forehead. He wore a very simple, very expensive-looking suit of some lusterless black material, and a high-collared white shirt that buttoned in a complicated way. When this man turned to address Rei Toei, Laney quite clearly saw the light of her face reflect for an instant in the almost circular lenses.

Arleigh's sharp intake of breath. She'd seen it too. A hologram. Something generated, animated, projected. He felt his grip relax slightly, on the edges of the cushion.

But then he remembered the stone tombs, the river, the ponies with their iron bells.

Nodal.

Laney had once asked Gerrard Delouvrier, the most patient of the tennis-playing Frenchmen of TIDAL, why it was that he, Laney, had been chosen as the first (and, as it would happen, the only) recipient of the peculiar ability they sought to impart to him. He hadn't applied for the job, he said, and had no reason to believe the position had even been advertised. He had applied, he told Delouvrier, to be a trainee service rep.

Delouvrier, with short, prematurely gray hair and a suntable tan, leaned back in his articulated workstation chair and stretched his legs. He seemed to be studying his crepe-soled suede shoes. Then he looked out the window, to rectangular beige buildings, anonymous landscaping, February snow. "Do you not see? How we do not teach you? We watch. We wish to learn from you."

They were in a DatAmerica research park in Iowa. There was an indoor court for Delouvrier and his colleagues, but they complained constantly about its surface.

"But why me?"

Delouvrier' s eyes looked tired. "We wish to be kind to the orphans? We are an unexpected warmth at the heart of DatAmerica?" He rubbed his eyes. "No. Something was done to you, Laney. In our way, perhaps, we seek to redress that. Is that a word, 'redress'?"

"No," Laney said.

"Do not question good fortune. You are here with us, doing work that matters. It is winter in this Iowa, true, but the work goes on." He was looking at Laney now. "You are our only proof," he said.

"Of what?"

Delouvrier closed his eyes. "There was a man, a blind man, who mastered echo-location. Clicks with the tongue, you understand?" Eyes closed, he demonstrated. "Like a bat. Fantastic." He opened his eyes. "He could perceive his immediate environment in great detail. Ride a bicycle in traffic. Always making the *tik, tik.* The ability was his, was absolutely real. And he could never explain it, never teach it to another ..." He wove his long fingers together and cracked his knuckles. "We must hope that this is not the case with you."

Don't think of a purple cow. Or was it a brown one? Laney couldn't remember. Don't look at the idoru's face. She is not flesh; she is information. She is the tip of an iceberg, no, an Antarctica, of information. Looking at her face would trigger it again: she was some unthinkable volume of information. She induced the nodal vision in some unprecedented way; she induced it as narrative.

He could watch her hands. Watch the way she ate. The meal was elaborate, many small courses served on individual rectangular plates. Each time a plate was placed before Rei Toei, and always within the field of whatever projected her, it was simultaneously veiled with a flawless copy, holo food on a holo plate.

Even the movement of her chopsticks brought on peripheral flickers of nodal vision. Because the chopsticks were information too, but nothing as dense as her features, her gaze. As each "empty" plate was removed, the untouched serving would reappear.

But when the flickering began, Laney would concentrate on his own meal, his clumsiness with his own chopsticks, conversation around the table. Kuwayama, the man with the rimless glasses, was answering something Rez had asked, though Laney hadn't been able to catch the question itself. "—the result of an array of elaborate constructs that we refer to as 'desiring machines.' " Rez's green eyes, bright and attentive. "Not in any literal sense," Kuwayama continued, "but please envision *aggregates of subjective desire.* It was decided that the modular array would ideally constitute an architecture of articulated longing ..." The man's voice was beautifully modulated, his English accented in a way that Laney found impossible to place.

Rez smiled then, his eyes going to the face of the idoru. As did Laney's as well, automatically.

He fell through her eyes. He was staring up at a looming cliff face that seemed to consist entirely of small rectangular balconies, none set at quite the same level or depth. Orange sunset off a tilted, steel-framed window. Oilslick colors crawling in the sky.

He closed his eyes, looked down, opened them. A fresh plate there, more food.

"You're really into your meal," Arleigh said.

A concentrated effort with the chopsticks and he managed to capture and swallow something that was like a one-inch cube of cold chutney omelet. "Wonderful. Don't want any of that fugu though. Blowfish with the neurotoxins? Heard about that?"

"You've already had seconds," she said. "Remember the big plate of raw fish arranged like the petals of a chrysanthemum?"

"You're kidding," Laney said.

"Lips and tongue feel faintly numb? That's it."

Laney ran his tongue across his lips. Was she kidding? Yamazaki, seated to his left, leaned close. "There may be a way around the problem you face with Rez's data. You are aware of Lo/Rez global fan activity?"

"Of what?"

"Many fans. They report each sighting of Rez, Lo, other musicians involved. There is much incidental detail."

Laney knew from his day's video education that Lo Rez were theoretically a duo, but that there were always at least two other "members," usually more. And Rez had been adamant from the start about his dislike of drum machines; the current drummer, "Blind" Willy

Jude, seated opposite Yamazaki, had been with them for years. He'd been turning his enormous black glasses in the idoru's direction throughout the meal; now he seemed to sense Laney's glance. The black glasses, video units, swung around. "Man," Jude said, "Rozzer's sittin' down there makin' eyes at a big aluminum thermos bottle."

"You can't see her?"

"Holos are hard, man," the drummer said, touching his glasses with a fingertip. "Take my kids to Nissan County, I'll call ahead, get 'em tweaked around a little. Then I can see 'em. But this lady's on a funny frequency or something. All I can see's the projector and this kinda, kinda ectoplastic, right? Glow, like."

The man seated between Jude and Mr. Kuwayama, whose name was Ozaki, bobbed apologetically in Jude's direction. "We regret this very much. We regret deeply. A slight adjustment is required, but it cannot be done at this time."

"Hey," Jude said, "no big problem. I seen her already. I get all the music channels with these. That one where she's a Mongol princess or something, up in the mountains. ..."

Laney lost a chopstick.

"The most recent single," Ozaki said.

"Yeah," Jude said, "that's pretty good. She wears that gold mask? Okay shit." He popped a section of maki into his mouth and chewed.